AF424423

THE HOLLOW CROWN SERIES VOLUME 1

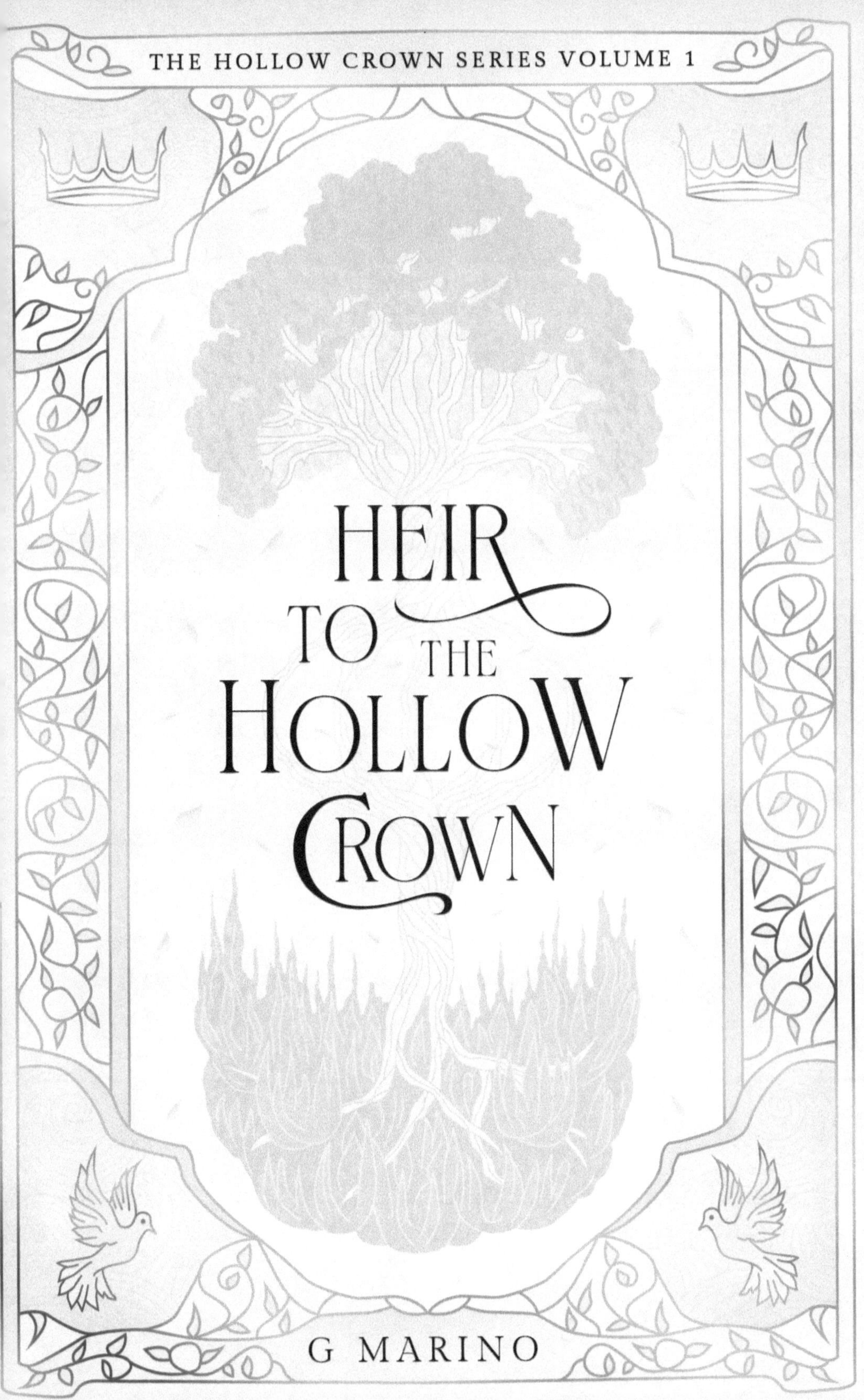
HEIR
TO
THE
HOLLOW
CROWN

G MARINO

To Nick—you are the heartbeat of Nalara and the compass I carry in every enchanted forest. Your unwavering support has made it safe for me to dream. You have always believed in me—sometimes more than I deserve. Thank you for guiding my steps to this place and patiently waiting for me to follow. I love you.

To Maddox—your existence reminds me that magic is real. You are magic, son. I hope more than anything that I make you proud.

In loving memory of Peggy Bresnick Kendler. You entered my life later than I hoped and left earlier than you should have, my kindred spirit. Thank you for seeing me in the way I needed.

AUTHOR'S NOTES

Thank you for reading *The Heir to the Hollow Crown*. Before you begin, I want to be honest: this is not a gentle read. It contains religious extremism, institutional corruption, mental illness (including derogatory remarks from the mentally ill individual about their own mental health), brief mentions of self-harm, and morally gray characters.
Reader discretion is advised.

A note about AI:

AI is quickly becoming prevalent in our daily lives. With it comes concerns regarding environmental impacts and the ethics behind its use in art. AI has been trained by human-made works for replication. I did not use AI in any part of the writing or editing of this novel. My use of an em dash or semicolon—and there will be a lot of them—is not indicative of AI usage and should not be seen as such.
Thank you to the real humans involved in producing this work:
Sam (Scrollwork Edits) - copy and line edits

Lexie (Selkkie Designs) - cover art, chapter art
Rachael (Cartography Bird) - map of Nalara
Manu (Devonstore on Fiverr) - character art
Morgan Teal - scene break art
Vanessa (Inkspark Digital) - interior formatting

Special thank you to my earliest beta readers.
Without you, this story wouldn't exist in the
capacity it does today:
Aubrey
Jasmine
Kate
Reid
Megan
Audrey
Nina
Michelle

ELVARN
PRYVETH
ALVIAN FALLS
VAELGUAR
THE GREAT LANDS OF
NALARA
MAPPED
IN THE PRESENT ERA
TO DISTANT SOUTHERN SEA

O THE UNCHARTED NORTH
LIRIWYN
THE SACRED GROVE
GALLIVARUM TEMPLE RUINS
THRYVOSS

PROLOGUE

Before the truth unraveled, before the crown and the prophecy and the boy with my mother's eyes, I was just Mallory, the girl who ran. I ran from my hometown and my parents' divorce. I ran from the boy I thought was forever. The truth is, I've run from everything my entire life. Even myself.

I told everyone that I packed my minuscule belongings and moved myself five hundred miles for a job, for a fresh start. This time, I wasn't running away. I was finally running toward something, though I wasn't sure what.

Back then, I didn't know magic existed or that I was destined to rule an ancient kingdom whose laws and customs I couldn't yet fathom. I couldn't possibly have known that the boy who followed me with quiet steps and unreadable eyes would hold my fate in his hands.

I didn't know much, looking back. I only knew how to run, and I was good at it.

CHAPTER ONE
MALLORY

I'm in my old bedroom, but not really. The walls are the wrong shade of blue, too dark despite the sunlight streaking through the shutters. I can't tell the time of day by the shadows on the wall; they're all wrong. The curtains are up just a bit too high. A pillow I don't recognize sits on the bed, and there's a lamp in the wrong corner. Everything is still, as if the world is holding its breath. Outside, a lawnmower growls. Downstairs, my mother is cooking dinner. The TV in the den is too loud—my father's doing. They spend far too much time apart, but I still live here. Which means they are still married. My life hasn't been torn apart yet, though I know it's coming.

My legs don't quite belong to me. They're mine, but shorter. Heavier. Harder to move. Every step feels like panic as I will my leg to rise and am met with an almost immovable force. The pressure builds and my bones ache. Slowly, painstakingly, I cross the room toward the desk sitting opposite the twin bed. I don't know why, but I am drawn to it—I need to be in its presence.

I remember this desk.

It looks different, older.

That doesn't make sense.

It's scratched and worn as if it had fallen too far back in time before making its resurgence. Something familiar tickles the back of my brain as I inspect the long-forgotten piece of furniture.

A bird sits on the desk, waiting to be noticed. Wooden, carved, its wings neatly folded into itself. It would be beautiful if it wasn't so alarming—its eyes are watching me.

I know this bird.

Though, not in the way you know your favorite song lyrics. Not even in the way you know your favorite teddy bear. In the way you know a word that you can't quite remember, but which is lying right across the tip of your tongue.

I pick up the hollow figure and turn it over. Nothing about the back of this bird raises a cause for alarm. It looks just as anyone would expect, but the weight of it surprises me. It shouldn't be this heavy. As I consider this conundrum of physics, the trinket grows impossibly warm in my hands, almost too hot to continue holding. A rattle resonates from deep within the bird's empty belly, shaking my hands. Or they're trembling on their own. The rattle echoes in my bones, an unremembered aching which suddenly feels as if it's always been with me.

"You have forgotten your name," I hear an ominous voice say.

No, not hear, feel, from somewhere deep in the recesses of my mind. I want to ask what it means, but my mouth fills with leaves. In my choking, I drop the dove and it rolls to the corner of the room. My chest tightens—it's not quite fear, but something more.

I beg myself to stop choking.

The truth hits me and, all at once, the leaves tumble from my mouth.

This isn't a dream—it's a memory.

My eyes open to the dim light of early morning. Long gray shadows dance across my small bedroom, bathing scraps of my saddened existence in a familiar, cold-blue light. My head pounds from whatever dream it is that now lies forgotten in the depths of my psyche. Forgetting my dreams is not entirely out of the ordinary, and neither is the emotional hangover that accompanies the loss. From below, sounds of cars honking and a street sweeper passing waft up through the open windows of my sixth-story walk-up. It's not much, but it's mine. Or, rather, this room is mine. My roommate, Vanessa, is working in the kitchen already, humming along to some Top Forty radio hit or another. It doesn't matter which; they all sound the same. I roll over to examine the clock on my bedside table. 6:27.

Swinging my feet to the floor with an exaggerated slowness, I groan. I have to be at the coffee shop in an hour or Chuck is going to kill me. Being on probation, I can't afford to be late . . . again. Not that losing my job would be the worst thing in the world—it's not like I want to be making lattes forever. Still, finding another temporary job to make up for the loss of income would be humiliating. While most young adults may not have their paths lined up to a tee, I am probably the only twenty-two-year-old in existence without even the faintest idea of their future. Vanessa is my opposite in every way. She will be starting med school in the fall, whereas I dropped out of community college.

My eyes scan the floor, searching for anything not disgusting, and land on a black T-shirt and a pair of blue jeans. Feeling grateful for the ability to dress down for work, I run my hairbrush through the knots in my long auburn hair and twist it into a messy topknot. It doesn't need to be perfect, it just needs to be up. I glance at my reflection before making my way to the kitchen. I know what I look like; there is no reason to linger.

"Good morning, my beautiful birthday girl!" The harmonious voice of my roommate calls to me before I can fully appear. She has an uncanny ability to predict my moves. It would be alarming if I wasn't so used to it.

Shit. That is today. My 22nd birthday. "The day that made the world a different place."

My mom never said "better," just "different." Even *she* had known from the moment I was born that I was nothing special. She'd always given me the sense that she would have rather not had me.

"I can't believe you're working today," Vanessa says, ripping me from my thoughts. She's pointing her spatula at me, flailing it about with each word.

"Yeah, well, it's just another day."

She rolls her eyes and slides eggs onto a small white plate. By now, she's learned not to push.

Vanessa is the kind of person you want to hate. The "girl's girl" all girls wish they could be. She draws envy and longing from every woman—and man—who has the pleasure of meeting her. Not only does her dark skin, tight curls, and symmetrical face speak to her radiance, her exuberant personality and whip-sharp wit dazzles the throngs of hangers-on she has collected over the years. Her perfection sometimes makes me sick. Still, she's the closest thing I have to a best friend.

"I love you, Ducky," Ness calls my pet name over her shoulder on her way out the door.

The first time I attempted latte art to impress her, it was a lump of foam that looked more like a duck than the lotus I'd intended. She exclaimed "Ducky!" the second she saw it and hasn't let me forget about it since. She thinks it's cute. I think it's infantilizing.

"We will celebrate tonight! Eat your eggs before they get cold, and get your ass to work before Chuck fires you. You're on thin ice as it is."

I scowl as warmth spreads across my cheeks.

It is a relatively warm day for mid-January in Poughkeepsie. Java Central is eight blocks away, which I usually walk, but today it's supposed to rain.

At least it isn't snowing.

After scarfing down the lukewarm eggs my friend had made, which I hate, I search for my keys, readying myself for the walk down to the parking lot. The elevator has not worked since the day I moved in. Not that I mind, I would probably choose to walk regardless.

We keep our keys on the credenza by the door. *Credenza.* That is such a Vanessa word. Her brilliant style is evident in every corner of her apartment, save the spare room—my bedroom. I wouldn't let her touch my stuff, though not for a lack of her trying. At least once a week she pitches a new feng shui idea.

My keys are not in the bowl, a typical occurrence due to my

continued lack of responsibility. Today is not the day to face the consequences of my actions. My mind peels back the layers of fog still hanging over me from last night's dream. Nightmare? Everything in my memory points to the keys being put away correctly. I don't linger on it, I don't have time.

There is only one other place my keys can be if they aren't where they belong. I try to keep my possessions in Vanessa's apartment minimal. Not that I have much anyway. My whole life has been relegated to a ten-foot-square room.

My bedroom is messy—another thing I wish I could say isn't a typical occurrence. But what twenty-two-year-old girl's room *isn't* messy?

Vanessa's isn't. A bubble of resentment creeps up my throat, and I squash the feeling with relative ease. It isn't a new thought. How does one compare a diamond to a pebble?

I find my keys, not on the dresser where expected, but on the floor in the corner of the room. Normally, this isn't a spot I'd consider looking if not for the bit of intuition clawing at me, telling me to check precisely in that location.

How strange.

I shrug my shoulders for no one's benefit but my own. It's not impossible that I just dropped them and refused to pick them up at that moment, swearing that I would remember later—I almost never remembered later.

Wrapping my fingers around the smooth surface of the slightly-too-large keychain, a comforted smile crosses my lips as I spy it—a dove. Another irregularity. Why had I been thinking about this dove?

The dove in question is carved out of ash wood. I wouldn't know by sight alone, and normally wouldn't care, but to Nana this bird was special. She explained that ash wood had been used as a symbol of protection for centuries, and that doves brought inner harmony.

"May your steps be guided by your intuition and protected by the mighty ash," she'd whispered as she'd slipped the bird between my outstretched hands.

A lot of good it's doing me now, Nana.

She was a superstitious old woman, my grandmother. It's a quality I am surprised to say I miss dearly. Nana is the only one who ever seemed to understand me, and the only one I feel guilty for leaving.

My drive to work is uneventful as always, being as short as it is. The monotony of a car trip is something I will never mind; it gives me a brief window of time in which to exist without expectation.

Despite the earlier mishap with my lost keys, I arrive at work early . . . for once. As soon as the car settles into park, rain drums on the windshield, eager for an audience. Rain reminds me that even the sky needs to cry sometimes.

From my position behind the steering wheel, I watch the droplets race. A car game I invented in my childhood, I would listen to the rain drown out my parents' arguments, while choosing two champion droplets to battle to the death in a race against my reality. If my chosen drop won, the fighting would stop. I mostly never won.

My mind reels back to the present as I realize the air around me has gone still. From the corner of my eye, a small cluster of water droplets, clinging together like nature's afterthought, hovers. No, not hovers—*rises*. Just a little. Just enough to make me doubt everything.

Are they moving upward?

Racking my brain, I try to remember the last time I'd taken my medicine. It hadn't been last night, or even the night before. First thing tomorrow, I will swallow one of those little white pills and two of the oblong orange ones. Drinking tonight will affect them, though it wouldn't be the first time the two mixed.

The rain has not moved upward; my mind is playing tricks on me.

Gravity is a concrete fact of life, and that is not how it works. Once I take my medication, it will all make sense. The sedative keeps me from reliving my hardest-to-swallow memories, which is precisely why I take it. It helps me sleep without dreams. And, when I forget to take it, it leaves me confused.

I am just confused.

All at once, time begins moving at its regular cadence and I let go of the breath I'd been holding. Collecting my apron and name tag from the floor of the passenger seat, my gaze shifts over the dash and my eyes lock on *him.*

His presence disarms me. The scowl, the hoodie, the look of distrust etched in his brow. Every fiber of my being wants him to look away, needs him to look away. He is watching me like he's studying every move I make. *I* should look away. But I don't. For whatever reason, I can't. Something about him feels like an echo— like a name I used to know. Familiar, yet cold and distant, but thoroughly unnerving. I shiver as an invisible wind beckons me toward the stranger. I want to follow, but fear pins me to my seat. He must notice, because his lips curl into a gentle smirk as he slips into the wooded lot behind the coffee shop.

I want to follow him, to discover this man's identity and why he was watching me. The danger of following a stranger into the woods, however, gives me pause. This is different though, *right?* It doesn't seem like he wants to hurt me. In fact, I think he *wants* me to follow.

My phone buzzes. A text from my manager, Chuck.
Shit.

"You're late. Again."

Chuck's disappointed voice shrinks me with how familiar it feels. When you're a child, you think the scolding ends at eighteen. That when the clock strikes midnight on that magical day, you are granted equality amongst the world's adults. Apparently I was very wrong.

"I know, I'm sorry. I lost track of time. I promise it won't happen again." The pleading is evident in my voice as I set my jacket on the counter. If I keep things moving, he might overlook this instance— it's worked before.

My boss's chiseled jaw clenches visibly and I can see his inner turmoil. Chuck cares about me, I think, in some way, and has over-looked many of my previous infractions. He isn't great at hiding his feelings, though I can't blame him. Even after years of practice masking my emotions, my facade still cracks occasionally. Writing me off for this breaks our friendship, but his sense of duty to the store is making the decision hard on him.

Another write-up would mean termination, and Chuck is a by-the-book kind of leader. Thorough and sometimes harsh, but always fair.

I brace myself as his blonde brows furrow. He's my boss and I have to respect his decision. Our friendship has saved me far too many times, as he has often given me an out—letting me stay later or scheduling me an extra day to give me the opportunity to atone for my sins.

This would've ended by now if he was letting me off the hook; he isn't cruel. My probationary status must've forced his hand in the matter. The higher-ups would see what he'd done, and it would mean trouble for him. He will stick his neck out only so far for his employees, but he wouldn't let them lower the ax. Even though it means the end of my employment, I *really do* admire his leadership skills.

Tears form in my eyes, and a fire rises in my throat. With every-thing in me, I manage the friendliest smile I can muster. My body can't cry if it thinks it's happy, right?

"Sorry, Mal. This is one time too many, and so soon after being placed on probation. You know I have to let you go. Turn in your apron, please." Chuck doesn't look me in the eyes.

Trembling, I fumble with the apron strings and remove the grayish garment with reluctance. Pushing the ball of fabric into Chuck's hands, I turn my back briefly and wipe my tears away. I can't let him see the evidence of his betrayal descending my cheeks.

When I turn back around, Chuck's mouth is moving again. There is a ringing in my ears as I try to make out his words. I can't quite catch them until the last one—"go."

Happy birthday, Mallory.

Escaping through the employee door for the last time, I make my way to the parking lot as fast as possible. I need to leave this place. The farther I get, the less it will hurt. Right? My thoughts return to the boy, realizing now in my post-confrontation haze who is truly at fault. I was on time. I *was*. He distracted me. *He* is the reason I am late.

My eyes begin to dart from tree to tree, scanning the woods where I had last seen him. He was gone. Of course he was gone. I had seen him leave, hadn't I? My chest tightens, a sharp iron coil held over a fire for far too long poking my ribs.

Who is he?

Inexplicably, I'm walking toward the trees. I should go home. I should cry, or call Ness, or pretend everything's fine. I should do any number of safe, rational things. But I don't.

Instead, my feet move like they belong to someone else. Like I am walking into a long forgotten dream. Each step crunches over wet leaves and brittle twigs. The cold air bites at my skin, but I keep going. I *must* keep going.

Maybe it's the way he looked at me—like he knew me. Like he'd been waiting.

Maybe it's because I've spent my whole life running, and for once, someone hadn't chased me.

He had *waited*.

And I want to know why.

CHAPTER TWO
MALLORY

The rain is coming down in sheets now. Not ice, but just as sharp. Cold clings to me like the jacket I forgot in the cafe, making it impossible to feel my ears. I know I should stop, that I won't find anything. The boy is long gone. Still, I have to keep looking—I have to find those eyes that gazed at me as if they knew me. Perhaps they do. Maybe even better than I know myself.

You're overreacting again. It was just some random guy trying to creep you out.

It worked.

But this doesn't feel like last time. It doesn't feel like I am inventing this.

Slowing to a walk, I examine the never-ending forest around me. This place shouldn't exist. Last I checked, this was a vacant lot about the width of a city block.

Getting lost is impossible. At least, it should be. But as I look around, I realize that I must have been wandering longer than I'd thought. Everything looks the same, the way everything sounds the same and feels the same in every forest that has ever existed. Dead trees, piles of old, slushy snow, and a lack of wildlife. *Yep*, just another forest in winter.

So why is it here? Where did it come from? These trees couldn't have grown overnight, but they weren't here yesterday. Were they? Is it possible I have been so absorbed in my own life that I completely neglected to look at the parking lot?

To be fair to myself, I don't drive too often. Maybe I *had* just imagined it as an empty lot. That's not exactly outside of the realm of possibility.

Branches snap and fall to the ground around me, twisting toward the sky as if cursing the heavens for the barrenness of winter. Picking one up, I feel a surge of pain as a small crimson puddle forms on the tip of my thumb. I stare at the shiny, sticky liquid for longer than necessary. I won't admit this to anyone, but sometimes pain feels good—a welcome disruption to the typical. Not so welcome that I would invite it myself.

Not anymore.

The grove opens to me with a cautious regard. It is living— breathing, almost. As if the trees themselves are fluctuating in and out, swaying with the nonexistent breeze. Ethereal. Sacred.

Am I dreaming?

My presence is both a welcome addition and a wary expectation. If I didn't know any better, I would think I belonged here. This is as close to peace as I can ever remember I've felt.

It dawns on me with a sudden shiver that I am unsure how long I've been walking. Every moment has bled one into the next as I'd been taking account of my surroundings.

I sit, letting out a sigh of frustration, and maybe a little contentment. The cold, hard, bumpy ground embraces my thighs. The earth underneath thaws slightly with the warmth of my legs. My jeans will be cold and wet later, but at this moment I do not care. My thoughts slow; the racing images of the boy, the woods, and my desperation to find meaning in the unknown fades as I breathe in the crisp, cool air. Nearby, songbirds sing. Their melodies remind me of a song my nana sang to me in childhood. Briefly, I wonder if they should have made their way south for the winter, or if they had simply returned too early. Either way, I am enjoying the company.

A distant ring tickles my ear—someone's phone. Considering

the possibility that the phone belongs to the boy in the hoodie, I stand up, ready to locate the source of the sound. That is until I do: my pocket. Only one person ever calls me.

"Hey, Ness," I say without checking the caller ID.

"What's up? Where are you?"

"At work."

"Didn't your shift end hours ago?" Vanessa probes through the phone.

Had it? I check the time. 4:32.

How?

"Um, yeah, but I decided to stay late to help with a few things. I can't say no to Chuck," I say, forcing a smile into my voice and hoping he hasn't reached out to her yet.

If Vanessa knew where I am and why, she would come looking for me. And then would come the voice. The one meant to be supportive, but which instead drips with disappointment, patronizing me. It's nothing I'm not used to, of course, but I do whatever I can to avoid the voice. Especially today. I think of it as my birthday present to myself.

"Okay," comes her usual sing-songy voice. "Well, get home! We can't start your party without you."

Shit. My party.

"I'm on my way, I'll see you soon. Can't wait to celebrate with you." It's another lie that I mumble into the phone, but knowing Vanessa, her desperation to turn me into a normal girl will allow her to believe it.

My fist clenches around my phone and I give it a rough shove into my back pocket. As if responding to an unasked question, the ground dispels the fallen leaves and jagged branches. The path is clear, and I run.

Getting to my car was quicker than I'd expected. For whatever reason, leaving a place has always been easier for me than entering. If I were a more intelligent person I would find some kind of poetic irony in that. Like Chuck would. Or the man in the hoodie . . . he seems the poetic type. Deep, brooding, insufferably cliche.

Another ten minutes later, I am sitting on Vanessa's bed, helping her choose the sluttiest black dress. Her words, not mine. "Slutty" sounds crass when I say it, like it senses my discomfort.

My birthday party isn't about me, not really. Not that I expected it to be. Vanessa's friends treat me well enough, but we don't talk unless Ness has forced us all into the same room. Which, admittedly, is relatively too often for my liking.

The doorbell rings.

"Can you get that, babe?" Vanessa asks over her shoulder while rummaging through her closet.

I don't reply. It isn't a question.

Opening the door, I see Brody, Jennifer, Nick, and Doug in the hallway. They always seem to travel together. They are inseparable —the Three Musketeers. You know, because "there were actually four of them." From the way Jennifer is hanging off Doug's shoulders, I would venture to guess they are on again. Not that I care. Hiding a wince at the display of affection, I smile and step aside, waving my arm in a sweeping gesture. It feels strange to match their energy.

"There are drinks in the kitchen." I don't tell them I have had three already.

"Vanessa," I yell down the hallway, "your friends are here!"

As if on cue, Vanessa steps into the living room, eliciting a wolf whistle from Brody. Her long black hair is elegantly tied back, juxta-posed against the skin-tight, low-cut crimson dress that falls just above her fingertips. She is stunning.

"*Our* friends, sweetie," she teases. She won't say it with company present, but she hates when I call them *her* friends. Her desire to meddle in everyone's affairs has deluded her a bit.

Smiling, I take my own advice and meander into the kitchen for a drink. And then another. And more yet. With each glass, I watch my supposed friends celebrate my birthday without me. I slip through the night unnoticed, like a ghost in the rafters. Never a participant, always an observer.

Another knock sounds at the door—more of Vanessa's friends. I play a doting hostess, showing them where the drinks are. The snacks, the cake. All the while smiling like I'm having fun. Why wouldn't I be having fun? It's my birthday party, after all. If I say it enough, and ply myself with enough alcohol, I'll believe it. Let's hope they believe it too.

One of the guests—short, quiet, with green eyes that flick past me before settling on the bookshelf—nods politely as he passes. Those eyes. There is a familiarity about them, but the man wearing them is a stranger. He seems like the kind of guy who won't stay long. He seems like the kind of guy who wouldn't be at this party.

Before I can linger too long on the stranger, another guest—a new friend of a friend of Vanessa's—corners me in the kitchen.

"Great party." He grins while bobbing around like a flailing chicken. "Thanks for the invite."

"Thanks," I reply tersely, looking behind him for an excuse to end the conversation before it begins. There must be something, because I hear myself make an excuse to leave. Since it's there, I pour another drink from a bottle of cabernet, a screw top, and exit the room, feeling the heat of his eyes on me. Maybe under different circumstances, on a different day, I would stay and finish our conversation. He is good enough to look at, and, I am sure, not nearly as shallow as he seems.

Settling on the couch, I watch myself live a life that is not mine. My body feels like it's floating, and I can't sense if I'm smiling or frowning. Minutes tick by while hours pass. The more I interact, the more I don't want to interact, and each moment I have to play pretend only adds to the torture. Tiredness overwhelms me and my bed calls to me from the other room. Whatever time I exit the party, the guests are all still in Vanessa's living room having the time of their lives. The sounds of thumping music and fits of laughter drift behind my closed eyes as I wait for the room to stop spinning.

Time moves on and, eventually, the house quiets.

My breath is ragged and heavy. Sweat slicks my back, yet I am shivering in the night air. My heart pounds in my ears as I make my way through a fog. If I didn't know any better, I would say the fog was purple, but that doesn't make sense.

I'm back in the woods, running faster than one would think possible. No, not running. Flying. I'm above the ground, circling now. I hear flapping overhead and glance up to find a pair of wings. They look too small to hold my weight, and they definitely belong to a bird. Before I think about it any longer, I begin the two-foot descent. Flying just above the ground embarrasses me for some reason—it's not like anyone is around to see.

As my feet touch the dirt, the skeletal trees of the forest bow to me, their branches scraping the ground. There is no sign of the leaves and twigs that previously littered the forest floor. The earth beneath my feet begins to hum, the vibrations propelling me forward, toward an illuminated path. Creation is shifting before me without so much as a second thought. My presence is not an unwelcome one; I belong.

The glade is bathed in starlight, and a symphony of sounds echoes in the cool night. A faint voice calls to me from a distance. The trees are speaking to me, whispering a name in a foreign tongue.

"Selowenya."

I'm not sure what it means, but I'm certain it's for me.

"Selowenya."

My steps trace along the long, winding pathway. Several intersections pop up, begging me to reconsider my actions, but the growing volume of whispers makes the decision easy. I must continue forward. At the end, when there is no more light and the whispering has quieted, I arrive in a clearing. The world looks different here, open and alive. A willow resides in a ring of the lushest grass I have ever seen. Lawns this well-manicured belong in the suburbs, and are usually painstakingly cared for—they don't crop up overnight in abandoned fields.

Magnificence radiates from the willow, its massive stature juxtaposed only by the beauty of its features. My fingers reach up to feel a tiny pool of wetness just below my right eye. Where I'm standing feels like the only safety left on Earth. The air itself is crisp and clear, as if it too understands the gravity of this place.

Examining the willow, I trace my fingers down its bark. Rough, jagged, and beautiful in a haunting, ethereal way. Circling toward the other side, I stumble upon a door, wider almost than it is tall, deeply set into the trunk. Above the roughly hewn shape, an empty plaque sits like it's waiting for its little elfin owner to come along in a moment and paint his name on his home. My eye catches on the object perched atop the plaque before I can investigate the door further. A bird.

A dove.

Nearly identical to the keychain I have clung to with desperation my whole life, its wooden head, not turned away in its usual manner, is looking directly at me. Those eyes. Something about those eyes. I've seen them before, although I'm not sure where. Instinctively, I reach toward the dove, wondering if it will reveal to me some deeper truth.

The moment my fingers graze the soft wood, I hear a small click as if a mechanism deep within the tree itself opened. A glow emanates from the wooden plaque, green and mysterious, beckoning me closer. Words, hidden before, become visible now. I recognize the language as the one the trees speak. Though I still cannot understand its meaning. I read the words aloud, as if reciting a magic spell.

"Naelyn doral selowen—asharil ven shalair."

The air is the first thing I notice. Duller, more mundane. I feel grass tickling my calves and remember I am still wearing my dress from the party. A sharp ache in my temple brings me back into my body. My eyes flutter open. I blink hard—once, twice, three times. The soft blue of the morning light envelops me as I sit up.

Where am I?

Pain. The ache behind my temple calls my attention. I shouldn't have had that ninth glass of wine. My stomach churns, and, before I can expel its contents in the grass, the wave of nausea is gone. I should lie down. I should find my way home. I *was* home. How did I get here?

Where is "here"?

Preparing myself to take inventory of my surroundings with careful movements, as not to disrupt the equilibrium I have found, my gaze turns to my left. Trees. Then to the right. Java Central. "Here" is the clearing on the edge of the parking lot. Something feels different this time, almost out of place. It isn't until now that I remember the feeling of grass. It's January, so the grass should be dead. It *was* dead yesterday. I look down with uncertainty, as if I expect the ground to jump up and bite me. I'm not sure what I anticipate, but it isn't this.

This isn't grass. It's moss, dotted with deep violet flowers, growing in bunches. Flowers that, despite their downturned petals, exude a sense of jubilation. I reach out to touch the carpet of vegetation, my fingers sinking deep into the plush surface of the moss. Whispers? I hear whispers. Telling me memories that aren't quite mine, but somehow ones I've lived. I can't pinpoint the sound, but trying to make sense of it seems much too strenuous in this condition.

A branch snaps in the distance, jarring me from my investigation. My eyes dart toward the sound, hoping to find its culprit. Blurry figures begin to take shape. There are two of them, positioned beside a tree. Not just any tree.

Standing in front of me, like a statue erected from my memory, is the willow of my dreams. The tree's giant trunk stretches upward, so far up it's as if the tree's crown touches the sky. Wisps of leaves, overhanging on all sides, encapsulate anything hiding under the foliage. Its magnitude catches me off guard—so much so that I realize I had forgotten the figures on either side.

On one side of the willow stands a man. Though I can make out no distinguishing features through the willow's umbrella. Judging by the whiteness of his perfectly coiffed hair, the man is older than my father by many years. His left hand is curled around a staff, jagged and unpolished. A nonchalantness is evident in the way he holds himself, as if the forest blooms for him. Pangs of longing stab my chest, the nausea of my anxiety indistinguishable from the sickness the copious amounts of alcohol tries to bring.

Warmth overcomes my body and I fight the urge to move closer to the strange man. I wonder how I must look to him, sitting in the grass alone in a party dress. Unless, of course, he is the reason I did not wake up at home.

Before fear can overwhelm my senses, a fluttering on the right side of the trunk grabs my attention and I whip my head around faster than I should. I brace myself for the rising acid. Swallowing hard, I resolve not to be sick in front of these strangers. There is a burning in my throat as my stomach welcomes the bile back down. I steady myself and squint through the leaves to look on the other side of the tree.

No.

I recognize that boy.

I recognize *those eyes*.

CHAPTER THREE
MALLORY

"Hello, my dear," the older man's soft, lilting voice calls out to me.

My body stiffens and my eyes don't leave the boy's figure. He won't get away this time, not without giving me answers. And not without explaining just *how* it is I recognize him.

"Come, child. We have much to discuss."

The boy smirks at my trepidation, taunting me to break eye contact first.

A sigh from the old man catches my attention as he shifts on the balls of his feet. Despite him being a stranger, I can't help but feel he is some authority figure over me. One that I don't dare disappoint. The pressure causes me to rise from my place in the field, clumsily, like I'm not in control of my body. I shouldn't be here. This doesn't feel safe. Still, I walk forward. One cautious step after another.

My hands shake. My voice stalls as I open my mouth to speak.

Who are you?

"Cat got your tongue?" the mystery boy asks with a wiggle of his brow.

Now that I am close, his features look softer. Handsome, even. The sharp skulking eyes are replaced with piles of sea glass. His dark hair contrasts brilliantly with those light eyes. Soft cheekbones frame his face and, to my surprise, I see a few freckles dot his nose despite the tan skin. Now that he is no longer wearing a hoodie and stalking me from a distance, I can admit he is quite handsome in a less-than-masculine way. Although he isn't my usual ruggedly handsome type, I am not opposed to the feeling that is telling me he and I will be spending a lot of time together. There are worse companions.

Say something.

"Wh-who are you?" My voice shakes.

My stutter elicits a full-blown smile. He can tell I'm flustered, and it amuses him. Everything in me wants to bite back, to show him a quick wit. But, before I can form words from the thought, the older man speaks again.

"Mallory, I am sure you have many questions. This is bound to come as a shock to you, but you have my word that you are safe with us."

Somehow, I find the courage to speak. "Where am I and how do you know my name?"

A smile, kinder than the other man's, crosses the old man's lips, a hint of pride in his eyes. "Let me introduce myself first, if you would. My name is Oskar Alborian and this is my son, Derrick."

Oskar gestures to his son, who gives a sharp wave, before returning his attention to me. "And you, my dear girl, are Mallory Nerezza, The Unrooted Queen. The Shadowbearer of Nalara."

What the hell is he on about?

I blink and wait for him to continue, hoping to magically find a semblance of understanding in his words.

"You didn't answer my question." My boldness surprises me.

Derrick's eyes look me over as the muscles of his mouth twitch. He is sizing me up like a lion would a gazelle. When I get the chance, I will smack that smirk off his ridiculously handsome face. That is, if I don't come to my senses and leave first.

"What my dad means is we need your help."

Odd. Is he being . . . kind?

The older man, Oskar, smiles softly, his wrinkles creasing. His weathered hands clutch a wooden staff, ornately carved and beauti-fully preserved with a waxy sheen. Gray hairs speckle his chin, matching the thick white patch atop his head. He has warm eyes—the kind that can be trusted.

"I'm sorry." I look directly at Oskar, ignoring his son. "I'm not sure what this is. I don't have any money if that's what you're looking for."

They don't seem like they're unhoused, but you can't always tell by looking. Still, that makes more sense than a father-son tag team going around assaulting women and sticking around until the morning to chat. Unless they found me here and are luring me away.

Oskar is not offended by my comment. And, what's even more perplexing, his smile widens as if he's in on the joke.

"Patience, my dear. Let's take a walk."

The three of us journey through the forest—despite every scrap of survival instinct screaming at me. My will to live in hypothetical crisis scenarios has forever been nonexistent. Who would willingly live in a post-apocalyptic hellscape fighting the undead when bullets exist? That struggle could end quicker than a singular thirty-minute TV episode.

The trees don't sound like wind or settling wood. They sound like a decision made long ago. Whatever my gut is saying to the contrary, the voices whispering in the trees around us intrigue me enough to propel me forward. Either I am finally fully losing my grip on reality—sorry Dr. Thompson—or there is more out there than my meaningless existence. The way my life has been going lately, either answer is just as likely, and I'm willing to take the chance. It will work out, or it won't.

As we walk, I take note of the moss squishing between my bare feet and wonder if I should bring it up to Oskar. I'm no horticulture expert, but January isn't exactly conducive to lush greenery. He might think me incredibly dull for noticing, or for caring, but if anyone has an answer, it's probably him. Or, at least, that's the image he invokes.

Around us, the forest seems to breathe. The wind is carrying the trees back and forth, the aisle of trunks looking more and more like a rib cage expanding with each inhale. It is much less intimidating under the quickly rising sun than I remember from my dream. Though there was a serenity in the dark that I can't name now. It is much too open; I am too exposed in the light of day. Birds chirp and squirrels scamper, as they would in any other forest. This might even be a pleasant enough place, had I chosen to come here willingly.

"What is this place?" I hear myself ask in a breathless whisper, as if speaking too loudly will anger the trees.

That makes both Oskar and Derrick smile. Their eyes sweep over our surroundings with pride.

"Home," Derrick whispers back. He doesn't say it like a man describing a place. He says it like a man who's been describing it his entire life and is only now standing in it.

I stop.

"You mean, you live here?"

They do *want money.*

This is too much—two strange men living in the woods I just happened to wake up in after a night of drinking. My mind races, searching for any scraps of memory from after I left the party. Nothing comes to mind except the dream. It is one that, unusually for me, I can remember. It had to have been triggered by flashes of consciousness as my body was being moved.

"Not exactly," the younger man chortles. He is getting pleasure from how uneasy this is all making me. Was it his idea to bring me here?

I look at Oskar, seeking answers to the plethora of questions his son just raised in me. His face gives away nothing. *Of course.* If he were an accomplice, he wouldn't give up his son. Why would he bring me here to tell me the truth?

"What my son means"—he glares at Derrick—"is that while this forest itself may not be our inhabitance, it is the doorway to our homeland."

What?

"Neither of you are making any sense. Please, just tell me what is going on and why I am here, and I won't call the police. I already told you I don't have money, and I don't do drugs. You've definitely picked the wrong girl."

Hopefully they do not know that I don't have my phone on me. It must still be on the charger at home. That thought triggers another series of questions.

"What did you do with Vanessa? Where is she? Did you hurt her?"

My mind swims with the possibilities. With the extent to which a man would go with a woman like Vanessa.

The men stop and turn in my direction, and the ease with which they are ignoring my concerns leaves a bitter taste in my mouth.

I am not safe.

"It is probably best if you follow us."

My feet stay rooted in their spot.

"I am not going anywhere until you tell me where Vanessa is."

Derrick rolls his eyes and gestures at me with wild, jerking movements as he speaks to his father in an unknown tongue. The sound each word makes is a long-forgotten lullaby, beautiful and haunted.

"Behave, son," Oskar responds in English before slipping back into that silvery, flowing dialect. Whatever it is, I've never heard it spoken before coming to this forest. The more they talk, the more I recognize the cadence of the words.

The trees spoke this language.

"Hello!" I sweep my hands in a wide arch overhead, determined to be as dramatic as possible. "What did you do with my friend?"

"Oh my god, *nothing*. Your friend is fine. I'm sure she's at home sleeping off that wild party you had last night. Happy Birthday, by the way."

The exasperation in his voice begs me to believe him. And I almost do, were it not for those last words.

"How do you know it was my birthday?"

"We've been looking for you for a long time, Mallory. And we did our homework."

It's not a threat, just a revelation born from a bone-crushing exhaustion. Whatever their plans with me are, they weren't flippantly concocted. There is effort in their words, in their movements, that surprises me. Effort that most wouldn't go through for an opportunistic crime, whether that be theft, or worse.

"My dear, you can ask as many questions as you want, and we will answer them all, but you must follow us before anything more can be discussed."

Agreeing with a nod, we walk a bit farther and stop mere moments later when we arrive at a clearing, the whole of which was invisible from where we'd been standing. A willow mourns in the center, its mass weighed down by leaves, bending to the earth, subjugated by its master.

Weren't we just here?

It's logical they'd walk me in circles to disorient me, but if they were looking to hurt me, surely they would do so farther away than the parking lot.

I turn to look, weighing my options. Maybe I can find someone to help me. If I can find a passerby with a cell phone, then I can call for help.

But there is nothing there. Where the lot once stood is no more than a plot of trees. If the willow is as deep within the forest now as it was in my dream, why was it sitting at the edge of the clearing when I woke up? Did I imagine it?

I'm going insane. My greatest fear is coming true.

"How did you do that?" I ask the men in a low voice.

"Do what, my dear?" the older man responds, cocking his head.

"We——" I can't think of how to form the words without sounding like I needed more of my medication. Maybe I do. Maybe this is all an alcohol-induced dream and I will wake up in my bed hungover, just as I had planned.

Before I can finish my thought, I hear whispers sound from deep within the willow tree's trunk.

"Selowen Varis Ephyrill." This voice sounds like it belongs to someone who is either an elderly woman or a small girl. The whisper is feminine, but indistinct.

"Asharil tréd myphin." This from a man—a deep tenor. He sounds stern, but not unapproachable, as if he has knowledge he knows you will seek. Knowledge he would happily bestow upon anyone who asked, if only they asked the right questions.

I cannot decipher their message, but I know it's for me.

Without cognizance of how, I find myself enveloped in the canopy of leaves. My fingers brush the rough bark as electricity runs through my bones. A heaviness overcomes me, and I find myself— just like the long-suffering giant—weeping.

The weight of a hand presses into my shoulder. Smiling at the touch, my attention shifts to the attractive man behind me. It's been too long since I've let anyone comfort me. Since I've let myself be seen. Moments ago, I was afraid of this man. But he is not the enemy. Some outside force brought me to this place for a purpose much greater than any man could invent.

Damn. That's some tree.

Embarrassed, I wipe the tears from my cheek as a laugh forces itself out. "I really can't explain that."

Derrick's green eyes peer into me like he's reading an obscure classic. I can't hold his gaze for long. Every flutter of his lashes feels like a white-hot knife in my chest. Blushing, I turn toward the older man who is standing just outside the willow's shade.

With his ever-gentle voice, Oskar tells me we are here for me to meet the mighty Willow. It is a test—one whose rules he does not explain. His tone makes it apparent that I have passed somehow.

"You heard it whisper?" Oskar asks, though it seems more like a wish than a question. His eyes search my face as if it is the key to his salvation.

"You heard it too? Both of you?" I feel less unhinged at the possibility.

"No, only certain people can hear the trees," Derrick states, as if this is common knowledge. His voice sounds nonchalant, but his face is giving away how much he cares.

"It is a rare, yet powerful, gift bestowed upon all the heirs of Nalara. It's a form of magic called Thalanorah—The Whisperer's Gift. This gift was bestowed upon the founding brother of Nalara who was born from the Willow's seed. Only the Selowen receive it."

Nothing he says makes any sense to me, but he's speaking to me like it should. Afraid to risk upsetting the stranger by asking too many questions, I stick to the easiest one I can find.

"Selowen?"

"Ahh, yes, the Sylvaneth name for those who are born with magic the Willow supplies. Of course, some practices are common between both Trees' lineages."

This has *to be a dream.*

Oskar continues, "My son and I are from the Asharil line, who cannot hear the trees—though most don't care enough to be disappointed. It was a gift imparted only to the brother with the purest heart. My child, the fact that you can hear their whispers, however faint, proves that you are indeed a queen."

That's right. He called me a queen when we first met.

Oskar bows to me slightly at the waist, his left hand still clutching the two-toned staff. He beckons Derrick to do the same. A sharp look of judgment dances across Derrick's face, but he obeys his father. Whatever moment we may have shared is long gone now, it seems.

"And . . . what is Nalara?" I ask, afraid to look out of place.

Oskar has given me more information in the past hour than I've learned since graduating high school, and all of it is as foreign to me as the concept of calculus.

"Above all, it is your birthright and the land I escaped to find you. It is the land you are destined to rule and the home Derrick has never known. The home where I hope he will settle down and find the kind of love his mother and I once shared."

Oskar's voice trails off, an expression of longing replacing the cheeriness with which I have grown familiar. Whoever she was, wherever she's gone, he loved her.

But that is in the past, and whoever this man thinks I am, he's mistaken. There is nothing even slightly royal about me, and the only thing I've ever led is a shift at the coffee shop. My future is not wherever Nalara is.

Nalara.

Even the name sounds made-up, like a poor replica from a story I knew as a child.

That must be it.

It hasn't been that long since I last thought of that story. More than likely, my alcohol-addled brain is throwing that to the surface as some kind of psychological breakthrough. The simplest explanation is usually the truth, right?

This is definitely a dream.

Before I can pinch myself awake, a feeling bubbles to the surface, one I wish I could overlook. Every fiber of my being is screaming out toward the tree. A ridiculous *tree*. I want to laugh and cry and scream all at once. This is my reality, or whatever new version I am about to embrace. And it's one where I can talk to trees . . . and they *talk back*.

CHAPTER FOUR
MALLORY

"Haven't you ever felt like there was more for you than this place?"
Derrick questions. "Like you belong somewhere else?"

Only every day of my life.

Are these strangers—these familiar strangers—right? Is Nalara,
whatever that is, the reason I've wanted to crawl out of my skin my
entire life?

Is this where I've been running?

My body tilts as something internal shifts, and I am overcome
with nausea once more. My hands flail, desperate to grab on to
something—anything—that can keep me upright. Nothing comes to
my rescue and I fall to the earth, scraping my left leg on the jagged,
exposed roots of the willow tree. Blood trickles. It's not a deep cut,
but I watch with bated breath, waiting for the pain. The pain is
underwhelming.

The two men stand over me. Concern is evident on Oskar's face,
but Derrick is looking at me expectantly. My bleeding won't derail
his line of questioning.

"I guess? Doesn't everyone feel that way sometimes?"

Of course, I have dreamt of moments like this my entire life.
But, through the painful teacher that is experience, I am a pragma-

tist at heart. This is too good to be true. Whatever reason they're telling me this, something is in it for them.

A quiet look of pity crosses Derrick's face as he studies me again. His eyes are not roaming my body, but I feel exposed. He is looking directly into my mind. It only feels that way, of course . . . unless he has some sort of Nalaran super magic. He *could* have some sort of Nalaran super magic—how would I know otherwise?

"Who exactly are you, and how did you find me?" I direct this question at the father. So far, he has proven more receptive to my curiosity, like he understands that I owe him nothing.

"You will have to trust us, child. There is more to this world than you could possibly fathom." Oskar's lilting smile grounds me. His paternal nature comforts me, a feeling I haven't had in too long.

It's not fair to use him to fill the void, Mallory.

We sit for a while longer, the men giving me a brief summary of the fairy tale world of Nalara. Fairy tale is my word, not theirs. The way they describe this country—kingdom?—sounds nothing short of a Brothers Grimm story. Though, hopefully, without the tragic endings.

It is clear to me that Oskar misses this place. His passion emanates in a flurry of feverish adjectives. Enchanting. Magical. Ancient. My disdain for my current surroundings only amplifies the intrigue. Could Nalara be all that he's promising?

When Oskar breaks from his impassioned monologue, I find my footing to interject.

"How do I fit into all of this, exactly? You say I am queen, but I am the furthest thing from it. I'm a barista. Or, I was until I lost my job yesterday. There is nothing I have to offer you that *I* even want."

"Ahh, yes. If you're looking at it from an Earthly perspective, I suppose that would be an excellent question. However, you need to provide nothing but yourself. You can't earn the crown through work alone, and you can do nothing here to deserve it. It simply is, and you simply are."

How pathetically evasive.

Sensing my reluctance he continues, "You will be tested with a far greater scrutiny than any you have yet to endure. But, you will not be asked to earn what is to be given, only to prove you can bear its weight. You are Mallory Nerezza, the Unrooted Queen. Our most sacred prophecy foretold your coming many years ago."

"I am queen of nothing," I want to say, but don't. Instead I nod, as if I understand.

"What does the prophecy say?"

"From foreign land, a child born, shall hold the crown while fate is torn. Daughter of Willow, child of Ash, a hero's flame will split the path."

My breath catches as the wind nods against my arm, a silent ode to my birthright. As much as I want to believe in destiny, the words are too ambiguous.

"That could mean anyone," I say, trying to be the voice of reason. "What makes you think it's referring to me?"

Derrick rolls his eyes—he would rather I shut up and accept my crown. What little girl never dreamt of being a princess, right? Swallowing hard, I fight the urge to cause a disturbance. The two of them wouldn't be able to take me seriously if I do—everything I do after that would be forever overshadowed by how quickly I throw tantrums.

Whatever, let them explain.

Oskar steps in graciously and provides a history lesson. He explains that time between the realms moves differently. Years ago, just before I was born, there was an uprising in Nalara known as the Sundering. The Sundering was a bloody battle instigated by the Emberguard, a militant operation bred from the Ashen Doctrine.

"Both walks of life in Nalara are equally important, but the Emberguard denies the Twinned Path, a tenant of peace in Nalara that even most of those who follow the Ashen Doctrine believe. My staff serves as a reminder to me, the Voice of the Hollow, that the Crown I serve reflects that path. That joy cannot bloom without sorrow, healing cannot exist without judgment, and order can only be formed with righteous compassion."

I stare blankly at the man.

Oskar goes on to explain the cause of the Sundering—an oracle child was born, and a prophecy foretold that he would be either the salvation or the undoing of the entire kingdom.

"The king and queen sent the child through the door. But fear overtook me and I did not go with the child. In that time, the war raged and peace vanished from the kingdom. When I could finally make my escape, generations had passed on Earth. It took far longer than I'd anticipated to find the oracle child's heir." Oskar paused with a pointed smile at me. "But here you are, at last."

"How do you know that heir is me?"

Oskar smiles but does not answer. I process his story as a heaviness fills the air. His passion makes it just believable enough that I decide to consider it, but there is a twinge of something behind his eyes, like this story was just a little too well-rehearsed. For whose benefit is this little show? A gut instinct tells me he isn't being completely honest with his son.

"So, what do you need from me?"

It is Derrick who answers, his tone teasingly ominous. "You're going to save us."

The muscles in my ears twitch as I fight the scowl growing on my face. The position I am in is certainly strange, but I can't be bothered to joke about it. My belief in a magical world of which I am high queen is already comical enough. But, despite the ridiculousness of the premise, it's one I do believe.

"How?"

"We need you to take your rightful place on the throne," Oskar answers. "It is only with your help that we can get home and begin righting these historic wrongs."

"And what if I can't?" My voice comes out shaky.

Oskar's face darkens. "Then the Emberguard will rule. They are close as it is, it won't be long until magic in Nalara weakens enough for someone to steal the crown."

This man has the wrong girl, I am sure of it. But the thought of escaping excites me—there is nothing left for me here: no job, no friends, no relationship. I don't think anyone would be too hard-pressed to see me go. And once they realize I am not who they were looking for, they'll leave me in peace in Nalara.

"How do we get there?" My voice is even, trying to sound precisely as interested as I should be—not too eager but also not entirely unfazed. It must have worked, because Oskar takes his turn to smile.

"We walk through the gate."

"How do we find the gate?"

"We are already here." He springs to his feet more spryly than a man his age should be able.

Oskar's jovial steps bound around the substantial trunk. He looks like a child playing with their favorite toy—the anticipation building for a payoff that, unbeknownst to them, will be less than promised. We come to our stopping point, the buzzing in my ears like I am standing near an electric fence. My body knows this place.

The door from my dream—which I'm beginning to understand wasn't a dream at all—stands in front of me, exactly as I had seen it. The bird sits in the same place, and those same words shine from their resting place.

Naelyn doral selowen—asharil ven shalair

I pass a quizzical glance to my companion, silently promoting a translation.

"It says, 'The keeper of the Willow shall enter—" Oskar begins.

"The Ash will rain judgment," I hear myself finish.

CHAPTER FIVE
MALLORY

A gasp escapes my lips. The ancient tongue that had been eluding me now came as easily as my own.

Maybe this is real.

Behind me, Derrick clears his throat. A rustling sound fills my stunned silence as Oskar shifts behind me and his antsy energy penetrates the air.

"How do I open it?" I ask the pair, hoping it will be Oskar who answers.

"Just knock, my dear, and it will open to the heir."

"That's it? A land of magic and mystery, and to enter all I have to do is knock." I shoot a pointed look at the old man, whose lips are pursed in a tight line. A laugh threatens to escape at the ridiculousness of the situation.

"Just go," Derrick urges.

With shaking hands, I squeeze my right fingers into a fist. Moments ago, this was a cute story from a fragile old man. Now, it's reality. What if the door doesn't open?

But what if it does?

Drawing my hand to eye level, I rap my knuckles quickly against the smooth door. Once. Twice. Three times.

Like I'm waiting for it to explode, I take a step back. My breath catches as the seconds pass. One. Two. Three.

A warm green light seeps through the seams of the wood. The wind stirs, picking up fallen leaves in a cyclic storm. An indistinguishable yet familiar scent fills the air, sweet and earthy. Slowly, begrudgingly, the door in the willow creaks open as the scent of lavender permeates the air before settling. The tree is warning me of my fate. With a matched reluctance, I step over the threshold.

I'm not sure what I expect: a sweeping vortex, a beam of lightning, a wormhole. I get none of that. There is a small flash of light as I push into a thick wall of air, where I am greeted with a forest that is the mirror image of the one I left. So much so that I worry I imagined the whole thing. Is it possible it didn't open at all?

Brushing my hands against the bark of the willow I'd just walked through, I notice the writing above the door is different.

"The gate shall seal with the prophesied steps."

Words written in my native tongue surprise me. By the absence of my companions it is evident I have safely crossed the portal.

Shit.

My companions are not through the portal yet. I'd forgotten all about them in the mystery of the gate, however long it had taken to step through, but I was sure they were right behind me. No matter, I can wait. After all, I am finally home. Regardless of their eventual surfacing, my path is set before me—I am here to stay. Besides, without them I won't have the pressures of the Crown looming over my shoulder. Maybe it *is* a good thing they haven't surfaced.

Resolving myself to a bit of light exploring—never too far from the view of the willow tree—I walk around the expansive trunk in hopes of surveying the other side. I realize I am still barefoot when I step squarely on a twig. Pulling the thorn from my heel, I roll my eyes at the nuisance. Finding shoes will be an urgent matter.

On the other side of the meadow, I expect the emptiness of the clearing back in the real world. Instead, I find myself staring at another tree. Not a willow, but somehow its mirror. Its rival. Its equal.

This tree is much taller than the willow, and not nearly as broad. Its leaves point toward the heavens with a sense of purpose—or arrogance. Before today, it would have been impossible for me to tell what type of tree I was looking at. It looks exactly like every tree I have ever seen. Today, though, I learned of an ancient prophecy and a magical realm with two sacred trees.

Ash. Judgment.

"Mallory!" It's the younger man's searching voice. Is that . . . concern? Is it possible he doesn't resent my existence nearly as much as he showed earlier?

"Over here!" I call toward the voice. "I found the Ash tree."

Derrick sidles up beside me, a low whistle escaping his lips.

"Wow. That is an impressive tree," he teases.

My eyes roll as far back as they can, but inside I want to chuckle. It feels good to joke with someone, even if it's with a stranger. I'm not sure I can even remember the last time I laughed. Derrick may be an arrogant prick, but he is funny—I'll give him that.

"Okay, but it *is* a pretty cool tree," I say mock-defensively.

Derrick chuckles, the corners of his lips pulling up to meet his eyes. It's a smile that belongs to a Greek god etched in stone long ago. Putting his hands in the pockets of his jeans with an emanating coolness, he looks around, surveying the canopy above our heads.

"This must be it," he determines.

"What is it?"

"My dad talks a lot about the Sacred Grove of the Twinned Trees. The gate must have led us here for some reason."

"What do you mean 'led us here'? Isn't that how doors work?" I ask while studying the trees. While both the ash and the willow tree are impressive in circumference and stature, they don't look like twins. In fact, I don't think they can look any more different.

"It's less of a door and more of a portal, really. Dad was wondering where it would lead us. According to him, it takes you where you need to go." His voice is low and ominous in a mockery of Oskar's sincerity.

My eyes roll again. "Do you take anything seriously?"

"Not usually."

"Where is Oskar anyway?" I ask an amused Derrick. "Didn't he come through with you?"

"Time works differently, remember?" He taps his finger to his temple before glancing toward the willow. "He'll be here soon, but we really should head back and wait there. He might think we left without him. I'm not going to lie, I thought you had bolted on us for a minute there."

He studies me carefully. "Luckily, I gave you the benefit of the doubt, which wasn't easy, you know."

A flash of concern crosses Derrick's face at the mention of Oskar, but is quickly replaced with a serene grin. He cares for his dad, I can tell. But there was a brief sense of trepidation in his demeanor.

Who are these people?

Just as we make our way to the gate, Oskar steps through. Serendipitous, and a good omen . . . I hope.

"Children." Oskar looks between the two of us. "Are you both alright?"

Being called a child by Oskar isn't nearly as infantilizing as I would have thought. In fact, I don't mind it. His presence is fatherly and warm, something I haven't felt in too long. If I was going to trust anyone without question, it would be him. Whether from years of practice as part of the royal council or inherent ability, he exudes an air of calm recognition. He *sees* me, and that's rare.

After a thorough examination of the clearing, we nestle under the canopy of the Willow tree as the three of us make a plan. Oskar quickly points out there isn't much I can decide until I learn what I will face. How can someone sit on the throne of a kingdom they have never known without lessons?

My elbow nudges Oskar's side when Derrick gets up to look for anything we can use to make camp. His years as a wilderness scout, and the long hours spent in the woods earning badges, are paying off, according to his father.

"I fear there may be those who will object to my authority." Hopefully my voice sounds as confident and regal as I imagine.

It isn't that I waited to get Oskar alone because I distrust the younger man, not wholly anyway. He's a cliche. Enigmatic, moody, maybe even a tad goofy—every male protagonist in a cheesy romance novel—and I can't get a read on him. Derrick is the kind of guy I would have trusted, before. He is the kind of guy I need to stop trusting. Oskar, on the other hand, is strong and consistent. Well-spoken, deeply grounded. He isn't a presence that comes by often and I find myself admiring him more and more. The sense that the two of us are more alike than we seem itches at the back of my brain.

"They might have some quarrels with your appointment, but fear not, my dear. I was an honored advisor to the throne for many years. If anyone can break through their wall of scrutiny, it's me."

"How long have you been away?"

"I'm not sure." His voice falters. "It is impossible to tell."

My head tilts to the left, silently imploring him to explain.

"There is no formula to how time runs between the realms. Sure, there are days and months and years here, but how they line up is unknown. On Earth, time is relatively linear, with a past, present, and future running concurrently, if science is to be believed. Nalara doesn't have science. It's unheard of now and forever will be. Why develop industry when you have magic?"

His weathered hand rests on my left shoulder. "Hopefully it's been long enough."

Before I can spend more than a moment pondering what he means, Derrick comes bounding up to us. He reminds me of a Chihuahua, with his anxious energy and constant need for attention. It's like he wants me to be aware he's upset that his father is spending so much time on someone else. As far as I can gather, it has always just been the two of them.

"What's the plan?" he asks, impatience growing in his voice as he stands above us, bouncing from foot to foot. "We can't stay here forever."

Before walking through the gate, I hadn't thought to ask for logistics. I hadn't bothered to consider the consequences. Someone needed me and I'd leapt through that door without a second thought.

Stupid girl. You wanted to be special.

"We go to Elvarn, see where the state of Nalara lies. Once there, we will come up with a plan to get Mallory on the throne," Oskar replies to Derrick—ever the wise councilman of his past.

"Elvarn?" I ask.

"It's the capital city of Nalara. It is where your palace, Thirawen, lies in wait for its ruler. From here, it is about a seven-day journey west if we walk continuously. Though there is no telling how long our journey will take us, there are a few stops we must make along the way."

Derrick looks at his father, shock etched on his face. "Dad, please tell me we aren't taking the Witherwalk."

"Yes, my son, we are." Oskar nods gravely. "It is the only way to Elvarn from the Grove. The Witherwalk itself is the only clearance anyone has to come to The Sight of the Twinned Trees. If we do not complete it, the consequences are more grave than I want you to know."

Without my asking, both Derrick and Oskar launch into an explanation of the Witherwalk's symbolic journey. Traditionally, it is started in Elvarn as a spiritual pilgrimage for newly appointed nobility. As the Voice of the Hollow, Oskar has completed this journey before.

"It is not for the faint of heart," he tells us. "It is a rite of passage Mallory would have had to take regardless—it is only fitting that it would be now. The Creators deemed it so, or the portal would have opened elsewhere."

"Besides," he says with a nonchalant wave of his hand, "we can use her trek to gain favor with The Order."

"Who keeps track of its completion?" I surprise myself by asking. "Surely this won't count without some kind of record?"

The now-familiar smile returns to Oskar's face with an alluring warmth.

"The trees."

"The trees?"

"You know as well as anyone that the trees whisper. Here in Nalara, an underground root network runs from the Twinned Trees to the Castle Thirawen, and everywhere in between. You are never alone, my dear." His voice blankets my anxiety only for a moment. "It is up to you to decide whether or not to trust them."

"Dad, quit scaring her."

Derrick scolds Oskar as if he was the child in their relationship. A stern heat comes from his words and his shoulders stiffen. I'm not sure if Derrick is a violent man, but I suspect, at this moment, he might be.

"It's okay," I interject to restore peace. "Tell me as much as possible about this journey. What am I getting into?."

Derrick gets to work building a fire while Oskar and I haphazardly assemble fallen logs into a ring for seating. The act of doing so reminds me of the campfires I had at summer camp every year. My parents, in the prime of their marriage, would send me away every summer to get rid of me. Not that I minded. Summer camp was the one place I could breathe without an adult looking down my neck. Even the counselors seemed to leave me alone. And anything was better than being with my parents.

When their relationship was good, it was almost worse. At least, worse for me. Being constantly at each other's throats kept them from ganging up on me. If they were speaking to one another without screaming, it was only a matter of time before the screams were set on me.

My parents are not bad people, just two people who never should have gotten married. The tension finally became too much, and they divorced when I was fifteen. I wish it had been sooner. Countless nights of my youth were spent dreaming of what it would be like to have a broken home. For many kids, it was a sad reality of their daily life. For me, it would have been a welcomed reprieve.

Embers fly through the air as Derrick slams the last bundle of twigs onto the fire, shaking me from my past. A warmth spreads through the air, bringing along with it the faint smell of marshmallows. Of course, that is just a memory, but I realize how hungry I have gotten, though I am sure by Earth standards it hasn't been more than a few hours. Here, night is falling fast. As if his circadian rhythm has already returned to Nalara's schedule, Oskar acclimates quicker to the time change than the two of us.

"Good night, children," he says with a yawn. "I think I will turn in for the night. You'd be better prepared if you both did too."

Smiling politely, I reply, "Good night, Oskar. It shouldn't be long for me."

That's a lie, and I know it.

As Oskar descends into the shadows, Derrick sits beside me with a hard thunk. Daggers shoot from my eyes as the log rolls slightly under his weight. In answer to my disdain, he grins back like a kid in a candy store. Welcoming the silence, I turn my face away from his, but not before rolling my eyes again. This expression is one that will be permanently etched on my face if he doesn't grow up soon. We sit in stillness for a moment, staring in opposite directions.

"The Witherwalk claims more lives than it saves, Mal." Derrick sounds somber enough that someone might think his concern was for me. It's the first time I hear something in his voice that isn't performing.

He called you Mal.

Not many people do, but I wish they would. Although, I never tell them. I think nicknames should be something you earn. It's unnatural to ask someone to call you a cooler name. Only try-hards try that hard.

"What do you mean?" I ask.

"Remember what Dad was saying about this being a rite of passage for you?"

That gets my attention, and I turn around to face him as I search for his eyes in the amber light of the fire. His voice is serious, something I don't take lightly from the jester of a man. Words fail and a small nod is all I can manage.

"That's because it's a test. And it is one that isn't meant to be passed."

Blinking in the darkness, I stay silent. Hopefully he can't see how nervous I am.

"You're not going to die," he says, trying to reassure me, "but it will change you, and maybe not for the better."

CHAPTER SIX
MALLORY

The clearing has become eerie since Oskar left our circle, the sound of owls hooting in the distance breaking up the constant chirping of crickets. It is cold, but not uncomfortably so. Whatever month it is now, it's not winter. Huddled against a stranger in a place unfamiliar to me, it dawns on me that I should feel afraid. Back home I would have.

I'm breaking all my own rules, but it's hard for me to see it that way. Destiny chose me for this place. At least, that's what they say. And I want so badly for that to be true. If it is, all my years of running would mean something. Maybe this is the finish line, or, at the very least, the right race.

For years, I've run from anything that got too hard to face. When my parents split, they sold the house and I was forced to shuttle back and forth between each of their condos on either side of town for a week at a time. It was then that I swore to myself I would never have a child. The part of my DNA that got whatever fucked-up gene they had wouldn't live on.

When I'd turned eighteen, I'd packed my room at my mom's house. By then, I'd stopped visiting Dad. He didn't really want me anyway when I was no longer the little girl he remembered, when I

49

was too hard to love. That night, I left town and never looked back. Back then, it felt necessary. Then I'd met him.

His name was Jeremy. We met at a bar I was too young to get into, and he was too old to be looking at me the way he did. But what does twelve years matter when you're young and in love? Or, I thought we had been. He was ready to settle down and start a family with his blushing nineteen-year-old bride within six months of meeting me.

At the first sight of something serious, I did what I always do. Manhattan called me, a single girl in her early twenties, and I answered. Once upon a time, I thought that was the right choice. But one thing led to another and I landed in Poughkeepsie with a shitty job and a half-interested roommate.

And now I'm here, wherever in the universe "here" is . . . if anywhere at all. This feels more right than anything I have ever done. Hell, the gate welcomed me through as its long lost heir. Would it have opened if I wasn't destined to be here?

A rustling noise to my right jolts me from my contemplation. Turning, I find Derrick sitting upright, staring off into the distance, as if trying to pinpoint what it is. When he notices me, he wordlessly puts one index finger to his lips and points into the distance with the other. My eyes follow his finger and settle on the inky blackness of the tree line, unable to make out shapes in the growing darkness. Derrick must notice my squinting.

Listen, he mouths.

Closing my eyes, I beg my ears to work harder with the loss of a sense. A distance away, I hear a faint rustling in the brush. The sound grows louder with each passing second, eventually overtaking the pounding in my ears. My heartbeat quickens and I open my eyes. To my surprise, Derrick is now standing, moving closer to the source of the disturbance. It takes me a moment to decide, but I get up and join him.

Instinctually, I grab his hand. My fingers lock through his before I know what I'm doing, finding comfort in their warmth. He looks down, eyes widening just a smidge. My hand retreats before he can ask a question. The look on my face begs him to stay silent and forget about this moment. Whether he hears my pleas or it's the thought of whatever animal is lurking in the bushes, he obeys, yet he doesn't stop smiling as he resumes his investigation.

We creep forward, as silently as we can muster, hoping to uncover the source of the noise. The rustling sounds like it is being made from an animal no bigger than a raccoon, but I wasn't about to let Derrick leave me alone to be eaten—just in case I am wrong. I look behind me. Oskar is still sleeping soundly. A chill runs down my spine. Should I wake him? The air stiffens and the pounding in my chest grows stronger.

A fragment of something catches in my peripheral vision. Indescribable, but real. Another flash of movement flutters in the opposite direction. Its proximity startles me and a jolt runs through me. Derrick looks unnerved. His skin, darker than mine, glows warmly in the yellow light as his emerald eyes search the fire. Without the ever-plastered smirk, he looks young—like a scared little boy camping with his family for the first time.

"Go from here. We wish to work in peace," a child's voice whispers in my mind.

"Did you hear that?" I ask aloud, not looking at Derrick. I'm afraid that if I look away from this spot, whoever is out there will grab me before I have the chance to scream.

"Hear what?" he asks back. He keeps his voice low—something I ought to remember.

I shake my head, a silent plea for him not to question my sanity. The voice was real, there's no doubt in my mind. Gathering the courage to speak, my voice carries out into the woods.

"Who are you?"

"Please. We are frightened. We mean no harm to you."

Derrick is staring at me now, his eyes wide as he steps back.

"I heard them this time," he says walking backward.

"We will leave," he tells the mysterious voice.

"Wait." The voice stops me as I turn. It sounds closer now, but I have seen nothing change. *"We will reveal ourselves only to you."*

When I stop, my companion gives me a puzzled look. He gently grabs my hand, incorrectly suspecting my change of movement has been triggered by fright. My heart kicks up into my chest and I grow warm despite the fire's distance.

He can rescue you just this once. No one would think poorly of you if you just let him take charge.

Despite the longing consuming me to retreat, and for no other reason than curiosity, I push his hand away.

"No," I say to him, my voice little more than a whisper, "they are speaking to me. I think they want me to stay."

Derrick looks at me, a question in his eye. Can he trust me? One foot draws back slowly, and then the other. A leaf crunches under him, as if to protest his withdrawal.

I turn away.

Hurry up.

A phantom hole forms on the back of my skull, where I can feel Derrick's trained gaze penetrating. I wipe my clammy hands against the fabric of the party dress I had forgotten I was wearing. The soft velvet does little to dry the dampness, but the warmth is welcomed.

"Please," my voice croaks when I hear the distinct creak of Derrick taking his seat on the log. I clear my throat.

Don't show your nerves.

"Please," my voice comes out stronger this time, "come out where I can see you. I promise I mean no harm."

Small figures glide forward. Three of them, I realize in the light. Each shorter than the last and none taller than an eight-year-old child. Though their frames are small, an ancient aura glows around them. Serenity fills the cold air between us and I draw in a strong breath. My pulse slows as I wait for their words.

"Mallory Nerezza, the Unrooted Queen," the shortest of the creatures begins, "for centuries we have awaited your coming. It was once foretold you would grace these woods through a portal from Earth."

"Fear not." It is the stoutest of the three who speaks now. "We were born to aid in your journey and are bound to your light by our sacred oath to the Twinned Path."

Magnificence radiates off of these . . . creatures. Whatever they are called, they are humanoid saplings. Each of them looks carved from the bark of either sacred tree. One looks to be carved somehow out of both barks, though not haphazardly fitted together like one would expect. Their hair glows with a green light—the light that seeped from the portal into the real world. Walking through that door feels like forever ago now.

"I am sure you have many questions." The third one's childlike voice perforates my thoughts.

There is nothing to do but to nod.

"We suspected you might," the first voice speaks again. "That is only natural, given the circumstances. You are likely wondering who we are, and how we are connected."

Again I nod. It's not a question.

"We are the Hollowborne. A race of beings constructed by memory magic and born from the bark of the Creators. It is our duty to defend this Sacred Grove of the Twinned Trees. Our magic is bound to its protection and therefore it is us who allows entry into this most holy place."

Oskar had said something about the Witherwalk being the only means of entry to this place. Are these Hollowborne the reason for the trials I am to face?

"Prophecy has foretold your coming and we've lain in a dormant slumber for quite some time."

"As you may have noticed," the Hollowborne continues, "there are but three of us in existence. One to walk the path of the Ash's fire and one for those burdened by the Willow. And, as for me? I am the Arbiter, the spiritual embodiment of the Twinned Path."

My body swallows hard as I force the gasp back into my lungs. The blanket of peace their presence laid on my shoulders slips.

Have I been burdened? Or, am I the burden?

As if reading my thoughts, the spirit speaks up again. "The path of the Willow is dark and painful, but that pain is essential to the harmony of Nalara and its people. Only once it can be truly embraced will the crown find its home. The Hollow Crown needs a ruler."

"Why me?" I ask the trio. "Why couldn't it have been someone else? Some other heir to the throne before me?"

My words are carefully chosen—they can't know the thought of the Witherwalk, from all that Derrick has said, makes me want to throw myself from the nearest cliff. That it is taking everything in me to keep my feet planted. I could run. I *should* run.

A sigh, and a soft smile, from the one who is presumably the Willow spirit (the shortest and widest of the bunch). "One cannot question fate. We must only choose whether to deny our destiny or let it give us strength."

What is my fate?

The fire crackles behind me, drawing my attention. Derrick, perched on one of the logs, stares intently at us. His features are sharp, on edge. I should head back before he gets too suspicious. The Hollowborne are watching me, their eyes following my thoughts.

"I really should be leaving. My friends are going to start to worry."

"Mallory," the Arbiter begins as I turn to leave, "before you depart, let us leave you with one last warning."

With a slow reluctance, my body faces the Arbiter.

"Hold loosely what you think you know," Willow begins in a quiet voice. "Sorrow clouds perception. Grief veils even the deepest wounds."

The Ash spirit speaks next. "Grasp firm your perception. You sense what is unsteady and right its course. Cling fast to what lies hidden."

"The scales demand balance. Balance demands justice. Justice demands sacrifice. Sacrifice demands truth."

The Arbiter's voice rings in my ear as I return to camp.

CHAPTER SEVEN
DERRICK

She moves quietly, Mallory. Rising from her spot, her hips sway in a way that isn't overly feminine, but I can see the appeal. She wears her long auburn hair down so it grazes just above the small of her back. The soft curls look messy after a night of camping in the woods without a tent, but not in a bad way.

It had been a rough night of sleep for us both. I suspect she spent her time awake, holding her breath, waiting for me to prove her right—waiting to be hurt. Despite what she says, I get the impression she spends a lot of time waiting. But it doesn't matter. My whole life was spent searching for her, waiting to bring her back to restore the dwindling magic of this land. A land that is my birthright, and hers too. At least, that's what dad has been telling me for years.

Mallory is right to worry. Where we come from, it is only natural for a woman to question men. It may not be much different for a woman here in Nalara. Where there are men there will always be an enemy to the well-being of women. Most of that on Earth is the result of religious interference, something not unfamiliar to this world.

Despite what she thinks of me, I made a vow to my father and the Crown to keep her safe and oversee her journey to the throne—no harm will come to her. It's doubtful she'd believe that from a virtual stranger, but she isn't a stranger to me. I'll have to work to earn her trust and I'm okay with that.

When we discussed the creatures last night, lying on opposite sides of the fire, gazing into each other's eyes through its orange flames, my inquiry was met with indifference. Of course it's normal, to be expected, even, but there was something about the way she grabbed my hand that shot a flicker of hope through my skin. For a brief second I thought that maybe . . .

I shake my head to clear the thoughts. Last night is in the past and I have to let it go, even if I don't quite know what *it* is. Dad will know what those things were and what they wanted with Mallory. He knows more about Nalara than anyone living. Or, he pretends well enough.

"Are you coming?" Her voice rings in my ear. Despite the tone, it is a pleasant enough sound.

"Yeah," I call ahead as I hurry my steps to meet her.

With all my pondering, I hadn't realized they'd begun the walk into the woods without me. It is impossible to tell which direction they are going, though I am sure my father knows. My childhood was painted with stories of the royal advisor, hard at work, keeping peace amongst the nation. He'd only ever told me tales of the good in Nalara, until recently. There is an innocence in being a kid that even *he* felt he couldn't corrupt with the truth.

In the morning light, her hair had shined like fire, though in the woods it is only coming through in brilliant bursts. She is nothing like what I'd imagined. All this time I was preparing for someone to lead, and she walks like she's trying to take up less space than she's owed. I don't know what to do with that.

"They told me to be careful of trusting others," I catch Mallory saying to Dad.

"Yes. That is a prudent warning indeed."

With a curt nod, a silence settles between the pair.

Quickening my pace, I settle to match Mallory's stride. Her lips press into a thin line, but she does not falter. Whether she feels confident or not, she exudes it in a way that makes me want to laugh. In a way that makes me want to make *her* laugh.

She turns to me. "Why were you following me that day in the parking lot? You could have come to talk to me. Why did you run?"

My cheeks flush and I turn to hide my face. I can feel her stare boring a hole in the back of my head. The truth is, I had wanted to, but I had been under strict orders not to talk to her . . . orders I may or may not have skirted a few too many times by ordering a coffee. She'd had to come to the grove on her own—Dad had made that abundantly clear—so he could determine her powers. I wasn't supposed to be seen, but when she caught me staring, something inside me had begged me to stand still.

"I don't know." I wish I could give her a better answer, one that makes me look mysterious or intelligent. "I guess you're just intimidating."

An eye roll.

"No, but seriously, I'm not sure. I knew it was important that we find you, but I didn't know how to approach you about a magical parallel realm. Be honest, would you have believed me or would have called the police because some creepy loser was stalking you?"

That part is true enough. How do you tell someone you are stalking that they are actually destined to be heir to a crown in a world of magic? Even if I could have spoken to her about it, she wouldn't have believed me.

She chuckles and it sounds like music.

"Fair enough," she replies and her features soften. A small smile dances across her lips, daring her to live in the moment for once.

Good, I've disarmed her, if only slightly. Maybe this will work out after all . . . maybe I can fulfill my promise.

It's then I realize I have no idea where we are going. We have been walking at least twenty minutes in this direction, whatever direction that is.

"Dad," I shout, toward his back, "where are we?"

"We are heading east, my child, to the village of Liriwyn."

CHAPTER EIGHT
MALLORY

Something about the journey to Liriwyn surprised me. It's not that it was incredibly long—we walked no more than an hour. Oskar told me when I'd arrived that the Witherwalk must take no less than seven days, but at this rate I am not sure how it will last that long. There must be more to this country than meets the eye, or more to these trials.

By the time we make it to the village, my soles are blistered and black with caked-on dirt. Derrick had offered me his shoes on the walk, but their size proved more of a liability than my feet alone. A village must have a place to buy shoes—with what money, I don't know. Maybe someone will take pity on me and loan me something now with a promise of repayment from the future queen. Not that I have any kind of collateral to leave in place.

Liriwyn is a bustling place, if the town center is any indication. Music flows from countless directions at varying volumes. The inhabitants, who look much more like humans than I would have thought, line the square. All of them are either dancing or milling about shopping at the various vendors' tents arranged along the perimeter. We may have stumbled upon a festival of sorts, but something tells me it is always like this. Each Nalaran we pass seems happier than the last.

"The Vale of Joy," Derrick whispers beside me.

"What?"

"That's what it means—Liriwyn. Dad says this is the happiest place in any known universe. Just look around. I'd say he is right."

Scanning the crowd once more, my eyes lock on a group of kids blowing bubbles through some rudimentary contraption. Each of them smiles, their laughter drowned out by the band playing a short way behind them in the center of the square. Wind and string instruments create a lively tune and a crowd forms, with pairs breaking off to dance.

In another section of the town, men mill about with steins of beer, their boisterous laughs evident when one misses the target on the dart board in front of them. Crowds of women, presumably their wives, watch and cheer as the competition continues.

This truly is a place where happiness thrives; there is not a single frown amongst the throng of villagers. A feeling like a bubble of light erupts in my chest. It boils up into my throat, eventually culminating in an uproarious laugh escaping my lips. I can't stop laughing. Why am I laughing?

Joy.

It's a feeling I can't remember having ever known. My limbs are light as air as I move through the crowd.

"Excuse me." A voice fractures through the layer of happiness surrounding me.

"Oh, I'm sorry," I say to the little boy out of habit. My meaning is nothing more than to express my understanding, but I can sense immediately I have said something wrong.

Silence fills the air. The music quiets and every conversation in the square stills. All at once, I feel hundreds of eyes on me. Unable to comprehend my faux pas, but understanding its magnitude, my face grows red with heat as I look down at the boy in front of me.

"Selowen," he whispers, not breaking eye contact. For a moment, panic flits across his young brows, replaced in an instant with a smile. Just as fast as he appeared, he bolts, leaving me alone to wonder what I had done.

Selowen—the Willow.

How could he have known of my bloodline, and why had it frightened him?

A muscular man saddles up beside me and wraps his arm around my shoulders. He smiles, euphoria leaking from him, and chuckles. A connection, like an intoxication, sparks between us instantly.

"Welcome, my friend, to Liriwyn! We couldn't be happier to welcome you into our fold." He smiles and I see nothing but my reflection in his teeth. They are so white they are almost blinding. "You will be treated as kinfolk when you are in our village, and you will be given the same opportunity at living a joyous life as any natural-born Liriwynian. There is, however, one rule in Liriwyn. One cardinal rule, if you will. We do not acknowledge anything to do with Selowen. The Willow, and all that it stands for, is cursed on these Ashen grounds."

"Oh," I say, "I'm so—"

Oskar shoots me a pointed look and quietly lifts his finger to his lips.

Don't apologize.

A smile replaces the curiosity etched in my brow as I heed the little boy's warning and remove any trace of discontent from my face.

"Can I ask why?"

"Of course you may! But first, come, come. We must eat! I am sure you are starving from your journey through the portal," the man says with an exaggerated wave of his arm, before pointing at my mud-covered feet, "and we mustn't forget to find you some shoes."

The stranger ushers us forward, like longtime friends, blabbering about something or other with Oskar. What they are discussing, I can't pretend to comprehend. The reminder to acquire shoes is welcome. In the anxiety surrounding the events of the last few minutes, that particular quest had slipped my mind.

"Hey." I hear a whisper as a sharp elbow jabs my ribs. "How did you do that?"

"Do what?" I whisper back like an elementary school kid being scolded by their teacher.

"Talk to him," Derrick answers.

I am not in the mood to play mind games.

"What?" It comes out colder than I mean, but I don't correct myself. He should understand my frustration.

"Mal . . . you were speaking Sylvaneth. Did you not realize that?"

"No, I wasn't. You know I can't speak Sylvaneth."

Silence. A quizzical look, followed by a slight nod. Whatever I said must have been wrong because he won't match my gaze. Why won't he believe me?

We follow along in silence the rest of the way. It isn't a long walk, but my newly remembered feet remind me with every step how far I've come. The roughly hewn cobblestones that make up the road jam into my wounds, eliciting small whimpers—I don't know how kindly they will take to me screaming in pain in such a happy place. With each step sending jolts up my calves, I hold my breath until we arrive.

It isn't long until we arrive at a home—best described as a manor of sorts. The garden is lush and perfectly manicured, with the same combination of moss and clover that had been growing in the grove back home. A pang grows in my stomach—at least there is something here that reminds me of home. Until now, I hadn't considered the possibility that I would be homesick. That I *could* be homesick.

A sweet, overly perfumed scent floods my nostrils, growing stronger the closer we get to our new friend's grounds. His lawn is ornately decorated with both flowers and statues, as if eager to make a good impression.

Coming up to the house, we are met with gazes from a variety of onlookers, some holding quiet judgment, while others more blatantly ogle. There are magical beings from every aspect of one's imagination—some beautiful and ethereal, some rugged and mighty. All focused on us. On me. I can't be sure they are regarding me with contempt, but that is what it feels like. Some avert their eyes as I try to meet their gaze, while others boldly return my stare.

A group of what I can only assume are guards standing erect flanking the crowds, two on either side. They are wearing plain gray clothes with a small red emblem above their hearts, depicting what looks to be fire engulfing a branch. From this distance, there is no way of knowing to which tree the branch belongs. As we pass, each of the men train their eyes directly in front of them, only dipping their heads in recognition when our host passes.

Who is this man?

Inside, the manor is much the same in the way of people; men and women from all species gape and gawk as I cross the threshold. I do too, but not at them. This house—though I can't believe this isn't the castle where I will don my crown—is immaculately kept, with vaulted ceilings held up by intertwined branches, arching unnaturally, letting in an abundance of light. Flower petals in shades of pink and blue carpet the floor, enchanted in a way that does not crush them beneath one's feet. Much like outside, the perfume is overbearing.

Our host pauses in front of the archway to the left of the grand staircase, making a spectacle of himself and our surroundings. An ornamental tapestry sits on the wall beside the magnificent arch, depicting a brutal scene of a man, clad in what looked like medieval armor, raising the head of his enemy in triumph. Surrounding him is a crowd of onlookers, cheering, dancing, and drinking in his honor. I look away, queasy with bile from my empty stomach. It has been too long since I have eaten, and I am growing weary quicker than I could have anticipated. Maybe this strange man will prove our salvation after all.

"Welcome to my humble abode," our host roars with passion. "I am Thalion the Joymaker, a title of honor bestowed on me by the Captain of the Emberguard herself. Please refer to me simply as Thalion if you would. I will be your host for your time here at Bloomhall, this magnificent feat of magic and nature I am honored to call my home."

Magnificent *may be too dull a word for this place.*

Thalion continues, "Consider my home your home, too. You will be given everything your heart desires while you are a guest."

A smile forms on my face, replacing any thought I had given to the tapestry. Who am I to frown on such generosity simply because I don't like the decor?

"My new friends, let us eat!"

The three of us follow Thalion through a grand gate, fashioned of iron and detailed with the same bluebells I am growing accustomed to seeing in Nalara. Even their downturned petals are triumphantly jubilant, a subconscious obedience to the Ash. Whether that is the magic or nature of which Thalion spoke remains a mystery.

Beyond the gate, a vast expanse of perfectly manicured lawn, complete with various statues and fountains sits waiting. Another gorgeous structure looms over the lawn.

He has a house as a gate to the main house . . . How rich is this man?

This inner house is more glorious than the first, and far more private. Tree trunks and vines intertwine in the four corners, holding up the robust brick structure. Nature and the work of Nalara combined into one, demonstrating the most beautiful parts of each.

Glancing toward each of my companions, I expect to see a mirror image of my own joy. Instead I catch a hesitancy in Derrick's eyes. His head swivels around, looking high and low, taking in every aspect of the sight before us. His shoulders sit high and tense. Our host has been nothing but kind this entire time.

Inside the manor, we are taken directly to a lavish dining hall. Upon arrival, my feet are immediately adorned with golden sandals—after my wounds are carefully washed and wrapped. On the table sits a feast, greater than anything I have ever seen, even in movies. Various meats, cheeses, fruits, vegetables, and breads line the table. My stomach growls looking at the spread, and I am forced to resign myself to common etiquette as I study the room.

Our company is not the only one Thalion will be enjoying, it seems. By the looks of things, we are the last to arrive. And it feels like we are intruding on something sacred.

"In the way of formal introductions to my new friends, I would like to say a toast and give a brief history of who we are and what we are doing here. For those of you who have heard the whole spiel already, bear with me. For those who are new, you're welcome." A twinkle shines in Thalion's eyes. He likes the sound of his own voice and he doesn't care who knows it.

The crowd silences until the only sound that can be heard is the scraping of forks against porcelain plates.

"I am Thalion the Joymaker, the proprietor of Bloomhall. More than that, I am the punisher of the sorrowful. The only way to drown out sorrow is with joy, after all. And that is the undertaking I find thrust upon my existence, drowning out the sorrow present in Liriwyn with all the joy I can manage to make. You are all here for one reason, and one reason only. Every being in this room is guilty of expressing sorrow in some facet within the confines of our beautiful village. You have all broken the cardinal rule of Liriwyn."

Looking around the table, no one seems anything less than perpetually happy.

Derrick looks around the table with his brow furrowed as he catches my eye.

What now, Derrick?

My attention turns from his gaze as Thalion continues to speak.

"Within the walls of my residence, you will be given anything your heart desires. You simply have to wish for it and it shall be done." A flash of something shines beneath his pearly smile as he lifts his glass. Whatever it is melts me into relaxation.

Maybe the Witherwalk won't be that bad after all. Thalion will probably be willing to help me out.

"With that being said, your joy can only be created and monitored within the walls of Bloomhall. This does mean, of course, that my guests are unable to be reacquainted with society."

Maybe not, then.

The room doesn't freeze the way I think it should. No one seems as disturbed by this news as myself and Derrick—not even Oskar, a fact that confuses me. Thalion, in the midst of his monologue, doesn't seem to notice our discomfort.

"But fret not, you will never want for anything, and you will soon forget the life you once resented."

I blink up at Thalion. If what he said is true, my companions and I can't leave— ever. We will be stuck here permanently rotting in the castle with all the rest. Not that I would consider living a life of luxury to be particularly miserable. There has to be a work-around for me, an exception for the throne's heir. Once I learn my lesson and live out enough of my sentence, he has to let me leave.

Thalion informs us he is the only one with permission to leave Bloomhall as his sacred duty as the Joymaker. There is some sort of spell on the grounds that keeps us in, so we shouldn't even try to escape. Even his daughter can't leave the grounds without him, and by the look of it, she isn't upset with the arrangement. That fact alone settles my nerves as I study the pretty girl seated on his left.

"The people of Liriwyn are allowed to exist outside of my court unless, of course, they bring sorrow to the village. Then they must accompany us here."

We glance at each other, Derrick and I, trying to telepathically communicate our desire to escape. I look at Oskar. There is a twinkle in his eyes that concerns me. He looks like he is not only at peace with this arrangement, but is excited by it. After dinner I need to ask him about it—he must have a good reason.

I take a forkful of something that looks to be haggis, or what I would imagine haggis to look like, and pretend to chew it thoughtfully, attempting to mask my dread. Not at the mush of minced meat I'm chewing—that's delightful—but at the thought of being a prisoner. A well cared for prisoner, but still. My past being the barometer for what's to come, I am not the kind of person who can just stay in one place my whole life. The impulse to move, to escape, is too strong.

I chew my food without tasting it.

I stare at the plate in front of me.

Chew.

Stare.

Chew.

I swallow and feel the burning in my eyes that tells me tears are coming. Blinking them away, I clear my throat.

"There must be a way out."

Please let that sound confident.

Thalion stares at me hard. His joyful exterior cracks for the tiniest moment, hiding underneath it something sharper. Not anger, I don't think, but something old and unsettling.

Mere nanoseconds later his typical expression is back, as if nothing out of the ordinary just occurred. He chuckles under his breath, his eyes meeting mine with a curious expression.

"Think happy thoughts," he addresses the table. "We must hold a positive outlook in circumstances such as these. There is joy to be found in every situation, no matter how bleak it seems at first. And, after a few days, you may find no reason you would want to leave. If you find yourself still longing for the world you once knew, search for the way out with glee."

His words hold little comfort. The optimism in his tone feels menacing. Sharp.

I won't stop looking.

CHAPTER NINE
MALLORY

The next morning we are met with the same elaborate table, spread with an equally as decadent offering as yesterday's, though catered now to breakfast fare. After a lazy morning in a bed bigger than any I've ever seen, food sounds wonderful. Ever a creature of habit, I take my seat in the chair I had previously chosen, hoping no one will be offended by my taking the empty spot.

Pastries of all sorts line the table, along with fried meats and various types of eggs in unearthly shades of pink. What type of creature laid those? On one end of the table are various pitchers of juice. At least those look familiar. Juice can't be that foreign a concept, can it?

"Good morning!" a familiar voice booms behind me.

I turn my head to glance through the door, not expecting a shirtless Thalion to be strolling his way into the room with a scantily clad woman on each arm. My eyes dart to the floor. I'm not a prude by any means, but it feels like I am intruding on something private. The three of them are buzzing from what I can only assume was a night—and morning—of passion. It feels wrong to witness the afterglow. I bite my tongue to keep from embarrassing myself.

Am I allowed to be here?

It's another moment before I realize it has been too long since his greeting.

Shit. I'm making it awkward.

"Good morning, Thalion, um, sir," I spit out finally without making eye contact. Maybe he will assume it's an Earthly sign of respect. I can only hope.

One of the women—petite and blonde with egregious curves—starts laughing. Not the kind of laugh that is dainty and polite. She lets out a hearty, thick laugh solely for the purpose of letting me know I am not in on the joke. I *am* the joke.

"Mirandel, enough!" Thalion scolds his lover. "Mallory is new to our home and she will become accustomed to our ways eventually. First, she must wean out the Selowen mentality. Sooner or later, she may be joining us for breakfast."

He winks at me.

A blush, not of attraction, rushes to my cheeks.

Oskar walks through the door and courteously issues a slight bow to our host, which is returned in the same somber fashion. Thalion escorts his beauties out of the room, leaving Oskar and I awkwardly staring at each other. He glances up at me with a look that shows he knows what he walked into.

"Good morning, Mallory," he says, with that same twinkle in his eye from yesterday. "I trust you slept well?"

"I actually did."

For once.

"Ah, yes, these beds are the pinnacle of comfort—I remember them well." He smiles fondly.

He's been here before. Why didn't he tell us?

Before I can ask, he is speaking again.

"How did you dream?"

Did I dream last night? I can't remember, though dreams themselves often tend to escape my memory.

"Actually I think I had a dreamless sleep for the first time in my entire life."

He quietly laughs at a joke only he knows. "I suspected you would."

My face shifts into a puzzled expression at his continuous lack of transparency. These guessing games piss me off.

He must be able to tell I am less than thrilled with how this conversation is going because he continues after a beat.

"Liriwyn bans dream magic. It is not allowed anywhere, as it is another practice that is for the descendants of Selowen. With your roots so deeply ingrained in the Willow, and your inability to remember how you got to the gate in the first place, I would be surprised if you didn't have some sort of dream magic."

Thalion had said there was magic, but nothing about different forms.

Of course there's different kinds of magic in Nalara.

I'm sure it's just like anything else, like any talent that exists; everyone is likely more inclined toward some forms than others. Whether by birthright or interest in the practice of the art remains unclear. Surely either my elder companion or the proprietor of this manor will explain soon.

But, while magic might exist, I don't have it.

"You're wrong. I don't have any kind of magic, as nice as that would be."

Another smile from Oskar.

Great. Another joke I don't know.

"My dear, of course you do. Magic in your world is subject to scrutiny, so it often goes overlooked. Though, of course, Earth does not have nearly the same magical content as Nalara. Once humanity strayed from the spiritual, magic dwindled with the rise of science. Magic is often called *coincidence* by unbelievers."

What does this have to do with me?

"Have you ever known someone whose coffee inexplicably tastes better, even though they push the same button you do? Or found something you have been looking for without even trying?"

He continues, "Magic in Nalara is both finite and infinite—it depends on the trees."

"The trees?" It feels ridiculous to speak of trees as if they are sentient beings. This entire experience thus far feels more and more like an alcohol-induced dream. Nothing is making any sort of sense.

"The Twinned Trees, Mal," Derrick's voice sounds from behind me. When did he walk in? "They are the source of the magic that keeps us alive. After the Sundering, magic has been waning—can't you feel it? Everything in our kingdom will die once those trees do. Which is why we need you. You are meant to save the magic that keeps us alive."

No, I didn't sign up to save a kingdom. I signed up to wear a crown—the one I was told I needed to wear. Oskar will tell me what to do once the crown is on my head. *I* won't be saving anyone.

The sick feeling in my stomach must be evident on my face, because both men are staring at me, concern etched on their faces.

"Mallory, my dear girl, are you alright?" Oskar asks.

"Yeah," I lie. "It's just a lot of information at once."

Both men nod gravely.

"It's okay, Mal," Derrick says while reaching for my hand, which I pull away. He ignores the rebuff and continues, "We will be with you every step of the way."

At least I won't have to save everyone alone.

But how does someone save a nation when they can't even save themselves?

The rest of the day passes rather uneventfully, with each member of our little party exploring a different area of the house. Derrick spends the whole of his time in the massive library, which looks like something straight out of a fairy tale. Oskar splits his time in two major areas. He is either in the parlor watching beautiful women dance or he is accompanying his son with research. If there is a way to escape, the two of them will find it.

For the most part, I spend the day wandering the halls with a glass of wine in hand. Every time I near the bottom of the glass, it refills itself—either with red or white wine, depending on what I want most at the moment. No matter how much alcohol I consume, I maintain my sobriety.

I can get used to this

There are many secrets to uncover in Bloomhall, I'm sure. They must be sprinkled between rooms of pleasure. One room I come across is an art studio where artists work in various mediums. The next room I stumble upon, its door opposite the art studio, contains a swimming pool that seems impossible. I meander down the hall, leisurely taking in the sights behind each door.

Two guards, marching in lockstep, round the corner and make their way toward the women, causing them to scatter. Perhaps they do have the good sense to understand that this is their prison too, and those guards report to the warden.

Without a word, the guards shuffle past me and continue what I can only assume are their rounds. Pairs of guards, different each time, patrol the halls at semi-regular intervals, searching for any trace of weakness in their "guests." What happens when they uncover a wrongdoer, I don't know. Though, it can't be that unpleasant in the house of the Joymaker.

A buzzing sensation runs through my hand as my wineglass refills itself—a pinot grigio this time—and I drift toward a room whose door is slightly ajar. Giggling sounds from behind it as I poke my head in. Whatever's going on sounds like fun. Thalion's back faces the door. He is kneeling on a bed that runs the length of the short wall, behind a woman with blonde hair and a perfect, heart-shaped ass. She must be Mirandel, the woman Thalion scolded at breakfast. A dimple sits at the small of her back, right about where the two bodies connect.

Beside them lay a group of attractive women who are made even more attractive by the way they are lazily kissing one another. Their hands move idly up and down each other's bodies. These are not kisses of love or of lust, but rather some kind of performance art. Filling the room are people of various genders. Some are in pairs, some with two or three partners, and some are alone. I don't linger too long on those who are solo, as they meet my eyes in a way that feels predatory, attempting to pleasure themselves to my likeness.

"Mallory!"

I snap my head back to the abnormally large bed. Too much

time was spent looking around the room, and I failed to notice when Thalion switched positions. He is now lying on his back with both the blonde and brunette from breakfast between his legs.

How long has he been watching me?

"Do you like what you see?" he asks, gesturing to the naked bodies.

My face grows hot as I try to avoid another survey of the room.

"Um," is all I can manage.

"You can join, if you want." He winks.

I drop my wineglass. Not bothering to clean the mess, I slam the door shut and exit the room with as much speed as I can muster. The heavy thud of the door does nothing to drown out the roaring laughter behind it.

Fuck. They're laughing at me again.

Ducking my head to hide my face from the creature milling about the corridor, my body tingles with something between embarrassment and excitement as I open the nearest door, looking for a quiet reprieve.

Deep breaths.

It's imperative I calm down. Whatever might happen in my flustered state could upset Thalion and ruin my chances of escape. He needs to think I'm a scared little girl—I *am* a scared little girl.

"You look like you've seen a ghost. Are you okay?" A feminine voice fills the room.

Looking up, a woman sits at a luxuriously ornamented dressing table brushing her hair. She is in a state of undress that suggests she is just getting ready for the day. Her bed is messy and a tray lies on the bed table, half-eaten eggs left to congeal into a pink goo.

"Yeah, I'm fine. Just a little lost, I guess."

Every bone in my body is begging her to believe me. Maybe it's because I don't want another person to laugh at me. Or maybe it's because I recognize her from yesterday's feast.

"Good."

Good.

The beautiful woman stands and crosses the room to me, my heart fluttering as she does. She grabs my hands and leads me to sit on the edge of the bed. My face warms. Maybe sitting on a bed with a pretty woman is not the best way to calm myself down, but at this moment, I can't care less.

"Ahh," she says nodding, "you witnessed my father's orgy? He likes to leave the door open for admirers."

He planned that?

I feel sick to my stomach knowing what I had seen was not an accident like I'd thought. And I feel even sicker still that I enjoyed watching. And maybe I enjoy that he wanted *me* to see it. Though if it's as frequent of an occurrence as his daughter is suggesting, Thalion probably does not care who ends up on the other side of his performance.

How fucked-up am I?

"Of course, I am not allowed in with his debauchery"—I hear the girl's voice somewhere in the distance—"but he permits me to hold my own."

My ears perk up at that and a flash of heat settles over my body, quickening my pulse as her voice comes back into the foreground of my mind. Images of her naked body flash in my thoughts, her ample breasts bouncing as someone takes her from behind. How do her lips taste?

Physically shaking my head to clear the thoughts, I hear her giggling. A beautiful, twinkling giggle that makes my stomach drop in longing.

"Don't get too excited," she says. "I am not that kind of girl. Not that I don't have my fair share of fun. I'm just a bit of a selfish lover."

She has to know what that statement did to me because she winks as she says it. If I was standing, my knees would have buckled.

"I'm Selyra." The woman extends her hand in greeting.

"I'm Mallory." I feel like a child in her presence.

"I know that, silly." She giggles again. "The whole house knows the new recruit, especially since you are so important."

Now it is my turn to laugh.

"I am *not* important," I assure her.

"I don't know about that, Shadowbearer."

Shadowbearer? Is that a title Oskar had mentioned?

Before I can form the question, there is a knock on the door.

"Come in," she says, not caring that she is half-naked.

A small, blue, pixie-like creature enters the room. This is my first time seeing any staff aside from the guards, but something in her demeanor tells me she is a servant—voluntary or otherwise. It makes sense that there'd be servants; some combination of labor and magic must be responsible for keeping this manor in its pristine condition. Oskar and Derrick told me magic is dying, and I imagine more and more labor is necessary as it decays. Facing the reality of that labor, however, feels like a knife to an otherwise perfect throat.

Does Thalion own slaves?

There isn't much time to dwell on the thought as the servant girl's voice comes out in a squeak. "Miss Selyra. It is time for you to return for dinner."

"Thank you, Destrada." Selyra's voice is laced with a kindness I have yet to see in Bloomhall.

"I should go—let you get ready." I stand.

Selyra smiles up at me. "Perhaps I will see you at dinner."

Perhaps.

My heart flutters a bit and I make my way out of her room and down the hall to prepare myself for dinner. Looking for her in tonight's crowd will be top priority.

The feast lying before us is more opulent than even our lunch was. The smell of roast meat rises to my nostrils and induces a growl from my stomach. Filling my stomach over the last few days the way I have has done a lot to reset my hunger cues. I have never seen this much food at once.

And, of course, goblets of wine and tumblers of whiskey are present, much like the glass I'd carried throughout the day, never running empty.

Thalion is seated at the head of the table, flanked by his

groupies. It wasn't long ago that I walked in on their . . . performance.

I *have* to forget it. The last thing I want here is to be treated like a child, though they need to view me as such for my plan to work. Or, for me to have any hope to form a plan. Details of a plan grow fuzzier with each moment I spend looking for answers to this place.

Arriving later than anyone else, I settle into my seat between Derrick and Oskar. Oskar is buzzing with energy, invigorated by his day. His glassy eyes look very much like someone in the throes of passion. It's possible he slipped into Thalion's party, but my stomach curls at the thought. I can only hope his excitement stems from the information he spent all day helping Derrick gather.

And, I'm back. I definitely don't want to picture that.

Derrick is his father's opposite in every way. Where Oskar keeps his cards to his chest, Derrick is quite the open book. By the expression on his face, I can tell Derrick's thoughts are elsewhere. He is carefully nibbling at his plate, which is shockingly bare, and staring into the near distance. I wouldn't be surprised if he hasn't registered my presence yet at all.

"How was your day?" I wave my hand in front of Derrick's face to get his attention.

Aside from my morning stop at the library, I haven't seen him. He had sequestered himself away during lunch, Oskar citing that Derrick would request a sandwich in the library while he worked.

"Relaxing," he replied. "I had intended to do some research on how to get out of here, but read a book for fun instead."

"What book?" I ask, intrigued by Nalaran literature and what passes for entertainment here.

"Just a book about the history of Nalaran royalty."

"And you read that for fun?"

Derrick looks directly at me for the first time tonight. "Yeah, it wasn't helpful in conducting an escape plan, but it was fascinating all the same."

"Fair enough," I say before turning to Oskar

I'm ready to ask the same question of the older man, but he is deep in conversation with the impish woman next to him. She's laughing as if Oskar has just told her the funniest joke she's ever heard. I don't know Oskar well, but I can't imagine anything he said would be that clever.

Maybe she was in Thalion's room too.

Down the table ran people of every gender, color, and species imaginable. Some faces I recognize from my journey around the manor today, but most are new to me. Each of them must have done something sorrowful to end up at this table, and I wonder how many of them are passers-through who are as ignorant to the laws as my companions and I.

They do look happy now, though.

Maybe I can find a way to be happy here too. If it's possible for me anywhere, it would certainly be here. There are worse existences than a life of luxury in a home where no responsibilities hinder my day. Every need provided for, every wish fulfilled.

Selyra.

My mind wanders to thoughts of the future. Painting Selyra's figure in the art room, curling up in front of the fireplace in the library while reading aloud to one another—stroking that beautiful blonde hair.

Mallory, stop. Don't get too comfortable.

I know I'm supposed to want out of here, but I can't remember the last time I thought about my future in the same way. Even my months-long crush on Chuck was more physical than anything. Before Nalara, I never planned my existence out for longer than a few weeks at a time.

My heart pangs at the thought, and I swallow before tears can form.

Maybe there is a future for me here.

Thalion clears his throat loudly and raises his glass in a toast.

"Cheers to friends and found family. As we close out another day of reveling in life's greatest pleasures, it is important that we remember what this is all about. To the Asharil spirit! "

"To Asharil!" the crowd echoes back.

A moment of silence follows as the crowd lifts their cups to their lips, then the hum of conversation returns in force.

Much like the square, every inch of this place feels vibrant. Alive. Living with the Dionysian leader of the village has its perks, I guess. Perks that, with every presentation, outweigh the captivity. Can you truly be captive in a castle?

Searching for a beautiful elven maiden, I scan the crowd. Men and women, all gorgeous, catch my eye but, no matter how hard I look, I cannot find Selyra.

CHAPTER TEN
MALLORY

I'm walking the Liriwyn square, barefoot on the cobblestones like before.

This time, each step isn't blinding agony. A cool breeze sweeps through the village and a shiver runs down my spine, though no one else seems affected by the wind. Daylight pours through the city center—it is just as raucous as I remember, but there's a different feel to it. Everyone seems distant, like I can sense them through an invisible fog, but they can't see me back. Once again, I am existing on the edge, observing life being lived around me.

I walk past the laughing faces, the roared laughter, the vivid art. Stall after stall, the world looks untouched. This is exactly the place I arrived at when I came to Liriwyn, though I didn't get as good of a look then.

Without warning or command, my body stops in the middle of the crowd. A guard, one I recognize as Thalion's right-hand man, looks at me hard. No one else seems to be aware of my presence, but the second I match eyes with him, he looks over my head to something behind me.

I turn and see a group of scantily clad women on the porch of what I can only assume is a brothel. Knowing the guard wasn't looking at me fills me with a wave of relief, though there's an unexplained edge to my nerves.

Again as if they have a mind of their own, my feet are pulled toward a stall on my right. This one looks no different than the rest. Jewelry lines the table, made of various metals and precious stones—more beautiful than any jewelry I have ever seen. There is a girl working the stall. She looks to be in her teens, a youthful aura about her despite the layers of wear on her face. Young as she may be, she has experience beyond her years that's culminated in a permanent tiredness under her eyes.

The girl glances up at me. The second our eyes meet, she darts hers back to her table. Much too quickly. She saw me, and I won't let the only person who knows I'm here ignore me.

Her hands shake as she fumbles with the trinkets. Her limber fingers carry the signs of craftsmanship, blistered and calloused. She made these pieces herself. All at once I become aware I'm dreaming.

Oskar said I shouldn't be able to dream in Liriwyn.

"See, Oskar?" I think aloud, not bothering to keep quiet with all the noise bouncing around the square, "I don't have dream magic. I'm dreaming in Liriwyn."

A small clanging of metal sounds as the girl drops one piece of jewelry onto another. She steadies herself against the table, still looking down, and hisses a "shh" at me.

I cock my head, silently willing her to look at me. When she doesn't, I decide to make her acknowledge me. Stepping up to the table, I pretend to busy myself with her wares, keeping my eyes trained to the spot where hers are looking.

"I'm Mallory," I whisper in the lowest voice I can manage.

"We know who you are," she bites back in a matching whisper. "We have been warned of you—the one who is fulfilling the prophecy."

"What do you mean? Who warned you?"

"You, of all people, should know it isn't safe here. Dream magic is highly *illegal in this town. Myself and a few others practice in secret, but your being here puts us in danger. No one would care to seek out a few lowly vendors, but the future High Queen of Nalara will always have a target on her back."*

"Who's looking for you?"

"Thalion's guard. He has enslaved a handful of Selowen worshippers from neighboring cities who were born with dream magic. In exchange for their lives, and their families being left unbothered, they patrol nightly. Some will overlook the everyday practitioner, but none will overlook your presence."

"I don't understand. If it's so dangerous for you, why are you here?"

Her body goes rigid at the question, like she is frightened to say too much. There must be a good reason to risk imprisonment.

"With practice, those with the power of dream magic can walk into any place in existence. Those of us who are young in our practice still can only control where we are about half the time. It's wise to live where you wish to practice until you can control it better."

"But why would you want to be somewhere you aren't welcome?"

A slow shake of the teenager's head is all I get by way of response.

"Okay, then answer me this: exactly whose dream are we in?"

"We are in Somnarel, the realm of dreams. It is a thin veil between the living and the dead. Everyone's consciousness comes here at night, but not all are aware."

"So everyone in Liriwyn dreams of this place every night?"

The girl dares a peek up at face. By now I have forgotten my pretense. I am looking for answers she'd rather not give.

"This isn't exactly one place. It is a realm that weaves interchangeably from one dream to the next. You, as a dream walker, can manipulate your surroundings and bring into this space anyone you wish."

She gestures her hand to a boy a few feet away.

I know that boy.

"He is the one who sent you to Bloomhall, a dignitary of Thalion's. It's not an accident that you are being held captive, Mallory. The Emberguard planned your arrest the moment they caught wind you'd entered Nalara. Thalion works on their orders, and everything that is done in his name is done in the name of the Sacred Ash."

My heart is beating so loudly I wonder if she can hear it. "If everyone is here, how can it be illegal?"

"It is not illegal to be here," she whispers in an exasperated tone. "It is illegal to wake in this realm within the village limits of Liriwyn. Dream magic can only be practiced by the seed of Selowen. Liriwyn would love nothing more than to watch the Emberguard destroy everyone with Selowen blood in their veins. We are not safe here."

I blink. Thalion had told us at dinner, during his drunken rambling, about the Emberguard, their sister faction. Their wish to uphold the path of judgment and passion had been clear, but I hadn't realized that would mean the complete destruction of those born of the Willow.

"Why would they want to do that?" The question comes out louder than intended.

She confirmed what I already suspected about the Emberguard.

A stronger chill runs down my entire body, though this time there is no wind. I dare to hold her gaze as she continues.

"That is why you are being held prisoner. You are a threat to their mission, the prophesied healer of the Hollow Crown. You are destined to rejoin the factions and unify the Twinned Path. They will do anything in their power to stop you."

"What about the other prisoners in Bloomhall? Thalion said that anyone who experiences sorrow is doomed to repeat their revelry forever. Most of them looked happy enough."

The stranger squints, looking at me hard.

"Mallory," she says slowly, deliberately emphasizing every word, "there are no other prisoners in Bloomhall. You are and your friends are there alone."

"Mallory, wake up. Open your eyes. WAKE UP."

CHAPTER ELEVEN
DERRICK

Mallory looks antsy this morning, her eyes darting from seat to seat as if she is expecting something to materialize in the empty chairs. Her hair is still a mess from bed and it looks like she hasn't slept well. She isn't one to worry about appearances, from what I've been able to tell, but her disheveled look has me worried. This imprisonment seems to be harder on her than the rest of us, and purposely so, if I had to guess—this is likely her trial, whether she's realized it yet or not.

In the last few days, she's been wandering the halls, opening random doors, and then just standing there peering into the room for minutes at a time before moving on. I don't think she saw me watching but, on the sole occasion I left the small, dusty room I had tucked myself into, I'd caught her.

I was working on a way to escape this godforsaken place. I was working on a way to save her. And she was taking a stroll.

"Mal," I whisper across the table, careful not to let our captor overhear. "Are you okay?"

"Derrick," she says with a grim expression, "what if things aren't what they seem?"

My eyes meet hers, studying the movement on her face. She

seems . . . different today, more serious. Despite our surroundings the past forty-eight hours, I had seen her smile more than ever before. Even when—

I want to support her, but at what cost? Pushing the cold lump of eggs around on my plate, I search for an answer. The gray walls feel like they are closing in on me. Mallory's sudden discontent is unsettling, an omen that something sinister is coming.

After what feels like too long a silence, I answer her question with my own.

"What do you mean?"

"I don't know." She shakes her head. "I had a dream last night that confused me. Oskar said I shouldn't be able to dream, but I did. That has to mean *something*."

I glance over at Thalion, who is sitting at the head of the table. It's unclear from this distance whether or not he can hear our conversation, but his menacing glare is pointed at us.

"Let's talk about this later," I say without looking away from our warden, hoping Mallory will get the hint.

"Fine." She doesn't follow my gaze. "We will meet in the library later." She gathers her plate and walks out of the room with it, leaving me to ponder her words.

As she makes her exit, my father takes her place at the table. He is looking, as usual, well-rested this morning. I don't know if the smile on his face is an act or delusion, but it's been a permanent fixture since our arrival. He has a history with this place—how much I don't know. Nothing he does is without meaning, though.

"Dad, have you noticed Mallory is acting strange? Something about her seems off today, but I don't know what. It's like she is waking up from a dream or something."

My dad smiles back at me. "I think she is adjusting beautifully."

"I hope you're right."

I know better than to question my father's wisdom. He isn't fond of it and it always proved useless.

"Have you talked to her this morning?" I asked.

"Not yet, but I did see her leaving as I was walking in. Why do you ask?"

I push my plate away, not bothering to mask my confusion at the words I am about to say. "She asked me to join her in the library."

Another small smile. "Then things are working out."

I stand, telling myself he's right. But I have been watching her for three days, and the girl moving through these halls is not the same one who'd grabbed my hand in the dark.

CHAPTER TWELVE
MALLORY

I find myself in the library before Derrick and decide to do a bit of reading until he shows up. Picking up a book titled *Law and Light of Nalara* off an easily accessible shelf, I look for a seat. A faded red chair sits next to a fireplace. As good a place as any. I examine the book in my hands as I sink into the worn leather. The thick tome is caked with a layer of dirt—I swipe my finger through and it clings to my skin.

The book settles open in my lap as I wait for my companion, but my nerves make it difficult to concentrate. No matter how hard I try to focus on the words in front of me, the letters swirl into unintelligible nonsense. I snap the book shut.

Where is he?

My impatience boils over and I rush to the door and pull it open. The solid wood door is lighter now than I remember, and I stumble into the hallway with the force of my push. The hallways are empty now, except for two guards planted at the end, and the lights are dimmer. Derrick rounds the corner at the far end of the corridor, passing the guards, who perk up at his presence. I wave my hand in a "hurry up" motion and he breaks into a light jog, easily covering the distance.

As he nears, I pull open the library door.

"What took you so long?" I ask as he crosses the threshold.

"I wasn't sure where you wanted to meet."

"I told you, the library," I say, following him through the door.

His expression remains blank—maybe a little confused.

"You know . . . where you spent all day yesterday?"

"I was in here all day yesterday, but I wouldn't exactly call this closet a library."

What kind of libraries is Derrick used to, that he doesn't find this one impressive?

I scoff, looking for the leather chair where I'd left my book. Instead, I find a roughly cobbled-together wooden chair in its place whose legs are at visibly different lengths.

It's happening here, too.

Once seated, I take in my surroundings again for the first time since Derrick arrived, the grandiose room with thousands of books now replaced by a room not much bigger than a broom closet.

I let out a sigh. "Oh."

"What's wrong?" my companion asks, the same concerned look still resting on his face.

"This has been happening to me all day."

"What has?"

"The disillusionment."

I wait for his response but he remains silent, his eyes questioning me.

"I had a dream last night," I say, as if that explains anything. "She told me this would happen."

Another silence as I wait for it to click.

"Back up," he says, in too rough a tone. "What are you talking about? What dream? Who's she? What illusion?"

I take a deep breath. This might be difficult for him to understand, but I have to try.

In great detail, I enlighten Derrick about the dream realm, Somnarel, and the girl at the jewelry stall whose name I didn't get. I recount her warning—that I am a threat to the Emberguard. When I get to the part about being alone, Derrick interrupts.

"Of course we are alone, Mal," he says in a low voice. "We have been alone here with Thalion and his daughter the whole time."

My heart leaps at the mention of Selyra.

At least she is real.

"Anyway," I continue, breezing past his interjection, "ever since I woke up, I've seen things differently. It started with my bedroom. Last night I went to sleep in the biggest, most comfortable bed I've ever lain in. My room was beautiful and comfortable. This morning, I woke up in a cold, gray room on a bed of straw."

Derrick's lips purse but he remains silent. I notice the judgment in his eyes but he nods for me to continue.

"Then it was breakfast," I tell him. "Yesterday was an incredible spread of pastries and fruit juice, smoked meats and quiche. This morning I chewed on gritty eggs that were colder than the water."

A look of realization slowly spread across Derrick's face. He must have figured something out before me, and I need to know what.

"Derrick—"

The door bursts open, a guard flying through in a rage. He grabs Derrick's arm before I can bring myself to react. A low growl escapes from the younger man as the guard roughly covers his mouth. Derrick is outmatched and knows it, but he puts up a fight anyway. Seconds later, my stomach twists as my companion is dragged through the open doorway. Standing to follow, I hear a voice coming from the corridor.

"Sit, Mallory," Thalion's voice rings through the tiny room.

At the authoritative tone, I sink back into my chair.

Thalion, our host—our captor—saunters in, a smug expression on his face.

How could I have missed it?

Green, pearlescent skin stretches across Thalion's frame, almost paper-thin like an iguana's belly. He isn't quite scaly, but I wouldn't be surprised to find out he is part reptile. He squints as he opens his mouth to laugh and his forked tongue flicks with delight. From far enough away, Thalion appears human—appears like every other Nalaran I've seen.

What is he?

Thalion snaps his fingers and a chair appears. He sits, crosses his legs, and rests both hands on his left knee. Every move is calculated; he knows how to intimidate and he's practiced carefully for moments like this. Watching me, studying me like he expects I will break into a run at any moment, he leans forward.

"So," he starts, "you broke the rules—already. I distinctly remember telling Oskar to make sure you did not use that dream magic of yours."

His lips curl like he smells something sour, and I can read the word that's practically on the tip of his tongue.

Selowen.

Before the disillusionment, I knew there was a law against the practice of Selowen magic—it's why we are here after all. What I failed to notice was the disdain that crossed Thalion's face whenever the subject came up.

"He said I wouldn't be able to, even if I tried," I said. "And, I didn't try! I promise, I really didn't even know I could do it until last night."

To my surprise, Thalion chuckles. His amusement disarms me.

"That son of a warlock. Clever, I will give him that much. Not directly defying my orders, just planting the seed of rebellion. Of course, he couldn't have known about that wretched jewelry girl. That was dumb luck on your part."

I think back on the conversation with Oskar. The smile makes sense now. He hadn't been laughing at me. He had been laughing at his own private disobedience. Oskar is the kind of man who can walk two lines—form allies and enemies out of the same men.

Before I can admire Oskar's brilliance much longer, I catch Thalion's last words.

The jewelry shop girl.

"How do you know about that girl?" I ask. "I don't even know her name."

Another sinister smile.

God, he's handsome.

Despite the newly discovered appearance, I can't help but admire Thalion's form. The apple doesn't fall far from the tree.

Selyra.

The jewelry girl.

My brain snaps back just as I see Thalion's mouth form the words "taken care of."

What did he do with her?

Thalion must mistake my silence for complacency, because he bolsters on.

"No matter. Though I had hoped your illusion would last indefinitely, I suppose it was bound to shatter at some point. This meeting was not due for another fifty years or so. I will just have to make the illusion stronger next time—let it seep into your dreams and memories."

Panic grips my body at the thought of him manipulating my memories. Manipulating my current existence is one thing, but something so personal feels violating.

"Where did you take Derrick?" I ask as I remember my friend's absence, with more than an ounce of guilt. That should have been my first question.

"He's safe enough—at least physically—though I do suspect some of my guards are having their fun with him somewhere. They hardly get any exercise and they *do* grow dreadfully bored."

He glances toward the door with a small smile, amused at the thought of Derrick's torture. My stomach flips.

If Thalion senses my discomfort, he breezes past it.

"You have a choice to make, Mallory." He grins, hopeful. "You can choose to exist here in bliss once more—an overindulgence of everything good: food, booze, sex, music, art—and live a comfortable life you will learn to love. I could even talk a certain daughter of mine into your bed on occasion. You will never remember having woken from the illusion. You will never remember this talk."

Is that really such a bad offer?

"Or"—the pleasantness drops from his voice—"you can live here with your illusion shattered—every day agony."

"What about them?" I hear myself ask. It's the right thing to do, making sure my companions are safe in the illusion too.

"They do not get the luxury of a choice, I'm afraid. They will not experience the illusion."

"Why not?"

"The illusion takes effort and, since they are from the Ash themselves, they have no magic we wish to squelch. They cannot enter dreams at will as you do and the sorrow—the weakness—of Selowen cannot overtake their souls as it can yours."

"And I will be here either way?" I ask, genuinely considering his offer.

"Yes, you will grow old and fade away in this house. I myself am a minor deity, something akin to a demigod in Earth lore. Nalarans are not immortal like me, though their lives span for centuries if they are not cut short by war or disease. You are half Nalaran, half human. We haven't seen one of your kind in centuries, but I would estimate you've got a good four hundred years or so left in this kingdom."

Four hundred years.

I never wanted to be immortal, never even wanted to leave past twenty-seven.

But I won't have to struggle anymore.

Four hundred years is a long time, too long for my human perception to comprehend. Would it drag on if every day was luxury? Would I grow bored of the sameness of joy?

"Consider it," he says, rising. "I will expect your answer by this time tomorrow."

He leaves, exiting in much the same grand fashion as he entered. I am left alone now with my thoughts—the gray room echoes my melancholy.

How can I survive this?

I would be a fool not to take the life of luxury, even if it's fake. Is the illusion of pleasure better than the knowledge of pain?

Can I knowingly leave Derrick and Oskar in this hellhole even if my future self won't remember doing so?

Do they deserve that?
Do I?

CHAPTER THIRTEEN
MALLORY

Dinner is uneventful. Derrick sits alone with his eyes downward. The pain he's in radiates from him several feet away. It's permeating the air around him like a blanket I can't see through.

For someone who hates sorrow, Thalion seems to enjoy inflicting it.

It's different now; seeing the feast hall in this light steals whatever appetite I may have had. Tonight, I make no appearances to enjoy myself. Not that I have to, since Thalion is not in attendance. But Selyra is. Does she know what a monster her father is or is she, too, under an illusion?

Studying Oskar, I am careful to watch him through this newly found lens. His jovial air has washed off, leaving an old man keeping every bit to himself, as one would expect. Thalion told me that neither Derrick nor Oskar experienced the illusion, but I suspect that, in some way, Oskar had. My stomach sinks as I realize I will have another four hundred years to figure out just who Oskar is, and that still may not be enough time.

"My dear boy," Oskar says to the room. I don't know if he won't meet his son's gaze or if he can't. "I heard what they did to you."

A moment passes, the silence heavy in the near-empty room.

"I suspect—" Oskar clears his throat. "I suspect very much that it was retaliation for my wrongdoings. They promised you would be safe and happy. I didn't break my deal—don't know how they found out. I'm eternally sorry, Derrick."

When did Oskar have time to bargain with the Liriwyns?

Derrick looks ahead, every bit someone who has seen too much. Someone who has *felt* too much. The trauma clings to his skin, almost as evident as the blood on his jaw. All traces of the amiable boy I sat with this morning are gone. He holds his gaze fixed on his plate and pushes the food around. Whether he wants something to do or it's an involuntary response to the attention, I don't know.

What did they do to you?

I want to be the hero. The kind of person who fights for others. The kind of person who wouldn't think twice about turning down this offer. But I'm not. I see Derrick's pain and hope I never have to feel it myself.

It's about time I feel okay too.

So what if I won't be able to save Nalara? I never wanted to in the first place.

Maybe I can talk Thalion into a deal. A contract of sorts. Anything that will keep Derrick safe while I am under. He will have to live with the trauma, but it's not impossible. If I can stop the wounds from piling on, I can give him a chance to heal.

What if I can save Derrick and myself?

Derrick catches me staring at him. The tears welling in his eyes beg me to reconsider. I've never seen a man cry and it's not something I want to see again. It's an unspoken social contract that when you see someone cry, they're placing the burden of feeling responsible for fixing them on you. Especially when it's your fault.

"Okay," I say. "we will get out of this."

"Fancy seeing you here."

Please go away.

Standing in the doorway, ready to exit the dining hall after Derrick and Oskar, I feel a dainty tap on my shoulder. My mind is begging her not to push this, but I'm sure she will. She knows I know she's here, and that won't go unpunished.

"Mallory, please can we talk?" Her voice sounds like magic, and it could be magic, for all I know. It's drawing me to her and, despite every bone in my body wanting to root to this spot, I turn to face the one person I want to see most and least of all.

Selyra.

Even with the illusion lifted, her presence is breathtaking and her spirit shines with warmth. Despite everything her father put me through, I am smitten with this woman.

Careful, Mallory. Don't let her cloud your judgment.

"Did you know?" My voice comes out less harsh and more tired than I meant it.

Selyra's face grows dim as she bites her lips, her hands fiddling with the ends of her long hair. "Mallory, let me explain."

"Why should I let you?"

"Please, just sit with me and we can talk about it." She extends her right hand out to me, tempting me to take it.

When I relent and wrap my fingers around hers, she leads me back to the table and we take our seats in a pair of chairs, our knees touching as we face each other.

"My father told me to come talk to you, to convince you to take his deal."

"Why does he care if I am happy living here or not?"

Selyra shakes her head sadly. "He doesn't. When you are under the enchantment, you are easier to manipulate. You will eventually forget your will to escape. My father is powerful, Mallory, highly regarded by the Emberguard. Those in power never truly wish to make you happy. All they want is to keep you occupied so you don't resist their cruelty."

Her face drops with something resembling embarrassment. My eyes trace the lines in her beautiful face, searching for I don't know what.

"Why are you telling me this?"

"I am a prisoner here too," she says with a small smile that doesn't quite reach her eyes. "When we spoke in my bedroom, I knew what you were seeing was an illusion—I see them too."

The confusion I feel must be showing on my face, because she answers my unasked question.

"Yes. I know about the illusions. I chose to have them. My father can pull himself in and out of them, so we can share some of the same experiences. Even when I'm in an illusion, I'm aware of it."

"I don't get it." Biting my lip, my voice grows soft. There is more to the story with Selyra and her father, but it's not my place. Still, I press on. "Why does he keep you in the illusion?"

"Well, firstly"—she gestures around the dingy room—"just look at this place without it."

She has a point.

"And, secondly, my punishment is in knowing that my existence is a lie and every person I meet is a figment of imagination."

"Why are you being punished?"

Selyra takes a second to gather her thoughts. She must have known this question was coming the moment she pulled me aside.

Tucking a stray piece of hair behind her ears, she inhales sharply. "As you've noticed, my mother isn't here with us. According to my father, she was just a whore he slept with in an orgy—yes, that part was real—and he didn't care for her beyond that. I have my doubts about that. My mother was Selowen-born and my father didn't know. He found out on the night she gave birth."

I want to ask how, but any interjection might derail the conversation, so I wait while Selyra collects her thoughts.

"The Emberguard, and the rest of those born of the Ash, see Selowen's sorrow as weakness. What they fail to realize is sorrow breeds compassion, and compassion breeds healing."

My hand rests on her knee, which is now bouncing with nervous energy. "Your mother healed herself after childbirth didn't she?"

A tear slides down Selyra's cheek as she looks at me and nods.

"And my father killed her for it," she chokes out.

Biting the inside of my cheek to keep myself from crying for a woman I don't think Selyra even met, I reach for her cheek. She nuzzles into my hand and I feel her tears flow over the back of my hand as her body heaves with unheard sobs. This is the most intimate moment I've had with anyone in a long time—and my clothes are still on.

"I'm sorry, Selyra." I don't know what else to say. What else can you say when someone expresses their deepest pain?

I tilt her chin so her eyes meet mine. Her pain hangs between us as we stare in a heavy silence. My hand lowers off her face and she gives me another pitiful smile. It's a look I never want to see on her again, and one I certainly don't want to cause.

"Mallory"—her voice comes out in a squeak—"you can't stay here. You have to find a way to escape. My father loves me, the bastard child of a one-time romp with a whore, and this is how he treats me. He cares nothing for you or your well-being. I don't know why he's kept you alive this long, and I have no idea how long it will last."

My face blanches as the blood rushes to my toes.

"I know he said you could live here for the rest of your life with me, and I would love nothing more than a true companion, but he is lying to you. It's not a matter of if, but when—he *will* kill you."

Issuing a silent nod, I rise to my feet in a swift motion. Selyra understands my intent and stands with me, throwing her arms around my shoulders in a welcome embrace. For a moment, the gray room melts around us as I dig the pads of my fingers into her back, willing her to stay with me in this moment forever.

"Maybe someday you can come back for me."

When I am a queen with an army, I will wage war to see you again.

The next morning, I skip breakfast and tiptoe into Derrick's room. His dwelling is even less impressive than mine, if that's at all possible. A lump of flesh lies on the ground, twisting violently. Though he's asleep, Derrick is not getting any rest.

"Derrick." I shake him.

No answer.

I shake him again.

A slight flutter of his eyelids, though, ultimately, they remain closed.

One more shake.

A piercing scream fills the air.

It is coming from Derrick, still half asleep—his body no doubt remembering the torture session from yesterday. Dropping to my knees, I scoop his head up into my lap. Stroking his cheek, I sing a song from my childhood.

> *"Light blooms softly,*
> *In the meadow.*
> *Life moves slowly,*
> *Where flowers grow.*
> *Peace moves mountains,*
> *From down below.*
> *Hope breeds longing,*
> *Where dreams all go."*

The screams quell and he opens his eyes, blinking hard.

"Mallory," he says with a start, "what are you doing here?"

He pulls his head out of my lap quickly, careful to hide his embarrassment.

"We need to leave," I tell him earnestly. Yesterday I might not have meant it, but seeing what Thalion has done to even his own daughter, I know it's what must happen. We have to escape.

"There isn't much time. Thalion and his lot will expect an answer from me today, come noon. We *need* to figure out how to leave."

Derrick steadies himself, looking like the hero in a fairy tale. His handsome features look flat and disjointed in this light. Like even the backdrop doesn't want him here.

"You need to stay away," I tell him, despite how much I don't want him to leave. "Thalion's men will be looking for you, and I don't think you will like the results if they find you."

"Mallory." His voice is quiet. "You don't have to protect me. My father and I need to be protecting *you*. It doesn't matter what happens to me. You need to get to the crown."

"Derrick. I am grabbing your dad and we are getting out of here. He's probably at breakfast by now. Let me go down and talk to him. He must have a plan. You said it yourself, he always has a plan."

Reluctantly, Derrick lets me go after promising to meet in the garden we'd entered through. In reality, Derrick says, it is an overgrown swamp with plenty of places to hide. Derrick promises he can handle whatever wildlife challenges him. I can't worry about his physical well-being for now—I have too much at stake to derail my focus.

With a goodbye, Derrick and I go separate ways down the stairs. I head to the ballroom, ready to face my captor, ready to fight the temptation that lies ahead.

To my surprise, Oskar is the only person at breakfast. He smiles at me as I walk in, anticipating my arrival.

Is there anything this man doesn't know?

"I sense you made a choice," he says in his usual, cryptic way.

"Yes," I answer, not giving more than I need to. "We need to leave."

I do not tell him that it is his son's agony alone that convinced me of my decision. That if I hadn't seen his pain, I would have chosen pleasure for myself.

"Ah," he said around a mouthful of food, "you made the *right* choice. I am glad to hear it."

He doesn't appear overly glad to me, but nothing in this place has been what it seems so far, so I shake the concern from my head.

"Yes," I reiterate. "We need to leave."

Oskar rises slowly, deliberately.

"You are right, of course." He draws the words out.

"So," I start, "how do we do this? How do we escape?"

"Oh, that part is simple enough, my dear. You just have to decide. And then, commit to that decision."

What does that mean?

"I have decided, Oskar. And your riddles are messing with my head. If I hadn't decided what I wanted, we wouldn't be having this conversation."

He shakes his head sadly. "No, my dear. There is still doubt in you. If you were truly determined, we would be free."

CHAPTER FOURTEEN
MALLORY

Doubt?

There *isn't* any doubt. At least, I don't think there is after that conversation with Selyra last night. There is nothing here for me but her, and she doesn't want me to stay.

My thoughts flash back to my conversation with the Hollowborne. They had wanted me to doubt, hadn't they?

And how do you stop doubting what you don't realize you are doubting?

Oskar had told me that leaving was as easy as truly wanting to leave. And I do want to leave. At least—I think I do. Derrick does not deserve to bear the brunt of mine and Oskar's choices, and Selyra had made it clear her father would kill me. There isn't any doubt of that in my mind.

Locating one's uncertainty is an arduously introspective process. My brain berates my heart which, in turn, interrogates my nervous system. It is a vicious, demanding cycle that keeps my body in eternal vigilance.

Do I feel okay about leaving?

Yes.

Do I want to leave?

Truthfully, no. Whatever small amount of time I could have living in happiness with a beautiful woman on my arm, I would always wish for it.

Oskar was right—there *is* a part of me that longs for the simplicity of the illusion. Sure, it wouldn't be real, but it would be easy. If I am honest with myself, that easiness is what I've been looking for, for longer than I'd realized.

How do I stop wanting this?

I walk the corridors, aimlessly looking for a way out, though I know I won't find one. There are too many obstacles in front of me. And I am not even sure what they are.

This isn't what I signed up for.

It dawns on me that my motivations may not be entirely selfless. At least, in the eyes of whatever magic continues to bind us to this place. Isn't that how magic works: through knowing the motivations of one's heart or something else as utterly cliche?

Isn't wanting to help others the purest motivation that exists?

I stop walking and hold myself still, my back pressed against a wall. I have to clear my head. My heart pounds in my ears as both options weigh over my head. Stay? Or fight for escape? This won't be as easy as saying I want to leave—I'll have to prove it. I'll have to do what I do best.

Run.

Walking out to the front lawn, I check for Derrick in our assigned meeting spot. We may have to do this without Oskar, who doesn't seem in any hurry to leave anyway. If he wanted to leave, I have no doubt he'd be able to. He has been here before.

My efforts find Derrick staring off into space. He looks so helpless, though I don't let him know that. There is probably some ego left that I don't wish to bruise.

"Derrick," I whisper to my friend, "we have to go."

"What did Dad say? Where is he—why isn't he here?"

"You know him. He gave me some weird non-answer about how I must not want to leave or something. He said once I made up my mind we would be free. It's all on me and I don't know what I am doing wrong."

Derrick blinks at me, the fear in his eyes making him appear much younger than he is. "You don't want to leave?"

"I do—of course I do," I say, almost pleading, not sure which of us I am trying to convince. Of course there is a part of me that doesn't want to leave, to face whatever trials lie ahead.

His face doesn't change. I can't tell if his expression is full of judgment or exhaustion, but I don't like it.

"Don't look at me like that. I want to leave . . . I just don't know how to want what comes next."

"I see," Derrick answers. "Your fear of what's to come is greater than your discontent with your surroundings. You will never move forward if you are too scared to take that step. And we can't make you take that step Mal."

He's right. I am terrified of the unknown more than anything, more than I am terrified for his safety. My mind runs into overdrive trying to convince myself that it's okay to value my safety above a boy I just met. But I know it isn't true.

I can lie to almost anyone, but I can't lie to myself.

"It doesn't matter, we have to leave anyway. If we don't try now, I'm not sure I'll have the strength to do it later. Plus," I continue, "we are almost there already. We made it out the front door with no issue. How much trouble can there be in crossing the lawn?"

The lack of guards worries me for the first time since we've attempted escape. What felt like a good omen now feels like a trap. Every day there are multiple guards lining corridors, and today, the day I choose to escape, there are none? Maybe more than what I thought around here was tied to the illusion.

Glancing down at Derrick tells me that at least the two guards I saw dragging him off were real. The evidence of their brutality is painted across his swollen face and scratched-up limbs.

"I don't think it will be that easy, Mallory, or we wouldn't have been trapped here."

Realization dawns on me the second the words leave his mouth.

I just have to want it.

"What if that is *exactly* what is keeping us here?"

He looks up at me silently, like he's waiting for my words to make sense.

"Someone told us we were stuck and we just naively believed them. What if our belief is the cage? We're not trapped, we just think we are—this is part of the Hollowborne's warning. *That* is what I should have doubted. From the beginning of our time here, I should have trusted my instincts."

For the first time since arriving, I feel hopeful.

"I hope that's it, Mal. I really do. But people usually don't make threats they can't keep, and I've seen firsthand the threats Thalion is willing to act on." He shudders hard.

I help Derrick onto his feet, his weight heavy in my arms. He hadn't let on how badly he was hurting but his limp gives me some indication as we lumber toward the gate. If he needs help to climb, I'm not sure I will be able to support him. If I'm right, he won't have to climb—we'll march through the gates with our dignity.

I hope I'm right about this.

The lawn that had once been a vibrant landscape of beautiful flowers and topiaries is now a swampy cesspool of muck and mire. Our feet make sucking noises every time we lift them to take a step. I'm glad I grabbed that rogue pair of boots on my way out the door or my sandals would be sunk into the mud by now.

Our surroundings slow our speed, but the real burden is Derrick's dead weight on my shoulder. He isn't a large man—quite the opposite, in fact, with his tall, gangly limbs—but my upper body strength is essentially nonexistent. With each labored step, Derrick lets out a heavy breath, somewhere between a grunt and sigh.

Eventually the two of us reach the towering gate, its substantial bulk insurmountable, reducing us to the size of ants in its shadow. If we can't pass through the door, we won't be able to climb this thing. Even if both of us were as healthy as possible, the stone surface would prove too slick to gain any traction.

Shit. Is it locked?

I have been so worried about how we would get through the door, I had forgotten to consider the possibility that maybe we truly *are* locked inside. There is a heavy-looking iron lock wrapped around the thick metal bars, clicked shut. My heart thumps wildly in my chest as I reach a hand out to inspect the lock. As my fingers move to grip its body and yank, they sink into its plush surface.

Styrofoam.

The lock is fake.

"Are you ready?" I ask, more to myself than to Derrick.

"As ready as ever."

I let go of Derrick. He wobbles a bit before steadying—I don't know how much longer he can stand on his own. With as much force as I can muster, I push my weight into the gate. The muddy ground squelches but the gate barely budges.

This is going to be harder than I thought.

I push again—maybe a centimeter of give this time.

"Derrick," I huff, "I know you're hurting, but I'm not strong enough to push this open by myself. I'm going to need your help. Can you do that for me?"

I hate asking him for more than he's already given, but if we get caught escaping it will be much worse for the both of us. Thalion may take back his offer and torture me too.

"I'll try, but I can't make any promises," he squeaks out.

My heart sinks. I need Derrick to give his best effort, pain or no. And the weakness in his voice gives me pause to believe there is any strength left in his body.

"You have to give me everything you can, or it won't work." My voice comes out pleading. "I know it hurts. I know you're not okay, but I need you. This door is too heavy for me to push on my own with all this mud around."

Softening my voice as I look into his eyes, I say, "When we escape I will find someone to heal you. I promise I'll fix this."

He matches my gaze and nods.

"On the count of three," I dictate. "One. Two. Three."

The two of us slam our body weight against the gate, eliciting agonized groans from Derrick. Under our combined force, the gate moves significantly. But it's still not enough.

"If we can do that one, maybe two, more times, we'll have it open." I tell him as his panting grows louder. "Just hang in there."

He says nothing but manages a small twitch of his head despite the grimace on his face. Standing up from the bent position he's in, he turns back toward the iron monstrosity with a determination in his eyes. When he has both hands firmly locked around a bar, he sets his jaw and gives another firm nod.

"One. Two. Three!"

Another strong push, and this time Derrick lets out a full-blown yelp. I push past his pain—I can't let it stop us now that we are this close. I have to start making sacrifices for the greater good if anyone is going to take me seriously as High Queen of Nalara. Once we get over the threshold, I will make good on my promise to find a healer, whether Derrick believes me or not.

"One. Two. Three!"

One last thrust and the doors open entirely, groaning in reluctance as they do. Derrick is lying on the ground, sweat and mud dripping from his exhausted face. We are so close to the finish line, there is no time to tend to his wounds now. Our difficulty is not over —we must escape.

"Come on." My voice rises as I plead. "Get up. The door is open. We did it. Get up."

Derrick attempts to stand and manages to make it to his feet without the support he'd once had of the gate.

One step.

Two.

On the third step, Derrick collapses again.

"Mallory," he says quietly, "I need you to go through. You are the one who matters most. You are the one who needs to save us. I am nobody in the grand scheme of things."

The air stills between us. I don't really know this man, but I feel like I owe him safety for enduring the torture Thalion doled out. Without me, he wouldn't be in this mess. Though, without him, neither would I. He and I are tied together somehow, by far more than obligation.

"No, you idiot." I spit the words with more force than I mean. "You are the only reason I even want to leave. If Thalion had promised to enchant you and Oskar, or at least leave the two of you unharmed, I wouldn't be fighting this hard to leave."

Sadness overcomes his face as he looks up at me. "You need to make it to the crown. I don't matter. Once you rule the land, you can come back for me if you remember."

Part of me wants to take him up on that offer, and another gnawing, nagging part drenched in guilt is telling me that I must stay with him, no matter what.

Why must you always do the right thing?

"No." I shake my head. "I won't be able to make it through the rest of the Witherwalk on my own."

That part is true enough. Nalara may be my birthright, but I don't yet understand it. Oskar told me of the Witherwalk, but gave no more than a cursory mention as to its logistics. My next trial is south, but how far eludes me. And what comes beyond that, I don't have the slightest clue.

"And," I add, "Oskar will never come with me alone. He will stay here with you, and you know it. He's the royal advisor, and I need him to advise. Without you safe in the castle, Oskar will be of no use to the throne."

The gate is open and all he has to do is go through it. His wounds may be deep, but the most painful part in all of this awaits if he can't step through the door. Earlier he'd said that I am too scared of the unknown, that it makes me willing to endure pain. Well, Derrick is so scared of the pain in front of him that he's unwilling to face what's to come.

"You just have to get through the gate, Derrick. That is the last thing I am asking of you and then I will go find a healer. Selyra said her mother was Selowen and healed herself. There have to be more healers out there, maybe even held captive in the villages in order to heal the Emberguard."

Why can't you want to get through?

Looking at the puddle of wounded flesh on the ground that calls itself Derrick causes something inside me to flip. I have a choice to make. Return to Thalion and accept his offer, or step through the gates by myself and figure out the rest, just like I have always done. I've made it this far—I have to keep going. If only to prove to myself that I can.

Can I actually do this? Should *I do this?*

My right foot crosses the threshold, then my left. I feel the boundaries of an invisible barrier, a slight resistance to my form exiting the grounds. Warmth overcomes me for a brief second as I break through. A levity washes through me and I giggle. Really, truly giggle like a small child. It dawns on me that this is the first time I have laughed since entering the grounds, despite the incantation on my senses. It's like my body knew whatever happiness existed was a facade.

Turning to look at the manor I had just left, I am more than a little surprised to see that once again it is replaced with the wonderful vision from the day I entered. There must be some form of magic that guards the ground's true identity.

I couldn't have known.

"Well done my dear."

My head whips around. Oskar and Derrick, both in perfect health, stand arm in arm behind me. Oskar's grin is plastered on his face, a mix of pride and relief. Derrick, ever his father's opposite, stands looking as stunned as I feel to see him whole again.

"What happened?" I ask the older man.

"You passed the first trial of the Witherwalk my dear, designed to test your clarity—your ability to sort through beautiful lies to reveal the harsh truth. It shows integrity to choose that truth, no matter the cost."

This should be a happy moment: one trial down on my impending journey. All at once, clarity washes over my body, flushing out the endorphins of relief I'd felt. My joy evaporates and in its place drops a blanket of betrayal. Oskar knew there would be trials like this and kept it to himself. Whether he was privy to the minute details of what to expect or not, he could have prepared me better. He purposely kept me in the dark.

What else is he hiding?

"Okay," I say. "I guess I can expect more of this?"

Oskar's grin grows wider than I would have thought possible. "Of course, my dear, though never in the same way twice."

Of course not.

A heavy breath escapes my lungs.

I should have taken Thalion's offer.

CHAPTER FIFTEEN
MALLORY

"Hey," Derrick whispers in a low voice as he grabs my arm, "you didn't have to do that."

The look in his eyes stops me cold.

"Do what?"

"Save me."

I didn't save him, not really. I saved myself. There was no way for me to know that stepping over the threshold would bring him and Oskar to the other side. And even less way of knowing his wounds would magically heal.

"It's nothing. I really didn't do anything."

"Yeah, but you saved my life. I thought for sure if you left without me Thalion would take it out on me. He would have killed me."

Now that Derrick is back in fighting form, I can't find the same sympathy for him I once could. He looks strong, he looks like himself, but his groveling is so out of character it grates against my skin. And why is he thanking me? He was there. He saw me leave him, didn't he?

"Don't mention it," I say through gritted teeth, mimicking a smile as best I can.

He turns to his father and the two of them discuss what Oskar had previously known about the situation. I can't hear what they are saying, nor do I want to, as I begin wandering toward the woods flanking the opening near the gate where we are standing. Bloomhall is nestled at the very southernmost point of Liriwyn, that much I had learned from one of Thalion's boastful speeches.

"The Ruins of Gallivarum are just south of here," I overhear Oskar saying to his son as he points lazily in my direction. "The next trial is there."

Knowing which direction to walk is just half the battle, but a challenge I may have to meet. Derrick has proven a liability to my cause and, while Oskar may yet prove to be an asset, he won't come without his precious son.

What good was Oskar in that trial?

He'd said these are trials meant for me alone, but as an advisor, one would think he'd be a little more apt to give advice. Besides, I am taking him at his word that he was the Voice of the Hollow. And I am believing his arrogance that he was good at it. Both these men are still relatively strangers. Even in captivity I'd managed to avoid speaking with them too often. Something feels off, and I need to trust that.

Continuing to walk deeper into the woods, two voices grow quiet behind me. Now that I am separated from my companions, I am alone with my thoughts. A darkness descends on the woods, the dense awning of leaves block out what little light remains in the day. Leaving the manor must have taken longer than I'd thought, or else its magic altered my perception of time. Either way, I am grateful to be done with that place. Continuing the Witherwalk is not necessarily something I aspire to—if it happens, it happens—but leaving Bloomhall means I'm free from carrying the burden of someone else's happiness.

I can barely manage my own.

Glimmering sparkles of illuminated bugs dance around, breaking up the ever-growing darkness. In Nalara, I am learning, the forest is never silent. Despite the lack of obvious fauna, it is always humming. Alive. From the leaves to the earth itself, everything is whispering and vibrant. Even the smell—a mix of pine and fresh morning dewdrops—tells its truth.

Closing my eyes, I allow the sounds of nature to bathe me in their radiance. A vibrant energy fills me and I am overcome with the chatter of the trees.

"Something new has come to Nalara."

"The prophecy will be fulfilled."

"We are doomed."

"We are saved."

The voices crescendo to a scream inside my skull. Emotions that are not mine swell and fill every pore of being. My stomach quivers as the pressure builds in my head, threatening to bring me toppling to the ground.

"Enough!" I scream to the void.

Silence follows. Whether out of respect for their new ruler or shock at her audacity, the trees hush at my words.

"Thank you," I say aloud to the darkness once more. To an onlooker it would look like I am speaking to myself. I guess, in a way, I am.

Continuing forward at a brisk pace, each step serves as a gentle reminder that I have no idea where I am going. It doesn't matter.

Anywhere but there.

My feet pick up the pace, running once again—this time physically—to an unknown destination. I forget about my companions as the exhilaration washes over me. The act of running itself is not the thrill, it is the pain that is so immediate it washes out coherent thought. When I run from something, I am safe, not by distance but by detachment. Although, this time, I find myself running toward something, rather than away.

What does that mean for my safety?

My feet ache, my lungs burn, and my eyes are growing weary. My body screams for the kind of rest that was stolen from me in Bloomhall. The kind of rest I was tricked into thinking I had.

Whatever momentum I had been carrying stops abruptly as my knees buckle, sending me to the ground. My palms hit the dirt and a dull pain reverberates up my arms and into my elbows. A familiar pain. Like falling on the concrete while playing tag at recess. Falling hurts like hell, but the nostalgia it brings is a certain kind of romantic. My childhood wounds in a new light.

I'm not a child anymore, and this isn't the worst pain I'll ever know.

I don't know if it is the sting of the fall, the lack of energy from the run, or something deep within me that causes the tears to roll down my cheeks. The trickles quickly turn to rivulets. My shoulders ebb with the sharp sucking in of every breath. Sadness.

No, I'm not sad. I'm exhausted in my bones.

The emptiness of the woods is finally catching up to me and I remember that Oskar and Derrick are probably camped out somewhere, warm and light, while I lie on the ground in the middle of the woods. For a moment—in weakness—I wish I was with them.

My choices are clear: I can lie in the middle of the woods alone and pathetic, or I can get up and *do something*.

Find a shelter, Mallory. That's Step One.

Admittedly, I am not much of a scout. Even if I had the capability to survive, I can't see more than a few inches in front of my face now that the lightning bugs have gone to bed. I am truly alone in the moonless night.

A spark of inspiration overcomes me and I speak into the stillness.

"Hello," I say with uncertainty to an unseen acquaintance. "I need help."

Silence.

"I know you can understand me." A beat passes before I add, "And I know you can speak. I've heard your whispers."

Nothing.

"Look," I say with an exasperated exhale, "I'm sorry I yelled at you earlier. I was overwhelmed and emotional, and you were all talking at once. Where I come from, the trees are silent."

"Pity," a deep voice booms from behind me, reverberating

through my bones. "We have a lot to say if the right person is listening."

I consider this, wondering about all that the trees must see.

What secrets can they tell?

"But now," the tree continues, "you only wish to listen out of greed. It's not that you care to hear our tales. You are fueled only by your own desire for safety."

I nod in the dark. They're right—they *are* my last resort.

"Why should we help you now?"

Do they know who I am? Do they know of the prophecy?

"I'm aware," I say with as much remorse as I can muster in my voice, "that I don't deserve your help—that much is true. But I am asking for your mercy after escaping Bloomhall."

The trees murmur at the name, as if Bloomhall's reputation precedes it, even out here. Once they settle, another long stretch of silence hangs in the air, taunting me.

"Come, let us help the girl," another voice hisses to the first. I can't pinpoint its location, but I smile to the darkness, hoping whichever plant spoke can see my gratitude.

"Fine," the first voice huffs again, "but when this backfires, let it be known that I was against helping *her*."

The way this voice spits the word "her" makes my blood run cold. They do know who I am, and they hate me too.

How many enemies do I have? How many more will I make?

"Thank you," I say, "You won't live to regret this."

"I wouldn't be so sure about that."

A beat passes. How do I respond to that?

"What is it you require from us?" The voice is growing impatient with me now.

"I need shelter. I don't know what dangers lie in these woods, and you do. Can you tell me where I can sleep tonight without getting hurt?"

A flurry of voices fly together at once, debating each other. I catch scraps of conversation but can piece together nothing concrete.

After what feels like several minutes of chaos, I hear another voice say, "There is an old Selowen temple not too far from here. Most people ignore it, so you should be relatively safe there."

"Your biggest danger," the voice continues, "is not any wild creature that prowls the woods. It is your fellow Nalarans. You are known by all but loved by few. There are many who seek to take you down before the crown touches that pretty red hair."

Chills run through me and I fiddle with my cuticles. I find a tender patch of exposed skin where a hangnail had been and squeeze hard. A jolt of pain runs through me, and I relish the familiar ache. I hadn't considered that there are those who would wish me harm before I've even hit the throne.

""I understand. Where I come from, the greatest danger to me is mankind—our dominant species. I wouldn't expect any different here."

I hope I sound more confident than I feel.

"Where is this building?" I ask the surrounding flora, pushing down how ridiculous it feels.

"It isn't much farther," the main tree speaks again, sounding suspiciously happier about this arrangement. "You are almost there. Continue walking in the same direction you were running and you will get where you need to be."

"Thank you." I stand, brushing dirt off the skirt of the green dress I had acquired from Thalion. He told me it was an old frock of his daughter's, which surprised me, as I am substantially bigger than her. But now all I can think is that it's the last remnant of what might have been if I'd stayed.

It seems silly to me that I can't get the pretty girl out of my head. We've spoken twice—I shouldn't feel like I owe her so much. Knowing she is just as much a prisoner as I was draws me closer into infatuation with the idea of her. Maybe when I can free her, which is the moral choice, something will come of it. Right now, she is behind me and I have to leave her there.

My thoughts return to the present. Running through the dark, the world blurring past me faster than I can register, had been one thing. But walking alone in an unknown place? The thought terrifies me.

I hope it's not much farther.

It feels like a lifetime before I reach the base of the temple. Or what I can only assume was once a temple. The decrepit remains are closer to a Grecian monument now than anything inhabitable.

My fingers fumble in the dark to graze the cold, unyielding stone. It's stable but worn from years of decay in a way that makes me think it's seen more than the elements. Much more.

"This is what you give me?" I shout up to the starless sky.

"What did you expect?" the familiarly deep voice responds.

How did a tree move?

"Who are you?" I ask. "*What* are you?"

"I am Fenric."

"Who" was a rhetorical question, but I suppose it makes some sort of sense that a talking tree would, in fact, have a name. Though, the name does not explain much.

"Are you following me?"

"Yes and no."

More cryptic puzzles. Great.

"You're a tree."

"Not quite." He chuckles with such force the ground shakes. "I am a dryad who has been watching these woods since the Sundering."

The dryad's voice grows quiet. "I was once a Nalaran myself, many years ago, who served in this temple until the slaughter."

Slaughter?

The word sits on my tongue like earwax, foreign and bitter. It doesn't belong, but once it's there, it can't be ignored.

"What slaughter?" My voice shakes as I ask.

"Many years ago, before the Emberguard took control of everything, we lived and worked in this temple in peace. I spent my existence worshipping the Sacred Willow, determined to bring its gentleness and beauty to the Crown. One night, the Emberguard snuck into the temple while we all slept and murdered us all in our beds."

"And there was no one there to stop them?"

A sad breath of air escapes the dryad. "No. We were naive and believed harmony would be the way forward. Before that night, we had never thought to employ any sort of guard—and the Selowen don't believe in combat. At least, we didn't back then."

"Why did they attack?" I ask the spirit.

"For no other reason than our bloodline. We were born of the Willow, born with a weakness the Emberguard would seek to eradicate from Nalara. A weakness that they have all but eradicated from Nalara. The Selowen have grown fewer in numbers, and are spread throughout to avoid detection."

My lineage is Selowen. I am an enemy of the state simply because I exist.

"How did you end up here?" My voice is steadier now with the realization that this *tree* is the key to understanding my birthright.

"The mighty Willow had mercy on my spirit and gave me life after death to continue in its service for all of eternity. Whether that is a blessing or a curse remains to be seen."

Fenric has raised more questions in me than my body has energy to ask. If an afterlife exists, surely to live in the form of a tree-inhabiting spirit is punishment. But that begs the question, *Does an afterlife exist?*

Shaking the thoughts from my head, I thank the dryad and make my way into the ruins. The ceiling is missing in more areas than it's not, littering the floor with debris. I find a secluded alcove, under what looks to be the remains of a stairwell. Sweeping my foot in a broad arch, rubble scatters with each pass. The clicks of the stones meeting one another echo loudly in the stillness of the night. It isn't going to be comfortable, but having my back to a wall will at least allow me to sleep.

My body is ready to give out on me—I have asked too much of it today. I lie on the hard ground, wishing for a blanket as blood trudges its way through my veins. Every inch of me vibrates like a familiar lullaby. I am too tired for fear—it won't be long until I succumb to sleep.

Outside, I can hear the trees whispering, though I cannot make out what they are saying.

CHAPTER SIXTEEN
MALLORY

A beam of sunlight shines through a crack, landing squarely on my closed eyes, beckoning me awake. Letting out an involuntary groan, my body protests my movements. In an attempt to avoid the sun, I roll onto my left side and open my eyes, taking a mental scan of myself. Every muscle feels like jelly but simultaneously aches with the stiffness of sleep. It's been too long since I've run like that. My head is pounding from a lack of water, and my throat feels like sandpaper.

A hangover without the alcohol—fun.

My bladder screams at me for release and I stand to find relief. The pain is overwhelming and my movements are quick as I exit the structure and scan the tree line, looking for a secluded-enough spot. After taking care of business, I walk back to my sleeping nook. My little alcove is easily accessible from the side of the ruins, as a large portion of the wall is missing, making the perfect window.

Sitting on the floor of my new room, acknowledgment of what I have done finally washes over me; I am alone, and I don't know what the next step is. Oskar had said our next stop on the quest was the Ruins of Gallivarum. These have to be those ruins, right?

Will they come looking for me? Do they even know I am gone?

I fiddle with a pebble between my thumb and forefinger as the cool grayness of my surroundings washes over me. In the early light of the morning, I notice details that were concealed in last night's darkness. The Ruins of Gallivarum, if these are them, are larger than I'd thought, but smaller than I had anticipated. Piles of crumbled stone lay scattered across the ground level. Stairs lead to phantom second floor landings.

What's holding them up?

Rising from the floor of my makeshift bedroom, an urge to explore tickles the back of my brain. Not all the debris on the floor looks like rubble. Most everything is covered in a thin layer of a grayish residue—probably soot from a fire—but there are hints of ivory frequent enough to garner a second look.

The nearest cluster is a few feet away and, when I reach it, I sink to my knees to examine what I am sure I recognize. My hand brushes away a layer of soot, and I am left staring into the empty left eye cavity of a fragmented skull. A shiver runs through my body, sharp and unsettling. These are the bones of the temple clergy. Perhaps even Fenric's remains are scattered somewhere throughout the decrepit shell of the temple.

Keep moving, Mallory. You can't save the dead.

My meandering leads me to discover a landing perfect for stargazing, hidden behind two walls that look to have once held a courtyard between them, with naked flowerbeds and a singular willow tree, much smaller than the one that brought me to Nalara. It isn't until this moment the thought crosses my mind that this place was once beautiful.

"Devastating, isn't it?" A voice, groggy and distant, comes from the tree as my fingers graze the notches carved into the trunk of the war-ravaged willow.

An arrow, broken midway down the shaft, is buried in the wood high above my head. I stare at the rusty tip, trying to find a visual point of focus as Fenric speaks again.

"This was, at one time, my favorite spot in the temple. Do you see that bench?"

My eyes scan the base of the tree and spot a slab of stone broken in two at the midpoint.

"That's a bench?" The question escapes from me with a scoff as I point.

Fenric's voice grows sharp. "Yes. That is a bench. Or, rather, what is left of one. My father built it before I was born, and it was the last thing I had of him."

"Your father worked here too?"

"Being a Brother of the Verdant Concord is a time-honored tradition passed by birthright from father to son."

The Verdant Concord. I remember Oskar mentioning them when I first arrived.

"My mentor, Oskar, who I was traveling with told me of the Verdant Concord and their beliefs. What was it like belonging before the fall?"

His voice grows almost wistful, "It was beautiful. We worshipped with the wind and the rain. All Brothers had the gifts to commune with nature, the same gifts I am quite certain you have."

"And that's how I can speak with you?"

A smile sounds in Fenric's voice, despite the lack of a face. "I am a dryad, and we can make ourselves known to anybody. But you, you hear the grass whisper and the flowers sing, don't you?"

My mind travels back to my time in the meadow. When I'd woken up, I could have sworn I'd heard the moss humming. The flowers in Liriwyn called to me, though I'd ignored their warnings.

"Yes."

Tracing my fingers along the cool stone of the broken bench, I ask the question that has been pulling at my mind.

"Are your bones somewhere in the rubble?"

A gentle breeze flips my long unbrushed hair into my face.

"No, I was Brother Supreme, the head of the Concord in Gallivarum. My remains were stolen by the Emberguard as a warning to the rest of those who worship Selowen."

A warning. The words thrum through my skull over and over again, begging me not to heed the message. My ancestors were killed and poor Fenric faces a fate worse than death.

"Fenric?" The question comes out as little more than a whisper.

"Hmm?"

"Do you regret spending your life in servitude of the thing that ultimately cost your life?"

"That isn't a question easily answered. In a way, I still live. What faith I had in my lifetime, I needed. What faith remains is hard to say."

Nodding, I turn my back to the tree and take in the sight of the Ruins of Gallivarum, imagining what they once were.

It is coming upon midday now, and I am once again entirely alone. My conversation with Fenric feels like it happened in another lifetime, as I was left to contemplate the choices that have led me here. Whatever faith Fenric had in life, was a faith I have never known for anyone or anything. Not even my companions.

Oskar and Derrick told me they were here for me—that I could count on them. If that was true, they would be here by now.

Wouldn't they?

When they discovered my absence, I can't be sure they weren't relieved. If the tables were turned, I certainly would have been. They've got what they wanted. Oskar brought his son back to his childhood homeland and is giving him a chance to grow old in the land that was stolen from him. Derrick will continue to make his father proud. Both of them deserve the chance to leave me in their past.

I hope they're not coming for me.

As my stomach growls and nausea falls over me. The world wobbles slightly, the ground once flat and steady now threatening to rise to meet my face. The pangs of an empty stomach feel familiar . . . almost enjoyable. It's been a long time since I have allowed myself to feel this hungry.

You're done with that, Mallory. You graduated from treatment and everything.

Besides, there is nothing better for me to do than spend the day finding something to eat. Getting to tomorrow means getting through today. And, today, I am starving.

Meandering to the courtyard willow where Fenric and I spoke this morning, I call out to the emptiness.

"Hello?" I ask the wind, but to no avail.

Perhaps he's not here and is not close enough to hear me.

Instead of waiting around to call into the emptiness again, I make my way toward the edge of the forest where the dryads and I had last spoken. The only sound that follows is the distant chirping of birds. Last night, the forest was alive. Its silence is disconcerting.

"Fenric!" I call into the emptiness again.

What did you expect, you stupid girl?

Despite his begrudging help last night, I'd thought our morning talk had made a difference in our relationship. Sure, we aren't best friends, but he'd told me more about his life . . . and his death. I'd thought that counted for something.

Before I can contemplate my social standing with the trees, my stomach grumbles louder than before, bringing with it the tinny taste of metal in my mouth. I *need* to eat.

Walking over, I noticed berries on a bush near the opening of the forest. Despite my years of summer camp, I am not a scout. And the only thing I know about foraging is, don't eat something unless you can positively identify it. I am in Nalara, a world so new to me I don't even know the names of most plants, let alone whether their fruit could kill me.

For the first time, I am completely alone.

Another realization hits me like a ton of my bricks.

I will have to kill and cook something if I want to live.

Death isn't something I have ever feared. On my worst days, it's even desirable. Though I'd prefer it as quick and painless as possible. Now, facing the choice of death by poisonous berry or by starvation, living seems to be the most comfortable outcome.

They say that pain is temporary, that you forget how you felt even a short while after the wounds heal. No matter how temporary, a painful death is something I don't ever wish to endure. My will to live is forever at odds with my desire for comfort.

The dehydration will probably get me first anyway, but I can worry about that once I silence the cavernous ache in my stomach.

"How does one catch breakfast with no tools?" I ask aloud to no one, hoping to catch the eavesdropping ear of one of the tree spirits.

First, I must take inventory of my options. Nothing in the forests of Gallivarum seems too foreign to me, a small mercy. My eyes follow a small blue bird darting along the treetops, while a family of gray squirrel-like creatures with antlers play along the forest floor. Birds will be too hard to catch for someone with no experience and no ammo—squirrels and rabbits too. Deer, if they exist here, are too big and require too much work to break down. I learned that much from the deer carcass hanging upside down over a bucket of blood in my neighbor's garage. That's one memory I wish I could forget.

Fish.

If there is a pond nearby, I can try to catch fish. Finding the fish will be the easy part. Catching them with no poles, nets, or experience will prove a challenge. Still, it is my best shot at eating today.

From everything I know, fish can be caught with one's bare hands, in a pinch. Rolling the sleeves of my green dress up to my elbows, I raise my hands to eye level for examination, like this is my first time ever seeing them. They are soft and uncalloused, clearly not the hands of someone who does hard labor.

I hope this works.

CHAPTER SEVENTEEN
MALLORY

Much of the next few hours are spent looking for a body of water but, despite my best efforts, the forest appears dry. The sun is high in the sky now, well into the afternoon, and I am nowhere closer to eating. My stomach is screaming at me and it takes everything in me not to double over in pain and give up the search. Dehydration is the stronger threat now, though. Every swallow feels like a hot knife slicing the back of my throat, and my head is pounding like a drumline.

Every inch of this forest has been combed by my walking in incessant circles. As fond as I have grown of the repetition of the woods, it may be best to keep walking. Whatever trial is meant to be here hasn't come yet, and I can't pass it anyway if I'm weak or dead. Oskar said each trial would be different from the last, making it impossible to know what to expect until I face it.

Bloomhall isn't looking so bad.

"Fenric," I pant, my lungs struggling as if full of ash. "Help me, please."

A strong gust of wind responds, knocking me to the ground. I sit, legs splayed and palms planted, waiting for my tree spirit guide to answer my call.

Faintly, as if from a distance, I hear a whisper in the wind, different from the dryads, whose voices are strong and mighty. It is a thin, girlish whisper, as if coming from someone no bigger than my pinky finger. A gnat buzzes around my head and I swat it away. It comes back, as if taunting me, dancing from eye to eye. My strength is fading and I wonder for a second if it's the gnat that is speaking.

That is an absolutely ridiculous notion.

My time in these woods alone, as short as it's been, is testing my sanity.

Psst.

I hear a taunting from somewhere below me.

Psst.

This time it's coming from above. Whatever it is—whoever it is—that is making this noise is moving. There is no longer any doubt about that. Why won't they still?

"Stop it!" I scream into the void.

It feels good to raise my voice again. Yesterday, I regretted yelling at the dryads. Now, it means they're listening again. This morning's conversation with Fenric feels eons away, and I can't be sure through the delirium of dehydration that it even happened at all.

A giggle erupts at my plea, slow and steady at first but gaining momentum. Whoever this is likes to play tricks. And I am a joke.

Not again.

"I'm serious," I say, finding my voice. Their laughing tweaks something primal inside me, something defensive and urgent. I am dying out here, and they are *laughing* at me.

Despite my indignation, or maybe prompted by it, the laughing continues to move around my head. Every time I turn my eyes to face it, it changes direction.

"This isn't funny. Cut it out." My voice comes out almost pleading.

All at once, a glow envelops me. This glow, unlike the others, is not green. It is purple—a hazy lavender mist bouncing off the trees, reflecting back at me. The gnat begins to grow. No, not a gnat. A woman. At full height, she stands about a foot shorter than me and is much daintier.

She is likely the most beautiful woman I have ever seen. Even Selyra's beauty pales in comparison. Long dark brown hair caresses her upper thighs. Her nose sits upturned, perfectly positioned in the middle of her face. Pixie-like ears frame her crystal blue eyes like something out of a painting. The woman is dressed in what I can only describe as an icy blue gown, with thigh-high slits on either side and a tight silhouette.

If it wasn't already, my mouth would have gone dry from embarrassment. Here I am, hair unkempt and dried urine on my leg, sitting on the ground in front of perhaps the prettiest and most put-together person who has ever lived.

"Apologies," she says through laughter, not noticing my appearance. "It amuses me a great deal when someone cannot find the object for which they are searching, despite its proximity."

Her age is indistinguishable—she looks young, but the way she speaks and carries herself tells me she must be, at the very least, centuries old.

"If it is so close, are you going to help me or just continue to laugh?"

It isn't that I mean to be rude, not outright, anyway. But someone who wishes to help others should do so without the theatrics. She owes me nothing, of course, but a bit of kindness goes a long way.

Her beautiful face twists into a frown, one that looks hardly used by the girl. She is studying me like I said something greatly offensive.

"Yes," she says in a soft voice. Her eyes search my face, no doubt looking for an ounce of joy to match hers. For both our sakes, I hope she finds it.

"There is a pond nearby teeming with fish. I will lead you to its edge and aid you in procuring lunch. That is your wish, yes?"

My stomach growls in response.

The woman nods.

"Follow me, then. It isn't much farther. You can eat and be on your way." Her tone now is harsh and her sentences abrupt.

Standing, I dust my hands off on my skirts, my palms sore and indented from the rough ground.

"I am Maryna," the woman tells me as I gain my footing.

"I'm Mallory." I step forward with an extended right arm.

"I know." Maryna looks at my hand but does not shake it. "I have heard tell of your arrival from the dryads surrounding my pond. As a species, they are not known to keep secrets."

Of course they aren't.

A warmth runs over me as I ponder what gossip they could possibly be telling. Hopefully nothing too uncouth.

"Oh, right."

She giggles again. Her laugh sounds like running water.

"I come from an ancient species of water nymphs. It may come as a shock, but the water in Nalara speaks almost as much as the trees."

Her eyes twinkle with a glint of mischief as she gestures to the small pond that now lies before us. Its beauty, like Maryna's, is unmatched by anything in these woods. Just above the water's calm, glassy surface, hundreds of nymphs, still in their small, bug-like forms dance through the air.

This wasn't here before.

"I thought water nymphs were more like mermaids, not fairies."

She shrugs. "Perhaps things are different in your world, but here not all nymphs are the same. Ocean nymphs are cousins to the sirens or merfolk. River nymphs, like my family and I, are exactly like what you see before you. You mustn't make such sweeping judgments of a world or culture you do not yet know."

"I guess that makes sense," I say, still not understanding.

"It's best not to dwell too long on our differences." She smiles warmly. "Come, let me help you find food."

Her voice calms me now, along with the sight of the water. Trudging down to the edge, I stare back at my reflection in the glassy surface of the pond. Seconds feel like minutes as I wait for her to show me what to do, but she hangs back, observing. Every fiber of my being is screaming in hunger and, without thinking, I reach my hand down into the pond. Something tingles my fingers as a pulse of electricity runs through me. The fish stay in place.

A hum of energy reverberates up one arm and into the other. Every life form in the pond has gone still, and the nymphs flying above like mosquitoes have scattered. My stomach curls in on itself, whether with hunger or in response to the newfound power, I can't be certain.

Something doesn't feel right.

"Ashawill."

Maryna breathed the word so it was barely audible. I'm not sure how I caught it with the rushing of blood in my ears, pounding to the beat of my heart. For a brief moment, the question of safety flits through my mind. However, all questions cease as I turn my head to look at her, hands still dipped up to the elbow in water. Maryna's body has gone ridged and her face pale, paler than her milk-white skin should allow.

"Maryna," I say softly, "are you okay?"

She shakes her head to clear her thoughts, and meets my gaze.

"Of course," she replies, her smile returning to her face. "You did wonderfully. You are so new to our world, I had not anticipated your magic to prove so . . . advanced."

Magic.

That feeling had been magic. Was she sure? My magic feels like an enchanted lullaby, not an electric shock. A shudder runs through me. If this is what Ash magic feels like, no wonder the Emberguard is so on edge.

"I thought I had dream magic?" I ask my beautiful new friend.

"And you still may. I wouldn't know. As a water nymph, my specialty is in water magic. It stands to reason you may have both. Aquenai—the practice of water magic—and Somnara both derive from the seed of Selowen. They rely on manipulation of that which is fluid."

"Wait—" My finger shakes violently at a point inches from her nose. "You said Ashawill. If water magic is Selowen in nature, why did you say it was Ash?"

Her flighty demeanor returns and she smiles a wide, cat-like grin. "Who said it was Ash?"

Holding on to the exasperated sigh that's threatening to escape, I do my best to match her expression. "Ashawill sounds a hell of a lot like Asharil to me, don't you think?"

"Huh, I guess you're right! I never thought of it like that."

My eyes narrow as another giggle escapes my new friend's lips.

"Well, then, what does Ashawill mean?"

Maryna shrugs convincingly. "You know, I don't think I actually know. It's just something we say when we get surprised."

Her explanation sounds genuine, but I'm not buying it. Still, there is no one else to ask until I see Oskar again.

Will I see Oskar again?

"Well, whatever it is, I caught myself some lunch." I point to the still-frozen fish in the pond. "Can you help me figure out how to cook it?"

Maryna starts on about how to build a fire, something I vaguely remember from when Derrick set up camp on our first night. She's rambling about skinning and boning the fish, but I can't concentrate on her words. If I didn't think a raw fish would make me sick, and if they didn't have eyes, I might be tempted to skip the cooking step altogether.

With the fire now successfully stoked into a small flame, Maryna orders me to pull as many fish as I'd like to eat from the pond. In all the commotion of the past several minutes, I'd forgotten my thirst. But looking at the water now, I am drawn forward onto my knees. My head dips low as I hold my hair out of the way, and I draw in a deep drink of the freshwater pond. Looking at me from directly below the water's surface is a fish, still suspended in the liquid right where I'd left it.

If I didn't know any better, I would think the fish looked scared.

After lunch, Maryna invites me to take a swim with her and some of her sisters. They've returned now that the life inside the pond has continued flowing. Her sisters, while beautiful themselves, don't hold a candle to Maryna's vibrance. There is not a male nymph in sight, but I suspect if they exist they'd be effeminately decorated as well.

Maryna is too polite to say it, but I know her invitation isn't out of pure altruism—even I can smell the stench that clings to my skin like clothing.

"Sure. I guess a swim could be fun," I say, wading into the water to join her and her family.

With every step, Selyra's gown tugs at my collarbones, as if her memory attempts to drag me under. Water is rapidly filling the porous cotton fabric, threatening to trip me as it sinks in front of me. By the time I am hip-deep, I can't move another step.

"You're going to want to remove your garments," Maryna calls, her head bobbing up from beneath the pond's surface. "They will only weigh you down. Why don't you take everything off, give them a rinse, and leave them out to dry?"

She's right. Staying clothed may very well be the death of me. Trudging my way back up to the shore, I begin removing my clothes, acutely aware of Maryna's eyes watching my every movement. My face burns red as I bend over, completely unclothed, and ring my garments of water. I toss them, rather haphazardly, onto the shore and jump into the water with as much speed as I can muster, convinced the pond will hide my shame.

"How does it feel?" Maryna asks when I reemerge from beneath the surface.

"Wonderful," I admit with a grin. She splashes my face and wiggles her eyebrows before diving back under. Fingers wrap around my ankle from below, threatening to pull me below the surface, but free themselves just as suddenly as they appeared. Maryna pops back up, roaring with laughter as three of her sisters swim around us, lazily backstroking in the afternoon sun.

The coolness of the water hitting my face reminds me that I'm human. My last few days have been spent surviving, and just barely. I lap up the water with my tongue like a dog and relish in its taste. When you are on the brink of dehydration, even pond water you are currently bathing in tastes like heaven.

"We can stay here as long as you wish," Maryna's heavenly voice rings out.

I begin to protest out of habit—she is just being kind—but stop myself. I have nothing else to do today, and no responsibilities I can think of. A trial waits here but, until it presents itself, there is nothing more I can do.

Just lighten up, Mallory.

Maryna and I, along with a few of her sisters, swim lazily for the rest of the afternoon. I don't know why, but I memorized her face. The exact shade of her eyes. The twinkle of her laugh. As if I know this is the last time I will see her happy.

One by one, her sisters excuse themselves to nowhere in particular, leaving Maryna and I alone in the pond. We swim until the sun tucks itself in behind the trees and the air grows cold. Shivering, I exit the water, no longer ashamed of my nakedness, and am, more than anything, thankful to have clean garments for tonight.

Maryna, with all the skills of a nature scout, makes another fire with the remains of the wood from lunch. For someone whose power is in water magic, she does know her way around a fire. Shaking myself dry in the newfound warmth, I dress myself by the glow of the orange light. Now that my nakedness isn't hidden by water or darkness, my movements are quick and imprecise. Once dressed, the two of us lie head to head in the grass, staring up at the sky. Unlike last night's sky, this one is alive with flickering stars.

This has to be a good omen.

"Mallory"—Maryna's voice cuts through the darkness—"why are you here in Nalara? What is it that you want?"

Her voice grows quieter and more hesitant as she speaks, like she is afraid of my answer.

"I was brought here," I tell her truthfully. "I don't know what I am still doing here, though. I had the chance to leave."

"Why didn't you take it?"

The air hangs thick and still in the darkness. My silence amplifies the feeling of isolation I've grown accustomed to the previous twenty-four hours.

"I panicked," I say, instead of being honest. How would she look at me in the morning if she knew the truth? "We had just escaped a monster's capture and I didn't know where I was going. I just ran."

Before I know it, I'm launching into the story of waking up in the clearing back on Earth. Maryna giggled at the word Poughkeep-sie, which made me laugh. The absurdness of the name is why I had chosen it in the first place. By the time I got to the part about Liri-wyn, Maryna was enraptured. Her many questions popped up at the oddest moments, but I took them in stride. Having someone listen to me this intently is not something to which I'm accustomed. It feels better than I'd imagined.

"NO!" Maryna shouts, loud enough to wake the dryads. "You were the one who escaped from Bloomhall? You might be the first person in history to escape Thalion the Joymaker."

News of my capture and escape has reached the forest beings, it seems. Though, Maryna's shock at my identity confuses me. Shouldn't she know my name and what I faced? It's possible she's just being polite. A kernel of self-doubt gnaws at me, but I push it down, not allowing it to outshine my moment.

"Was he as scary as they say?"

I shrug for no one's benefit but my own. "Most of the time, I was under some sort of incantation that kept me from seeing reality. I thought I was living in a fancy castle with everything my heart desired. Even after I learned the truth, I imagined I could stay and build a life with his daughter."

A quiet *hmm* sounds from the grass on the other side of my head.

"Selyra. That's her name." My hands rub the fabric of the now-clean dress I'm wearing. "This is actually her gown. It's the last thing I have to remind me of our short-lived love story. As imagi-nary as it was."

Maryna's breathing is somewhere between a snore and a sigh, and I can tell she's fallen asleep. As I finish my story, I am grateful for the silence that falls. Tonight, as my eyes wander around the sky, studying the stars, I am not alone.

CHAPTER EIGHTEEN
DERRICK

It's been two days since Mallory left. She just took off running while Dad and I were figuring out our next steps, and didn't even bother telling us where she was going. Dad thinks she headed south to Gallivarum to start the next trial, that something was pulling her there ahead of us. What's more peculiar than Mal adventuring alone to unknown locations is that Dad insisted we wait a day or two before following.

Gallivarum proper, the city that is no more, is a four-hour walk, according to Dad, and the temple ruins sit on the very northernmost edge of the forest, on the outskirts of town. Catching up to Mallory should have been easy. We should have moved as soon as we could to catch up, but for whatever reason, we took a detour to a village too small to have a proper name.

Now, we are preparing to leave the little inn we've called home the last two nights. The anticipation has been making my skin itch. Mallory is out there, and she needs us. She needs to know I wasn't lying when I said I'd be there for her.

"Dad, let's go." He's nestled in a chair by the fire in the main room. He hasn't left that chair once this morning.

Receiving nothing more than a *hmm* in return, I walk the few steps from the front door to his chair and crouch to meet his eye level.

"My son," he starts in the voice he puts on for the benefit of others, "you are too impatient. Everything will work out as it is meant to. The trees have destined it, and they are the divine authority by which the Crown was built."

"I know, Dad. I've heard the stories of the Trees of Creation my whole life. I've seen you spark flames from your fingers on a whim. It is not my intention to question their judgment, or yours, for that matter, I just want to help my friend."

Dad grips the knob of his walking stick with both hands, a thin line forming from his lips. His eyes trace the outline of my face like they've done a thousand times, as if they're searching for proof I am actually his offspring.

"We have waited long enough, son. If you would like to forego the rest of your healing to find the girl, then we can. It is almost certain she will still be in Gallivarum when we reach the ruins."

My stomach drops. Dad is pretending this pit stop was for some divine purpose, but he and I both know the truth. Thalion the Joymaker left me pretty rattled, though the external scars healed the second Mallory walked through the gate. Stagnation won't bring me any solace, however. There's no point in harping on old wounds.

"Dad, I can't just keep sitting here. The memories won't fade if I do nothing to replace them. I am alive. I am whole. That's all that matters moving forward. And we *have* to move forward. Mal needs us."

The old man, who has been old my whole life, stands and points toward the door with an open palm. My legs straighten to match and I am left staring at the top of his head. He hates that I'm a head taller than him, even if he won't admit it. Too proud. That's one trait I hope he didn't pass down. The full head of white hair at his advanced age, on the other hand, is something I will take from his genes gladly.

"Derrick, we will go. But I need to warn you. By now, Mallory will likely have completed her second trial. I do not know what it is or how it's changed her."

Grimacing, I nod.

"Well, then, let's find out."

CHAPTER NINETEEN
MALLORY

No dreams, no dream magic, and I wasn't alone while I slept. That's about the best night I've had so far in Nalara. Yawning, I sit up with an exaggerated stretch. My muscles are still sore from the run here but, with the food and water I found with Maryna's help, they are screaming at me a little less today.

"Good morning," I say with my eyes closed, basking in the dawn sun.

There is no answer.

My eyes fly open in response to the nothingness, and I check behind me where Maryna had been sleeping. An empty spot greets me, without so much as the indent of her body or a nymph-shaped dry patch in the dew. Whipping my head to the left, I look toward the pond.

Nothing.

Had I imagined Maryna in my dehydrated delirium?

Imagining her existence would be my preferred reality. At least it would mean I hadn't been abandoned. Though I can't explain the pond—my head isn't pounding from thirst, but there is no trace of water here.

Something about Maryna had to be my trial.

She'd come and gone with the will of her magic, but for what lesson? Starting the Witherwalk with the last, and therefore most difficult, trial would undoubtedly mean the trials should grow easier with time. But this easy, this soon? A pit forms in my stomach at the thought, walking the fine line between hunger and nausea.

Yesterday afternoon, somewhere between the races and the chicken fights, Maryna and her sisters gave me lessons on the forest's vegetation. My fears were a tad unwarranted. As it turns out, most berries are safe to eat, but the red—the red berries would prove a slow, agonizing death and provide lots of vomiting.

A bush near my alcove teems with purple and blue berries, ripe for the picking. It isn't the best meal, but with the amount of fruit, at least I won't starve.

Boredom, it seems, may be the end of me after all. The pit buries itself deeper into my stomach, stretching and pushing until it is in the shape of Maryna. She hadn't owed me her kindness, but she had given it. And then she'd left, stealing away into the night without a word.

Goodbye, Maryna. Thank you for saving my life.

I try to call the dryads and the water nymphs both, but neither will answer. I don't hear their whispers at my passing like I did before. I guess it's true that you'll miss life's little nuisances when they are gone. But now that I am alone, I long for Fenric to chastise me or make an offhanded remark.

Hours pass and night comes on quickly, leaving me alone once more in my makeshift room, my body screaming at me for a substantial amount of food and water. The stars are gone tonight.

CRASH.

"Fuck! Keep it down."

"Sorry."

Noises not far from my sleeping arrangements jolt me awake.

There are people here.

My body stiffens subconsciously as I worry whether the instigators of the noise can hear how loudly my heart is beating.

Another sound, a banging this time, echoes in the alcove. My alcove. Silence follows for a moment and then I hear whispers. I am not sure how many there are in total, probably just the two, but they are men—that much I can make out.

Could it be my friends, finally coming to my rescue?

The sound grows louder, closer, and my fight-or-flight instincts kick in.

Run.

With as much stealth as I can manage, I crawl out of the alcove, making sure to stay as close to the ground as possible. If I hit rubble with too much force, it will send the men searching in my direction. When my elbows touch grass, I stand and stumble through the night toward the wood.

Two trees, not more than a few feet into the forest, merge to form a makeshift lean-to. I crawl under and settle in. There is no possibility I will fall asleep anytime soon. My heart is still hammering in my throat, and whispered prayers to the tree gods escape my lips. I sit, on edge, breathing as shallowly as I can muster, watching the darkness in front of me.

What happens if they find me?

CHAPTER TWENTY
MALLORY

"Mallory!" a voice somewhere in the distance calls my name. The morning sun is barely peeking over the treetops and a shiver runs through me. The sound is too far to determine its direction but close enough I recognize that it's definitely my name.

My heart pounds wildly and my body stiffens—more people than I realize know who I am. Anyone could be out here looking for me.

"Mal!" another voice, closer, more familiar.

Only one person calls me Mal.

"Derrick!" I shout into the emptiness, forcing my voice to carry as far as it can from the safety of my shelter.

Silence follows.

They must not have heard my call. With as much precision as I can muster, due to the errant twigs everywhere, I crawl out from under the tree's tented roots. My hiding spot is magnificent in the light of day. It is easily visible, so staying here too long wouldn't do me much good anyway. But now I don't need to stay.

My body straightens as my feet find their footing. They propel me forward toward the hope of a reunion.

"Derrick! Oskar! Is that you?"

"Mallory, my dear," I hear Oskar's voice—closer now.

As fast as my feet will allow, I run toward the familiar voice. Without warning, my body meets the soft skin of Derrick's shoulder, the momentum causing us to tumble to the ground. It is a few moments before I can breathe again. My body still aches from exhaustion.

I look down at my friend, now fully beneath me, and take in his features and the musky scent of soap.

He must have bathed.

The thought of Derrick in the shower and the embarrassment of our collision makes my face grow hot. My hesitation must be evident, and it is Derrick who ends our mistaken embrace. He pushes me off with a firm, but gentle, touch.

"I . . . am so sorry," I stammer, unable to look him in the eye.

"Excited to see me?" he asks with an immature wiggle of his eyebrows.

"Not *that* excited."

"Clearly you were—running at us like that and all."

I roll my eyes and huff with a dramatic flair. It does feel good to hear his voice again, I'll admit. My pain at the young man's absence had grown unnoticed with all the chaos of the past few days. As fun as Maryna and her sisters had been, they couldn't make up for the connection Derrick and I had garnered in the past week.

"What took you guys so long?" I punch his shoulder harder than I mean to.

"Ow," he says, rubbing his wound in an exaggerated way. "It doesn't seem like a few nights in the woods changed you all that much."

An inquisitive look must cross my face, because Derrick cocks his chin in his father's direction.

Oskar smiles at me in his usual way— warm, but wholly unreadable. Our time apart has not given me any clarity on my royal advisor. Not that I thought about him particularly much while starving to death. Still, there are depths of hidden knowledge I still haven't discovered how to coax out of him.

"You ran off, my dear. What would you have an old man like me do, chase after you?" He lifts the cane in his hand as proof.

I *had* forgotten that Oskar needs a cane to walk. It makes sense that he wouldn't be able to keep up with me—I'm a third his age and I was running at full speed. There really is no way for me to know how far I travelled that night. Another wave of embarrassment curdles in my stomach; the familiar streak of heat burrows deep in my chest.

"Oh, I'm sorry, Oskar. I didn't think . . ." I trail off, hoping he will catch my intention.

"It is alright, my dear. No harm was done, after all. I am just grateful you are where you needed to be and you waited for us before departing."

I smile at him graciously and turn my attention to Derrick, who is still rubbing his shoulder.

"Baby," I tease.

"Hey, it hurts," he whines back in a playful tone. "You almost took me out."

"You wish." I grin like a toddler.

He laughs and throws his head back slightly.

I missed that sound.

It's been days since I've taken my medication, and I notice laughter in a way I haven't before.

The three of us make our way to the ruins—me leading with my newfound forest exploration skills. Watching Oskar nimbly glide through the trees gives me pause.

Something doesn't add up.

How can he move this efficiently, but it has taken him days to reach me? It's almost like he had wanted to take his time. Maybe someday, long after the trials are over, he will finally be honest with me. For now, he's here and that's all that matters.

Now that everyone has gathered their bearings, I lead the pair to the ruins and show them the alcove I'd called home.

"This is where I was hiding when the two of you were fumbling around in the dark. If you had just told me you were here, I wouldn't have had to hide in the woods."

The two men look at each other, sharing a silent moment of confusion between them.

"That wasn't us, Mallory," Derrick says in a hushed voice. "We just came through this morning."

Terror steaks through me like a bolt of electricity. If that wasn't them, then I was in real danger after all.

Thank God I moved.

"Well, that's alarming," I say, trying desperately to keep my composure for my audience.

Oskar nods. "Quite right, but we are here now, and it doesn't matter anyway. You will not be here tonight to encounter them again should they return."

That helps ease my mind—until it doesn't.

"Where will we be?" I ask. "What is next for us?"

"We journey to Vaelguard, your third trial."

"Third?"

A twinkle reaches Oskar's already bright eyes. He reminds me of Santa Claus, just with a much slimmer figure, and the Witherwalk is his Christmas Eve.

"You remember I said Gallivarum was our second stop in the Witherwalk?"

I remember—now. But which trial had I faced? I've barely spoken to a soul in days.

"The world went quiet on you the past few days, did it not?"

Maybe it was my body screaming at me to provide it with basic necessities. Maybe it was the loss of a new friend. Maybe it was my preoccupation with my emotional turmoil. I had forgotten the dryads. They'd brought me here, led me to safety, and shown me a place to sleep.

Derrick looks between his father and me, like he's watching a schoolyard bully make taunts. The usually smooth lines on his face are pulled into a concerned half-smile.

"I guess," I answer the rhetorical question. "I was speaking with the spirits in the woods who led me here, but they have been quiet since then. How did you know?"

His elusive smile once more lights up his face. If he wasn't an elderly man, I might consider punching him.

Maybe I'll find a reason to punch Derrick instead. His smug face could probably use it.

"And you met the water nymphs, I assume?"

My heart skips a beat. *Maryna.* I swallow hard, searching for the words to form an answer. Instead, I find the question I had lost.

"Ashawill."

"What was that?" My mentor raises an eyebrow. He creeps toward me, both hands extended, proving little need for the stick in his left hand.

"That's what she said when I did my magic. *Ashawill.* What does it mean?"

An expression I have never seen on anyone takes over Oskar's demeanor. He looks both proud and disgusted, excited and terrified. My mind flashes back to the look on Maryna's face. There was no misinterpreting her feelings—she had been scared.

"Dad?" Derrick asks from his perch on one of the self-suspended flights of stairs.

When Oskar doesn't answer, Derrick questions him again. "What does it mean?"

"The One of the Twinned Spirits," Oskar says quietly, eyes focused on something in the distance above my head.

"So?" Derrick asks. "Isn't that a good thing?"

"Yes and no, my son. It's a term given to those born of Selowen that demonstrate Asharil powers. It means her blood is tainted, something that sat on the throne twice and has never been allowed since."

"I don't understand," I interject. "Isn't that a good thing, if I am to wear the crown and rule the nation? The Twinned Path led by a Twinned Spirit?"

The older man shakes his head slowly, his ever-present smile etched with a grave solemnity. He looks older now than even his hundreds of years.

"You don't understand, Mallory. Two spirits living in one—it's an abomination. Those born Ashawill always make history books, and not usually in a good way."

My head spins. Is there some unknown evil flowing through my veins?

"How can that be? There are thousands of children born to parents of both the Ash and Willow. Surely they must be Ashawill too."

"That would stand to reason, yes, if magic was inherited in the same manner as human DNA. But as it is, magic is partly inherited and partly gifted."

"I don't understand."

"It's like this." Derrick stands and walks toward his father and me. "A child cannot inherit the gifts of the Willow if both their parents are born of the Ash, and the other way around. So in that case, of course they are inheriting Asharil's magic. But, if a child has a parent from each bloodline, the Hollowborne give them their powers accordingly."

"According to what?"

Derrick shrugs.

"No one knows for certain, my dear girl, but it is to be assumed the Twinned Trees have a method with which they decide. Maybe it's a prophecy, maybe it's a plan. And maybe it truly is at random."

"What about me—what about people like me? Ashawill also have to be chosen by the Hollowborne at birth, right?"

Oskar's eyes sag a little as he answers. "Yes—they are, but not always for pure reasons. The Trees have a plan. Sometimes that plan involves creating an unprecedented evil to ultimately benefit Nalara."

"So I am destined to become a villian?"

"Not necessarily. The theory stands that those born with the gift of both sacred magics must guard themselves carefully from ruin. Influences of evil are more effective on the Ashawill, but so are influences of good."

"This is supposed to be the second-to-last stop on the Witherwalk." It's not a question.

"Yes." Derrick agrees. "What does that matter?"

"Well, when does a quest ever get easier as it goes?"

"I guess you're right," he concedes with a furrow of his brow. "It makes sense that if this stop is meant to show you whether you are Ashawill or not, it would be too late on the journey to change anything."

"Ahh, yes. I see what you are getting at," Oskar chimes in. "This rite of passage is designed to test the very core of your being and expose all your flaws. A leader is only as strong as their greatest weakness."

"But who designed it like that?" I ask. "It seems a flawed system to do it this way."

"No one designed it, Mallory. You know that."

Do I?

I think back to all I have learned in Nalara.

"Everything comes from the Twinned Trees," I say numbly. "The root network communicates and writes the laws. No one but the universe itself designed this quest."

"Precisely."

I stare blankly at the pair in front of me. If it is the Creators of this world themselves who will judge my ability to rule, what does it say about me if I fail?

"Mallory"—Oskar's voice cuts through my thoughts—"this discovery is not a curse for Nalara. Everything comes together for the good of Nalarans eventually. Our faith in the Creators' plan mustn't be abandoned."

Not a curse for Nalara, but maybe a curse for me.

I will choose to be good.

"Okay," I say, looking into his eyes intently. "I am trusting you."

CHAPTER TWENTY-ONE

DERRICK

Mallory looks paler and more reserved than normal as we journey to her next trial. She seems deflated in a way I have not seen from her yet. Moody, maybe, deeply saddened by some unknown history, but never hopeless. I miss her sass and her razor-sharp wit.

The few days without her were harder than I expected. Running off like that doesn't make any sense to me—why couldn't she wait? She saved my life from Thalion and then completely abandoned me. Completely abandoned the two people who understand what she's going through.

After what Thalion did to me, I changed, I'll admit it. When we were in the middle of it, I shriveled up into a pathetic shell of myself. Having a few days to think about it set my mind clear. What I'd felt and gone through had been real, and my reaction to it had shown me a lot about myself. And my father.

I shudder thinking about what could have been—what *should* have been. She might not have wanted to hang around, but I will never be able to repay her sacrifice. A life with everything she could ever want, every whim catered to, every desire fulfilled. But she chose me.

Other than Mallory's change of demeanor, the walk is uneventful. We stop halfway and eat some of the provisions Dad and I brought with us. She eats hers ferociously, wolfing down both portions we'd allotted her in a single sitting. If only she had been patient, or less selfless—whatever it was that had possessed her to take off like that—she wouldn't have had to starve alone in the woods the last few days.

Mallory sits opposite me after finishing her lunch, keeping her eyes downturned. She can't know how she comes across to others—guarded, reserved, like a bear caught in a trap. This is a person who freely gives her trust; you're just never sure whether or not you've earned it yet. And that may be the most dangerous thing about Mallory Nerezza.

As I finish eating, Dad finally enlightens us on the journey that lies ahead. The hairs on the back of my neck stand at attention. I know this voice. Nothing good ever follows this tone.

He knew about the first two trials and he didn't tell either of us. Dad always has a plan and I never know if I am a part of it. Not that I mind; he'll always tell me when he's ready. He adores Mallory, and why wouldn't he? Although I know it's in more of a "daughter I never had" way than "a girl I'll always want" way, I can still relate. He wants her on the throne just as much as I do . . . I just don't know why.

"Children," Dad says in the grandest of storytelling voices, "let me tell you what we will be walking into. We are going to the city of Vaelguard, the Emberguard's headquarters. This is a city full of judgment and fire. Punishment is a spectacle, as law and order are tenants of the Ash tree and those who worship it. The seeds you sow in Vaelguard, you must be ready to reap."

He continues despite Mallory's slack-jawed expression. "Long ago, at the forming of Nalara, an ancient tome split from the Sacred Trees—half of its pages deriving from each. In the Tome were the sacred beliefs we hold dear today. Two brothers were born from the trees, born from the earth itself, and each picked up half of the sacred text and took it as sacred truth. It wasn't until three centuries later that their ancestors assembled the pages into one book and the Twinned Path was forged as intended."

I thought I knew all of Nalara's history. I've heard enough bedtime stories to have each one memorized. Why haven't I heard this one before today?

My eyes never leave Mallory. She sits in a dazed trance. I remember being that same way as a small child, eager for every new story. I would squeal in delight with each voice my father put on.

Now that I am here, in Nalara, I'm not so sure if I believe in its message anymore. It used to be a fairy tale, something to keep me on the right path, balanced between empathy and order.

Dad always told me, "Magic carries a heavy burden, my son. Only those with the purest intentions should practice."

I can't help but wonder what the burden of Mallory's newfound magic will be. Or what the Crown will demand of her to exercise its powers on the land.

A rustling sounds as Mallory picks at the grass. She might not even realize she's doing it, but the way her cuticle-bitten fingers touch the ground makes my spine tingle. How can she be so blissfully unaware of the attention she grabs?

My dad clears his throat and I whip my head to meet his gaze. He gives me a look that tells me to settle down as he continues. "The ancestors of the brothers came together and formed the Order of the Twinned Path. It was then that they devoted their lives to maintaining harmony between those whose fire and passion and judgment ruled them, and those who let their compassion be their guide. When they formed the Church, they each weaved together branches from the Trees of Creation into a crown. The Hollow Crown."

Mallory's breath catches audibly in her chest. She pretends she doesn't want the crown or the responsibility it demands. I don't believe her. Even now, she sits listening to my father talk about the crown with a grin so wide I can see her back teeth. She can't know how loudly her face betrays her when she isn't aware of what it's doing.

"The first ruler was like you, Mallory. He had both Ash and Willow flowing through his veins. His magic made him powerful. And, yes, he did well with it. You see, my child, the crown is not as much a status symbol as it is the conduit of the source power that governs Nalara. The Hollow Crown demands a worthy leader."

"How do I know that's me? How does anyone know that's me?" Mallory says, sucking in her breath. She looks scared, almost childlike.

"The prophecy has named you—a child of Earth, a daughter of Willow—who shall return the kingdom to its rightful harmony. That prophecy was issued eons ago at the forming of Nalara. Before the first ruler even took the throne, the portal to Earth was formed."

Chills run down my spine as I begin to grasp the magnitude of what this prophecy means not only for Nalara, but for the girl I have come to know.

CHAPTER TWENTY-TWO
MALLORY

After learning Nalara's history, and my role in it, Oskar explains to us the trial that awaits me in Vaelguard. He describes the citizens of Vaelguard to be stoic, pragmatic, and ordered. I think they sound cruel. What is a world where people can't have empathy? They have taken the fire and judgment of the Ash's words and twisted it to a level of extremity the Creators couldn't possibly have meant. Kindness is seen as weakness, and this trial will require that I don't show any weakness.

Unlike the first two trials, this one is to be organized. One where I will be tested in front of Vaelguardian citizens of all ages. Oskar promises that even the youngest of them will not be on my side.

Moving through the woods, we see posters on trees, calling for the cleansing of the Ashen bloodline. On some of them, a portrait of a stern-looking woman stares back at me, her hair in a tight bun. Below her face the writing says *Join the Emberguard today*. Something unsettling wrestles in my stomach, but I can't quite place the feeling. The further into the forest we travel, the more posters dot the trees.

After resting for the night midway, we reach Vaelguard early the next morning. My heartbeat is surprisingly steady knowing the challenges I will face. Since this trial is required for me to gain my crown, I have to believe I can beat it. The only way I got out of the first two was sheer dumb luck. That can't happen again.

The Hollowborne had warned me that doubt was necessary. That I must question everything and trust no one.

I should have listened to them.

With those words in my head, I cross the threshold into the city. The city itself is immaculate—not a brick out of place—and every building is made of the same gray stone. If I didn't know we were still in Nalara, I wouldn't believe it. There are no grass lawns, no ornate wooden statues or symbols. The sameness would remind me of a cul-de-sac in the suburbs, but with the dreariness, it looks more like a military base than anything. Or, at least, what I would imagine a military base to look like.

That same woman, hair still tightly in a bun, is now in different poses on larger posters.

"All hail Asharil."

"Sorrow is weakness. Maintain your strength."

Shuddering at the dystopia, my doubts settle on Oskar as he leads the charge through the well-planned city limits. He was forthcoming this time, a shock. What did he have to gain in his transparency? Or, rather, what do I have to lose? He had said the Witherwalk would change—but not harm—me. Was he honest in that as well, or was it yet another veiled half-truth?

Oskar raps the knob of his staff sharply against a stone door directly in the center of the grid system we'd been following. The resulting sound is a low thud so quiet I am not sure the inhabitants of the building can hear. But hear it they did. Two soldiers dressed in armor open either door and greet us with a stoic expression and no words. On their lapel is the same emblem that adorned Thalion's guards in Bloomhall. There is not a hint of emotion in either of their eyes as they follow us in and close the doors behind them.

"You are to report to Thessara Draxen, our Chief of Command. She is waiting for you in her office to administer your trial."

Nodding as gravely as I can manage, I attempt to match their sincerity. Neither guard says anything, but the taller of the two looks down at me with disgust. It's like he can smell the Selowen in my veins. I want to react, to give him an attitude for the rude expression, but I know it will only set me back in the eyes of the Emberguard. And I need to be on their good side for this.

Emotion will get you nowhere, Mallory.

We follow the guards up a winding set of stone steps. As we ascend, we pass several landings. At each, I can't help but doubt the staircase goes much higher. But higher it goes. This is a defensive tower, if I had to guess—not that I have ever seen one.

Once we hit the top landing, we arrive at an ominous arched doorway with two solid wood doors enforced with iron. The designs are too sparse to be decorative, and Vaelguard is too regimented for them not to be utilitarian in design. It takes a bit of force, but the guards slowly open both doors and usher us in. Once we are just inside the boundaries, the pair slip out and slam the doors behind us. A breath of wind passes through my hair and a reverberation runs through my back. The nearest door misses me by an inch.

This room, while sparsely decorated, screams importance. A map is spread on a large round table, and small figurines whose significance I do not know, are strategically placed in various quadrants, lined in formations I can only assume are effective. Who are their enemies and will the Willow even fight?

She knows what she's doing, I'll give her that much.

"Mallory," the chief's voice rings out from the monstrous wooden chair seated at the far end of the table. She doesn't lift her head, not that our entrance was quiet. "We have been expecting you since the time of your arrival through the Earth portal. Now, we typically like to have an order to these things, and you are working against the system. This act of insubordination does not bode well for your trial. But as it were, there are five trials to the Witherwalk and we would have been third either way. So I will allow this indiscretion—this time. If you make it through this trial, know that any future disregard for protocol will not be looked upon as favorably."

I hold my head high and stare at the chief, her tight dark brown bun bobbing as she continues to scribble whatever it is she deems more important than me. My silence raises her head and I meet her stare, daring her to continue scolding me. She is as calm as one would expect a war general to appear. It's imperative I match the icy demeanor if I want her to take me seriously as the future High Queen of Nalara. Despite my best attempts at inner peace, a flicker of rage boils just underneath the surface of my skin.

I didn't choose this.

I was brought here against my will and told this was my destined path for millennia before I was even born. My fate has always been out of my hands. Whatever she wants to think of me, she is wrong about this.

"Noted," I say in an indignant tone, still not dropping my gaze. "Just remember, *Thessara,* if I make it through these trials, I will be your queen."

My cheeks grow hot with attention as Derrick and Oskar look at me with more than a hint of shock. With one man on either side, there is not an inch of me that isn't holding scrutiny. Still, I persist. Whatever they anticipated me saying, it clearly wasn't that. But I am not that same Mallory who got fired on her birthday. I am no longer the Mallory who used to run from reprimand. I've been through too much now to allow myself to be spoken to in this manner. A queen does not bow to a commander.

"Until you receive the crown, you are to call me Draxen, like the rest of my guard." Her eyes narrow slightly, but she gives nothing away.

"I am not the rest of your guard."

"In Vaelguard, I outrank you. Remember that. You will refer to me as Chief Draxen, the title I fought for and won. Do you understand?"

"What is to be my trial?" I ignore her question, surprising myself with my own audacity.

Thessara looks me up and down, a slight smirk shining behind her eyes. She may not like me, but she respects me.

Good.

"Your trial will be quite literally that. Except you will not be the one on trial, as much as I wish that were the case. No, unfortunately, you will be administering the trial of two prisoners of Vaelguard."

That doesn't seem too bad.

I tell the chief as much.

The smirk returns. "Oh but I haven't told you the best part. You will be judging with Ash's sacred flame. Meaning that, as congruent with Vaelguard law, one of the prisoners must be put to death."

Silence fills the room. My stomach drops at her words as bile rises in my throat, threatening to upturn the contents of this morning's small breakfast. What will my companions think of me if I have to cause someone's death? My facade is cracking, I know it. I can feel the look of terror on my face, but I can't make it go away. I can't pretend to be okay with this.

Thessara appears delighted by my hesitation. She said it was Vaelguard law, but that doesn't stop me from wondering if this trial is a special occasion. Oskar had said this trial would be in front of the entirety of Vaelguard—attendance is mandatory.

How do I stop this?

As if reading my thoughts, Thessara's smug voice fills the room, her eyes trained on mine with a sniper's precision.

"You can't escape this trial, Mallory. If you should falter in your decision, you will be held prisoner alongside the men you are to condemn. You will grow fonder and fonder of them—they are not bad people—and, eventually, you will wither away, unable to free any of you by sentencing the other to death."

My heart beats twice its normal rate. I can't go back.

I shudder visibly under Thessara's gaze.

"No, I will do it."

Derrick's pained expression hits me from the corner of my eye. I know what he's thinking, that I am betraying myself. But this isn't unlike the future decisions the High Queen of Nalara will face. Sometimes sacrifice is necessary. If there is anything I have learned in my time away from Earth, it's that. It was the sacrifice of my personal happiness that freed Derrick from a life of unyielding torture.

How dare he judge me for what the universe has made me.

Oskar, in opposition to Derrick's countenance, looks as calm as I have come to expect. He obviously knew this trial was coming, just as he knew the specifics of the last two. His presence here will prove comforting. At least he understands the burdens of nobility, though he's never faced them himself.

"Excellent," she says. "Let us eat, then, and gain sustenance. Your trial shall begin at dawn."

Night passes slowly. I was left alone in a sparsely furnished room to toss and turn with the implications of what is to come. There may be a reality where I can justify my actions to my companions. But I will always have to live with knowing myself capable of something so heinous, even if it was forced upon me.

After breakfast, Thessara takes me behind a curtain on a large wooden stage in some central room of the military building we have yet to exit. One of the guards throws Derrick roughly into a front row seat by the elbow. Another of her soldiers escorts Oskar to the seat on Derrick's right with more care, whether as a sign of respect or due to Oskar's ailment, I'm unsure. My eyes scan their faces as I peek out from behind the curtain, with all the nerves of opening night in a local theatre production. Only, this isn't a show. At least, not for any rational person. My stomach curdles at the thought that my trauma will be someone's entertainment.

"The trial will begin in an hour's time. You will sit, like any other judge, in front of the prisoners and listen to each of their arguments. You will then make your ruling, but your job does not end with the verdict. Whomever you select to be worthy of the death penalty will be tied to a stake and consumed by fire."

My face must contort with the disgust that runs through me, because Thessara utters a deep, breathy laugh.

"And the one lighting the pyre will be none other than the future High Queen of Nalara, the Shadowbearer."

Shit.

Thessara leans forward and I catch a glimpse of something threatening in her eyes. Something vaguely familiar. Something almost *reptilian.*

My stomach curdles again and it takes all my concentration to hold my composure. The chief is trying to rattle me, trying to get in my head so I fail the trial. I can't let her win.

"It is the only way for your divine justice to be served as bearer of the Hollow Crown." She straightens with a smirk. "Far worse awaits you when you take your throne."

One hour.

This isn't truly murder, right?

They are prisoners, after all, so one of them must have broken a law that leads to death. Vaelguard honors those who face the consequences of their own actions—the prisoners knew what they were getting into when they made their decisions.

CHAPTER TWENTY-THREE
MALLORY

The hour came and went faster than I would have cared to admit. I enter the stage dressed in ornamental robes emblazoned with an embroidered ash tree on the right panel and a brilliant orange fire on the left. Both prisoners are dragged onto the stage with bags covering their heads. I sit behind my judge's bench, perched high above them. Whether they are nervous about their fate or not, I cannot tell.

Guards stand like statues on either side of the stage beside the prisoners. At Thessara's command, the guards spring into action, dragging each man to his respective table set on either side of the platform. A single chair faces me at each small table; the whole of Vaelguard fills the benches behind them. With unnecessary force, the soldiers throw the men on their chairs and remove the bags.

An audible gasp escapes my lips and I look to where Derrick and Oskar sit in the crowd, hoping their eyes will provide some clarity.

Identical twins.

Not only must I condemn a man to his untimely death, I have to make his brother watch. No one will win this case.

The guard in front of either brother begins to speak simultaneously, uncharacteristic for the stoicism the Emberguard is known to convey. What they have to say is irrelevant to these proceedings and I hold my hand up to wave them silent.

You are in control. This is your courtroom now.

Having been given no instruction as to how I am expected to conduct this hearing, I must take matters into my own hands. Clearing my throat with an exaggerated force, I address both brothers.

"You will each be given a chance to prove yourself innocent in the eyes of Vaelguardian law. I will then deliberate on the earned consequences of your chosen actions. One of you will pay for his crimes with his life."

The promise of death sends a whisper through the audience, and they lean forward, ravenous hyenas ready to pounce on the carcass I devour.

Raising my hand once more to the crowd, I turn to the brother on my left. His hands are untied now and he is free to move about the floor, though closely flanked by a guard. I gesture for him to approach center stage and begin his tale.

"Your Highness," he begins with a deep bow.

I am struck with an unknown emotion at those words. *Your Highness.* Of course, I knew the day would come when I'd hear those words, but this feeling of power at the deep reverence comes as a shock to me.

The man continues, "I am guilty of the charge of murder."

This will be easy.

"You see, I am captain of the forty-third battalion of the Emberguard. My scouts received intel of a planned assassination of the heir to the Hollow Crown by the Riftclan—the sworn enemies of the Twinned Path. They follow neither the Willow's nor the Ash's instruction."

Okay, maybe not so easy.

The crowd murmurs again and I feel thousands of eyes focus on my face as the captain's message settles over me. Why they're gazes all swung to me simultaneously is no secret. *I* am the prophesied heir to the Hollow Crown. This man took a life that was determined to take mine. Exonerating this man despite his clear

betrayal of orders may mean failure in the eyes of the Emberguard, but how will rewarding loyalty be treated in the eyes of the
people?

"Please continue."

"An adversary of the Crown was making their way from
Thryvoss to Elvarn ahead of you. They passed through a small
town to the west, and I took leave without following protocol in
order to stop them. I acted outside of orders. I acted alone, and I
would do it again in a heartbeat even knowing you may sentence me
to death."

I struggle to keep my face neutral while tears threaten to spill
from my eyes. My being in Nalara—my existence—has made more
enemies than I could even think possible. The Emberguard has
themselves been many of them and this man would choose to see
me on the throne. I am the reason he might die, and not because I
am the one rendering the verdict.

"Is there anything else you feel necessary to disclose to persuade
me in my decision?" My voice, regal and commanding, surprises
me. If no one can hear the incessant beating of my heart or see the
sweat dripping down my temple under these blindingly bright lights,
I would be surprised.

"My commander would not heed my warning, did not believe
my intel, or did not care whether or not the Riftclan succeeded. It is
no secret that the Emberguard holds disdain for the throne of the
Twinned Path and, therefore, the one who inherits it. There are
many who feel you are too Selowen to rule with the justice that
disorder deserves, but I am not one of them. The Sacred Trees
made their decision on you millennia ago, and I believe in their
plan. Even the mighty Ash chose you. I am honored to have made
this sacrifice in your name."

Motioning for the man to take his seat, I nod. I know nothing
about either man except what they tell me—I was not briefed on
their relation to one another, their names, or even their crimes.
Though I suspect being twins is their greatest crime.

Can anything this man says change my mind?

I turn to my right and motion for the next man to rise.

"Your Highness," he says, in a voice much softer than his brother's, "I am guilty of using forbidden magic."

Okay, this might be easy again.

"In Vaelguard, as with most of Ashen territory, the magic practiced by the seed of Selowen is forbidden. Anyone born from the Willow residing in Vaelguard is put to death for treason as soon as they are discovered, unless they choose to surrender their gifts and live the rest of their days in servitude. I, myself, am not naturally gifted with healing magic, so I used a forbidden spell to the same effect."

"Why would you risk your life for a bit of healing magic?" Surely he knew the consequences.

"For my daughter. She is a young girl who is sick, sicker than any healer in Vaelguard could cure. In our city, dying from illness means succumbing to the weakness of Selowen. Warriors die in battle. Warriors die with honor. I could not sit idly by as my daughter slipped away into a shameful death. By healing her, I knew I would be trading my life for hers. I have made peace with that fact, and would make the same choice again and again."

Before me stands a man whose only crime is loving his daughter. Wanting her to die in battle doesn't sit well with me, but this is not my culture and these are not my customs. He saved her. Maybe it was rooted in shame, but even the unwillingness to let his daughter's name be shamed is love, right? He was protecting her.

My father wasn't even willing to hold my hand.

More tears threaten to escape, the heat stinging my eyes. I brush a hand across my face, hoping to surreptitiously catch any stray tears before they hit my cheeks.

Don't let your jealousy make this decision for you.

Looking at the man now, I motion for him to continue. The crowd has gone silent, and I fear they can see the thoughts written all over my face.

"I will die graciously, if that is your will, to give my child the honor of a hero's death when she grows old enough to fight. Because of what I did, she will see the battlefield, and maybe beyond. I will trade my dignity for hers every time."

"Is there anything else you wish me to know?" I ask the man.

"No, Your Majesty, this is all that is relevant."

"Thank you," I say to them both.

Addressing the crowd, I stand from behind my bench and say, "Now I will take a recess to deliberate on what I have heard. I will come back with my ruling."

Thessara seethes beside me. She'd been so silent this whole time, I'd forgotten her presence. Watching the frustration dance on her face gives me pause. Her expectation that a decision would be flippantly made leaves a bitter taste in my mouth.

What's the trick?

"It is traditional that your judgment be rendered now," she hisses, low enough that only I can hear. The crowd is standing to stretch their legs already, her warning too late.

Turning my head, I steady my gaze to match hers. "With the information presented, I am unable to render a swift verdict. And I would rather be correct than to be hasty in my judgment. Isn't that what the Ash stands for?"

She nods almost imperceptibly. Her judgment is not questioned often. While she may be in charge here in Vaelguard, I will someday soon be in charge of Nalara. Despite her insistence otherwise, I outrank her and she knows it.

My eyes catch Oskar's and I wave, beckoning my companions from the front row. The guards on either side of the men stiffen as they stand, but one glare has Thessara motioning to release them. Once the pair has made their way onstage, I lead them behind the velvet curtain. If anyone can help me make this impossible decision, it's them. They've gotten me this far and I trust Oskar's judgment more than my own.

"Mallory," Derrick says, brows furrowed, "you can't do this. You have to tell them they are both free to go. Or give them prison sentences. They don't deserve to die just because some fucked-up legal system tells them that what they did was wrong. Since when is the law the same thing as morality?"

He's got a point, this gentle man with a heart of gold. Morality *should* triumph over law, but it doesn't. Not here, and not yet. When

I rule the nation, then I can change the system. Until that time, I have to operate under its rules.

"My boy," Oskar tells his son gently as he rests his hand on the young man's shoulder, "she can't do that. It would show her as a weak leader and would lead to questions of her judgment when she becomes high queen. These trials, and what occurs in them, will not stay isolated to their cities. Word spreads quickly in the kingdom, and this will move much faster than any idle gossip ever could. Right now, the people's perception of her matters more than anything."

A muscle works in Derrick's jaw as he stares daggers at his father. I can feel the heat of his fury from here, but Oskar doesn't seem to mind it. As Voice of the Hollow, Oskar consulted on many nearly impossible situations. He understands that the world is not as black and white as humans tend to make it.

If this were the first trial, I could understand Derrick's point. It would be my inclination as well to fight the inevitable. Whatever torture Thalion had imparted on Derrick back in Bloomhall clearly hadn't affected his humanity.

When will you learn, Derrick?

"I understand your frustration, son, I do. In a perfect world, no one would die here today. But this world does not run by the same laws as Earth. The Sundering has destroyed even the ways of old— these are the new rules by which we must play. Mallory will not be allowed to leave without making this decision. Without lighting the match and setting the blaze. She would become a prisoner of the system herself until the decision is made. Our high queen would be rotting in a jail cell, and the Emberguard would love nothing more."

"How do we know Draxen won't throw her in prison anyway?" Derrick's voice rises, half yelling, half pleading. "If she relishes in the idea as much as you say, she can't be trusted."

Don't trust anyone, I know.

"No my son, the Emberguard is far too focused on adherence to the outlined structure. Emotion is quite literally beaten out of children of Ash in military cities like these as a core tenant of the education system. Whether she wants to or not, she will uphold her promise and let Mallory go once the decision has been made. Unlike her brother, Thessara Draxen doesn't lie."

Brother? Thessara has a brother?

Suddenly the reptilian features make sense.

Derrick is still fuming with his righteous indignation, pacing back and forth. As much as I want him to be right, I know he isn't. This isn't the moment for indecision. Before today is over, I will kill a man.

"Your father is right, Derrick." I catch his arm as soon as he passes close enough to do so. "I *must* make this decision and I need your help."

With a scowl, Derrick jerks his forearm out of my grasp. He won't be a part of this, and I can't make him. My attention turns to the older man.

"How can we help, my dear?" he asks. "What do you need?"

"I have my ideas, but I need to run them past someone. I need to make sure I am making the right call. Draxen and the other guards won't hesitate to take my crown if I make the wrong decision. In their eyes, there is a right answer. This isn't a test of whether or not I can make a hard choice. To them this is a test of how aligned to the Asharil spirit I am. There is no margin for error."

Oskar agrees as Derrick throws his hands up in exasperation. While I understand Derrick's hesitation, I am not sure I like this side of him. Nothing I can say will convince him of my course of action. This time, I can't consider Derrick's feelings to make that choice. He may have been the only thing that saved me from Bloomhall, but I have to push that aside.

I don't owe him anything. He owes me.

Rolling my eyes at Derrick's sulking face, I turn back to his father. If only one of them is going to make sense, only one of them will get my attention.

"Oskar, what is the normal penalty for using forbidden magic? Is it death?"

"In almost all cases." Oskar's smirk lights up his face, wheels turning in his head. "I see what you are driving at. That man admittedly knew the outcome of his actions would result in his death."

"And of the soldier?" I ask, though I know the answer .

"Protecting the Crown is the soldier's only job. Where that threat comes from, they do not differentiate. They will die by their sword for the Crown."

I acknowledge the words and clear my throat.

"Then I think I have my answer. Oskar, would you agree that the Emberguard would place a higher significance on the Crown than a child's life?"

"Yes, I do believe that to be the case."

"It's settled, then," I say, avoiding Derrick's gaze.

He opens his mouth to argue, but I ignore him and make my way to where Thessara stands, arms folded as she watches our deliberation. Whatever he thinks I am doing and however he feels about it will have to wait. The only way out is through. And the only way to get through this is to push down every feeling that pokes at my conscience.

"I have made my decision," I say to the Chief Commander of the Ember with as much authority as I can muster, stopping directly in front of her. This close, with my best posture, I realize for the first time the significance in our height difference. Badass Commander Draxen is three inches shorter than me.

Interesting choice of stature for the head of an entire military operation.

"Let's get back to it, then." Her too-white teeth shine with an almost bluish tint.

Back on the stage, both men remain in their previous positions, each just as deep in contemplation as the other. They don't look fazed by the proceedings, but neither of them look at the other. Instead, their eyes are trained straight ahead on my judge's chair where they are met with a sad smile. It is one thing to face your own fate, it is another thing entirely to face the fate of those you love most.

"I will begin swiftly so as not to worry either of you any longer than necessary," I tell both men. It is a small mercy for what is to come.

Addressing the now-quiet crowd back in their seats, I say, "I have been looking at this as a decision between two men and, in doing so, I have been naive. This was posed to me as a singular trial, one versus another. That may have been an attempt to persuade my Selowen spirits to shine through.

"Well"—I pause with a flourish—"I am not purely Selowen and cannot be tricked so easily."

Draxen inhales sharply behind me. This is news to her, and it's caught her off guard.

Good.

The crowd starts to murmur as I push on.

"This is not a trial of one brother versus the other. It is a trial of each man against the laws of Vaelguard. And, after much deliberation, I have come to understand that what I am being asked is impossible—neither of these men deserves to die above the other."

The audience gasps, and I see relief cross Derrick's face. I can't let myself linger on that handsome smile too long. What's coming next will break my heart to see painted on his face.

"You cannot do that, little girl. Your task was to condemn one of these men to death for their actions. If you do not complete the trial, you will not be permitted to leave Vaelguard." Thessara's voice carries loudly across the stage.

It is minutes before I can quiet the room.

"Do not hear what I am not saying." I raise my hand in her direction while still addressing the crowd. It is much easier to look out into the sea of faceless bodies than the two identical men standing before me. "I simply said that I cannot condemn one of these men over the other. This revelation does not mean I am unable to condemn either of them."

"This man," I say, pointing to the man on my left, "betrayed orders and foolishly acted on impulse. When he enlisted in the Emberguard, he knew death was a real consequence of that decision, and he made it anyway. When he acted outside of orders and disobeyed his chain of command, he knew death was a real consequence of *that* decision, and he made it anyway. His actions were noble and I owe him a debt of gratitude that I cannot repay."

My breathing falters as I turn to look at the man. "For disobeying direct orders and acting outside of your role by murdering an adversary without mandate, I sentence you to death by fire.

"Thank you for your service and your noble sacrifice in my name." My voice drops to a whisper.

Right now, I have to avoid looking at Derrick. The betrayal I know he feels isn't something I can face. Not yet. Maybe not ever.

Please don't hate me forever, Derrick.

"Now," I say to the crowd again, "my verdict is that one man mustn't die in place of the other. Neither man deserves it more."

"This man"—I point to the man on my right—"knowingly used forbidden magic. While his cause may be valiant, he understood the wages of his action would be death. In that moment, when he chose to give his daughter life, he brought death to himself. The wages of his sin is death, and he must pay what is owed. His daughter will be immediately enlisted in the guard to await the hero's death her father promised her, whenever that may come."

Stunned silence falls over the room. I can't tell if I have passed the test, but I know I made the right decision in the eyes of these zealots. If I were to choose one man to die over the other, it would not be on the virtue of law and order, it would simply be on my own biases. And those biases are largely Selowen.

"Well then." Thessara stands from her place beside me, looking more than a little impressed. "It has been decided. Both men shall suffer the consequences of their actions. Mallory Nerezza, the Shadowbearer, will light the pyres upon which these men will burn as dusk falls. You are all expected to be in attendance. Dismissed."

The audience shuffles out and I hear fractures of arguments being had. Some are proud of the decision that was made while most are unhappy at losing their bets.

What kind of sick person bets on a life?

Thessara turns to me. "That was an interesting decision. One I most certainly did not suspect you were capable of making. Mercy on either man would have shown weakness, though I would have let you pass your trial had you shown mercy to the soldier for his loyalty to the Crown. I commend you, Mallory Nerezza, future High Queen of Nalara."

With a bow of her head, Thessara makes her way off the stage. I hadn't considered that she would allow me to pass the trial if I allowed one of the men to live. The reality seemed to be only that she'd expected me to make a choice, and therein lied my decision to defy orders in a way that would fulfill the objective. I was so focused on passing her test, I had forgotten there were lives on the other side of my decision. My body flushes with a white-hot pain. The contents of this morning's breakfast roil in my stomach as I come to terms with my decision.

I am going to kill two men with my own hands.

Derrick and Oskar make their way onto the stage. Their guards have allowed them freedom now that my trial is over. My mind moves faster than my legs as I run to Derrick.

I want to beg him to understand where I was coming from. That I'd been so nearsighted I had forgotten the ultimate goal. Political chess comes at a price, and it was one I was willing to pay until the bill came due. I want him to see the reason for my actions, that I played smart. I want him to hold me as I let out my emotions onto his shoulder. I want him to *see* me.

But he brushes past me with a cold look on his face. Not anger, not disappointment. Betrayal.

"Congratulations, my dear." Oskar hugs me. "I regret to say I did not see that coming until the very end. You made a wise and calculated decision that paid off a great deal. News of what you've done will spread to every corner of the land. You are fierce, fair, and decisive. That kind of leadership is just what Nalara needs."

"Thank you, Oskar." I try to keep my voice calm. Hysterics will not do any good now.

I have to get ready to light the pyres.

CHAPTER TWENTY-FOUR
DERRICK

"I don't get her."

Dad looks back at me, that same ridiculous expression of mischief plastered all over his face. He isn't the least bit concerned that Mallory will be murdering two people in the next half hour. She insists she needed to make the choice, but she didn't even try to find another way.

"She made a wise and difficult decision, my son. Draxen and her army were expecting to see a weak worshipper of Selowen on that stand today. Mallory showed no weakness in their eyes, no mercy for disobedience."

"But does the Emberguard's opinion of her matter more than her humanity?" My hand curls into a fist, begging to punch something. On one hand, I curse the Witherwalk and those goddamned trees that put her in the position she faced today. On the other, I don't know the girl who will light those fires.

Mallory Nerezza, the barista, would never be able to stomach the thought of condemning anyone to that sort of fate. She may be broody and sulking and sarcastic, but she's never cruel. Her cleverness never outweighs her kindness. At least, it never used to.

"Some things are worth the sacrifice, son. You will someday learn that more painfully than you would ever hope."

My dad's ominous forewarning doesn't stick with me long. From where I am seated in the courtyard outside the main military building, I see two guards walk in lockstep with Commander Draxen behind Mallory. Two more guards lead the pack, each holding a twin brother by the elbow, wearing the burlap bags over their heads. A pit forms in my stomach as I watch the guards tie the men to large wooden stakes in the center of town.

A crowd is already forming, many getting here early to make sure they have a front row seat to the execution. Congregating to witness the pain of others isn't new. It's a centuries old sport where I come from, but in my time, the manner of spectacle has evolved. There will always be wolves waiting to watch their prey struggle.

Logs are placed under each of the men's feet as the bags are ripped unceremoniously off either of their heads. Both brothers look at one another as Mallory drops a match on their respective pyres. She didn't hesitate, that's what gets me. It isn't her decision that haunts me, that I can almost understand. There was no hesitation.

I bury my head in my hands, palms firmly pressed to my eyeballs until bright lights erupt in my vision. Mallory may be able to stomach what she's done, but I can't. The world grows darker and my mind goes blank of everything except the burning smell of flesh and the screams.

CHAPTER TWENTY-FIVE
MALLORY

It is our final day in Vaelguard and I spend it exploring the city that I had barely gotten to see before the trial. My mind is actively working to bury the sound of screams and the burning of flesh it has recently experienced. Every so often, my fingers tremble in the same way they had when the match was struck.

The brothers stared into one other's eyes while the flames engulfed their bodies. I had made their worst nightmares come true. Each of them had been prepared for their own death, while being aware they might face the death of their best friend instead. My decision brought into reality both scenarios. A lump forms in my throat and I swallow hard, considering which fate is worse.

Why did I drop the match?

My fingers let go, I remember that much. But the moments leading up to it are nothing more than a blur. What I do remember, with an odd clarity, is that Derrick looked away before I struck the match. He was already looking away.

After everything I've seen in my time in Vaelguard, the buildings now exude a cheeriness I hadn't noticed when I'd arrived. What was the pinnacle of plain, gray repetition now looks like ordinary life—

like any other city back on Earth. There isn't the characteristic flora of Liriwyn or the mystic allure of Gallivarum, but this place has its own charm. Whether the newfound appreciation is genuine, or whether it is the manufactured outcome of seeing everyday life after the spectacle of a double trial, I don't know. Frankly, I don't truly care to dissect my own psyche at this moment. Instead, it would be nice to have someone with whom to share this revelation.

Derrick isn't speaking to me. And, while I can understand why, I ache for his cold shoulder to warm up. His anger at me is misplaced and acting like an insolent child won't erase the burden I carry. It won't erase his responsibility in all of this. After all, it was him outside my car that day—the one who started all this.

He's just mad at himself. It'll blow over when he realizes that.

Oskar, on the other hand, has been downright jubilant. He is gushing my praises. It's really quite annoying, actually. I'm glad someone understands the decision I faced, but it is the wrong some-one. Oskar has stood by rulers facing worse, so I knew he would be with me. Derrick is a good man, one not yet tainted by the allure of power. He's never faced anything quite like this. I'm not upset at him for his life's ease. But he shouldn't be judging me for my difficulty.

Still, being in Oskar's good graces gives me the confidence to believe that perhaps, despite my reluctance, I will make a good ruler. And, of course, I will have him by my side to make the truly tough choices. Derrick will come around someday; I have to believe that I mean more to him than two random strangers.

As I meander the city, I notice a group of children playing a game that looks similar to soccer. War might be this city's motive, but I can appreciate that they let children be children too. What child doesn't want to play in the park on a summer's day?

My rash condemnation seems nothing more than a mistaken jump to conclusions. Vaelguard's adherence to law and order brings a calming structure to their everyday lives I can admire now, seeing it up close. That kind of structure would be helpful in my own life, and in my life as ruler of Nalara.

Maybe those trees know what they're doing after all.

A little girl kicks a ball and it lands at my feet. Running after it, she stops short when she locks eyes with me. There is a hesitancy in her movements—she saw yesterday's trial. She saw me light the match. She's scared of me, and I don't blame her. With a small, tired smile, I kick the ball back to her. The girl scoops it up without a thanks and flits back to where her friends stand waiting.

I can't let the little girl's judgment bother me now. It's time to meet Derrick and Oskar back at the city center to begin our journey forward. The men had taken it upon themselves to gather supplies so I could clear my head. Not that it helped any.

"We need nothing from you, my dear, but to rejuvenate your spirits for the journey ahead. You have two more trials to face, and you need to be sharp," Oskar had said before leaving me to my own devices.

After Thessara made use of me, my trio was no longer given refuge in the military building. Instead, we'd been relegated to a dank-smelling inn, the only one that would take us—for a hefty price which, somehow, Oskar paid. After the trial, but before the execution, the innkeeper sold us three rucksacks to take with us on our travels.

This morning it was Derrick's responsibility to fill them with food and clothing. Oskar, on the other hand, had tasked himself with finding other, more magical, necessities. He cannot go a day without informing us of his importance to the kingdom—he was once second in command to the high throne, you know.

""Are we ready?"" I ask the group when we reconvene, taking the bag as Derrick thrusts it into my hands without looking.

Derrick shrugs, keeping his eyes trained on his left foot, which is kicking circles in the dirt.

Look at me.

"Yes, my dear," Oskar replies, "I believe we have everything we need and a few things we don't."

He lets out a small belly laugh at his own joke. It reminds me of the jokes my grandfather would tell and laugh at when no one else did. A fleeting tug pulls at my chest but I push through it.

"Then let's get going."

According to Oskar, my next trial is to take place deep in the forest. Although, most places in Nalara are deep in the forest. This one, though, he told me would have a waterfall. A waterfall sounds too peaceful, too easy. It sounds too much like a hero's quest in a long-forgotten fairy tale for my liking.

What's the catch?

My life is too dull to be the chosen hero. I've never gone into battle or faced a mortal foe. There will be no feast in my honor when I take the throne. No parades or exultation. All of Nalara will question my every move until I can gain their trust, if that's at all possible.

The Hollow Crown, if Oskar is to be believed, is a conduit for the Sacred Trees' magic. It is that magic that created, destroyed, and will heal Nalara. I am but a cog in a well-oiled machine. When I receive the crown, it will amplify what is already inside me. It will hold a mirror to my soul and the wishes of my constituents, nothing more. My reign will be dictated in the same manner as my existence.

A cobblestone path stretches across the entire expanse from Vaelguard to Alvian Falls. Unlike the entrance from Gallivarum, this path is not littered with those godforsaken posters. We do not have to stare at Draxen's ominous expression. As far as I can tell, our path is clear and straight. It should prove easier than any leg of our journey thus far despite the increased distance.

We travel in relative emptiness. The grass sways with a slight breeze that carries with it the scent of lavender. I can hear whispers in the distance—probably the trees—and the songs of the birds flitting overhead. Dusk will fall soon and the sky is bathed in a golden blue light that warns of a mild evening. Since we aren't buried deep under the canopy of leaves, we should be warm enough without needing shelter for the night.

"My legs may carry me another hour, maybe two," Oskar says to us both. "We will need to rest for the night then. Alvian Falls is five or more hours from where we are, if my memory serves."

"I understand." My voice is steady. It makes sense that the old man can't carry on as far as his younger counterparts. What I don't tell him is that I myself could use a rest. Not because of any physical exhaustion, but because the heat of the sun is burning too close to my skin for comfort. It's possible I'll get sunburn, but that's not my worry.

"Dad—if you need a break, we can stop for the night now. I don't want you hurting yourself."

"Yes, if you wouldn't mind, I could use a seat and a cup of water."

Derrick fishes through his father's pack, which had been on his left shoulder. He pulls out a flask of water and tips it into the old man's mouth. I hadn't noticed until now Derrick's strength—and not because he carried both packs on his back without complaint for hours. His concern for his father is admirable, and envy-inducing.

There was a time I thought maybe I would get to see that tenderness given to me. That time has passed. Derrick's given up on me.

"There you go, Dad," Derrick says with concern in his voice. "You need to be taking care of yourself. You remember what the doctors said don't you?"

Oskar nods at his son with pride in his eyes.

"If you need to rest, tell us. I will stop a million times if it means you're okay."

Doctors?

It dawns on me that I don't know how sick Oskar is. He walks with a cane, sure, but his exuberant personality masks his condition, whatever it is. This isn't the time or place to ask, however. My lips clamp shut to stifle the curiosity.

Derrick looks up and catches my eye. He gives me a small, sad smile. That boy can say so much using no words at all.

"Derrick, I—"

"Don't worry about it." His voice is louder than necessary as he shakes his head.

"No," I beg him, "let me explain. It's important to me that you understand—"

He rakes his fingers through his shaggy hair. "I understand, Mallory, and that's the problem. I just don't agree."

Do I need him to understand or do I want him to agree?

We stare at each other for a moment. A moment too long. The sadness that fills his eyes tears into me like a bullet, ripping my gaze from his. He might have a point, but I can't let him know.

"Let's go," I tell Oskar. "Break time is over."

The two men scramble to their feet, Derrick holding out his arm for Oskar to

stand.

Our party painstakingly makes its way forward, stopping to let Oskar rest every ten minutes or so. Derrick and I remain in silence with one another while Oskar regales us with stories of his time in Elvarn. If Oskar notices the tension, he doesn't let on.

"It shouldn't be long now," Oskar says to me when we are sitting alone, waiting for Derrick to find firewood.

"What do you mean?" It's still a few hours to the falls.

"We are almost through the trials. How are you feeling?"

I allow myself to let out a louder sigh than I normally would. Derrick isn't here—I feel safe to speak my mind.

"You are doing wonderfully, my dear. There is nothing one could experience on Earth that would prepare them for anything quite as emotionally taxing as the Witherwalk."

"Thanks," I say with a sheepish smile. The nail of my index finger digs into the ripped cuticle on the thumb beside it. "I can't make heads or tails of my progress. Every task feels impossible not only to complete, but to understand. Starting at the end had to have put me at a disadvantage."

"I understand the feeling and, to be honest, I would be concerned if you weren't having trouble coping with the responsibility." Oskar's voice is somber. "This rite of passage is notoriously difficult, even by Nalaran standards. You are doing better than even I could have hoped."

Derrick is back with the wood, clearing his throat to announce his arrival. He stands above where Oskar and I sit on the cobblestone path, his hands covered in mud from holding the bundle of sticks he'd plucked from the ground. When he gathers wood, he makes sure to only take what has already fallen off. Something he sticks to even when he doesn't think the trees can feel pain.

"Let me help you with that," I tell him as I stand and reach my hands out to help lighten his load. "You gathered the wood, so let me start the fire."

"No, *Your Highness*." The way he spits the words *Your Highness* stops me cold and my face grows hot as I push down the snarky response forming on my lips.

"We wouldn't want the future High Queen of Nalara hurt, would we? Besides, I doubt you even know how to light a fire without a match."

Take the high road, Mallory.

"Well, then, you'd better hurry. Her Majesty needs her beauty sleep."

We arrive in the Alvian Forest as the sun begins to rise, after far more breaks from Oskar than I could have anticipated. We'd left camp hours before first light in anticipation. The sound of the falls grows louder as we get deeper into the forest. When it is almost deafening, I brush the foliage back and drink in the most glorious sight I've ever seen. The water itself is aquamarine and just as brilliant as the gem itself. Every drop of liquid reflects light as it speeds down the side of the cliff.

Emerald green moss cascades around the water's basin and vivid florals burst up through the luscious grass. I feel like I've stepped into a post-impressionist painting—something I've dreamt of doing since I was a little girl.

The breeze picks up, whipping my hair into my face and lifting the frayed hem of my dress. Every fiber of my being relaxes, every sense enticed without overload. I spin around like a little girl at a daddy-daughter dance and allow myself to feel at peace in this moment.

Sooner or later, the trial will come.

Live in the moment.

"Welcome my child," I hear the trees whisper.

The waterfall screams "Come play with us."

Derrick eyeballs the scene hesitantly. Something's wrong. He's known to be hypervigilant, but the face he's making isn't capable with the vision before us. It's as if his body hair is standing at attention, the way he's constantly rubbing the back of his neck. A concerned expression sits on his face. Under normal circumstances, he would be enjoying this place the most out of all of us.

My feet slow to a halt, my dance with the wind at an end. I stop, out of breath, and follow Derrick's line of sight to the top of the waterfall. Whatever trial I will face lies hundreds of feet above my head.

"How do we get up there?" I ask Oskar between pants.

"I suppose, just like anyone would"—he smiles—"we climb."

Nodding, I touch my flushed cheeks, hot from the long trek here. My heart beats faster than it should, faster than when I run. This is no state in which to climb.

"We should rest first," I tell both men as they stare at me. "Oskar, I am sure you could use it."

They know it's a lie. They know I am the weak one now, but they both acquiesce.

Throwing myself down on the supple grass, I take off my boots. As comfortable as they've been on the long walk here, it does feel nice to finally remove them. One never knows whether or not they'll need to make a hasty getaway in the middle of the night. I sink my toes into the ground, feeling the soft earth beneath my soles. The sun is growing in the sky now, and the day is starting to warm. Cool water entices me in, and a lie with both feet dipped into the pool.

Without warning or any indication of what is happening, my

feet plunk on hard ground. Disoriented by the whiplash-inducing movement, I survey my surroundings. The river is louder here and a mist is spraying up at me, the rushing water tumbling to the rocks below.

However it is I got here, it's obvious why. My fourth trial has begun.

CHAPTER TWENTY-SIX
MALLORY

Derrick is on the other bank of the river, looking just as puzzled as I feel. His dazed expression gives way to his slackened jaw as he stares into the empty space above my shoulder. There is nothing but a rickety bridge between us, the kind of bridge made entirely of rope, where you have to cling to either side for balance.

"Come here, Derrick!" I yell over the deafening roar of the running river.

"Mallory, no. I can't." Terror laces his voice as he finally meets my gaze. His eyes are wide as he quickly, and almost imperceptibly, nods his head.

"Why not?"

His frantic tone and wild eyes are enough to make me spin on my heels.

Nothing.

"Derrick, there's nothing there."

"Wha—" He stops and straightens up, somber now. "You don't see that fire?"

"What fire?"

Turning to look again, the forest behind me is untouched by anything remotely resembling a flame. Hunter-green bushes dot the bank, leading to a path I can only imagine is the way off this cliff. A light breeze blows past me, the cool air tickling my neck.

"You're scaring me." My voice shakes. Whatever this trial is, it's different from the others. Derrick is the one hallucinating, and the one who needs to find his way out of the situation.

My blood rushes to my feet, cold terror washing over me.

I have to convince him. I have to earn his trust, just like every other citizen of Nalara.

"There is nothing over here, Derrick, I promise. Please just cross the bridge. We need to find your dad. He'll know what to do."

Derrick stands frozen, his pale skin looking every bit like a marble statue.

"I get it, okay. You think you see something over here, and it's terrifying, but there is nothing here. Trust me. This is our only way out."

"Mallory"—fear drips from his voice—"you need to trust *me*. I don't know why you can't see it, but the fire is growing. Fire can't cross water. You need to come over here."

He believes what he's saying.

If I can't convince him from my side of the bridge, I have no choice but to cross. And, once there, I can persuade him to follow me back. He'll stay trapped if I don't make him see the truth.

My hands grab one of the top ropes as the bottom one digs into the soles of my bare feet. Coordination isn't my strong suit; I won't be able to walk the bridge like a tightrope. The whole thing can't be more than ten feet across, but it feels longer. Each step I take is like walking backward three.

"Be careful, Mal. One slip and your body is tumbling down the waterfall."

My heart catches in my chest, and not out of fear at his words.

Mal. He called me Mal.

It's been days since I've heard that word. He's the only one I let call me Mal—I've always hated it. Mal means "bad" in French, and my high school classmates never let me forget it. When Derrick says it, it doesn't feel like he's calling me bad or wrong. It doesn't feel like he's othering me the way the rest of them did.

When we get through this, I will tell him as much. I'll even apologize if I have to, to hear him say it again.

Right now though, I have to concentrate my efforts as I near the end of the bridge. The tension causing my feet to hover inches above the moving river slackens as my left foot hits the opposite shore. Derrick runs to hug me and I hold his embrace a moment longer than necessary.

I missed you, Derrick.

He pulls back, a hand on either of my shoulders, and spins me to look at the opposite bank. From this side, clear as day, I can see a raging fire that now engulfs the bushes near where I once stood. Whatever this magic is, it's the reason for my trial.

He did see the truth. And this time, I listened. Maybe it wasn't purely altruistic, my crossing the bridge, but it served its purpose nonetheless. From this side of things, I know what my trial is. Saving Derrick . . . again.

A wall of stone rests behind the two of us. There is no way down from this side. Crossing back over is our only option if we want to find Oskar.

Like he'd been reading my thoughts Derrick says, "Let's just stay here until the fire dies down. There is no rush. It can't hurt us."

I shake my head as my panic grows, "I'm not worried about our safety standing here."

"Then why are you trying to throw yourself back in harm's way?" He grabs my elbow and turns me to face him, concern filling his eyes. Looking up at him through my lashes, I feel his breath on me as the air grows hot between us.

We could stay here and talk . . .

No, Mallory. You have to pass your test.

Pulling my arm from his I shake my head. "I don't know where Oskar is. He could be in trouble. We need to find him."

The spark of fear on Derrick's face grows, eyes wide and mouth agape. If there is one person whose safety he cares more about than mine, it's his father's—whom he seems to have forgotten all about in the chaos.

"You don't have to come."

"Mal, you are not doing this alone. I promised my father I would protect you, and that means that right now I have to protect him too."

"Are you sure? You're safe up——"

"Yes."

"Okay." I take a deep breath. "Let's do this."

I instruct Derrick to wait where he stands while I cross the bridge for the second time. He may have called me Mal, but that doesn't mean I'm back in his good graces just yet. Hopefully, sacrificing myself, should it come to that, will earn his trust back. Clearly, I'd rather die than have him distrust me. Making quick work of the rope bridge, I am on the other side in seconds.

"Okay." I pant for air despite the ease of crossing. The fire is evident now, the illusion broken. "The rope barely held my weight. You need to test it first."

His lip tightens into a determined line as he grabs hold of the ropes on either side of the bridge. With one foot planted firmly on the ground, he picks up the other and carefully places it on the bottom rope. He leans his weight forward.

SNAP.

In a flurry of movement, Derrick flings himself backward as the guiding ropes swing violently—though they remain intact. The same can't be said for the leading rope. One end remains tied to my shore, while the other dangles freely over the cliff's edge.

Who decided to put a bridge right on the edge of the waterfall?

"You're going to have to use your arms."

He hoists himself up in response, grabbing a rope in each hand. His biceps beneath his tunic as he carefully bends his knees. Left hand forward, then right. Slowly but surely, he is making his way toward me. For a split second, he loses his balance and the world stops. Even the fire raging behind me gasps for breath, its warmth fading and then returning twice as fierce.

Derrick recovers—and then some. His fumble must have given him a second wind because he is closing in on me fast. The second his feet touch the ground, his knees buckle and he collapses in a heap at my feet. His shoulders heave with unheard sobs.

My knees meet the earth near his, and I wrap my arms around his back. In any other instance, I would nuzzle my head against his neck and weep with him. This time, I have to be strong. We have a mission to accomplish, and the ticking clock of a roaring blaze.

"Derrick, I am so proud of you. That was incredible." I cup his chin in my hand and turn his face toward mine. "But we have to go. The fire will only get stronger."

He stands, brushing his hands off on his knees and nodding. Red welts where the rope cut into his flesh sit neatly across each palm. Without a wince of pain, Derrick balls his fists at his sides.

"You're right," he says without even a hint of a sniffle. "Let's go."

Ahead of us now is not a wall of stone but a wall of fire. The flames lap at the sky, reaching taller still than Derrick's six-foot-three frame. Every moment we hesitate to move is a moment closer to the fire completely engulfing us.

There is a small section where the flames are lower, creating an opening of sorts. I nudge Derrick with my shoulder and gesture with my head. He returns a knowing look. My eyes squeeze together tightly, and I take a deep breath. Bending my legs and pleading a silent prayer, I leap the two feet into the air.

Please don't hurt me. Please don't hurt me.

Thick tendrils of warmth no longer lick at my skin. The air around me stills and grows quiet while the scent of lavender rushes in. Seconds feel like millennia.

My feet hit the ground with a quiet thud and I snap my eyes open. Turning, I see Derrick staring at me in disbelief. I motion for him to follow but he just stares at me like maybe he thinks I'm not here all the way.

"Come on." I'm tired of begging for his trust.

Derrick shakes his head and watches the flames dance between us.

"Mal," he says, "I can't do that—that magic, or whatever it was. I don't have that. I can't *do* that."

More hidden magic.

He was born of the Ash, fire magic in his veins. If I didn't know

I could move fire, maybe he doesn't either. It's got to be worth a shot.

"You're just going to have to try while you still have the chance. That spot won't stay open for long."

Come on, Derrick. Just move.

No matter how strong the voice in my head grows, I cannot make him move. Finding a way to move the flames is my only option—maybe I can manipulate them on purpose this time. Testing my theory, I reach my hand through the fire and it parts ever so slightly, forming a cone around my arm. I motion for Derrick to reach for my hand and, when he meets mine, I pull him through.

He doesn't make it.

Instead I hear his scream sharp as teeth, clawing its way into my rib cage. Flames dance on his flesh and scorch his clothes, his hair. The sound of his scream is visceral, and loud enough to drown the sounds of the rushing water.

Water.

Without another thought, I leap forward, thrusting Derrick with both of my hands back through the flames as forcefully as I can manage. The resulting splash gives me a brief moment of comfort —until I watch the river pick up his body.

The waterfall.

I just wanted to end his suffering the quickest way I knew how. I wasn't thinking about the waterfall. I wasn't thinking that I could dampen the flames with my cloak. I wasn't thinking.

In slow motion, Derrick's body hurls toward the edge of the cliff. There is nothing I can do now. No way to stop the inevitable. I was so worried about the flames, I had forgotten the fall.

Tears sting my eyes.

What have I done?

I blink through the freshly formed tears as they fall, one after another, with no end in sight. When I close my eyes, all I can see is Derrick's body engulfed in flame. I squeeze them tight and push my palms into my eyelids as hard as I can, begging to erase the picture now etched in the darkness. Opening my eyes, I realize I've been transported to the foot of the falls—just in time to see Derrick's body tumble over the cliff. He looks unconscious. I hope that he had that courtesy at the very least, and won't feel the sharp rocks waiting to impale him. But he had felt the heat of the fire engulf his body. And that was my fault.

The world moves in slow motion. Out of body, floating high above the pond, I watch myself run to where Derrick's body lies floating in the water. I sit helplessly outside of myself as I watch my struggle to drag him to shore. I see, but don't hear, Oskar scream for the life of his son. He drops his cane and runs to my aid with the speed and agility of an athlete. But he isn't here to help me. He's screaming at me, something incomprehensible.

My consciousness slams back into my body and the roaring of the waterfall is all I can hear. I look up at Oskar's mouth, hoping I can read the words he's saying.

He is staring at me, venom in his eyes.

"How could you do this?" His anger is somehow worse than anything else I've experienced today.

"I-I'm sorry." It's all I can manage to say.

Nausea rolls through my stomach as I look down at the scene in front of me. My legs are covered in Derrick's blood. My hands shake as my gaze settles on Oskar.

"Truly—"

Oskar cuts me off.

"How could you do this to your own flesh and blood?"

"What?"

He's not making any sense. The chaos of the last few moments must have him in a state of delirium. His only son died right in front of his face; that's bound to drive anyone mad.

"How could you do this to your brother?"

The ferocity in his words cuts through me like a knife. The ground shifts under my feet.

Brother?

Before I can ask anything more, Oskar raises his hands and points behind him.

"Just go!" he bellows.

Leaving is the last thing I want to do right now, but I follow the old man's orders. I run. My mind and my body are numb, but some unseen force propels me forward.

I don't run long before a tree root trips me and I land on my face, lying crumpled in agony.

This is the least I can do.

Derrick will never feel pain again—he'll never feel *anything* again.

Why didn't Oskar tell me that Derrick is—*was*—my brother?

What could he possibly have had to gain with his secrecy?

Oh god, I was going to try to kiss him.

My stomach reels again at that thought as I shudder. I don't know which truth I am trying harder to ignore.

Sitting up, I put my head between my knees like I've been taught. White-hot lava pours out of my eyes. I can't stop it. I shouldn't stop it. This is my fault. I hadn't trusted Derrick enough to listen, and he'd paid the price.

I killed my brother. I killed my friend.

Oskar had said I wouldn't get hurt, and I had naively believed that meant neither Oskar nor Derrick would be physically harmed.

Something about this feels wrong. The fire couldn't touch me. Whether that's by my own magic or the design of this test, I don't know. All I know is, of the two of us, Derrick should be the one facing his friend's death.

The words of the Hollowborne echo in my mind.

"The scales demand balance. Balance demands justice. Justice demands sacrifice. Sacrifice demands truth."

Whatever this trial was meant to prove, it had succeeded in that much. I made a sacrifice and learned the truth.

I just hope it's a truth I can face.

CHAPTER TWENTY-SEVEN
DERRICK

"Alright, Mal, enough resting. It's about time we get on with your trial."

Mallory bolts upright, looking every bit like she's seeing a ghost. Her skin has gone paler than usual, and even her freckles have lost their color. A gentle wind blows her hair around her face as the smell of lavender grows strong.

"What did I say?" I ask.

She doesn't answer. I'm the one who is supposed to be mad at her, but now it's like she has something against me. Though, it doesn't look quite like anger . . . It looks like fear.

"Cat got your tongue?" I try to tease her with my old joke. Those were the first words I ever said to her that day in the clearing in Poughkeepsie. God, that feels like forever ago. She'd rolled her eyes at me back then, and I'd instantly fell for her. That same girl doesn't sit in front of me anymore.

Mallory just stares at me blankly, skin pale and eyes wide. These trials have been hard on her, harder than I think any of us anticipated. It makes sense that she'd be nervous to do the next one, but she wasn't this skittish earlier.

Dad makes his way over to where we are sitting in the grass, his eyes twinkling in their special Oskar way. Mal glances to him and then back to me a few times in quick succession.

"Ah, I see you've woken up, my dear. It's time I explain everything."

"So let me get this straight"—I look between the two of them—"Mallory did her trial in a dream, and somehow you remember it, Dad?"

"More or less."

"Okay, can you expound upon that?" I take up the tone I know he hates. If he is going to beat around the bush I am going to be a pain in his ass.

If my remarks have struck a nerve, Dad doesn't show it. He maintains his mysterious "wise old mentor" demeanor. I know as much as he does that it's a show for Mallory's benefit, or maybe being back in Nalara has caused the sudden uptick in theatrics.

Fine. If he won't take the bait, I will get my information elsewhere.

I look at Mallory instead. When our eyes meet, it's like she's seeing me for the first time. She studies me as if I have answers to a question she hasn't asked. If she wasn't so distressed, I could kiss her right here and now. This is the softest her features have ever looked —the most she's ever let me in.

"What about you?"

She shrugs without speaking. This is going to be like pulling teeth, I can feel it.

"Do you know what's going on?"

She shakes her head and I believe her.

"Okay, Dad"—I'm back to trying the tone—"explain it to me like I'm five. Why exactly do you two seem to be in on some kind of secret?"

"Don't be dramatic, Derrick."

Me, the dramatic one? There is no time to counter his argument, I just want answers. I bite my tongue and seethe in his direction as hard as I can. Years have passed since I've last lived with my father, but I remember how to get under his skin.

"Very well." My father lets out a heavy breath. "If you must know, this trial tested the limits of Mallory's Ash magic and her ability to display compassion. It showed her the epitome of what she can do both metaphysically and psychologically."

"So it *was* a dream?"

"In a sense. It was a dream come to life, manipulated by Mallory's subconscious. I'm not even sure she realized we were in Somnarel, but everything that happened, *everything that was learned,* was real."

He turns to Mallory at that last sentence and the fright on her face grows. Whatever happened fundamentally changed her.

"You mean—"

My father cuts her off. "Yes, my dear. Those events happened. Everything that was felt—and exposed—is true."

Tears are streaming down Mallory's face before my father can finish his sentence. My heart pangs a bit and I reach to wrap my arm around her shoulder. She's taken care of me quite a few times since we've met. It's my turn to take care of her.

When my fingers brush against the cloth of her gown, she shrugs me off, takes my hand, and places it back by my side. I can't pretend not to feel the sting of rejection.

"Mal, it's me. Your friend. And I thought that maybe someday, even in the far-off future, we could be more than that. I just want you to know that I am here for you, whatever you need."

What I said was the wrong thing, apparently. She turns her back on the both of us and I listen as her wailing grow louder. It's the kind of crying that hurts to hear, the kind where you're gasping for air while desperately trying to calm yourself down.

"Can't you tell me what happened?" I turn to Dad, hoping he'll give me some information to heal Mallory's pain.

He shakes his head and issues me a small, defeated smile. This is the most human he's looked in a while. Of course, he's not human.

"It's Mallory's story to tell. If and when she wants you to know, she will tell you herself. I can't break her trust by revealing the contents of her innermost workings."

Mallory clearly isn't ready to tell me yet and I won't push her.

"Well, can you at least answer me one thing?"

"I can try, son."

"How is it that you remember what happened, but I don't? Was I there?"

"You were there."

So Mallory is acting strangely around me because of what happened in her trial. I wish I could remember what I did and apologize for whatever it was. There is no part of me that would ever want to hurt her on purpose.

"That still doesn't answer my question. Why do I not remember?"

"Derrick, you were there." Dad's voice grows stern, like I'm being scolded for sneaking an extra cookie. "I can tell you no more than that. It's Mallory's story to tell and that's final."

CHAPTER TWENTY-EIGHT
MALLORY

Every time I've used dream magic before, I've known I was dreaming. The world generally gets hazy in Somnarel. The flight over the forest, meeting the girl in Lyriwin's town square, those all felt like dreams. But this was different, this felt *real*.

Oskar keeps telling me my powers are getting stronger, that the closer I get to the crown, the more I will learn about myself. I know he's right—he usually is—but I had thought a stronger gift would make my dreams more recognizable, that I would have more control over manipulating them, not less.

Keeping my distance from the two men, I sit alone in the meadow, far enough away from the water that I don't touch it, but not so far I am completely alone. I can't bear to be alone right now. But I can't bear to look at Derrick either. Every glance in his direction is a reminder of the companionship I lost, and *why* I lost it. He's alive—I can almost overlook the grieving of his death—but our relationship will never be the same.

"I thought that maybe someday, even in the far-off future, we could be more than that."

He wants more, the same "more" that I had. And I can't give him that. Either he's a cruel bastard or he's as clueless as I was. He grew up knowing Nalara, hearing its history, and learning its language. Why would Oskar keep from him that his sister was the prophesied heir who would bring peace to the kingdom?

What are you hiding, old man?

By now, I have cried every tear my body can produce. A thirst rises in my throat as my head pounds with the loss of so much fluid.

Behind me, a branch snaps. I know it's them by the weight of the air, but I don't look back. Oskar asks if it's time to continue our journey, but I can't face it yet.

"I don't know," I say, still not turning to meet their eyes. "This might be the end of the road altogether. Going on doesn't feel possible."

Derrick sucks in a breath, and I turn to look at the man standing over me. He contemplates my words and nods, blinking back tears.

"I'll set up a camp," he says. "And I'll spend extra time on it if you think we'll be here longer than a night."

I smile and thank him, digging my nails into my knees as hard as I can. Pain is the surest way to keep fresh tears from falling.

I am exhausted.

As if understanding my silent plea, Derrick turns on his heels and ambles toward the forest, looking like a scolded puppy. There will be a time he learns the truth about us, though not before I get a chance to talk with Oskar.

Taking the opportunity to be alone with my mentor, I make my way to where he is sunbathing in the grass. I look up, noticing the sun's pastel rays cutting through the thick white clouds.

Funny, I guess I never looked up at the sky—I would have remembered these clouds.

"Oskar?"

He smiles up at me and pats the ground beside him. I lower myself to the empty spot in the grass and press my shoulder against his. His kindness in not standing to face me does not go unnoticed. Looking at him would be too hard right now.

"I have questions," I say, after too many moments of silence.

"I thought you might. What I told you back there was life-changing."

It isn't funny, not really. And yet, a laugh, somewhere between a scoff and a giggle escapes me. Oskar's flippancy is unusual.

"That's one word for it."

"I suppose you want to know whose lineage you and Derrick share."

"Yes," I say, my voice layered with anticipation. "I think I deserve to know."

"Well, my dear, if you were wondering if I'm your father, the answer is no. Derrick *is* my biological son, but you are not my daughter."

Mom.

"My grandmother, my mom's mom . . . She is from Nalara, isn't she? She gave me my wooden dove, the same one that was on the portal door. She knew I would find it."

"Yes, she comes from Nalara."

A beat of silence passes between us, the awkwardness lingering like a blanket on my skin.

"So . . . you and my mom?"

The thought is almost too gross to consider. Oskar, by looks alone, appears to be much older than my mother's fifty-three years.

"Yes. Your mother and I were a bit of an item in our time."

"And Derrick doesn't know?"

"No, he doesn't know."

"Then who does he think his mother is?"

Another silence is followed by Oskar's quiet voice.

"I told him she died in childbirth with him."

"Why?" My voice is tense. I haven't seen her in a few years, but the last I knew, my mother was very much alive.

"Your mother and I were in love from the time we were young. We grew up together. Best friends turned lovers."

"That's not right. If that were true, it would mean . . ."

"That your mother grew up here too? That she is rather older than she would have you believe?"

"By hundreds of years?"

Oskar's laugh echoes through the clearing and I worry its volume will attract Derrick's attention.

"How old do you think I am?" he says through his laughter.

"I don't know—I just assumed you were really old. Thalion said Nalara is the oldest known kingdom, and the prophecy dates back millennia."

"Yes, Nalara is almost as old as time itself, if the legends are to be believed. And the prophecy that foretold your coming is indeed ancient. But your mother and I lived together here until we were not much older than you."

Twenty-odd years in Nalara could be centuries on Earth, for all I know, and vice versa. There seems to be no rhyme or reason to equivalency calculation, if there even is one. Our time streams don't run parallel.

A question lingers. It's *the* question. The question whose answer is the key to my existence.

"Why did it end?"

Oskar blows out a breath.

"When your mother fell pregnant with Derrick, we were overjoyed. I was going to propose and we would move to a small village in the South." His voice is warm at the welcome of the pleasant memory. As he continues, his voice grows colder. "Before any of that could happen, we were informed by the Oracle—the leader of the Order of the Twinned Path—that she would carry the heir to the Hollow Crown that was promised by the oldest prophecy known to Nalara."

Mom knew she'd bear the heir. She'd lived in Nalara.

"I don't understand. You told me that the oracle child was sent to Earth centuries again and I am a descendent of his bloodline. Was that just another one of your half-truths?"

He stops for a moment and raises a hand to his eye. I can't see it but I imagine he is wiping a tear.

"I did say that in front of Derrick. It's the version told here in Nalara as a child's bedtime story. History here, much like on Earth, grows into a thing of legend as time passes. That version is what your mother and I grew up believing as well."

"Then why did you let me believe it if you knew it wasn't true?" My hands clench into fists from their place on my belly.

"Derrick can't know about your mother—not yet. I didn't want to tell you the full truth only for him to start asking questions."

That doesn't make sense.

Right now, though, I can't question his logic. I want to get back to hearing about my mother.

"Okay. So Mom was pregnant with Derrick—" The implications of that phrase sit hollowly in my stomach. "—how did I get here?"

"Well, upon hearing the declaration that your mother would carry our savior, the king placed a bounty on her head and created the Emberguard. They thought if they could kill her while she was still with child, they could stop Nalara's downfall. What they failed to account for was the fact that their refusal to accept destiny ultimately created the fate from which they ran."

His words carry above the sound of chirping birds, isolating in my brain.

"What do you mean?"

"That king was a coward and his actions to stop your birth created a chasm in the Order. Those who sided with the Emberguard attacked those who spoke against the One Tree regime. Those whose ideals aligned solely with Selowen created the Verdant Concord—though their means of rebellion are never military.

"The Verdant Concord is small in numbers and deeply hidden," Oskar continues. "You remember Gallivarum, I trust. Those ruins were once their most sacred temple, where the connection to the Creator Willow was strongest. When the Emberguard attacked, those that survived fled into the woods. They live among occupied cities, trying to hide their magic."

"What about the Order? Surely they must have done something."

Oskar's breath catches as he says, "No, my dear. They have sat idly by watching this play out. They let the king and the Emberguard cause the Sundering."

There is an edge to his voice, bordering on anger.

"Why? And what happened to the king in all this?"

"The king still listened to the Order, and the Emberguard

turned on him because of it. They killed him in his sleep—no execution, no trial."

"Wait. The Emberguard? That doesn't sound like something they'd do. Trials are kind of their thing."

Oskar's weight shifts as he shakes his head beside me.

"Mallory, my dear. That trial was rigged. Their deaths were decided from the moment they were accused. If they had denied their crimes, they would have faced a fate far worse than death by fire."

I shudder, but let him continue.

"The newly liberated Emberguard believed that Nalara should no longer be a kingdom united by its Creators. It was their mission to see each city create its own laws and customs according to the traditions of its founding tree. Of course, the Emberguard would also seek to occupy any cities that did not worship the right tree—Asharil. The Order, spurred on by the Oracle, was convinced that was the will of the Twinned Trees, that interfering would upset the gods.

"Before any of that took place, your mother and I went into hiding together," he continued, his voice catching. "I loved her, your mother, more than anything. More than my own life—I was ready to push her through that portal myself, but she wouldn't have it."

Good to know Mom's always been stubborn.

"When she gave birth, we were both surprised to see a baby boy —the prophecy has always spoken of a female. Your mother thought that if we could convince the king to take her childbearing abilities, he would let us stay in peace. She would give up the big family that she always wanted to keep him safe."

Oskar's voice trails off. We are left, sitting in silence, letting the cool afternoon air wash over us.

"What happened?"

"Your mother was taken by the king. He would not listen to her begging. It wasn't enough that she'd sworn not to have any more of my children. He wanted her for himself. Since she hadn't borne the prophesied child, he would make certain that when she did, it would be his to raise."

"So my father's an evil king?" I blanch at the thought.

At that, Oskar lets out a small chuckle.

"No, my dear. Your mother is resourceful and full of ambition. It is one of the many things I admire about her. Determined to strike a deal with the Hollowborne, she stole away from the castle—I don't know how—and met with them in the Sacred Grove."

"What deal?"

"She would give them her firstborn daughter if she were permitted to return to her family and live in peace."

Her firstborn daughter.

Me.

"In their infinite wisdom, the Hollowborne rejected the deal. They foresaw what would happen if the king got his hands on you. What damage he would have you do, not only to yourself, but to the whole of the kingdom."

"What did the Hollowborne do instead?"

"They opened the portal to Earth, sending her through and promising her safety. Of course, I didn't learn of this until much later—long after she had abandoned her family."

A quiet falls between us, one that I dare not disturb. If I ask the wrong question, his sadness may turn to anger. He wouldn't speak to me then, and I need to know what he knows.

"You may be wondering how that leads to today. After learning of your mother's betrayal, I made it my mission to avenge our son. She hadn't abandoned us, of course, but I didn't know that then. Years before his murder, I had taken a position in the king's court—one I had been groomed for since childhood, but had run from. I neglected my responsibilities in favor of your mother. When she left, I had nowhere else to go."

"I don't understand. How did Derrick grow up on Earth?"

"I lived as an advisor for many years, so long that the king trusted only me with his most sacred intel." Pride flows through Oskar's words. Even now, he won't dare let me forget how important he once was to the Crown. "The king had discovered the Hollowborne's treason about six years into my tenure. Until then, we had thought your mother was still hiding in Nalara, gathering allies against the Crown throughout the state."

That doesn't sound like the mom I know. What did leaving Nalara take from her?

"When it was safe to do so, I took Derrick through the portal. The Hollowborne had gone into a deep slumber, awaiting your arrival. What I didn't realize then, is that only you, Mallory, could open the door to the portal to return to Nalara.

"When I realized we were stuck, I used a spell to alter his memory. Natural memory magic is extremely rare—and extremely illegal—but is capable of being mimicked with the right spells and potions. Having been in the palace, I had access to the confiscated materials."

In the distance, I hear Derrick's footsteps. By the sounds he is making, he is struggling to carry a heavy bundle of sticks. He swears under his breath as he drops one, the sound carried by the wind.

"We don't have much time," Oskar says to me, sitting up to look into my eyes. "I regret some of the things I did while trying to protect my son. Please, let's keep this between us for now. There will be a time he learns of his past, but it cannot be today."

I stay quiet, hoping he will assume my silence to be compliance.

"Mallory, it is important that I hear it from you. It is important that you agree."

"Yes," I say. "I will keep this from him."

CHAPTER TWENTY-NINE
DERRICK

Every time I pick up one stick off the ground, another tumbles out of the stack in my arms to take its place. I curse under my breath when I realize one is missing. Why I can't just leave it well enough alone and bring what I've got back, I will never know. There's got to be a metaphor in there somewhere.

Mallory and my father are lying in the grass near the pond at the foot of the waterfall, but on the opposite side from where *every-thing* happened—Mal's words, not mine. Their voices carry in the wind, but I can't make out the words. When I get close enough to understand, they halt their conversation as if they were talking about me.

There's nothing I could do about if they were. Besides, whatever Mallory just went through was traumatizing—from what I've gathered—and I'm glad she has someone she can talk to about it. Even if it's not me.

"Alright, you two," I say to the pair. Standing over them, I look down at the beautiful girl I am glad to be able to call my friend, if nothing else just yet.

I give Mallory's side a playful nudge with my boot. Hopefully she's not still upset with me, so I can apologize for how I treated her after Vaelguard. I can't imagine what she's going through with all these trials. Even if I don't agree with the outcome, she did what she thought was right—and that's what matters.

"Hey!" she exclaims with a giggle. "That hurts."

"Yes, I'm sure it does." I roll my eyes. "Come on, up you get."

Clasping her right hand with mine, I pull her to her feet. My heart stills with the contact and the bright smile that has returned to her eyes. I wasn't sure I would ever see that smile again.

Ever since I was a small child, I would sit on my father's lap and listen as he regaled the story of the Chosen Hero of Nalara. Of course, having never been to Nalara as a child, I'd thought it was nothing but an old man's fairy tale. For the past twenty-four years, I have heard tales of the Witherwalk, never imagining the young woman who would face it.

My father always said this was not for the faint of heart or those with a weak constitution. He described trials, carefully crafted by the universe itself, that would test each individual based on their own needs. Some leaders were tested with swords and fire. Others with temptation. You would never know what you were walking into.

It seems the trees, fate, the land itself—something conspiring against her—decided she needed to be broken and put back together, piece by piece. And all I can do is watch.

These are the toughest trials, according to my father. The physical implications of losing a battle are only temporary—even dying itself ends. Many men have lost their lives on this journey but many more have paid a greater price with their sanity.

I look at the girl in front of me. She is busying herself with setting a place to light a fire. Once upon a time, not long ago, I could tell what she was thinking. Her face read like a book. Right now, that face gives no indication of what is going on inside her mind. There is no way to tell how she is handling the pressure of these trials.

CHAPTER THIRTY
OSKAR

Mallory asked for the story of her beginning. Really, it is the beginning of everything for us all. My revealing all that I had may still prove a mistake. She shouldn't have been told. Not yet. Not in that way. Despite knowing my son's death was a farce, I lost my composure. It will not happen twice.

It is Mallory's duty and birthright to save us all. Her pigheadedness cost her brother's life and I cannot abide that. If she had listened to Derrick he would still be alive.

From now on, I will be watching her more closely and keeping Derrick at a distance. I've done nothing to fan the torch he carries, but perhaps it is time I stop ignoring it.

Now that Mallory understands her lineage—that she is not alone in this world—maybe she will stop acting like she is.

CHAPTER THIRTY-ONE
MALLORY

When Derrick returns, he nudges me up off the lawn. He insists we begin putting together camp, and I don't blame him. With the sky growing darker, if we don't start now, we won't get set up before nightfall.

"I'll make the fire," I volunteer.

It wasn't long ago that I had never been camping in my life, not really. Not like this. It wasn't long ago, in fact, that I was an only child living in a big city on Earth—learning to prepare a campsite will be the least of my revelations this week.

"That works." Derrick shrugs as he jerks his thumb over his shoulder, indicating the spot where he'd dropped the gathered wood. "Since we may be here another night or two, I also gathered enough leaves to make a shelter. I can get started on that while you work on the fire."

He calls over to Oskar, who is still lying in the grass. "Dad, can you come help me? I just need you to hold this while I string it together."

Oskar obliges, slowly rolling over before coming to his knees and pushing his weight on his staff. The two men amble a ways away from where I am working. Their voices hush as they grow farther.

The isolation is more welcome than I anticipated. Facing Derrick—and Oskar, for that matter—will be different moving forward. Derrick isn't going to stop flirting, and I can't even tell him why it makes my skin crawl now. And Oskar, knowing that my mother loved him and Derrick more than the idea of me—I don't see how I can forget that easily.

My mind wanders as I try to concentrate on lighting a spark. My hands are going through the motions, like they can't quite connect to the action itself. Like some unseen force is controlling my movements. Fire is a bad omen now, after everything, and I'm not sure what could have possibly compelled me to volunteer for this task.

Haven't you lit enough fires for one lifetime?

When the spark catches, I sit back and swallow my nausea. *It was me.* I dropped the match and looked into the eyes of those men, and later watched as flames consumed my friend's body and his corpse tumbled down the falls.

How could I not have known it was a dream? It felt so real. And, what I learned from Oskar *is* real. So he was there, not just as an observer the way Derrick was, but as a participant. Would Oskar still remember the dream if he hadn't been involved? Would Derrick remember if he hadn't died?

Derrick's voice cuts through my thoughts, sounding as chipper as ever. That boy truly is a walking exclamation mark. I don't even think he's mad at me anymore—not that we've talked about it. But it's like something has restarted the clock on how he feels about me. It's like he's forgotten Vaelguard completely.

I was too hard on him when I woke up, I know that. But I could do nothing more than sit in the grass staring at the person I'd just lost, alive and well. And his confusion when he'd said those words and I hadn't said them back was palpable. This could all be explained if I was allowed to tell him the truth.

Just talk to him.

As if with a mind of their own, my feet respond to my thoughts. Standing, I inch my way to where the men are finishing their work and watch as Derrick quips a joke, Oskar's laugh in response filling the night air.

They look so calm, and I can imagine this moment is a snapshot of their lives before they had the misfortune of meeting me. Before they spent all their time worrying about how I would perform in my trials.

They were the ones who came looking for you. They asked for this.

I take a small step backward, hoping to escape in silence. The last thing I need is for Derrick to look up. As I am lifting my other foot, he catches my movements out of the corner of his eye and tosses me a wide grin.

Just my luck.

"Mal! Come here, what do you think?"

In front me is a makeshift structure, strung together with some sort of twine Derrick must have gotten from Elvarn. The slightest breeze would be enough to send the entire shelter tumbling to the ground.

"Looks good."

"I know. I'm pretty proud of it." He places either fist on a hip in mock triumph.

Despite my best efforts, a giggle escapes me. He really is just my goofy older brother, and I'm sure eventually I would've figured that out. His amiable mood comes as a signal to make my move.

"Hey, can I talk to you for a sec?" I glance at Oskar and back to Derrick. "Alone?"

The smile drops from Derrick's face, his brow wrinkling for an instant before smoothing out.

"Yeah." He cleared his throat. "Sure, let's take a walk."

Oskar smiles, his teeth bright against the quickening darkness of nightfall. If he's afraid I will reveal the truth to his son, he doesn't show it.

"It is getting rather late for an old man. I think I will lie in this beautiful tent and let the two of you walk and talk amongst the stars."

My stomach curdles at the tone in Oskar's voice. It's one thing to keep Derrick in the dark, but it's another thing entirely not to dissuade his feelings.

Derrick and I walk in silence for a few yards. He looks over at me, still walking, and asks why I called this meeting. I feel my eyes roll deep into the back of my head. Does this man ever stop joking?

"Well," I start, "I wanted to explain myself. I know you were mad at me about the outcome of the trial in Vaelguard."

He stops in his tracks and looks at me, disappointment etched on his face in the moonlight. A tiny piece of my heart cracks open.

"That's what this is about?"

"What else would it be about?" I ask in a tone I hope comes across as confusion.

I can't have that *talk right now.*

Derrick kicks the dirt at his feet and looks down with his hands in his pockets—his nervous tick. I don't think he is even aware he does it.

"Nothing, I guess. Anyway, what were you saying?"

"I just want to explain where I was coming from. I know you don't agree, and I'm not asking you to. I'm just asking you to give me a chance. To listen."

Derrick gives a brisk nod and continues walking, at a much faster pace than we had been.

I follow after him, hoping to catch up. We need to be on an even footing for this.

"The challenge presented itself as picking the lesser of two evils, the most righteous of two wrongs. It was an impossible choice, but it was a choice that had to be made."

"You could've just—"

"No, I couldn't," I interrupt him as my voice whines with desperation. "Don't you think I thought of every way out? This isn't about the choice I made, is it?"

"I guess I don't know that answer. Maybe I don't know you as well as I think."

My stomach jolts. If only he knew how accurate that really was.

"So, it's true—you don't trust me?"

"I thought I could, but lately I don't think I do."

Any traces of the kind, sweet Derrick that existed moments ago are gone. But this conversation needs to be had.

"You can trust me, Derrick. I'm still the same person you thought I was."

"I don't think Earth Mallory would sentence anyone to death, let alone pull the stunt you did. You were asked to choose one man to die, and you chose two. There is no extra credit in the trials, you know."

"Earth Mallory," I say, ignoring the obvious bait, "wouldn't *have had* to send anyone to death. Her only choices were what to wear in the morning and what to watch when she came home from work.

"And," I continue, "whose fault is that?"

Stopping short, I watch as Derrick's shoulders slump. He follows suit and spins on his heels, the light drained from his eyes.

"I didn't *make* you do anything Mallory." There is a sad tiredness in his voice. "I gave you a chance to come here, a chance to mean something and make the world better than it is. Things have turned out a little shitty, but let's not pretend you didn't want this."

I swallow hard, carefully choosing my next words. "Maybe I did want this—"

"No, there are no maybes. Don't stand there and pretend you didn't jump at the opportunity to mean something. You might not have wanted the trials, but you wanted to matter. And don't act like the Crown's power hasn't been calling to you. You're acting like you already wear the thing."

"Where do you get off talking to me like that?"

My voice is loud now, almost a yell. The quiet of the forest around us only amplifies my words.

"Someone needs to say it." Derrick's tone matches my own. "Someone needs to show you who—what—you are becoming."

His words are laced with an anger his face doesn't reflect. No clenched jaw, no squinting eyes. If he wasn't yelling, I'd think he was hurt. His face shows the softness of betrayal in the dying light.

"Derrick," I say with a level voice, "I am becoming a ruler. A leader makes hard decisions that no one else could ever dream of making, and still gets blamed for her choices. A leader understands the sacrifices necessary to maintain an orderly kingdom. If I want to make a difference, I have to play by their rules until the time comes to change them."

Derrick scoffs. "What do you know about being a leader? You've been here all of two seconds, and think you understand what it takes. We haven't even reached the capital yet, Mallory."

Silence hangs in the air between us. It's too dark now to see his features, but I can feel his shoulders tense and his eyes narrow. This talk isn't as productive as I'd hoped. If I'm being honest with myself, it wasn't well-thought-out anyway.

Swing and a miss.

"I'm going to sleep." I turn around.

"Fine. Run away when things get hard. You're really good at that."

CHAPTER THIRTY-TWO
MALLORY

It's foggy now, our fight last night, but any trace of it is gone from Derrick's attitude this morning. He wakes me up just before dawn with the sounds of his movements.

Rolling over and squinting my eyes to keep the appearance that I'm still asleep, I watch as Derrick's back gets smaller. He's walking into the woods—probably to find food. If he had woken me up properly, I would have volunteered.

Once he is far enough away, I roll onto my back and open my eyes. Waking up in the cool, damp grass reminds me of the morning after my birthday. My excitement then was palpable, learning about my true home and the role I was destined to play. Looking around now at this fantasy realm, I can't help but be overcome by a creeping numbness. The change of scenery hasn't helped the way I had anticipated. It hasn't soothed the ever-present ache.

I'm a good person, damnit.

Why can't I find where I belong?

My tired eyes look toward the waterfall, subconsciously locking in on a single spot. I can still feel Derrick's weight in my hands as I dragged him to shore. I can still see the fear that was plastered on his face. I can still hear Oskar's shrieking cry telling me that I am a monster.

I clutch at my shirt, willing the cavity beneath to fill with air. My free hand grips the ground as mud curls around my fingers, barely registering the squelch as my hands claw deeper.

From somewhere in the distance, I hear whispering. It's the trees. But I don't recognize their voices or what they're saying; I've grown too accustomed to hearing their idle chatter.

The world spins beneath me as colors blur. A queasiness fills my stomach, exacerbated by the scent of lavender. What was once a welcome reprieve on a hero's journey is now an ominous token of death.

Before I know it, I am heaving.

My heart is pounding in my head.

THUMP.

THUMP.

THUMP.

Curling tightly in a ball, I collapse. My shoulders hit the mud and I can't be bothered to care about the mess I am sure is getting in my hair.

I'm not scared this time. Even if I could, I wouldn't call the ambulance to take me to the hospital again.

Breathe in for four. Hold for seven. Breathe out for eight.

Do it again.

Do it again.

Do it again.

At the end of the fourth round, I have finally gotten my breathing back into its normal rhythm. My therapist's breathing exercises have never worked that well before. I would be shocked if I had the energy. Lying back, I raise my left arm straight into the air. I pinch my bicep—something to short-circuit the overwhelming urge to cry. A sharp pain jolts through my body. It worked.

Now that I am under control, I allow my hands to fall to my stomach, breathing gently in the way I've been taught. My eyes flutter open to find an audience watching my panic. Derrick and Oskar stare down at me, worried expressions stretching across both their faces. A still quiet haunts me, as if the world itself is watching me too.

As if to confirm, a bird—something like a vulture—circles high overhead, waiting for the inevitable. My eyes snap shut.

"Mal, are you okay?"

They'll go away if you pretend they're not here.

"Mallory." This time it's Oskar.

With my eyes still closed, I nod, trying not to wince at the way my tangled hair catches on the grass below me.

"I'm fine," I tell them both. "I promise. This used to happen all the time. It's nothing I can't handle."

My eyes open and meet Derrick's. His concerned expression doesn't budge. I sit up, cradling my knees in my arms. The last thing I need from him is pity. Yesterday, he was distrustful of me. If he earns I earn his trust back, I want it to be on merit.

"Seriously, Derrick, it's not a big deal, so please don't make it one."

"Sure," he replies numbly. "Whatever you say."

Oskar interjects. "We were hoping to get a consensus on whether or not we will be moving to our final task today."

Not caring if I come across rude, I scoff. The only good I am to them is when I'm sitting on the throne. It's possible that Derrick is genuine, but Oskar's feigned concern makes me sick.

"I don't know Oskar."

"We need to know how to prepare."

"All of this is moving too fast, and there's too much not being said. This whole thing feels ridiculous, like some kind of hazing ritual."

The man's gentle features settle on my face, studying me. He may not like my answer, but he's prepared to accept it.

"I know, my dear. A plethora of new information has been heaped on you—and this isn't even half of it. Once we get through these trials, there will still be work to do."

"What kind of work?" The mud under my body groans as I heave a sigh.

"We must convince those few still left in Thirawen to accept you. And once we do, we must face the Oracle."

Great. More for me to do.

"And even then, you will have one final trial. While The Order of the Twinned Path may accept you—though even that will prove difficult—it is an entirely different matter whether or not the Crown itself will accept you."

With that, I throw myself back on the ground and roll over on my side with the intention to lull myself to sleep. The pair continue their discussion, and I'm sure they take issue with my withdrawal.

"Well, hello there, Your Highness," Derrick's teasing voice chirps as I wake to his eyes staring into mine.

"Have you been staring at me?" I ask groggily.

"No, of course not. I'm sitting here eating lunch and I heard you stirring."

"Okay." My body aches from the stiffness of sleep as I sit up.

"Not everything is about you, you know? Other people exist, Mallory."

I fight the urge to roll my eyes. Arguing is the last thing on mind, even playfully.

"There's some lunch left over if you'd like. Dad didn't want to make any extra, since he didn't think you would be up."

"Unfortunately, I can't sleep forever." There's a bite to my voice I can't control. Instead of letting it win, I busy myself with trying to get the now dry chunks of mud out of my hair.

"I think he just got upset about throwing out breakfast. He probably figured if you woke up, you could make your own food."

"Well sorry I'm such a burden," I mutter under my breath, still focused on my hair.

Derrick scoffs and I look up. He puts on a pained expression, teasing me with my own words.

"Come on, Mal, don't be like that. I know things are weird, but we'll figure this out. After all, it's *my* fault you're here, right?"

"I guess that's true. You actually owe me—I deserve to be cooked for," I say with a giggle in my voice. He's broken through the grogginess; I'm willing to call a truce.

"Good. Go wash your hands and I'll get you something to eat, Your Highness."

I'm glad to know part of the truth—I believe what Oskar told me about my mother. Though I have so many unanswered questions, I wouldn't know where to start if I were to get him alone again.

Despite my gladness at, for once, being in the know of pertinent information, I wonder what would have been without it. Of course, not knowing something doesn't mean that thing stops being true.

CHAPTER THIRTY-THREE
MALLORY

With the remains of lunch cleared away, the three of us discuss our next move—there is one more trial to face before reaching the castle and learning my fate. Deciding it best to wait until morning to continue our adventure, we opt to remain another night in this clearing. Derrick's makeshift tent is holding up, much to my surprise, and we have enough food to last through noon tomorrow. Oskar assures us that, despite Derrick's reluctance to remain in such a vulnerable position, wildlife in Nalara is the least of our concerns tonight.

Except wildlife isn't my concern.

The voices I heard in the middle of the night in Gallivarum could still be out there, following us to the castle, waiting to strike. Both Derrick and Oskar still maintain that it was not them that intruded, and I can't be sure it was just random burglars. What could they have been looking for in a decrepit temple?

They could only have been after me.

I shake the feeling of unease bubbling up in my throat. This time, I'm not alone; the men will protect me. Or, at least, they'll try. Oskar's injury will prevent him from being much help, and there is nothing about Derrick that screams "physically inclined to beat up a stranger." He looks dark and mysterious when you see him from far away, but once that smile cracks his face, his inner sunshine pours out. Even at his angriest, his features are soft.

Despite my begging, Oskar is either unwilling or unable to tell me much about this trial. He says it will be more of a challenge than what I've already faced. That thought terrifies me—I've already murdered two strangers and my own brother, what more could possibly be expected of me?

This is wrong.

"Why would it get harder?" I ask Derrick when we are alone.

"What do you mean?" He cocks his head.

"I mean, if I am doing the Witherwalk backward, wouldn't the easiest task be last for me?"

A smile dances on Derrick's lips. "Maybe you're special."

I want to push him and tease back, but it feels wrong with our newfound dynamic. He is my brother, but he'll take any sign of friendliness as reciprocal to his advances. It's best to stick to conversations dealing with the task at hand until we can sort out our relationship.

"I'm serious, Derrick. Why does it feel like the tasks are getting more difficult instead of easier?"

He considers my logic for a brief moment.

"I don't know, Mal, maybe the universe adjusted for you. Maybe it's just the stops that are backward and not the tasks?"

"Maybe." I mull over his answer. Something inside me disagrees with his rationale. It doesn't *feel* right.

Derrick wakes us at dawn's first light. I don't know how he does it, but his body seems in complete control of its own schedule.

That's got to be a form of magic.

"Hey, Derrick?" I ask as we assemble our stash of collected objects.

"What's up?"

"What . . ." I try to consider how to ask this delicately. "What do you do?"

He looks up at me, amused. "What do I do? What do you mean, what do I do?"

"Sorry." I'm flustered now, embarrassed for some unknown reason. "I mean, what is your magic? Do you have any?"

His head droops a bit before he shakes it. "No, not really. I mean, I've learned over the years by the spells my father has taught me—nothing innate or special. Not like you."

Yeah, so far my abilities have been really cool.

"I mean, I don't really see what's awesome about what I do. Oh, so I can walk into other people's dreams and talk to the trees."

I mock myself with a laugh, but Derrick does not return it. He cocks his head to the side and looks at me with questioning eyes.

"What?"

"Nothing," he says in a soft, sad voice—a voice one would expect when their parents are telling them about their divorce. A tone I wish I didn't recognize.

My shoulders heave with a sigh. Just once I wish I could ask either Alborian man a question and get a straight answer. Derrick doesn't see the resemblance between himself and his father, but from where I am standing, it is uncanny.

"Whatever. You were looking at me weird."

He chuckles. "Oh, I get it now, you're just super defensive this morning."

I roll my eyes as blatantly as I can manage.

"I wasn't looking at you weird," he says defensively.

"Whatever you say."

"Come on, you two, quit bickering." Oskar's voice cuts through the tension. "It isn't much farther to Pryveth."

"Sorry, Dad!" Derrick calls. "We'll be right there."

Turning back over his shoulder, Derrick stares at me, hard. "Mal, I don't know what happened here, but I don't like what this place is doing to you. You're different. I can't put my finger on it just yet, but I feel a different energy."

I shoot daggers into the back of his skull as he walks away. This boy doesn't know me. He knew me on Earth for all of five minutes, and we've spent half our time in Nalara apart. Yet he thinks he is capable of judging me—that he's *allowed* to judge me?

Both men walk toward the woods. I follow behind, close enough they know I am there, but not so close they think I'm listening. I *am* listening, but only because I need to know what Derrick is telling Oskar about me.

"I'm worried about her, Dad."

His faux empathy isn't fooling me, and Oskar is intelligent—he'll see through it too.

Why would he care about me?

"Don't be, son. The Witherwalk demands sacrifice. It is intended to mold your very existence to fit the needs of the Crown. Someday soon, Mallory will come second to Nalara in her mind."

"What if she doesn't need to change? The Witherwalk is making Mallory care only about herself. Isn't that worse?"

That's not true. I've only thought about others this entire time.

Derrick in Bloomhall, Maryna and Fenric in the forest, the Emberguard . . . every trial has taken into consideration how it affected everyone else involved.

"Not to the Crown, son. Mallory will be a Nalaran. For all intents and purposes, Mallory and Nalara will be one and the same. There can be no future kingdom without her. Her actions may seem selfish now, but are only meant to serve the greater good. She must become worthy of the Crown."

"And she couldn't have been worthy before?"

Aww, that's almost sweet.

I hear the smile in Oskar's voice as he responds. "The Sacred Trees designed this ritual—they know what they are doing. Their magic created the whole of Nalara and they sacrificed some of themselves to set a path forward for our deliverance. *Mallory* is that deliverance. All the kings and queens that came before were an homage to what was to come. Our savior is here."

"I still don't like it," Derrick grumbles. "She is a person, half human, with her own thoughts and feelings. Why should she put Nalara first? What does she owe us?"

What do I owe Nalara?

"You do not have to like it, son, but you must abide by her reign. With this last task, the Witherwalk will be complete. Once she passes this trial, she will face the deliberation of the Order and, ultimately, of the Creators."

"And what if she fails, huh? What if she fails the trial or fails to win over the hearts of the people of Nalara?" Derrick pauses. "What if the Crown rebels?"

I knew it. He doesn't think I am good enough to rule.

"I understand your concerns, and I have them too. But the prophecy—"

"What if the prophecy is wrong? What if it's not even about her?"

"My child"—Oskar's voice grows quiet—"it is her. They tried to kill her mother."

"Wow," Derrick says in a matching tone. "Does she know?"

"I don't see how she could. This world and its history are all new to her."

Liar.

"That's true. Even though I was born on Earth too, I had you. I had all the stories and history of this kingdom."

Maybe not all of them.

"Yes, it is sad how her mother left her clueless about her origins. When her mother escaped Nalara, her grandmother and I went to find her. We tried to convince her mother to come back to Nalara and fight. Her grandmother betrayed me and took Mallory's mother deeper into hiding on Earth before Mallory was even conceived."

Derrick, why aren't you questioning this?

The story that Oskar is spinning to Derrick is much different than the one he'd told me in the clearing that day. About the oracle child sent to Earth centuries ago, whose lineage eventually spawned me. Even Oskar himself admitted that's the accepted lore throughout Nalara.

You are smarter than to fall for this.

Derrick runs his hands through his dark, shaggy hair. It has grown quite a bit since we've arrived, and he has gotten into the habit of playing with it when he's nervous.

"Wow. That has got to be a lot to carry, even if subconsciously. I guess you're right—learning all this now has to change a person."

"Yes, and what's more, the land itself remembers her story. These trees carry her family's legacy and destiny rooted deeper than someone like you or I could ever hope to fathom."

Derrick mumbles in agreement. He still isn't happy with the answer he was given, but he's accepted it. Just as he always does. Any question he ever has is quelled with ease. He won't push an issue, even if he should.

"Go easy on her, Derrick. She is meant to save us all—even if it means losing herself."

CHAPTER THIRTY-FOUR
MALLORY

We walk about an hour west of Alvian Falls to Pryveth, where my last trial waits. This is the final major obstacle between me and my crown. After that, all I have to do is convince the Oracle to allow my coronation.

No big deal.

Pryveth is the kind of cozy little town straight out of a medieval fairy tale. There are quaint cottages and townsfolk milling about the dirt floor. Somewhere deep inside me, my make-believe-princess heart aches to stay. I suppose that now it's not make-believe—I *will* be royalty.

The smell of fresh bread wafts toward my nostrils, greeting me like a warm hug. My stomach growls, reminding me that, despite having enough food in reserves, I haven't eaten yet today. Not only can I use the sustenance for whatever awaits, I long for the euphoria that only baked goods can bring.

"Do we have any money?" I ask the pair of men, ignoring their answer as I realize for the first time that I haven't exactly had a normal experience. We haven't existed or traveled like typical Nalarans. For a kingdom I will soon rule, I know nothing about the everyday life of a typical person here.

Not much different than most leaders, I guess.

My thoughts float to the last time I was in a bakery. Nessa and I had been finishing up a shopping day—her idea—and she'd decided to treat me to a pain au chocolat from our favorite patisserie in Old Town.

Vanessa. After all this time spent in Nalara, this is the first time my best, and only, friend has crossed my mind. Despite how self-serving Vanessa is, she is a better friend than I deserve. When I forgot to bathe or eat, she was there. There were nights I couldn't get the tears to stop falling, and she held me every time. I can't begin to hope she would ever understand what I've been through since I left.

I wonder if she's worried.

A giggle escapes my lips as I realize that I hope she's not. I wish she would forget my existence entirely. I wish the magic of Nalara had seeped out through the portal and erased every trace of my existence from whatever realm I had inhabited. It would be easier for us both if she'd never known me.

I'm brought back to attention with the realization that Derrick is staring at me. His mouth is moving, but I can't make out the words.

"What?"

He begins to repeat himself.

"Oh, no. I wasn't looking for anything specific."

He opens his mouth as if to protest, then closes it and opens it once more. "Why did you ask if you knew what I said?"

"Sorry," I apologize, shaking my head. "It's just a thing that happens to me sometimes. My brain needs a minute to catch up."

"Okay then."

God, I hate this judgment.

"I'm hungry. Can we find something to eat?" I won't give him the satisfaction of explaining myself to him any further.

Let him think what he wants.

Oskar informs us Pryveth is a town he frequented often in his youth. There is a tavern nearby whose proprietor would welcome us with open arms and a pint of ale. We set down a path of winding streets, ducking into an alley tucked between two modest cottages.

A wooden door, ragged from years of wear, sits at the foot of the alley. Behind it, patrons shout and roar with laughter. It seems promising enough, though its surreptitious nature gives me pause. Still, we push forward.

My hands grip the wrought iron door pull and the surprisingly light door swings open with ease. Inside, wooden chairs and tables, haphazardly arranged around the room, teem with bodies. This place may be hidden, but from my inability to find a single open table at first glance, I gather it is well-known.

The clanging of the door brings dozens of eyes to meet ours and the conversation stills. As we move further into the room, hushed whispers trail us. At the opposite end of the room, a grizzly-looking man wipes mugs with a dirty rag behind the bar. He looks in every way your stereotypical barkeep—down to the tattoos on his arms. These tattoos, though, depict ancient glyphs and symbols that, not for a lack of trying, I can't make out. Whatever they say, it is not in Sylvaneth.

"What do you want?" the man growls, with far more force than necessary.

"Hello, Wolfric," Oskar says from behind me. "I'm rather surprised at your being here. I would have thought you'd have given up on your little tavern years ago."

"Oskar." Wolfric's eyes narrow at my mentor. "Why are you here?"

Oskar pushes on, ignoring the man's deflection. There is something familial about how these two men address one another, though their appearances are not similar.

"We're hungry," Oskar says with a hint of amusement in his voice.

He sounds like Derrick.

In a million years, I would not have imagined Oskar to ever be the taunting type. He's typically too above the escapades of the commonfolk.

"Eat somewhere else," Wolfric spits out the words. "You know you aren't welcome here."

"Now, Wolfie, is that the way to treat your big brother?"

Derrick and I exchange glances. I mouth the word "brother" and Derrick responds with a shrug. "I dunno," he mouths back.

This is pissing me off.

While this banter may be playful or hostile—I can't tell which—I am done sitting idly by while it continues. I will no longer be a bystander in this conversation. Or, for that matter, my life. *I* will be high queen, *I* make the rules. And I am hungry.

"Hi, Wolfric," I say with my best smile, hoping to charm the crotchety old man. "I'm Mallory. Mallory Nerezza. We are just passing through your little village on the way to the capitol, where I will take the throne."

He doesn't answer, but his frown deepens.

"Now, if you could be a dear and get your future high queen and her friends some food and ale, that would be much appreciated." I consider batting my eyelashes, but don't want to cheapen my authority.

Wolfric doesn't move. He stands in that confident way, much like Derrick, and looks me up and down.

I guess the apple really doesn't fall too far from the tree.

Grinning like I just said something funny, Wolfie matches my gazes. He throws his head back and laughs for much longer than necessary. My fists curl, but I have to learn to control my temper as heir to the throne.

"You?" he questions when he catches his breath. "You're the heir? You expect me to believe that a weak little thing like you is the prophecy's Chosen One?"

"Oskar," Wolfric continues, turning toward my mentor, "of all the ludicrous beliefs you've ever had, this may be the most ridiculous by far. I heard tell of your journey to Earth, but thought it simply a thing of rumor. And, here you are, standing in front of your only kin with this pathetic *human* you think to be our salvation?"

The way he says the word *human*, like it feels disgusting in his mouth, makes my skin crawl. I open my mouth to speak, but Derrick feverishly shakes his head. He may be wise to stop me from interfering between brethren. With a growing reluctance, I clamp my mouth shut, eager to attack with my words at the slightest provocation.

"Now, brother," Oskar says with a hint of fire behind his voice, "you may have lost the faith, but I have not. You and that faction you're rumored to be in cahoots with are an abomination to the Crown and to the prophecy. This girl is our destiny."

"Whatever you say, big brother. Go sit down, I'll get my wench to serve you."

The three of us scramble for seats in the dining area. There's a small table tucked off into the corner, difficult to reach and meant for two. Derrick spots an empty stool and scoots it as close to the table as he can manage. It's not comfortable, but it'll do.

A busty woman, clad in a corset meant to amplify her endowment, brings three steins of beer.

"Wolfric said whatever you want is in the house."

He can't hate Oskar that much.

The three of us order lunch—turkey legs for Oskar and I and a minced meat pie for Derrick. When the woman returns with our food, her eyes are red-rimmed.

"Are you okay?"

"Yes." She wipes her eyes and puts on a crooked smile. "I'm absolutely fine, darling."

"You don't look fine. Please tell me what's wrong?"

"Oh, you know how it is for a girl in these parts. Especially one who looks like me." Her eyes drop to her endowment.

Why would it be any different for women in Nalara?

"What happened?"

She shakes her head and tries to giggle her tears away. "I'm just a silly girl. Don't worry about it. Enjoy your food, hun."

A patron across the room calls for her attention. She excuses herself, and I watch her retreat behind the bar, my food untouched.

She reaches up to grab a mug hanging from the wall and her boss's meaty hand paws at her rear. I don't know him that well, but this shocks me coming from an Alborian. Something inside me snaps and I see red. Before I know what I'm doing, I am making my way to the bar.

"Hey!" I shout, drawing attention from every person in the establishment. "Get your hands off of her."

Wolfric's stunned expression pisses me off. He has the audacity to look outraged, after what I just witnessed?

It's about time I speak up.

"I mean it. Don't touch her." The eyes of the patrons, including those of my companions, grow hot on my body, but I don't care.

"Mind your business, little girl," Wolfric growls, "or I will have to see you and your friends out."

"Kick me out, that's fine. Why would I want to be a patron of an establishment in which you treat women like they are second-class citizens? In front of the woman who will be in charge of the entire nation soon enough, no less."

His raucous laughter fills the room. Several men join him from their seats. I glance at the women amongst the crowd, all with their heads hanging and their hands folded in their laps. Whether out of shame at my outburst or the societal embarrassment of being a woman, I do not know. Either way, I don't have their support.

"Get out. Before I throw you out," Wolfie growls.

I look at my friends sitting at our table. An expression I can't quite read hangs on my brother's face, while Oskar's is twisted in fury at his own brother. No. Not at Wolfric. At me.

Moments later, we are tumbling through the door, ushered out by Wolfie and his posse.

"And stay out!" The proprietor yells the cliche line to our back before slamming the door.

"What was that, Mal?"

"I don't know. I've never done anything like that before, but it's about time I did. How that woman was treated isn't fair. If that's how he is willing to handle her in front of customers, what could he possibly be doing in the privacy of a locked room?"

This isn't about her. It's about you. It's about him.

With a shudder, I pull myself from the past. I am not ready to go there, not yet—maybe not ever.

"Did you have to make a scene?"

I blink at him in disbelief.

Et tu Derrick?

"I don't understand." My voice comes out flat and even. "You insist time and time again that you are morally superior to me in every conceivable way, then you jump down my throat when I risk my neck to help someone? If I am to be queen, I need to be able to make a difference. It's not only my right as 'savior of Nalara' to speak my mind, but it's my moral obligation as a woman."

"Not like this, Mal."

Do I even know this man?

How can he justify what we saw in there? Or is he just so hell-bent on my downfall that he will be in opposition to everything I do, no matter how noble?

"I don't know you," I snarl.

"I'm beginning to think maybe you don't."

"Oskar"—I turn to my mentor—"you understand where I'm coming from, right?"

Oskar maintains a study gaze, boring into my soul with his eyes, but he doesn't speak. The two men walk off and I am left alone.

CHAPTER THIRTY-FIVE
DERRICK

"What's wrong with her?" I ask my father when we're alone.

We left Mallory standing in front of my uncle's tavern. The tavern with no name by the uncle I didn't know existed. But that's an argument to get into another time. Right now, we have to discuss whatever the hell got into Mallory back there.

Dad keeps walking without a word. Typical and not unexpected, though I had hoped we could discuss this together. I know he's growing weary of my constant complaints about her, but something is seriously wrong with Mallory. He insists it's just the trials doing what they were designed to do. And he won't tell me if it's a permanent change. That alone is enough for me to suspect it is.

As we exit the alley and step out into the quaint village center, my shoulder brushes against someone. I am briefly reminded of the same thing happening to Mal in Liriwyn, but I shrug the worry off.

"Oh," I say. I'm sorry."

"No, I'm sorry. I wasn't looking where I was going." A handsome man smiles at me, dressed in a fine white linen, like he is due to be somewhere important very soon.

"I'm Derrick." I extend my hand, pretending to be braver than I am.

"I'm Jorin." He takes my hand and shakes it. His smaller physique hides his strength—his palm feels warm and soft in mine, but his grasp is firm, like he doesn't want to let go.

For the first time since coming to Nalara, my mind moves away from Mallory and I blush. Jorin can't see how flustered I am, so I glance at my shoes as the heat spreads through my face.

"Nice to meet you," I try to keep the conversation going.

Jorin grins, a goofy, haphazard smile. His smile is infectious and . . . intoxicating. I bite my lip, half from nerves, half to draw his attention. It works. His eyes move down toward my mouth before snapping back up to meet my gaze.

"It's really, really nice to meet you," he says with a wink. "I've gotta get going, though. See you around?"

My mouth goes dry. "Yeah, maybe."

"Good," he says as he walks away.

I never thought of what I would do when Mallory took the crown. I've been so focused on getting her there that I never stopped to think about myself. With all that power, she won't want someone like me around. Maybe I'll come back here, find Jorin or someone else to settle down with. I'm twenty-four, still young by Earth standards. My being a bachelor at this age would be scandalous in some parts of Nalara. Best not to move there, then.

It's not like everyone here marries young, but if one chooses to marry for love and not out of contractual obligation, it is usually done by their twenty-seventh birthday. Still plenty of time for me.

I turn my attention back to my father, whom I had forgotten in the heat of our exchange

Don't mind me." He smiles knowingly. "I'm not here or anything. Wouldn't want to intrude on you and your new *friend*."

I laugh—Dad's used to this sort of thing. My mind jumps from one thing to another faster than I realize what's happening, and if I am not looking at something, that something ceases to exist.

"Sorry, Dad, you know I don't do it on purpose."

"I know, son. It's nice to see you smiling again."

"It's nice to smile. I've been so worried about Mallory, I haven't had the chance."

"You are not her keeper. We are here to guide her, not control her."

"I'm not trying to control her." My smile drops. "I just want to make sure she is safe and that our plan works. You keep reiterating the importance of getting her to the throne. I don't want to fail."

His mouth contorts into a grim smile, his age showing on his face.

"I know, son. Our plan is still intact."

CHAPTER THIRTY-SIX
MALLORY

I'm left standing in the alleyway alone, with the roar of diners in the tavern mocking me. Derrick and Oskar make their way through the alley and out into the sunlight. Once there, Derrick collides with a handsome stranger and the two of them spend far too long exchanging pleasantries.

As soon as Oskar and Derrick are out of my line of sight, I spring into motion behind them. They will be discussing this, and I need to know what they're saying.

"Our plan is intact."

What plan?

Stopping short while the two of them continue forward, I roll the word around in my head. *Plan.* I knew there was more to their hospitality—something sinister.

Why do they want me on the throne?

The Hollowborne warned me of unearned trust. Could it be they were referring to the Alborians all along? I've seen what Wolfric is willing to do, but could Oskar be that deceitful? He hasn't yet told me an outright lie, just omitted parts of the truth he didn't think were necessary.

Who is he to decide what's necessary?

My legs grow heavy with the urge to move as my instinct attempts to override whatever part of my brain is responsible for rational thought. It's a fight to keep them rooted in their spot.

Be rational, Mallory. Be calm. And, most importantly, be smart.

It's likely the father and son duo knew I would be eavesdropping, hoping they could run me straight into whatever awaits in my final trial. Not this time.

The Mallory who runs died in those fires.

Taking deep breaths of the crisp midday air, I examine my surroundings. Cozy shops line the town center, looking almost indistinguishable from the homes. Everyday people mill around outside the shops, moving in groups, gossiping like nothing's wrong. Unlike the manufactured joy of Liriwyn, the citizens of Pryveth are truly content.

Looking past a group of women, arm in arm in pairs, who whisper as they pass, I notice that some cottages appear to serve as both home and storefront. Everything about this place is charming, a perfect replica of a renaissance faire.

I deserve some time off.

In all the chaos of the trials, I haven't gotten to just exist. My actions have all been calculated to pass my trials. I've yet to do anything just for the fun of it, and once I take the crown, it is unlikely I will ever get this chance again.

My stomach growls, reminding me of the lunch I hadn't eaten, and I follow the scent of bread to the baker's shop. Oskar had managed to scrounge up a handful of coins, different in size and color, whose names I don't know. Surely one of them will be enough for some kind of pastry.

Walking into the bakery, I am greeted by the scent of freshly baked loaves and a warm burst of air. Loaves of different sizes and shapes line the baskets around the open room. They invite me in and a kindly, plump man with a mustache greets me with a smile in his voice. He helps me decipher the coins in my outstretched palm —the small silver is worth the most, the red ones with bumpy edges and a hole in the center are worth the least, and the green one with one of the Sacred Trees on either side is a special coin reserved only for tithing at the altar. According to him, I'm missing a few more Nalaran coins, but I have plenty for a long, thin loaf of bread that catches my eye.

Thanking the man for his hospitality, it dawns on me how strange it must be for an adult person to ask about the singular currency structure of the entire kingdom—though he did not ask where I came from. Word travels fast and, while he didn't say anything about it, he probably knows who I am. Nibbling the bread, which is softer and more delicate than any cloud could ever dream of being, I leave the bakery in higher spirits than when I entered.

Maybe food does fix everything.

The next storefront I walk through is an apothecary of some sort. Jars of potions and ingredients litter every table. Some I recognize, others are foreign. The room gives off an earthy smell, thanks to the candles strewn about, casting a dim glow. Beams of light emerge from the shadows and catch on crystals placed deliberately on shelves around the room. I examine the room and am startled by the sight of a woman sitting behind a desk, her long gray hair showing signs of aging.

"Hello," she croaks in a voice far younger than I expected. "Can I help you, dear?"

"No, I am just admiring the selection."

I run my hand along the edge of a table laden with dried herbs, bundled tightly and labeled for specific purposes. One bundle of sage and lavender reads "love," another with rosemary and cinnamon sticks reads "good fortune." I never believed in any of this stuff on Earth—but if smudging works anywhere, it would be Nalara.

The old lady with the young voice watches me carefully as I make my way around the shelves lining the room. Her eyes follow every movement—every time I pick up an object or turn my head. A heat—likely the sheer embarrassment I feel at being perceived— permeates the room.

After what is probably only three minutes but feels like a lifetime, she breaks the silence. "Mallory Nerezza."

I stop cold in my tracks, not daring to look at her. Maybe I misheard, or maybe, if I don't turn around, she will stop talking.

She doesn't.

"You, Mallory the Shadowbearer, are the heir to the timeless prophecy."

My hands fiddle with a small yellow crystal that I pretend to be particularly interested in.

"Be careful who, and what, you trust."

What does she know?

Slowly, I turn, expecting her to be right behind me. She isn't—she's still at her desk, but her eyes are rolling back into her head as if she's being possessed by a spirit.

"You, daughter of Earth, will take the throne. You will rule this land for a short time before bringing peace to our beloved kingdom. And you will die a young woman, defending your title. Before your thirtieth year, you will be immortalized in history."

My hands tremble harder than they ever have before, and I drop the crystal to the ground. It cracks neatly in half, taunting me with some unseen force.

With my eyes still squarely on the woman, I back toward the door. She opens her mouth to continue her prophecy and, just as sound begins to invade the quiet, I yank open the door and stumble out into the street.

Everything is as it was. Not a soul has batted an eyelash toward this woman's shop. Every passerby ignores it, like it's invisible to them.

Whether it was a prophecy or a threat, I do not know—I do not care to know. She is a stranger to me, one whose magic felt dark, twisted, hollow. Her spirits, or whatever they were, may have been guiding me as a friend. I don't care. There are much better ways to tell someone difficult information than to scare them half to death as they're looking to give you money.

A chill runs through the air and down my spine. What was once a quaint and cozy village is looking more like a haunted house.

"Mallory!"

My head swivels around, scanning every woman's face for the voice I recognize but can't quite place.

"Mallory!" the high-pitched sing-song grows distant.

How could I ever forget that voice?

My ears must be deceiving me. It's impossible that she would be here, impossible that she would even know I was here. The noise leads me to another shop, this one not in the row of cottages with all the passersby. What looks like a cabin perches in front of me on the edge of the wood, an external representation of the horror I feel.

What's in there?

Boom.

My heart beats heavily in my chest, out of its normal rhythm. A clammy coldness licks the palm of my hands. This cabin doesn't belong. This cabin has something to do with my next trial, I can *feel* it.

"Mallory," a man's voice calls from behind the closed door as I turn to leave. This voice from my past is one that I can't forget, not even for a second.

Dad.

Galloping into the shop at full speed, I'm greeted by an empty room. There is no way I misheard that voice, but I see no one. Mind games like Thalion's or what I experienced at the river must be behind this.

Oskar will know what to do.

Turning back toward the door, I find it shut—which is odd, because I know I left it open in my haste.

I must be more forgetful than I realize.

A pressure builds in me, mimicking anxiety, as I reach for the handle. I know what's coming before I even try.

Locked.

Nothing in Nalara has been simple. Why should this be any different? My final trial, adjusted for the direction of the Witherwalk, if Derrick's theory is to be believed, will be the hardest one I have to face . . . until I get to the castle.

Not wasting time looking for an alternative means of escape, I survey the room for options. Windows? There is one on either side of the cabin, bookending the empty room. As expected, they are locked as well. Their panes are several inches thick; it would take too long and too much energy to punch my way through.

There *has* to be some means of absconding from my current predicament. My eyes run along the length of the floorboards, searching for some kind of latch—or any indication there may be a trapdoor. After several moments, I drop to my knees and press my left temple into the floor, hoping something will catch my eye as my gaze runs along the floorboards.

Nothing.

"Mallory!" Derrick's voice.

"Derrick!" I shout back. "In here! I'm stuck, everything is locked, and there's no way out. You have to help me."

My voice comes out with more panic than I intend.

"Don't worry, Mallory, we will get you out of there. Just hang tight."

"Hurry!" I yell toward the door.

"Okay, just don't touch anything, and especially don't speak with anyone."

There won't be any chance of that.

Dropping to the floor, I cradle my knees in my hands. After all this time—all these trials—I find myself alone again. There was once a time when solitude was a preference, a refuge from the mundanity of everyday life. Now, the isolation is haunting, perforating into my bone marrow. It's a reminder of the responsibility that will be placed on my shoulders, and mine alone, in the coming weeks.

"Mallory!" my father's voice calls out again. "Can you hear me, Marshmallow?"

And especially don't speak with anyone.

"Darling girl," my grandmother's voice lilts through the air. My heart leaps into my throat at the sound. There are so many questions that hang in the balance between us. I bite my lip to keep from responding.

"Mal." This one is Derrick's.

He can't be back already. That's impossible.

"Derrick"—my voice comes out hoarse—"I thought you were going to get help?"

"Mal, there is no help. I'm sorry, I tried. Whatever this is, it's a trial. You will have to get through it alone."

My heart sinks to my toes as the blood runs cold through my body. Of course this is a trial. Another one that I am unequipped and unprepared to take on.

"Mallow," my dad calls again, and I can't help but roll my eyes. Even here he is using the pet name he came up with when I was six. If I wasn't afraid I am in danger, I would be embarrassed. "It's okay, sweetheart, you can stay here with us as long as you need."

"Dad, where are you?"

Vanessa's voice answers the question—the voice that led me to this cabin in the first place. "We're right here, Mal. Can't you see us?"

Mal?

"No," I answer to the open room. Whether I should be concerned or elated to hear her voice, I do not know. "This room is empty, I can't see anyone or anything."

"Just follow the sound of my voice, darling girl."

"I'll try, Nana."

And when I find you, we'll have words. Why didn't you tell me about Nalara? Why did you let me grow up without a true home?

The voices echo at me, one after the other, a cacophony of people I hold the most dear. I can't make out the direction from which a single voice is coming—they are layering together in a way that just produces noise.

"STOP! All of you, shut up!" I would regret my words if I could see their figures. "I need one of you—and only one of you—to speak at a time. You're confusing the hell out of me."

"Marshmallow, you know I don't like that tone."

"Sorry, Dad," I grumble. I'm twenty-two years old and the heir to a crown, for God's sake, and the man still acts like he can control me.

"Alright, Dad, keep talking so I can follow your voice."

"I'm *right here*, Mallory. Stop playing around, you know I don't like your games, you get too into them."

What does that mean?

But I ignore his words—don't take the bait—and instead focus on the sound of his voice. His deep baritone is coming from over my left shoulder, by my best estimation. I turn to face him, but he isn't there. No one is.

"Don't ignore me, I am your father."

This time, he sounds farther away. I take a step forward and then another until I am face-to-face with my reflection in the window.

Outside?

"Dad. Seriously, where are you? If anyone is playing games here, it's you."

A flash forms on the windowpane, and I catch a glimpse of my father's bright, lofty smile. From here, I can make out the faint, ghost-like outlines of him, Vanessa, and my Nana. Only Derrick is missing.

"Where's Mom?" I blurt out with little decorum. He doesn't like to speak of her—their divorce was messy—and I know it. But now isn't the time to spare his feelings.

Now also isn't the time to sift through the turmoil raging in my chest. This is the first glimpse of Dad in years, and he hasn't changed. He even still looks exactly the same, with just a touch more salt-and-pepper coloring in his hair.

"It doesn't matter," Dad's voice comes out clipped. "She's fine."

Of course he didn't, not really. He never does. And I know him; he will shut down and refuse to speak if I push him any father. If I want information, I am going to have to swallow the growing resentment lodged in my throat.

"What are you doing here?" I ask instead, changing the subject. "How do I get you out of there?"

It is Nana who answers. "My darling girl, haven't you realized it yet? We are not real. We are simply a manifestation of your heart's desires, brought about by your magic."

Of course. Dream magic in the real world once again.

"Well then, why am I talking to you? What is this trial meant to test?"

"My darling, that I don't know."

Right . . . because I don't know.

My frustration grows as the seconds pass, and I know I will not get the answers I seek in any manner of straightforwardness. A groan escapes my lips before I change my line of questioning.

"What do you want, then?" I rest my hand on the glass, hoping to form some sort of physical connection to the people I once held most dear.

"Mallory," Vanessa's whine chimes in. "God forbid a girl wants to say hi to her best friend. I've been lonely without you."

Have you, though?

I shake my head. "Nessa, you aren't real. You're just a figment of my imagination telling me exactly what I want to hear."

And especially don't speak with anyone.

"Derrick warned me about this. He told me not to speak with anyone. I shouldn't even be talking to you. You could be dangerous, for all I know."

My friend rolls her eyes through the window as I back away.

"Derrick!" I shout as loudly as I can, moving to the front door. My fists pound in a useless flurry, shaking the cabin beneath me.

"Mal, I told you, I'm working on it," Derrick's voice comes from the other window.

Are you though?

Running to the other side of the cabin, I peer through the window and nearly jump out of my skin. He is standing on the other side of the glass, nose pressed against the pane. At least he's real.

"I see my family," I tell him through the glass.

His face drops into a grim expression. "You didn't talk to them, did you?"

"No, of course not." A lie, yes, but what will it hurt?

"Dad wants to know what it is that you see in there? I can't get a good look from out here."

"That's just it, Derrick, there is *nothing* in this room. Nothing but me and the voices."

I laugh, not a sound of pleasure but of incredulity.

Maybe I am as crazy as everyone said. As I've always thought.

"I don't know what you were supposed to do then, Mal, but I do know that you are the only thing that can unlock the door. It has to be you who frees yourself, or you'll fail."

Throwing my hands up in exasperation, I stomp my feet, feeling every bit like a child who doesn't like their mother's answer.

"A lot of good you two have been."

My frustration only grows as I walk toward the middle of the room. If the Alborian men can't help me and won't keep me company, I might as well talk to the people I actually care about.

Arriving at the opposite window, where the figures had just been, I find the frame empty. Derrick's presence can't have scared them off. They must want something if Oskar and Derrick are so adamant I don't speak with them.

"Dad? Hello, are there?"

No answer.

"Vanessa?" The desperation in my voice grows. "Nana?"

They've all grown silent on me. Slinking back to the other window, resigned by the fate that I'll have to communicate only with Derrick, I peek out and see the two men wobbling away from the cabin.

"Great," I mutter to myself. "All alone with nothing to do."

Once upon a time, this would've been heaven. What changed?

I sit in maddening silence. I lie down. I sing—anything I can think of to keep me occupied until Derrick returns. *If* Derrick returns. I decide physical activity will keep my mind off the haunting silence. I pace the floor, do jumping jacks, sit-ups— nothing works.

Sometime after an hour passes, I hear the phantom ticking of a clock.

Tick.

Tick.

Tick.

That's it. I'm going mad.

It might not be the isolation that kills me, or the lack of basic human needs. If I die in this cabin, it will be because of that damn clock.

They say boredom is the mother of invention. I don't feel inventive, I just feel like I want to wrap my fingers around Derrick's neck and squeeze. *Hard.* If he hadn't walked away from me at the tavern, he'd be in this room too. If it were their lives at stake, they would have no problem finding an external solution. Is Derrick that petty? He's so upset that I defended a woman, he feels the need to punish me?

Thinking about what happened back in the alleyway, my resolve steels. How fucking dare he? Heat rises up my neck, kissing my ears. An anger that will do me no good now.

"Don't shoot without a target." My nana's words, delivered in a scolding tone ages ago, ring in my ears so clearly I almost look for her vision in the window. But I know she's not there. This one's me —my memory. Of that sweet day at the pier when I was so upset I hadn't won the largest pink teddy that I jumped straight into the harbor.

My grandmother was right, of course. Unbridled anger does nothing more than harm its wielder. For a productive outcome, there must be a focus. A target. A plan.

If I get out of here—*when* I get out of here—I will use that anger to form a plan. A plan that will ultimately clear the rift between us. A plan where Oskar tells Derrick the truth . . . or I do.

Without the ability to see the clock, I have no idea how much time is passing. All I can do is count the ticks. I make it to somewhere in the two thousands before giving up; counting the seconds will do me no good if I can't use that data.

The light outside is growing dim. It must be hours since I've entered, and I'm hungry again. But there is nothing in this room to sustain me, aside from the wishes for my loved ones to return in their spectral form. Between long stretches of nothingness, I return to their windows and call for them, hoping in earnest desperation that someone will save me from my own company.

After far too long without luck, I curl into a fetal ball under the window. My bladder is screaming at me, but there is nowhere to find relief. At least, nowhere I feel comfortable.

I awake in the cabin, exactly where I'd fallen asleep.

Is *this a cabin?*

Perhaps this is an empty shop and its proprietor will come rescue me. The type of building I'm in doesn't matter. I am still entirely and painfully alone. The only reprieve is that my bodily functions seem to be under control . . .

Did I wet myself last night?

If I did, there is no indication. Maybe the magic of the trial keeps the cabin tidy, a theory I am sure I will have to put to the test soon enough.

There's a haze in the room, one that wasn't here yesterday. It's somewhere between a fog and a smoke. Just a weird shimmer of film in the air. As soon as it comes, it disappears, and I hear voices.

They're back for me.

"No, Dad, this is awful. I have hated every second of being here with her!" Derrick yells to Oskar. The pair are standing outside, far enough away that I shouldn't be able to hear, but their loud voices carry with the wind

"My boy, you know this is necessary. Once we have her on the throne, things will work out. Trust the process—have faith in your old man."

This isn't the first time I've heard the pair of them allude to some grand scheme. It won't do me any good now to listen to this fight, but I can't escape it.

"She's nothing but a selfish coward." Derrick's voice is laced with resentment I'm not sure he deserves to feel. "Why should we help her get to the throne, if she doesn't deserve it? Nobody wants her there. You've heard the whispers all over town and the threats of assassination by the Riftclan."

"You may be right, son, but the Founding Trees in all of their omniscience requested her on the throne. Who are we to say they're wrong?"

With that, Oskar glances over to where I stand in the cabin, out of Derrick's line of sight, and winks at me.

He wants me to hear this. But, why?

"She's just a child, Marjorie," I hear my dad's raised voice. A voice I wasn't certain I'd ever hear again. Leaping toward the opposite window where they'd been previously, I cling to the windowsill as tightly as I can, so as not to lose them.

"I don't care. Look what she has gotten herself into. You know as well as I, she isn't capable of any of this. She's gotten to the last trial on pure luck—which is exactly why I never told her about any of this. Nalara is better off without her."

"You're right," my father concedes, "she doesn't really know what she's doing. Not that she ever has. And God knows she won't stick around long enough to listen to advice."

"Ed, you have to agree, our lives have been easier since she left."

"You're not wrong."

"We are better off leaving her here alone. She will rot in this cage and we both, as well as the whole of the Nalaran Kingdom, will be better off for it."

Nana, why are you saying this?

My lips quiver as I hold back the hot tears welling in my eyes. My grandma was always the one who believed in me most, the only one who ever made me feel seen. I thought for a moment Derrick would give me that also, and I understand now that's not possible. I just didn't think I'd lose my Nana too.

"Yeah, I guess that's true." Dad sounds less reluctant now. "All she's done is wait for someone else to save her. It's her perpetual curse in life—she's never faced anything head-on in order to save herself."

He looks sad for a moment, pondering his disappointment. But his urgency fades and he looks almost relieved as he says, "Let's find breakfast before we go. Celebrations call for pancakes."

Every muscle in my body grows limp. The floor spins out from under me, and some unseen force drags me to the ground. The impact of my collapse causes my torso to lurch backward.

A jolt courses through me as I sit up in terror. My heart thuds like a drumline in my ear. My back, despite the lack of a blanket, is soaked in sweat. The rhythm of my breathing is jagged and shallow, as if my lungs haven't been working for days.

Oh, thank God.

My bladder is screaming at me again and I am forced to decide which corner of the room I will use as a toilet. I *will not* be here long enough to decide where to defecate.

Responding to my body's urges clears my head some—I am in a lot less pain. Though, with the numbing of one pain comes the awareness of another. My stomach is eating itself in hunger, the remnants of my half-baguette lunch long gone.

My circumstances are still bleak, with no great prospects as to a means of escape. But, at least what I'd overheard yesterday wasn't real.

It felt real.

If my powers are supposed to be growing like Oskar says, I should be able to pick up on my dreams quicker now than ever before. Though, I suppose it may not be my awareness that is meant to grow, but the dreams themselves. Maybe they exist in this capacity to teach me what I need to learn but am too afraid to seek out myself.

"Mallory."

I pause. A cold chill runs down my spine, tingling every vertebrae. I'm not dreaming—I know that—so why am I hearing my own voice?

At a slow, reluctant pace, I move to the window, finding myself staring into my own eyes. This specter is different, clearer and more vivid than the rest.

A chuckle escapes my reflection's lips. I'm not looking through the window—I'm looking into a mirror.

My eyes stare into those of the other Mallory, daring myself for once to soak in every aspect of my face. The freckles, the wrinkles, the faint scar on my cheek from where I crashed my bike the first time I rode without training wheels. This girl is every bit of who I am, and somehow stronger—more beautiful. She is the version of myself that I wish I was. The type of person who doesn't resent themselves through the looking glass.

I try to open my mouth to speak, but find I have lost my voice.

"You stupid, stupid girl. You went off into the unknown with two strange men. Men who have done nothing but berate you and insult your intelligence. And you eagerly let it happen."

That's not true.

I stare at myself, unable to form any word or gesture that could possibly convey my thoughts. Though, I suspect mirror-me knows exactly what I'm thinking. For once, I shut up and listen.

"Don't worry, I know why you did it," mirror-me says with a wicked grin. "Poor little Mallory, always feeling like nobody cares. Always chasing attention and labelling it as affection. The girl who is so unloved."

I want to wipe the pouty lips right off her face.

"But there's a flaw in that plan"—her smile tightens, like a hyena ready to pounce—"and it's glaringly obvious if you would take even a miniscule moment of introspection. You are not wanted here. No, you are *needed* here. They don't like you, but they like what you will do for them."

I grit my teeth and tighten my fingers into a fist.

Bullshit.

"You aren't a hero, you aren't a queen. You're a pawn in someone else's game. You're a placeholder for what comes next."

Despite the boiling in my blood, this isn't anything new. It's the same thing I've been telling myself every day since arriving. The same thing I've been telling myself for years.

"You're wrong," I snarl the words. "Whether or not I am wanted now, I *will* make a difference. After I take the crown, I will usher in the era of peace the prophecy predicts. This time is different. This time, I won't run."

"It won't be different, Mallory. You said that about college, about Jeremy, about working at that pathetic coffee shop. And, guess what, you were wrong—just like you're wrong now. This is just another thing that will make you run."

Fire overtakes my veins and my fist strikes the glass.

Once.

Twice.

Three times and shards blow outward. It is no longer a mirror I've struck, but a window once more. The same green glow that I've seen time and time again in Nalara fills the room, obscuring my vision for a brief moment before it fades and I can orient myself again.

"Mallory," Oskar asks, "are you okay?"

I've never been more glad to hear that voice.

Spinning on my heels like the damsel in distress that I am, I hide my bloody knuckle behind my back. A smile, this one genuine, lights up my face. Derrick and Oskar are standing just over the threshold —whatever it is I've done has broken the spell.

"I'm free?" My voice catches as a sob threatens to exit my throat. "I'm done . . .At last, my trials are over."

My shoulders sag as I bury my face in Derrick's shoulder. His body stiffens underneath mine, and I know I shouldn't do anything that would play into his fantasies.

"You'll have to fill me in on the details of your trial later, Mal." Derrick can't be too mad at me still. "Let's get you some food first."

I nod into his chest. Food first and then to the castle.

I'm going home.

CHAPTER THIRTY-SEVEN
MALLORY

Whatever I expected of Elvarn, it wasn't this. The capital is not a city at all—just Castle Thirawen. There is no fortress surrounding the cool, white walls, and no moat either. It is just . . . a building. One whose doors you can walk right up to. I know Oskar said things have been sparse here since the Sundering, but I would have expected a guard or two. At least a magic barrier of sorts.

We slip right through with no resistance.

A breath escapes me as I drink in the sight. Every inch of the castle is made of solid white marble with gold veining. While it's not in its prime, Thirawen is a piece of art nonetheless. Ornamental vases of contrasting gold and black marble adorn every corner, and dusty paintings of kings and queens of old line the walls.

Derrick sizes up the room, much in the same manner as me—I can see the shock I feel plainly written across his face. The juxtaposition between his appearance and his father's is almost comical. Oskar is unfazed, bored even, at this beauty.

I hope I never look at this place like that.

"Welcome, Your Majesty, to Castle Thirawen, the seat of the power of Elvarn that governs Nalara." A butler bows before gesturing around the main hall. "We are honored to be in the presence of the highest prophesied heir."

I look around at the smattering of servants that occupy the foyer, each pair farther apart than the previous two. Perhaps they are trying to make the space look less empty, but all they succeed in is reminding me how much I have to build.

"Please," I say, "call me Mallory. I am not your queen until I have taken the crown."

The butler bows and turns to Oskar. "Sir Alborian, we have prepared your old living quarters. Will your son be accompanying you?" He glances at Derrick, then at me. "Or will the two of you require a room together?"

Derrick's ears perk up, and I nearly choke.

"No." I clear my throat and say with force. "I will very much be sleeping alone, thank you."

"Very well, Your Majesty." He catches the look on my face and hesitantly adjusts. "I mean, Mallory. Perhaps you would like to get acquainted with your new home. Please allow your attendant to show you about the castle."

At that, he waves over a young girl, probably not much older than fourteen. Orange markings decorate her pale, mint-green skin. They look to be some sort of tribal symbol, though different from the markings of Wolfric's tattoos. I make a mental note to ask about them later, as surely they carry some kind of cultural significance.

The girl bows.

"Your Majesty, it would be my honor to escort you to your chambers. Would you care to first explore the dining hall—you must be in need of sustenance from your long journey?"

Thankfully we had been able to find a small cafe in Pryveth that had been able to serve the three of us before we'd left for Elvarn. In the one-hour trip to Castle Thirawen, I had not found myself in need of food or water

"No, thank you. I smile at the girl. "What is your name?"

"I'm Ivy, Your Majesty."

"Ivy, how is it that I have an attendant already? Surely you couldn't have possibly known of my coming, nor prepared for it on a skeleton crew in a few weeks' time if you had?"

"I come from a long line of Lirae, a species not too different from the Nalarans—although you've undoubtedly noticed my skin."

I dip my head, both in understanding and as a silent bid to continue.

"In Liraen society, there is a group of children in every generation called the Lineth that are hand-chosen by the Hollowborne. Each new generation is taught to be in service to the Crown and the Order by their mothers. This practice has extended as far back as the prophecy itself."

She dips her head in her in return, a symbol of submission. A question forms on my lips but is just as soon pulled away by my mentor's voice.

"The Lirae is a matriarchal society. The prophecy speaks of a female heir and, despite the past kings of Nalara, they believe that prophecy grants superiority to women. In their culture, only women are permitted the honor of service to the monarchy. Men are relegated to second-class citizens only good for their life-giving . . . elixir." Oskar looks down on Ivy, uncomfortable to be sharing this knowledge—though I doubt it's nothing she hasn't heard time and again.

"Yes, Your Majesty. Sir Alborian is correct. I was a chosen Lineth from birth, the youngest in the class. When you arrived in Nalara, the Oracle himself plucked me from among the ranks. I do not know what I did to deserve the honor, but I am forever grateful for it."

"And you're a servant?" My words float from my mouth with as much care as possible. Much of my career was spent in serving others; I understand the implication.

"Not exactly—" The girl hesitates over her words with a slight air of offense. She would never speak on it, of course, with me being the soon-to-be high queen and all. "What I do is more important than simple servitude. I am your right hand, and will die a hero among my people."

There is a look in her eyes that alludes to seeing more—doing more—than she's let on.

"Ivy, tell me . . . why did they choose you?"

"I swear it is true when I say I do not know. I am nothing—no one—special. There were five of us in my generation, as with all generations before us. I am the first and only of my kind."

The reason why is obvious—there is only one of me. Only one heir. And, unless something happens to Ivy, only one attendant is needed. Would it be impolite of me to ask if the program will continue to exist?

"The rest of my class will retire with a place of honor on their twenty-fifth birthdays and, when they do, will live the rest of their days wealthy and cared for on the island."

The Chosen One has to work for the rest of her life, but everyone else gets nobility? How is that fair?

"And the Oracle selected you himself?"

"The Oracle only conveys the Hollowborne's message. And, of course, the Hollowborne receive their instruction from the Twinned Trees. I have been chosen by the Creators themselves to remain in service to you, the Shadowbearer—the bringer of peace."

A knot forms in my throat, threatening to choke me. All eyes are on me, adding to the pressure the prophecy presents. My hands grow clammy contemplating that every move going forward will be scrutinized by the court. Saving the whole of Nalara is one thing, but saving little Ivy? That's an entirely different form of responsibility.

Sensing my anxiety, like she is likely highly trained to do, Ivy steers the conversation in a different direction. "Are you ready to go see your chambers?"

"Yes." I am breathless once more. "Please lead the way."

The staircases, not unlike everything else in the castle, are a thing of beauty. There is one on either side, leading to a large hallway at the top. The lavishness screams of nobility, echoing something I saw in a princess movie as a child. I follow Ivy's careful footsteps as she ascends the right staircase, careful not to ruin the gold runner that shines underfoot.

We make our way past several landings to the top floor. There are no hallways that connect here. Just one wooden door, painted gold. Carved into the door are the Twinned Trees, their roots inter-twining at their base as the trees sit in opposition to one another. The Ash's leaves extend upward, beckoning to the sky above. The Willow is upside down, its leaves defying gravity, yet pointed with just as much purpose to the unseen sun. In the branches of the Ash, a crown is carved, a stoic reminder of its duty toward justice. At the bottom of the door, hidden within the Willow's foliage, a bird. A dove. *My* dove.

My mind flashes back to my childhood room where Nana gave me the dove keychain—an odd gift for an eight-year-old. I get it now. My grandmother knew of the prophecy, which means she knew about this door. She knew I would come.

"Would you like to see inside?" Ivy asks, ripping me away from my thoughts.

"Yes," I breathe.

She steps forward and slides an intricately shaped golden key into the lock, and with a turn of her wrist the lock mechanism clicks into place. She opens the door and I step into the most ostenta-tiously fabricated room I have ever had the pleasure to lay my eyes on. My room has its own sitting room, larger than Vanessa's entire apartment. Plush couches of deep, rich purple tones envelop a coffee table perhaps larger in surface area than my parent's dining table.

I've never been the type to dream for fancy things—they've always been out of my reach. Wishing for what you can never feasibly acquire is a fruitless endeavor.

A giddy giggle escapes my lips, one that I am glad Derrick and Oskar aren't here to witness. Ivy will need to be made aware of the discretion I expect in my chambers, if she isn't already.

Moving past the sitting room and down the hallway where I am greeted with three separate doors, I push open the one on the far wall, directly at the end of the hall. Welcoming me is a bedroom similar in size to the sitting room. Why a single bedroom needs to be the size of a small apartment, I cannot say. A large, circular bed sits in the center of the room, adorned with golden sheets and more pillows than imaginable.

The next room contains a bathroom that, while sparse in its furnishings, matches the grandiosity of the rest of the suite. A large claw-foot tub big enough for at least two stands as the focal point. Other than that, there is a toilet, which is a bit rudimentary in design comparatively, but painted with gold foliage. A large basin serves as the sink, above which is a mirror that is much larger than could ever be necessary.

But it's the third room that truly takes my breath away—it is nothing but an oversized walk-in closet. There are full shelving units, and a table in the center with drawers, reminiscent of something one would find in a lingerie store on Earth. A chaise lounge, soft and fluffy, sits next to a dress form wearing a sparkly gown.

"Wow." For the second time today, I am left breathless.

This is a real-life fairy tale castle.

The trials of the Witherwalk seem far away now.

"Isn't it wonderful?" Ivy asks from the doorway. Having been deeply enraptured with my surroundings, I had forgotten she was here.

"This room is beautiful. It looks like something out of a movie."

"What's 'the movie'?"

I giggle at her at her well-meaning ignorance. "Never mind, it's just an Earth thing."

A flash of curiosity crosses her face but she dutifully remains silent. This is the perfect opportunity to establish some goodwill between myself and my attendant. She is obligated by birthright to be here, that doesn't mean she shouldn't want to be too.

"Would you like to hear more about it? Earth?" I ask the child staring up at me with pleading eyes.

"Yes, more than anything. What's it like?"

For a moment, I am left contemplating her question. A child shouldn't know of the horrors of war, famine, rape, and political espionage . . . but she isn't just any child. It is likely she grew up with knowledge of the Sundering and its genocidal implications. Still, it's better to only give her the best parts.

"It's a lot different than this—more advanced in many ways, though I suppose there was a time it very closely resembled Nalara in its infrastructure and lack of technology."

"Technology?"

"Movies are an example. They are plays that are trapped forever within . . . a painting of sorts. You can watch the same play with the same actors in the comfort of your bed, whenever you'd like."

"What magic produces those?"

The corners of my lips quirk as I try to hold back a smile. Ivy's naivety and wonder at what has become mundane to me is endearing.

"There is no magic on Earth. It's all science that has propelled us so far forward; everything is in perpetual motion. And everyone works most hours of most days for most of their lives. I'm really coming to appreciate the slowness of Nalara."

"How did they get by without magic?" Her head cocks to the side, with a sincerity only a child could have.

"Well, we don't really know that it's missing. There are some who practice witchcraft and call on old deities, but most people take that to be nothing more than silly superstition."

"Wow. How many deities? Surely it can't be more than just your founding trees."

Another smile threatens my lips. "There are thousands of deities that millions of people worship. There are monotheistic religions, those that focus on a singular God, and each of them think their idea of God is the only correct idea of God. But there is not a single person on Earth that possesses the truth. Not like here."

Ivy's brow furrows, but she doesn't ask any clarifying questions.

"It is a very different kind of life than having proof of your Creator." My voice catches with an emotion dredged up from the depths of my childhood.

"Thank you for telling me, Your Majesty."

"You're welcome, Ivy."

CHAPTER THIRTY-EIGHT
OSKAR

Mallory took the transition quite well. By her account, she had done a wonderful job in her last trial and she took pride in her performance. The greatest outcome of which is my being back in my home, the one whose presence I can never forget. Every detail, corridor, and missing speck of mortar is still fresh in my mind after all these years.

Derrick is not as eager as I am to be here, it seems. He was given a modest, but comfortable, suite in the servant's quarters—at Mallory's behest. Knowing my son as I do, his reluctance to his chamber's modesty surprises me. Perhaps his sister has rubbed off on him quite a lot more than either of us anticipated or realized.

The council chambers are untouched by the cruel hand of time, with both thrones exactly where they've always stood. Of course, my seat beside the king's throne has long since been removed. No matter, another will replace it beside the queen shortly. Derrick enters the room with a quiet discretion, much like every room he has entered in the castle thus far.

"My boy, I am happy to finally have the opportunity to show you where I spent so much of my life. Soon, you will see me hard at work as Voice of the Hollow once more."

"I'm happy for you, Dad."

He tries to smile, but his body betrays him. His fingers twitch, trying to find a place to settle, his anxiety evident from the way he shifts his weight from foot to foot. He will never admit his troubles to me, but a parent always knows.

"Relax, son. Everything is going according to plan. We are here at the capital, and Mallory will make a speech to the Order where she will prove her worth as queen."

"And what if they reject her? What then?"

"They won't, you have my word. Having been a member of the Order at one point, I was groomed for exactly this."

"What changed?"

My expression remains neutral. He isn't ready yet to know the secret I've kept from him all these years.

"Life had other plans for me—my faith wavered and I was unable to perform the tasks necessary to service the Twinned Path. That is all behind me now."

He studies me quietly, waiting for me to say more, though he knows I won't. Everything he has ever learned of Nalara has been at my will. Questions are usually left unanswered.

"Okay, Dad, but it has been a long time since you've been here —longer even since you've known them. Your sway might not be as powerful as you think."

"Maybe not" I smirk. "But I do know their core tenants. Those haven't changed in nearly a millennia. And I know how to write a compelling speech."

"You're not going to let her write it herself? Surely, that is what will be expected."

"I will merely guide her in the way she should go. There is no margin for error—we need her on the throne."

CHAPTER THIRTY-NINE
MALLORY

Derrick and Oskar are embroiled in a heated discussion upon me entering the council chambers. The click of my heels on the solid marble floors alerts them of my presence.

"Wow, Mallory, I . . . You clean up nice."

Through whatever magic exists in Nalara, my gown fits like a glove, gently caressing my breasts in a way I know is attractive. Under any other circumstances, I would be beaming with pride at the compliment. But not this one.

"Thank you," I said to my brother. "You seem shocked. But you haven't really gotten a chance to see me try."

"I guess when you're traveling across the country on foot you really have no use for a ball gown and heels."

His observation makes me chuckle. The old Mallory would never have believed she would walk as many miles as I have simply to play dress-up in a castle. And before her coronation, no less. There isn't a bone in my body that feels natural about this, despite my adoration for my clothing.

"You look lovely, my dear," Oskar says to me.

Bowing at the waist, I give him a half-hearted curtsy. There was no reason on Earth for me to ever be this formal. The more I learn about this place, and my role in it, the more foreign it feels.

"Well," Oskar interrupts, clapping his hands together. "We must make preparations for your meeting with the Order."

A grim nod is all I can manage.

It looks like playtime is over.

"Yes. Of course, that is the next task. Tell me what you need me to do."

"The Order will be here in three days' time, the customary timeframe for any noble upon the completion of the Witherwalk. You will be expected to craft a speech befitting a ruler regarding what you've learned and the impact of the journey. Ideally this would have been completed prior to the trials, however, given your . . . unique . . . circumstances, we will be short on time."

Shit.

The last time I attempted public speaking, it had not gone well. My age had played a factor, as I had been a sophomore in high school, but more than that, my speech had been wholly inadequate. And that had been written months prior and edited frequently.

There is no way I can do this.

"Don't worry, my dear," Oskar says, reading the worry on my face. "Despite never having written a Witherwalk speech, I have a great deal of knowledge on the subject, and the libraries are filled with every deliverance that has passed the lips of a ruler since the dawn of the Twinned Trees."

"Thank you, Oskar." His offer humbles me. There is no way through this without him, that much is abundantly clear.

The three of us leave the chambers and adjourn to the dining hall. Having opted to be shown straight to my suite, I had yet to discover the hall. With Ivy attending to other matters at my request, Derrick and Oskar lead the way, making me feel utterly inept. Servants, roughly six or so, can be seen dashing through the halls about their business. Despite the discrepancy in staffing size, my mind wanders back to my stay in Liriwyn. This time, though, it's real. That's what I'm choosing to believe, anyway. My dream magic has proven my incapability of differentiating dreams from reality anymore.

I can't even trust what I'm seeing.

Bloomhall's dining room had been adorned in a substantially different manner than this. Where Thalion had one long, grandiose table fit to paint a tableau, Thirawen's hall resembles a fine dining establishment more than a castle. Round tables, clothed with thick white linen and surrounded by plush, purple, oversized wingback chairs are strategically placed around the room.

Looking for any indication of where I am meant to sit, I find none. There is no head table unmistakenly reserved for the Crown or tucked away into an obscure corner. Not that I mind dining with everyone else, I am just unsure what the impropriety of seating myself will convey. As queen, my every move will be calculated.

Don't let them see you falter.

Oskar gestures for the both of us to join him at a table closest to the window.

Good taste, Oskar.

"Do we . . . just sit anywhere?" My hesitancy is evident in my voice, making me sound as weak as I feel.

Oskar's mouth hooks upward.

"Yes, we just sit anywhere. That is to say, anywhere that is not already occupied." He laughs at his own joke.

Smiling politely, I tug on the chair to Oskar's immediate left. His back is to the window—he's missing the view, though I'm sure he's grown weary of seeing the mountain peaks over the forest of evergreen trees. Surely, one would expect they'd miss it after so long away. Oskar, however, doesn't strike me as one to have ever enjoyed it.

Derrick takes the seat across from me. Something in his appearance gives me pause. He seems reluctant at my being here despite his insistence that I come.

"What's wrong?" I ask.

"Nothing," he mumbles.

"You can't lie to me, Derrick. It's written all over your face; there is something irritating you."

"It just . . . doesn't feel the way I'd hoped." He runs his hand through his hair with a sigh.

"Yeah, I understand," I admit. "Not having had the luxury of bedtime stories about the palace my whole life, I was left to my own imagination. Thirawen exceeds my expectations in every conceivable way, but I can imagine why it doesn't live up to yours."

He gives me a pointed look, one that's laced with offense.

"No, it isn't that." He makes a face. "Something feels *wrong*. I thought I would feel different—like I'd accomplished something by escorting the legendary heir to her throne. But I just feel hollow."

"Well," I huff, unfolding my napkin onto my lap, "my journey is of no concern to you any longer. And, for what it's worth, *I* feel great about it."

He nods half-heartedly, not meeting my eyes.

"Let's eat!" Oskar breaks the tension. "I'm starving, and we will all need our strength for tomorrow."

The three of us dine leisurely—the first time in all our journey where we've had nowhere else to be. No plans for scavenging food or building a fire to prepare for the grueling miles-long walk we'd take after a pitiful night's rest. It is finally time for me to sit and enjoy the presence of the company in which I find myself. Perhaps it is in these moments that I will come to finally learn where our kinship lies.

A small, spritely girl, looking a few years younger than Ivy, waits on us. She is struck by my presence, clambering over herself to speak the next word. It hits me briefly as she talks, the age of her servitude. Surely her and Ivy are the exceptions. Or perhaps Nalarans reach adulthood at much younger ages than I'm accustomed to. Either way, it is something I plan to look into after my coronation.

When dinner is finished, I retire to my chambers, eager to sleep on a mattress for the first time in weeks—who would have guessed I'd miss my hand-me-down twin mattress?

Tomorrow we begin writing my speech, Oskar and I. Something about this process feels juvenile—like a class project. But if this is what is demanded of the High Queen of Nalara, this is what she shall do.

After a long soak in the claw-foot tub, I slip into the most luxurious silk pajamas of my dreams. They are even purple—my favorite color. Despite multiple clothing changes, it still shocks me that these clothes are perfectly tailored to my measurements. Some deep-seeded insecurity told me the clothing would all be designed for someone much smaller than me. A stereotypical princess.

Crawling into my massive, larger-than-king-size bed, I find a comfortable position propped between mountains of pillows. Like a toddler crawling into mommy and daddy's bed after a bad dream, I relax, and sleep comes quickly.

I'm standing at the podium in the council room, waiting to give my speech. The room is empty, the Order should be here by now.

Climbing down from my lectern, I approach the open doorway. A tapping sounds at the window. Trying to ignore it, my hand reaches for the now-closed door's knob, ready to start the search for my audience.

Locked.

With no other option, I turn and tiptoe toward the sound at the window. Drawing back the illustrious velvet curtain reveals a small dove, helplessly and repeatedly flying into the pane.

Dreaming about doves is a good omen.

Now open, the dove flies through the window, circling the room's perimeter.

Once.

Twice.

Three ti—the bird drops mid-lap with no warning. As if it has swallowed stones and suddenly anchored itself to the floor.

My feet move faster than I think possible in a dream, but I am too late. It's dead.

Grief for this animal seems arbitrary. Flying inside was a dangerous feat for it to undergo, though I can't tell if it knew that. And three laps? This bird was going to die anyway.

A heavy fog rolls in over the distant mountain range, heading right for the castle. The sweet scent of peaches fill the air, carried on the wings of the billowing fog. Its shade is somewhere between a dark purple and an emerald green—if it weren't so ominous, it would be beautiful.

My hands fumble with the window clasps as the fog barrels ever closer, gaining momentum by the second. With the window finally latched and the curtain back in place, I turn to finish my original task. I have to speak to the Order.

As soon as my back is facing the window, another rapping sounds on the glass.

They're looking for shelter—whatever the fog is, is killing them.

Deftly, I pull back the curtain once more and find another dove looking for sanctuary. In a sweeping motion, I throw open the window to let this one in, praying to the Trees for its safety. My prayers, not for the first time, prove fruitless. As soon as it enters, this dove, too, inexplicably drops dead in midair. The body of the first is nowhere to be found.

Before I can make it back to the door, the pungent odor of stone fruit fills the room, choking me. The fog is thick, almost impossible to see or breathe.

I am left wheezing as smoke fills my lungs.

CHAPTER FORTY
MALLORY

Jolting awake with a gasp, a hearty cough escapes my chest as I hack on the taste of peaches. My door swings open.

"Your Highness—" Ivy's voice slips in through the cracks of early morning light. "Are you alright? Did something happen?"

What is she doing in my chambers this early?

"Ivy," I manage when my breathing returns, "I'm fine. Sometimes my dreams bleed into my waking hours."

She gasps knowingly. "Right. You are a Somnara, aren't you?"

Nodding, my hand still rests on my chest, hoping to recover oxygen—or whatever exists in Nalara's atmosphere— back into my now shaking body.

"If it would please Her Majesty," she says slowly, like she is scared to offend, "I can procure for you a potion to stop your dreams."

What good is sleep without dreams?

"No, thank you, Ivy. Your generosity does not go unnoticed. It means more than you realize that you would care to see me comforted—duty or no. If you don't mind, I need to rest."

Before she can respond, my hands gesture a shooing motion. It's not polite, but the constraints of politeness don't hold as tightly to a queen. Ivy curtsies deeply and backs out of the room, never breaking eye contact.

Despite Ivy's retreat, sleep does not come again. Parts of me are nagging to decipher the meaning of last night's dream, screaming for secrets to be uncovered. Oskar may be able to help. He seems to know dream magic better than most, despite not having it himself. In fairness, he understands almost everything better than most.

It dawns on me that, in all this time, I haven't bothered to ask what Oskar's magic is. Or if he even has any. Those of us born from the Willow's bloodline are more inherently magically inclined, but the line of the Ash tree still bears some magical fruit.

It's at least twenty minutes before my pulse slows and my mind has the freedom to drift elsewhere. In forty-eight hours, I must recite a currently unwritten speech. Somewhere deep within the heart of the castle, I imagine Oskar and I will spend the day sequestered away, doing nothing but drafting my words through careful consideration. Now that we've reached Elvarn, it is likely Derrick will make himself scarce.

As far as he is concerned, I am no longer any of his business. Oskar's judgment about keeping our mother secret from Derrick may have been wiser than I'd thought. If these are the actions of a friend, how much more scrutiny would come from a brother?

Swinging my legs to the ground, I feel the sensation of cold wood under my feet. Unlike the rest of the palace and its barren, foreboding walls and floors, my apartments are more inviting—more like a real home. After only a few days, moving from this place would be a heartbreak of the worst kind, should it ever get to that.

"Ivy!" I call out to the sitting room, testing to see if the girl is still here.

How could she have possibly known of my nightmare?

"Ivy?" I call for her again.

No answer.

This matter can wait . . . for now. Pushing my questions from my mind, I take myself to the closet and dress for the day. In Nalara, it seems, pants of any sort are frowned upon for women. Which doesn't seem unexpected. There are, however, a pair of black leather stockings and a simple brown tunic hidden away in the back corner. Dresses are certainly beautiful, but pants are forever more practical.

Due to the time of day—pre-dawn—there is no way to be certain if breakfast will be ready by the time I arrive downstairs. If there is a wait for food, I'll explore instead. Arriving in the dining room, my suspicions are confirmed. There is a plain wooden door tucked into the corner at the back of the banquet hall, inconspicuously allowing access to the servant's wing.

Individual rooms down the servant's hall act as coordinated pantries for various food items. Some hold grains, like rice and barley, while others hold fruits and vegetables. There is even one fashioned into something like a walk-in freezer. Like everything else, it is powered by magic and not electricity.

What other magics are Nalarans capable of?

It dawns on me once more that I know very little of the magic systems here—I barely understand my own powers. Which tree is responsible for the magic necessary for daily tasks? One would assume by their very natures that it would be Selowen. The magic of Selowen worshippers seems far superior to the Asharil. But if that were the case, surely the Emberguard wouldn't hold all the power.

The warm smell of something wonderful leads me down the hallway and into the kitchen. A robust woman, looking everything like one would expect from a typical chef, is busy at work cracking eggs. Standing in the doorway, I watch her movements. That is, until she glances up and catches me in the act.

"Now who are you then?" she asks, her accent indicating she is not from this region. I can't place it from any city on my travels, though I have yet to see even a map of Nalara.

There is so much I have to learn.

"Oh." Her brusque attitude startles me. "I'm Mallory."

"Mallory . . ." She waves the empty eggshell in her hands, and a bit of its snot runs onto the counter.

I'm taken aback by her question. Surely everyone in the castle knows who I am.

"Sorry, Mallory Nerezza," I say, hoping to clear up her confusion.

The chef stares at me like she's waiting for more.

"And what are you doing here, *Mallory Nerezza*?"

"Breakfast wasn't ready, so I thought I'd further explore my castle, being the future queen and all." There's an attitude in my voice I know I shouldn't give on the first meeting, but this woman works for me and is already challenging me.

She looks me up and down, haughty judgment shining in her eyes.

"Well you're not queen yet, are you?"

"No." My cool reply accepts her challenge.

"Then you are not to be in my kitchen."

"And," I ask, "once it's my kitchen?"

Pushing past my own question, I continue. "Actually . . . since I am the heir to the throne, am I not heir to the castle—and all that's in it—as well?"

A scowl crosses her face, but whatever she thinks of me is her business. Though I doubt it's pleasant. Right now, I must maintain my rank in front of the other servants milling in and out of the room.

"No matter. I will leave at your request. You may think you have the upper hand here, but I can assure you, you don't. Fear and control are no way to govern."

On my way out the door I add, "But don't think I won't use them if necessary."

With that, I exit completely, this time from a different door than the one I entered. Another hallway adjoins the kitchen, this one leading to the servant's quarters. Derrick's room should be around here somewhere. The thought pastes a silly grin across my face.

Good. He can't possibly get in my way from down here.

The hallway leads to another set of servant's stairs, which deposit me in the middle of a grand foyer. A ballroom and my council chambers connect here, like a miniature entrance hall.

Vastly different from the woodsy, tangled supports of Bloomhall, stark-white Romanesque columns standing strong in each of the four corners of the room. Admiring architecture is a favorite pastime of my mother's, and the thought of her causes a panging in my chest. She may have lied to me about my existence and allowed me to feel responsible for my ostracization back home, but she is still my mother.

Miss you, Mama.

While what I experienced in Liriwyn will haunt me forever, my appreciation for nature as a form of decor can be attributed to that illusion. A redecorating may be in order post-coronation.

Hoping to find any form of greenery, I resolve myself to explore the gardens after breakfast—and, of course, after speech writing. As an ineloquent orator, this *presentation* will be the last of its kind in my tenure as queen. Oskar will suffice to handle any future announcements.

Breakfast comes and goes, and Oskar and I find ourselves huddled together in the library, piles of books scattered on the tables and floor surrounding us. It is his belief that I must learn as much as I can today regarding Nalaran history. We need to find a leader who inspires me—one whose ideals I can replicate before the Oracle and the rest of the Order.

Of the six we've studied, none have piqued my interest.

"No matter, we have one hundred and fourteen more to go. You will surely find someone who resonates with you, even slightly."

The mother tongue of Nalara, Sylvaneth, was all that had been spoken before the Crown was established. For centuries, no one had ruled the land, and harmony had existed. All creatures had been one. When the Brothers had established the Sacred Texts—which have since been hidden in catacombs under the castle—each religion fought for dominance over the Twinned Path.

Those who believed in Asharil hoped to gain afterlife through its fiery judgment, as promised in the Ashen Doctrine. Selowen worshippers, on the other hand, saw introspection as the true enlightenment. When the two halves were merged, the Brothers assembled their closest alliances to form the Order. To remain in harmony, the Order created the Crown. And, since its inception, the Order, and, to a greater extent, the Hollowborne, have hand-selected each monarch.

One of these rulers has to appeal to me eventually.

"Anything yet, Mallory?" Oskar asks as I close the book on the fifty-sixth queen, Julinera the Gentle.

"Not yet, Oskar. You said it yourself, there are a plethora of rulers, the odds are in our favor. And, if not, I already have a few that might be worth settling for, if need be."

"Yes, I said that hours ago, but our time is quickly dwindling. In your studies, I am confident you have uncovered the importance of the Order in this process. We must respect tradition, or risk giving up the Crown."

"How can they do that? I am prophesied to sit on the throne. Isn't this all a formality?"

"Yes, my dear, you are destined to bring peace to our nation. But even what is fated must be earned."

My shoulders bristle at his tone. If he notices, he makes no comment.

"Now, Mallory, you must focus . . . please."

"Yes, sir," I grumble.

Spending the next two hours researching every monarch since the formation of the Hollow Crown, I get a small sense of how long Nalaran live. In the millennia since its founding, there have only existed so many rulers—the crown extending their lifetimes exponentially with its power. Some ruled for thousands upon thousands of years, while others merely centuries. No one knows how long the crown will grant its wearer life.

At one point in the process, early on, I had prematurely selected the fifteenth king, but in an effort to exhaust all my options, Oskar insisted I continue my research. Unsurprisingly, he was right. After extensively reading about each of the one hundred and twenty rulers, I select the seventy-third High Queen of Nalara.

"Are you *sure*?" Oskar questions me. "Queen Veyrissa?"

"Yes." Indignation escapes in my tone. "You asked me to choose who I would like to emulate. It is her, above all else."

"You may feel her to be a kindred spirit." He looks tired. "And, be that as it may, that was not wholly your task. It is important that the royal you wish to emulate be well respected and beloved."

"Queen Veyrissa *is* who I respect the most. Her reign, although short, was impactful to the Nalaran people." I slam the book shut, ready to defend my position to my mentor.

"Do you, perhaps, mean queen Veyrintha? It's an easy mistake to make."

His question does not deserve a response. Instead, it elicits an eye roll from me. If I were to argue on whether or not I mean what I say I mean, we would continue our back-and-forth for a while, which would only prove to be useless.

"It is time to begin writing." The words escape my lips before Oskar has a chance to inquire again. "Let us start with a few questions of mine regarding the requirements for this oration. How long must this take to present and how will Veyrissa fit within its context?"

"Well"—Oskar clears his throat—"it should be as long as necessary. You must tell your story, and the lessons it's taught you."

I chuckle at that. "My story can fill a book. That will not be happening when I am on the podium. Provide to me, if you will, a condensed version of what I *must* include." The weight of my upper half leans forward from my elbows, squarely placed on the table as I look up at the old man.

"Let them *see* you. Let them recognize your labor in service of the Crown and, ultimately, of the Sacred Trees. Use . . . Veyrissa's . . . story to express your future intentions as queen."

Smiling at him in response, I ask, "That wasn't so hard, was it?"

Over the next few hours, I draft and redraft my document until it meets Oskar's expectations. It takes him a while to accept, and even longer to become nominally okay with Veyrissa the Ardent as my chosen role model. We get something halfway passable on paper by the time dinner is served.

CHAPTER FORTY-ONE
DERRICK

Mallory and my father spent the whole of yesterday tucked away in the library, working on her presentation. Neither party invited me to participate, not that I'm sure I would have gone anyway.

Most of my day is spent in the servant's quarters, getting to know those who work and live with me. Being relegated to the basement will not deter my resolve to be of service to the prophecy. Mallory did not explicitly delegate me to servitude, but there is no doubt in my mind she wants me as far from her as possible.

In the kitchen, I came across the cook. She is a lovely woman with a rough, yet beautiful, exterior. The kind of person who knows who they are and won't let anyone tell them otherwise. That's something I appreciate in a woman.

"Do you need any help?" My hands rest on the counter beside her cutting board as I lean over to inspect her work.

"No, thank you." She beams up at me as she chops a flurry of vegetables.

"You sure? I've always wanted to learn how to cook. Now that I'm stuck down here, you might as well put me to good use."

"Alright then, wash your hands." She points to the sink with the tip of her knife without looking up. A small smile forms on her lips, but I ignore it. If she'd wanted to me to notice, she'd have looked at me.

She proceeds to demonstrate her technique for chopping onions cleanly, and even goes so far as to teach me to julienne carrots.

"What are we making?" I ask as she grabs a parsnip from a pile and places it on her cutting board.

"Just my world-famous vegetable soup for *Her Highness*."

Chef notices my bristling at Mallory's name, but asks no questions.

"I know she's a friend of yours and all, but I had a run in with her in this kitchen that left a bad taste in my mouth." She glances over at me to gauge my reaction, knife still in motion. "There's something about her that doesn't sit right with me—acting like she already owns the place."

"Yeah," I grumble my agreement. "I don't know what's gotten into her lately. She wasn't like this before."

Chef pauses and points her knife at me. "Maybe she was, and she's never had a reason to show it. Power corrupts, that's true, but it also illuminates the already corrupt."

Is it possible this is Mallory's true identity hidden beneath the surface? The bigger question, I suppose, is whether or not Mallory herself is aware of how she's acting. Maybe she just doesn't know what she's doing.

CHAPTER FORTY-TWO
DERRICK

After my run-in with the chef yesterday, it took longer than I expected to come to terms with her assessment of Mallory. Before all this, before the trials, Mallory was awkward and non-confrontational. Now she picks a fight like she expects everyone to treat her a certain way. Maybe she thinks she deserves it. And, maybe she's right, but I can't let her go that easily.

A future between us is out of the question. She's made it abundantly clear that, for whatever reason, I am not who she wants. She's made her choice, and I have to respect it. What I can't respect is my father's obsession with sitting back and watching her ruin herself. It isn't fair to Mal to play with her like she's a pawn in whatever game he's playing.

Weeks ago, before all this started, before I frequented Java Central to keep an eye on our high queen, my father came to me. He was so excited to have found the woman he was looking for.

"I found her!" He'd come barging into my apartment on a Sunday afternoon. Normally, I kept the door locked, but my roommate, Ned, had gone out to grab a six-pack at the local corner store.

"What?" I pulled my headphones from my ears and looked up at him. "Dad! Where's your cane?"

"Don't bother with that now, my boy, I came over here to tell you as soon as I learned the news. We found her!"

I remember thinking my dad was losing his mind, that maybe it was time to send him to some sort of inpatient treatment. Not that I could afford it.

"Who, Dad? Who did you find?"

"The heir!"

He stood in front of me like he was hoping I'd jump up and join in his celebration.

Turning off the TV and standing for whatever medical emergency he was having, I asked one more time, "Who, Dad? What heir? You're not making any sense."

"The heir to the Hollow Crown . . . she's here!"

It took hours of convincing for Dad to get me to believe his fairy tale. I hadn't even realized he'd been searching for anyone. Either way, I had to check her out to make sure both she and my dad were safe.

Weeks later, I was officially on board with the plan.

"Now, son, she is the key to peace in Nalara. We must make sure she is crowned, or the rest of the prophecy won't fall into place as it is meant."

"How do we do that?"

"We must aid her through the Witherwalk and through her bid for the Crown. After she is accepted by the Order, we can move on to Phase Two."

Phase Two, my father explained, I would learn once the coronation had taken place.

This morning is as good a time as any to try to catch up with Mallory before her speech. Her attendant, Ivy, who seems to not be with her much, is standing idly in the middle of the small foyer at the top of the servant's stairs. As a young girl, much younger than most of the staff, she keeps to herself.

"Hi, Ivy," I say as I approach.

She smiles at me with a curt nod and continues looking forward. As a friend of the future queen, I've noticed much of the staff holding me to a higher regard, despite the fact that my room is next door to theirs.

"Ivy, can you help me?"

"Yes, Sir Alborian. What do you need?"

Heat flushes over my cheeks as I grimace. "Please, Ivy, just call me Derrick."

She nods again, this time looking at me. Her arms, once held clasped in front of her, relax now.

"Okay, Derrick. How can I help?"

"I haven't gotten a chance to speak with Mallory since arriving. Her and my father will likely get started on their speech writing, but I want to catch her before they do."

Ivy's face drops, looking like a long-forgotten pet puppy left out in the rain.

"She asked me to show her the room where her crown is being kept. When we got there, she ordered me to inform your father and return to the foyer to await further instructions."

"I don't think she meant that you just had to stand here."

"As a Lineth, I must do exactly what my queen commands."

Poor, young Ivy, having been groomed into servitude her entire life. It would be an insult for Mallory to deny her services, but I can't imagine my friend would feel right having someone attend to her every need. She probably thinks she isn't deserving.

"Thanks, Ivy. I'll go look for her." Turning back a few feet away, I say, "Give her a chance—she'll likely surprise you."

Outside the crown room, I watch from the doorway as Mallory leans over the glass case holding the crown. Something in the air keeps me from entering the room, some unseen promise that what I need to know can be found from the hallway.

Her eyes study the crown, moving back and forth to each point. The crown itself is unlike anything I've ever seen. It is not opulent like the rest of the jewels lining the room, though its simplicity speaks volumes. Entwined twigs from both trees wrap around to form a circle, fashioned in such a way that it resembles its golden counterparts.

This seems like the Mal I know, breath taken away by the natural juxtaposing the ornate. Her hands stroke the glass protecting the crown longingly. Soon that crown will sit on her pretty red hair and maybe then the girl I know will come back.

"Beautiful, isn't it?" My father's unmistakable voice fills the room before he emerges from the opposite entrance.

I duck back in the doorway, hiding only out of instinct.

"Magnificent," Mallory whispers, looking at her mentor. "It's like it *knows* I'm here. I can feel its power calling to me."

A twinkle forms in my father's eye. "Ahh, that is exactly what I'd hoped to hear when Ivy told me where to find you."

He props his cane against the glass and places his hands on Mallory's shoulders from behind. "In two days, you will earn this crown, and shortly after, I will place it on your head. It will be my greatest honor in life, a moment I have hoped for since learning of your identity. Nothing matters more to me than this."

The two embrace and my father ushers the future high queen out the door with a smile. He didn't know I was here when he said those things. It wasn't just for show.

Curiosity getting the better of me, I tiptoe into the crown room. My father and Mallory should be halfway to their destination by now, but I don't want them to come back and think I'd been spying. Still, I *had* been spying, and I need to see what it is that compelled me to do so.

Every step toward the crown makes my stomach curdle. A nausea-induced sweat slicks my back and palms as I try to grab on to the glass. Almost doubled over in pain, I look at the crown. From this close I can see how gnarled and jagged the branches are, how little they mesh. The twigs are loosely intertwined like the wood itself is fighting, separating at the seams.

Flashes of memories that aren't mine enter my head, one after the other. I can't quite place them; everything is too much of a blur. A high-pitched wailing enters the room, surrounding me with the deafening sound on all sides.

Like my circuits are overloading, everything around me goes black.

CHAPTER FORTY-THREE
MALLORY

"Alright, Oskar, what did you think?" My mentor, posing as a makeshift audience, sits opposite me.

"It was . . . fine, by all accounts," he says delicately

"You hated it." A groan rumbles in my throat. "What was wrong with this one?"

"Nothing is wrong *per se*—I just don't believe it. Which makes me uncertain, a feeling I really can't sit with."

"Okay . . . so, what needs changed?"

"The phrasing itself is fine—good, even—but your delivery falls flat. There is no passion behind your words. No emotion."

"But this *is* how I'm feeling. Everything on this page mirrors my feelings. What else can I do?"

"You must try. While, factually, it may be all true, you aren't conveying that well enough. It feels overrehearsed."

Maybe because it is?

We have been at this for hours. The Oracle and the rest of the Order will be here in less than a day. Oskar has had me write and rewrite this speech countless times, asking for a recital twice per draft. This specific draft has finally made it to the third recital, the first to do so. He had led me to believe this was *the one*, but his critiques are relentless.

Throwing my hands up in exasperation, I rub my face and say, "Maybe I'm just not cut out for this. It's entirely possible I'm not meant to be here after all."

Oskar looks at me and scowls. He has been more than patient with me through this process, a courtesy that threatens to wear thin.

"Nonsense, dear girl. You are exactly where you're needed most. Fate has a peculiar way of finding us, but it is never wrong."

Groaning loudly, I stomp my feet on the aubergine rug. It seems the castle knows of my love for the color; it's popping up more and more throughout the place.

"Let's take a break," I tell him while I'm walking out the door, not giving him even a margin of opportunity to object.

Breathe in.

Breathe out.

It grows increasingly likely, my need for spirituality or medication, though they are much the same thing.

My parents never forced me into a church building on a Sunday morning, nor the big religious holidays either. They taught me to lean on my own understanding, that my intentions matter most. While it's still a tenant I hold dearly, that belief will not help me in Nalara.

Here, the existence of a deity is not in question—the Creators are, even now, at work within the kingdom. It isn't a matter of believing in the divine, but in examining their actions and motives. That's why there are three major factions. And the Riftclan, of course—the religionless faction on the outskirts of society. As far as I am aware, they are little more than a ragtag ensemble.

After a few minutes collecting my thoughts, I head back to the council chambers for another round of rehearsals. There has only ever been one thing that stands between me and the crow. Myself.

This time is different. This time, I will win.

I deserve that. *Nalara* deserves that.

Oskar and I finish practice at ten o'clock at night. I wonder if, like so many other things, the concept of time in Nalara has seeped into the cultures and customs of Earth. There is so much here that echoes my former existence, it can't possibly be coincidence.

As I ascend the stairs on my way to bed, I see Derrick make his way up from the lower levels. His presence startles me, as the black mop of hair ascends the stairs. In a momentary lapse of judgment amidst the chaos of preparations, I had forgotten his existence. That awful chef woman is with him, the two of them giggling up a storm as they head to wherever their final destination may be at this hour. Derrick doesn't see me, so I tuck my chin to my chest and scurry up the stairs.

She's a little old for him, but I guess there's someone for everyone.

Tomorrow is the most important day of my life. I can't let thoughts of my *brother* keep me up at night. He doesn't deserve the honor.

It is myself and Oskar, along with the Oracle and six other members of the Order who cluttered into the council chambers at noon. A handful of servants, whose chores could be put off, are scattered around the perimeter, Derrick among them. Looking at my brother's face should calm me. It should give me something other than myself to focus on. Instead, my nerves boil into my throat, threatening to make an appearance. His presence reminds me there are forces, both known and unseen, that would threaten my place as monarch.

Just as the double doors are being closed, a boot steps into the room, stopping one of the heavy doors in its tracks with a loud thud. A familiarity creeps over me at the sight of the militant brown boots. Beside them, another set of shoes peeks through the doorframe.

No. It can't be.

Thessara Draxen and her twin brother step into the room in which I will give the most important speech of my life. As he catches my eye, Thalion flashes the sinister smile I'd seen in that wannabe library. My heart jolts into my throat at the sight of it as a flitter of hope runs through me. But my hopes are dashed as Selyra is no one where to be found. It makes sense that even if Thalion had brought her with him to the castle, she wouldn't be in this room. My speech is a matter of the state, confidential to only the influential and the lowest of the castle's staff—someone has to serve and clean after the elite.

As soon as I get into power, I will make sure they all receive raises.

Without warning or any time to clear my thoughts, Oskar stands and introduces me to the small crowd.

"Ladies, gentlemen, and all the rest, it is here that we witness history, thousands of years in the making: our prophecy-born princess. Hoping to bear a child without the scrutiny of the Crown, her mother stole her away to the planet Earth, where she lived peacefully until her twenty-second year."

I steal a quick glance at Derrick, who looks unfazed. It's possible Oskar told him about my heritage without revealing our shared maternal line.

"That little girl," he continues, "has grown up to be a beautiful, intelligent, remarkable woman who will be a fearless leader. It is with great honor that I introduce to you, Mallory Nerezza—Heir to the Hollow Crown."

Stepping forward, I give a small curtsy, remaining uncertain of proper etiquette, though this can't hurt. The members of the Order bend their heads in a show of reverence, with the rest of the room following suit in much grander fashion. My nerves get the best of me and my mouth feels like chalk. Every swallow sends spikes to the back of my throat.

The Oracle speaks first, removing their hood and training their eyes on mine. "Child, I have spoken to the sacred Ash, who has told me of your ruthless judgment. And I have spoken with the sacred Willow, who speaks of your deep sorrow. The prophecy declares that a child of Earth will be Nalara's salvation. It has been long believed to be you. The Order has been tasked with keeping track of your growth, waiting for just the right moment to offer the crown. It is your duty to prove that the time is now."

The members of the Order grumble their agreement from behind the Oracle. None of them have removed their hoods, as it is a sacred right reserved for only the most powerful amongst their ranks.

Thessara stands, arms crossed, watching me. The smirk on her face dares me to prove her wrong.

"Oracle," I say with surprising confidence, "I would be honored to prove myself to you and your fellow members of the Order."

Bowing again, while maintaining eye contact, I continue, "Let me speak to you in a way that may help convince you of my right to rule. I look forward to your acceptance and a long, prosperous relationship between us."

The Oracle smiles, and they bow slightly in return and replace the hood on their head. All seven of my visitors take their seats.

CHAPTER FORTY-FOUR
OSKAR

The young woman of whom I have become quite fond takes the stage. Her royal attire exudes confidence and class, though, despite our frantic training schedule, my nerves remain at attention. She must bare her soul to the most powerful beings in Nalara, to usher in its deliverance.

She may prove incapable.

Mallory clears her throat and unfurls the scroll she has been clutching all morning. Her fingers delicately caress the now dry ink she had been so impatient to wait on.

"To the highest esteemed individuals of my ancestral nation of the Kingdom of Nalara, I beseech you to consider my prophesied ruling."

Her stiff shoulders and wobbling posture elicit no emotion from the crowd. This is uncomfortable for her, as I expected it would be, but she must choose to give this her all. My involvement now goes no further than catching her eye as she glances around the room, mentally nudging her to let her guard down. She looks down, flustered, but has thankfully gotten the message—perhaps there is hope in her following instruction after all.

"It is true," she continues, "that I have spent most of my life blissfully unaware of this realm's very existence."

She should have removed the word "blissfully." The Oracle will not take kindly to its use. Despite my warnings, she continually acts on her own accord. Perhaps I would be wise to remain hopeless in that endeavor.

"That does not mean, however, that I wish to remain forever ignorant of the customs and procedures of the Crown of Nalara."

Her rhythm grows steadier with each sentence and she stands straighter.

"I am not here to beg you to consider someone wholly unworthy. In years past, there were candidates for the Crown campaigning against one another. Today, that is not the case. While I am not historically the most well-fitted candidate, I am the only one."

"If our first queen, Queen Elythra's, blood runs through my veins—and the blood of all her children is the blood of my ancestors—then it is my right, and my obligation, to lead this nation. The prophecy that foretold my birth also foretold the resurrection of peace in Nalara."

The room is enraptured now, speaking words of confidence over Mallory's oration. Murmurs echo about the chamber, all of which are in assent to her words. Even Commander Draxen and the Joymaker look pleased.

"Leading our great nation is not a duty I take lightly, and I will spend the rest of my days living up to the expectation inherent to the position. But like Queen Veryissa before me, I come to this throne nothing more than a humble servant."

Queen Veyrissa the Ardent garners this response in every room her name enters. Like Mallory, she was born Ashawill. Unlike Mallory, her influences were not out for the good of the Crown. Her reign was the shortest in history. She was only fifty-years old when she took her own life. Veyrissa sacrificed herself for the Crown, but that isn't the way history books or children's stories tell the tale. Her name is a stain on the monarchy, and better left forgotten.

"I understand the trepidation of assigning an outsider to rule over your beloved kingdom. There comes a time, however, when those who were not born of its soil should be given the same opportunities as its native citizenry. While I was not born in a home in Nalara, I *am* Nalaran. Nowhere has ever felt more like home to me. I give my life to serving the nation that has called me with open arms into its fold."

Mallory's eyes are glassy now. Whatever she's done to manufacture the proper emotions is working.

"Furthermore, I have overcome untold obstacles before gaining the opportunity to set foot in this magnificent castle. Obstacles that have informed my view of the world, and of myself—I am not the same girl. The Mallory that spent twenty-two years on Earth is no more and it would be unwise to move forward with judgments of the past."

She looks around the room to gauge reactions now that her speech is nearing its conclusion. Though whether or not there is more up her sleeve, as I suspect there is, remains unkown.

"I fear you would be doing Nalara a disservice to exclude me from the Crown simply by virtue of my upbringing. The Sacred Trees make no mistakes, and it is by them I have been granted the privilege of restoring order and harmony that has long been missing."

Mallory is giving no indications she's finished.

"In truth"—this is off script—"when I came to Nalara, I had no cognizance of my own being. And not in the sense that I was unaware of Nalara's existence—though that is true. On Earth, my existence was that of a lonely, broken girl who would rather run from a challenge than face it head-on. The trials I have had to endure have uncovered a capability and strength I never knew existed."

Derrick squirms at his sister's admission. He can't see that her transformation is for the greater good, though that may be my fault. Pertinent information will be revealed as necessary, and no sooner.

"I was weak when I arrived—there is no shame in that. In fact, I hold my weakness as a badge of honor and a touchpoint on which my growth was founded. Becoming one with the magic and spirit of

Nalara is what has fueled my strength. I deserve to pass that back to the people."

She bows and sits down. The Oracle stands in her place and recites the customary twenty-four hour waiting period for deliberation. Historically, all twenty-four hours are rarely needed. Mallory's performance today is now in their hands.

CHAPTER FORTY-FIVE
MALLORY

My heart thunders in my chest like a drum. The Oracle and the rest of the Order have gone into their chambers to deliberate on my fate —on the fate of Nalara. A queasiness creeps into my stomach and I squeeze the webbing of my thumb hard enough to keep it at bay. Another lesson passed down from Nana, though my luck with it is infrequent enough that I might as well not try.

Derrick and the other servants follow the Order as they exit the council chambers. Thalion and Thessara exit behind the rest, whispering to one another as they pass. Whatever the two of them have to say about me is not my business. All that remains now is my mentor. Facing him, knowing his disappointment in my straying off script, is unthinkable. But face him I must.

"Oskar," I hesitate to say, "what did you think?" My question echoes the sentiment I'd repeated countless times as I'd rehearsed for this moment. Not that I'd known I would go rogue—I had just spoke from my heart like he'd said, and that's what had come out.

His eyes shift back and forth, searching my face for the answer. "What I think doesn't matter. Our fate lies in the hands of the Order now. They are the highest religious authority in Nalara. Their word is law—even when it contradicts that of the high queen.

305

You must be aware that no matter how *good* you are, you will always be under their watch."

The Twinned Path is the foremost religion in Nalara, that much is clear to me. What I hadn't considered is that the Church would come before the Crown.

"They have a deep connection with the Sacred Grove. The Twinned Trees see and know all, as I am sure you are aware by now. You cannot escape their watch and, by extension, the Oracle's judgment."

"Why am I needed, then?" The question hangs between us like a dare.

"You, my dear, exist to bring hope to the people. As the Vessel, you will act as a conduit for the Trees' magic. The more powerful you are, the more the Trees can do through you. Nobility cannot be handed to a member of the Order, past or future. Only once in history has this ever occurred, and it shall never be permitted again."

He means Veyrissa.

Oskar glares at me like he's reading my mind. After a moment, his face softens and his head bobs in a slow nod. No wonder he was against my mentioning her.

Too late now.

"Well, it's in the past. There is no use dwelling on what could have been," I say, trying to act confident.

"Yes," Oskar agrees. "We must simply wait and hold faith."

Alone in my chambers, I pace the floor. While it is one thing to realize there is nothing more to do, it is another thing entirely to accept it. Floors below, the deliberation on my fate—which was once, quite literally, set in stone—leaves my blood running cold.

Take a walk, Mal. Get some fresh air.

It has been days since I've seen the outside of the castle, never having gotten to explore the gardens due to all my work. Now that there is nothing to do but wait, there is no better time. Sitting with the trees has become a sort of balm to my soul when it grows weary.

Maybe that means I do belong.

Descending the stairs, I fantasize about my life in a year's time. With the crown on my head, adoring countryfolk will sojourn to the castle for my wisdom and blessings. There will be feasts and balls with lesser nobility—none of whom I've met. In my fantasy, I am far wiser than I am today and have returned *all* magics back to the people of Nalara.

Between reading of long-dead rulers, I snuck a law book or two off the shelves behind Oskar's back. He wouldn't have been pleased to learn of my "slacking." From my research, I discovered the forbidden magics, outlawed in various times throughout history for one reason or another. Necromancy, mnemosyne arts—memory magic as Oskar informed me of that day at the falls—and blood-binding. By this time next year, I will understand and agree with the laws or dissolve them. Misuse of any gift is bound to happen. Why should that mean the gifts the Creators gifted their people should be illegal in their land?

By the time I reach the back garden, my anger is tipping to an irrational level. Were the Trees as omniscient or omnipotent as they are said to be, they would not allow their creation to be cast aside simply by virtue of the powers they were endowed. Contemplating further action against those who uphold these arbitrary laws, I am reminded that none of this can happen until my trial ends.

This will hardly be my last trial.

The back garden is more like a hedge maze than a true garden, though flowers rest in planters at each dead end, their vibrant yellows and oranges looking like fire against the dark green hedges. Although I am not currently here for a romantic tryst with a secret lover, I wouldn't be opposed.

If Selyra's in the castle, I'll meet her here.

In the center of the hedges sits a fountain with ornate carvings of the same materials spread throughout the castle. Despite the redundancy in materials, the fountain is breathtaking, depicting both Trees in the center with their roots intertwined, water flowing from their branches. In any other circumstance, I would admire the craftsmanship, but right now it feels like a mockery.

Sentient trees are supposed to have brought everyone and everything into existence. On Earth, that theory is laughable. Though I suppose it's no less credible than a floating man in the sky no one has any proof exists.

What happens if you try to chop the tree down?

I'd assume, of course, they are magically protected, but I make a mental note to research whether anyone has tried and to what effect.

A giggle interrupts the silence, coming from somewhere in the hedge maze behind me. The sound twitches in my ear and my body stiffens like a deer on high alert. If I move, my position will be disclosed to whomever the giggle to belongs with no gain to myself. If I don't, my eavesdropping will be successful, but more easily spotted. Weighing my options carefully, my indecision effectively makes the choice for me.

"I didn't know you two were *that* close," a female voice says.

"We aren't really." That's Derrick.

"Well, you are on a first-name basis with the future high queen. Most would say that's fairly close."

Heat tickles my ears.

"I guess, but I don't really know *this* version of Mallory. She wants nothing to do with me anymore, and eventually she will just be someone who I used to know." His voice is ladened with sadness —it almost makes me feel guilty.

"That's too bad," the mysterious voice replies. "She should be grateful to you for all you've done. Keeping her safe and all that."

Biting my lip stifles the snort that threatens to escape.

And here I was, almost feeling sorry for you.

The thought of Derrick parading around the servant's quarters masquerading as the knight who saved the damsel in distress blanches my skin. He makes me sick. Whatever this game of his is, I hope he wins—it's the only thing he has. My future is bright, and he knows that. Maybe that's what all this is about.

Their voices fade into the background, the two of them finding their way out of the maze, just missing me.

Thank God.

Trying to gather my thoughts back to the previous topic, I speak aloud. It's something I've found myself doing more frequently than I'd like, as I'd been hoping to leave that particular habit back on Earth. My newfound importance, and existing in a world that itself spies on me, is reason enough not to let every errant thought out of my head.

To prove my point, the wind stirs. A faint whisper of a word passes my ear, but I can't make it out. It is in a language unknown to me.

"Hello?" I call out to the wind.

Nothing but silence follows. A paranoia stirs in me. *Are they talking about me?*

"Hello?" A little more forceful this time.

The wind stops blowing, leaving me in the still quiet of dusk.

CHAPTER FORTY-SIX

MALLORY

Today is the day.

The Oracle and the rest of his minions will be rendering the verdict to decide my merit for the Hollow Crown, a day that once felt like it would never come. Upon approving my reign, the coronation will be set to take place in a month's time. This is a fairly quick turnaround, by my estimation, though no reason was given as to why.

It is only fair that the fruits of my labor are realized after the work I've put into this endeavor. Hours from now, they will be. My opinion may change once I get the crown, but for now it is all I can think about.

"Your Highness," Ivy's voice drifts into the closet where I am getting dressed.

"In here, Ivy."

Cracking the door open, Ivy peeks in with a wide grin on her face. "Hurry! They have finished their deliberation and are ready to render their verdict."

So soon?

Receiving an answer this early in the process can't mean anything good, can it? Deliberation will do me no good—it is time to meet my fate. Dressing in a hurry, I sprint down the stairs. Some of my constituents may be appalled by my lack of decorum, but that's a matter for another day.

Without so much as a knock, I barge into the deliberation room. Every eye meets my form in the doorway, but that isn't of concern. Slowing my pace, I make my way toward where Oskar and Derrick stand at the foot of the table. I am happy to see the room absent of either of my previous tormentors.

What is Derrick doing here?

"I'm sorry," I pant. "I heard you had made your decision and came as fast as I could."

Oskar grabs my shoulder to steady me. "Yes, my dear, they finished *mere* moments ago. Whatever little birdie told you must have been watching intently—that news has not yet left this room."

My cheeks blaze with warmth. Oskar's eyes are now waiting for the name of my informant; I will never give it up. He won't go after Ivy, even if he suspects her, without my confirmation. Looking nonplussed as usual, the members of the Order go about their business, but shock and disgust mingle on Derrick's face. I know I shouldn't care, but that look sends embarrassment rippling through me.

Never mind him, Mallory. Focus.

"Well, yes, they must be on top of it." I aim my answer at the group sitting around the table, not letting them see my confusion at how quickly Ivy was able to secure this information. She should be more thoroughly vetted; her training has left her a valuable asset that's been neglected.

The Oracle stands, beckoning me with their bony hand to sit in the chair at the head of the table. Crossing the room with my head high, I sit where instructed.

"Mallory Nerezza." The Oracle's haunting voice booms louder than necessary. "After careful deliberation, we have come to our conclusion—as you somehow know."

The Oracle's eyes narrow as they get to the end of their sentence, telling me silently that this topic is far from finished. I remain quiet, waiting.

"We have spoken to the Hollowborne—the voice of our Sacred Gods. They warned of a coming power so great that it would disrupt life in Nalara as we know it. This future, they say, cannot happen without you on the throne."

Holding my breath, I wait for the words I know are coming.

"The Order is not keen on change, you must understand. Our doctrine comes from the core tenants of the Twinned Path, which may not be disrupted in our name. We feel your possession of the crown will pose a threat to those tenants.

"Ultimately, though," they continue, "We act as messengers to the will of the divine. If it is in their design that you shall don the crown, then so be it. It is with our great reluctance that we offer you the Hollow Crown and appoint you High Queen Mallory, the Shadowbearer."

My stomach jolts as my own words come rushing back to me. They don't want me. They *need* me.

"I humbly accept the crown and will do everything in my power to live up to its expectations. Despite your reservations, you are making the best decision to benefit Nalarans for generations to come."

The Oracle nods and returns to their seat, with other members of the Order looking at the table, willing me to leave. Oskar's beaming face is in complete juxtaposition to his son's.

Scowling at Derrick, I make my way toward the older man, ignoring his presence. He can keep his pretenses; that doesn't make them true.

"We did it!"

Oskar's effervescent smile lightens my mood. "You did it, my child. I am proud to be standing before the future Queen of Nalara, and humbly offer my services as Voice of the Hollow, if you will have me."

"Of course." I don't hesitate even slightly. "I wouldn't be here if it wasn't for you. You taught me more about myself in the last several weeks than anyone I've ever known."

"No, sweet girl. Your journey was one of growth and is entirely reflective of your inner self. My involvement was merely a nudge or two in the right direction."

"Well, thank you regardless. And, of course, your advice is always welcomed in my court. Now, let's go celebrate!"

Derrick is still with us and, knowing he would never be the first to move toward a truce. So much of himself has been kept from him, is it any wonder he feels the way he does?

"Derrick," I hear myself say, "would you care to join us in celebrating our victory?"

He looks at me hard, his eyes narrowed in thought. He's judging me, though why remains unclear. There is a marked sadness hiding behind his rough exterior expression.

"Sure, why not?"

"Great, then it's settled." A feigned cheerful tone creeps into my voice. "Let's all meet in the bar downstairs for drinks in two hours."

The pair agrees to meet me and my legs carry me as fast as they can to find Ivy. She deserves to hear the good news—if she hasn't already. Which reminds me that I intend to ask her how she overheard their session and had the time to come to my room within "mere moments."

CHAPTER FORTY-SEVEN
MALLORY

Outside the room used for deliberations, I overhear Oskar and Derrick begin a conversation. They must have assumed I'd made it out of earshot, because as soon as I leave, Derrick blurts out a question that stops me in my tracks.

"You think how she is behaving is normal? Can you honestly look me in the eyes and tell me she isn't going down a dangerous path?"

My eyes squeeze shut as I will my ears to work harder.

"Derrick, I understand your concern. She will be well supervised under my tutelage, but your feelings for her are overshadowing reality."

"I don't have feelings, Dad." He sounds flustered. "Her behavior *is* different."

"You watched her for two weeks before her twenty-second birthday; you can't pretend to know her with any level of certainty."

"Dad, it wasn't just watching from a distance."

"What do you mean by that?"

"I just—" He's gearing up to lie. "—would order coffee from her and we'd chat from time to time."

How pathetic.

Derrick and I had never met, never spoken, until that day in the woods. And the only time I had ever seen him had been the previous day when he'd been staring me down in the parking lot. That feels like it was ages ago—if he ordered coffee from me with any degree of regularity, I would have recognized him that day.

"Son, you were under strict instructions not to engage. You could have ruined the whole plan."

The plan. Had I heard them reference a master plan before? It feels real, but I can't pull an exact instance from my memory. The further we move from the trials, the fuzzier they seem. Though, trauma generally does that to a person.

"Well, the plan worked, Dad—you got her here. You got her in front of the Order, and you got her the crown. When does the plan end?"

"The plan ends when Nalara is saved. You know that."

"Doesn't simply putting her on the throne save Nalara?"

"Not according to the prophecy, I'm afraid. There is a second part, lost to time and unknown even to the Oracle, that must be fulfilled for Nalara to find peace."

"What is it?"

"A sacrifice."

An audible gasp escapes my lips, and my hands rise to cover it later than they should.

From the way their conversation ends abruptly, I am sure the pair heard. Whether they realize it's me outside the room or not, I don't know. But I'm not sticking around to find out. I take off running down the stairs—it's faster that way—and head to the farthest part of the building that would give me a plausible deniability. That just so happens to be the kitchen.

Great.

"Hello, Chef," I say as I attempt to glide into the room looking nonchalant. "Have you heard?"

"Heard what?" she says roughly, not looking at me.

"The Order has deemed me worthy of the crown. I will be high queen in a month's time." I don't tell her that the Order has their reservations about my leadership. She doesn't need that ammo.

"Oh goody." Sarcasm drips from her voice.

"I thought I might as well get you going on the menu for my reception." A bright, teasing smile lights up my face. "But I would like to first set up a tasting to select from your repertoire."

She looks up from her busy hands and glares at me. "Just because you are about to run the country does not mean you run my kitchen. Can I get a please or a thank you?"

"Let's set something up to go over the menu for my coronation's reception, *please*." I hurl the final word like an insult. Whatever I did to this woman to make her hate me is in the past. If she can't behave like a decent person, I will match her attitude. And, if need be, there are more cooks than one in the kingdom.

"Who taught you manners?" It wasn't a question.

"I suggest you learn to speak to me with respect before I become queen—it would do you good to remember who I am. Further disrespect will not be tolerated. Especially as I have done nothing to you that warrants this behavior."

Chef turns her back without a word and goes back to whatever it was she was doing. That is my invitation to end the conversation. If I take it, I will look weak—easily controlled by my subjects. If I don't, I risk looking power-hungry too soon after receiving the Order's blessing. There is nothing I can do to win in this situation.

Chef has served her purpose as alibi anyway.

CHAPTER FORTY-EIGHT
DERRICK

A week has passed since the Order granted Mallory the crown, which has only served to stroke her ego. Her eagerness for the crown has grown with each passing day as she flits about the castle demanding preparations, poor Ivy following dutifully in tow. Mal acts like people will like her more once the crown is on her head. They may act like they do, but those that engage out of fear are no better than those who would openly despise her.

If I were being honest, I could say how badly my heart breaks for her. She had a friend in me and decided to throw that away for the first scrap of "belonging" she was fed. My father did plenty to stoke the fires of power-hunger, promising her the one thing she wants more than anything—love.

She could've had that with me, and she tossed me aside without so much as a second glance. And has yet to provide an explanation as to what she saw in her trial that caused her to push me away so hard. But push she did, causing an irreparable tear between us. We will never get back what we were building.

Mallory Nerezza is an insecure little girl masquerading as a ruler who will lead Nalara only out of her own greed and insecurity. The most dangerous leaders are often the ones who can't see their own issues.

My mind has been made up for weeks that the prophecy must be wrong, though that's blasphemy to say. According to my father, however, the prophecy is simply incomplete.

Dad had explained that the second part of the prophecy, lost to almost all, depicted the need for a sacrifice. The problem, though, is that the prophecy was lost so long ago that we don't have any other information. Most factions did not believe in its existence, let alone in its relevance.

The Riftclan is the only faction that still retains any faith in the back end of the prophecy. All others who heard of its existence chalked it up to being something akin to a children's fairy tale. Finding the lost half of the prophecy is the only way to move forward and bring peace, and magic, back to the kingdom. Dad is truly on the Twinned Path, so why he believes a notion only accepted on the fringes of society, I will never know.

"Good morning, sleepy head," a feminine voice murmurs in my ear.

Smiling, I turn to see Darcy—Chef to most people—has woken up. I give her a deep kiss and run my hand down her cheek in response.

"Good morning, beautiful."

"You didn't sleep well again last night. Nightmare?"

Nodding is all I can do. Who knows how she would react if I explained my dreams. Mallory being the primary subject would not go over well.

"Sorry if I woke you again."

"Don't be sorry. I'm just worried for you."

A deep smile crosses my face as I close my eyes. Darcy is tender and caring. She may come across as a bit brusque, but she has proven to be an excellent judge of character.

"I promise I'm okay. A few bad dreams here and there are nothing to be concerned about."

"If you say so." She strokes my arm absentmindedly. "But if you need to talk about anything, just know I'm here."

I give her a peck on her nose and she giggles.

"I know."

With that, I roll out of her double bed and make a face. She loves when I wriggle my eyebrows at her, and I love hearing the giggle—it's deeper than Mal's but just as rewarding to coax out.

"My dad is waiting for me," I say quietly. Bringing up Dad or Mallory is something we try to avoid. Darcy won't admit to it, but I get the feeling she's jealous.

"Okay," she says sadly. "Go ahead."

I throw my shirt over my head and blow her a kiss. She catches it and places it to her lips.

Darcy may not be my forever girl, but she is fun for now. And, most importantly, she is nothing like Mallory. She is smart and self-assured, but cares deeply for others. There is no forced, false altruism in her decisions. She simply does what she believes is right, with no further deliberation. If she liked Mallory more, I would attempt to get them together so her good traits could rub off. God knows Mal needs them.

"Dad!" My bounding into the room catches him off guard. "Your favorite son is here."

My dad waves a hand at me, annoyed with my antics already.

"Mallory," I say to the would-be queen who is standing in the center of the room clothed in a poofy yellow dress, surrounded by women with sewing needles and pins. "You look fluffy today."

She scowls at me, and I grin in response. It gives me a certain sense of satisfaction to be able to annoy her so deeply and so quickly. Especially after a week of distance.

"Why are you here?" she asks, an edge to her voice.

"I dunno." I shrug honestly.

Mal's eyes narrow, indicating that I'm doing my job.

"Dad, why am I here?" I grin at my father with my best schoolboy grin.

Dad gave me no indication of what to expect, or that Mallory would be here. From the looks of it, I'm barging in on coronation planning. Something I had yet to be invited to in the last week. Something I would rather not be invited to again.

"You are here, son, because I think it is time Mallory and I reveal to you a secret you should know."

Mallory looks like she's about to be sick all over her seamstresses.

"Now?" she whispers.

"Well, not exactly at the moment, no. But I did want to make you both aware of the dynamic moving forward."

"What dynamic?" I joke in an attempt to lighten the tension. "Does this mean I will stop being treated like an outcast who has been relegated to the basement?"

"That is precisely what it means, son."

The answer, while unexpected, intrigues me.

"Well that's . . . something." Coherent sentences won't come; even I can't make light of this.

"Yeah," Mallory says, "I didn't know this was happening yet either."

Mallory has, by this point, found herself a chair and has shooed the workers away. Her normally pale skin looks sickly and I can't help but be filled with anxiety at the thought of whatever she's hiding. Nothing about that girl is good, which is what makes her so damn alluring.

"Well, then. Now that you both know what is on the agenda, we will meet for dinner," Oskar said. "It's been awhile since the three of us have dined altogether. This will be the perfect opportunity to reconnect."

"Make sure there's wine," Mallory chimes in.

"We can make that happen. Now, son, your presence is not necessary for the remainder of this gown fitting. We shall see you in a few hours."

CHAPTER FORTY-NINE
MALLORY

Red wine fills all three goblets on the dining table. Derrick isn't here yet, but I had gone ahead and ordered his—I'm already on my second glass. Ever since our conversation this afternoon, there has been a pit in my stomach that nothing can fill. Oskar hadn't told me he was going to include me in his revelation to Derrick.

Oskar is sitting on one side of the table, across from two chairs smooshed closely together. It is almost comical how much more room he has afforded himself in this situation. It's almost as if he is attempting to physically distance himself from the two of us. Before I can say anything about it, Derrick comes in and sits down beside me.

"I see Mallory has already gotten ahold of the wine she wanted." His tone is malicious.

"Yes," I respond, ice in my voice.

"Okay, then, I guess I'll just talk to you, Dad. Are we ready to get started or what?"

Derrick's ever-present cheerfulness pisses me off. He was told he would receive life-altering news and he comes to the table with nothing but a smile? That is so typical of him—no real problems, floating through life with a supportive father and an empty calendar.

Yet he has nothing but opinions about how I spend my time and make my decisions.

"Yes. Now, what I am about to tell you might take some adjustment, but please know that I have chosen here and now to inform you of what I've kept from you all these years for a reason. This isn't a flippant or callous decision; there is strategy here.

"I will also have you note," Oskar continues, "that Mallory, of course, could not have known this without my telling her, and she was under direct orders not to disclose this to you until I was ready."

A quick glance is all I can manage, hoping Derrick won't see my nerves. His eyes dart back and forth between his father and me, his body shifting in his seat—so close that I can feel the brush of his thigh against mine.

This will be awkward.

"Let me first start by saying, I love you and I have only ever kept information from you for your protection. If you knew what it took to get us to this point—all the sacrifices I've made—you would understand.

"I think it is only fair to you that we start from the beginning, Derrick. You weren't born in Brooklyn. You were born here."

"What? Where?" Derrick's fervor is alarming.

"You were born in Thryvoss, your mother's hometown."

He didn't tell me that part, but I'm the one who knew—knows—her. Surely he should have felt inclined to disclose this information to me.

"Okay." Derrick hesitates. "What does that mean for us today? I mean . . . that's as life-altering as promised, but why did Mallory have to know it first?"

"In due time, my boy, in due time. We went through the portal in the Willow tree when you were eight years old. I wasn't aware of its existence until then, but it was how your mother escaped eight years prior. You see, she was wanted by the king's guard at the time. They took her to force her to procreate with King Malchior in order for him to sire the girl of the prophecy. He and his men, the Emberguard, did not believe the girl should come from Earth —they believed her bloodline should stay pure and sired from power. Malchior's belief that he alone could control, rewrite, fate is what ultimately led to the Sundering and the downfall of Nalara. The day your mother ran away was the day the magic started dying."

Derrick places his elbows on the white table cloth, leaning in as if it would help him make sense of what he's hearing.

"If I was eight, how do I not remember it? Surely that would be something I would have even the faintest recollection of."

Oskar looks at me for solace and, finding none, faces his son's gaze once more.

"Before I took you through the portal in search of your mother . . . I did some magic."

"What kind of magic?"

"A magic that, if it leaves this circle, I could still be tried for in Vaelguard today. I performed a ritual to invoke memory magic, taking from you all that you knew of your homeland and replaced it with generic memories of a typical American eight-year-old. It's why your youngest memories don't quite feel like your own."

"Dad!" Derrick's yell causes diners at several neighboring tables to try to listen in. "That stuff is dangerous, you have *always* said that."

"Yes, I know. And it is. You will never be able to regain the memories of your youth. Those who are not innately mnemosyne are cursed with an inability to reverse their magic, and that's what makes it risky. "

Derrick balls his left hand into a fist as a muscle in his jaw twitches and his eyes grow dark. With him being this angry now, I shudder to think how he will behave once he learns *the* truth. A breath of anticipation leaves my lungs and, hearing it, Derrick turns his attention toward me.

"And you," he says with hurt in eyes, "how could you not tell me? I thought we were friends."

He isn't looking for an answer, not really.

"Now, son, I know this is a lot to take in, but I think it is important that you learn the rest."

Trees give me strength.

I take a gulp from my wineglass, hoping to steel my nerves and find the courage I need to face what's coming.

Leaning back in his seat and folding his arms, Derrick nods at his dad to continue.

"When we came to Earth, I was hopeful to find your mother—and find her we did."

"So she's not dead?"

Oskar glances at me and, for the first time since I've known him, I sense his nervousness.

"No. She is not. But I don't think she remembers your existence either. I am pretty sure she has had some form of exposure to memory magic herself. And, at a future date, I would love to learn who cursed her, and make them pay. Until that time, though, I will finish my story with no further interruptions, if you don't mind."

The question on Derrick's lips dies immediately.

"When we found her, your mother had a life on Earth. She was married, with a beautiful six-year-old daughter, and she had forgotten about Nalara. When I tried to talk to her, she introduced herself to me as if we were meeting for the first time."

Which explains why she never told me.

"That experience is enough to drive even the strongest man to despair. Despite the heartache, I had to continue being strong for you. Wiping your memories accidentally allowed you to walk away without knowing your mother's betrayal. I do not regret my actions in the matter."

My heart pounds so loudly it must be audible. I bite my lip and close my eyes, waiting for the realization to set in.

"Wait," Derrick says after a moment too long. "That means that I have a sister."

"Yes."

"How could you not tell me that I have a sister?" His voice is growing frantic. "We have to go back to Earth. You have to help me find her."

"There is no need for that."

"Why not?"

"I have already found your sister and she is doing remarkably well in life."

"Where is she? Can I meet her?"

Oskar's crooked little grin returns to his face as both hands clasp around the knob of his new walking stick.

"My son, you have met her."

"Where is she? *Who* is she?"

"Derrick . . . why do you think I told Mallory? Why do you think she's here?"

CHAPTER FIFTY
DERRICK

Rage.

A white-hot rage courses through my veins. How could he have told h*er* before his own son? Why does that bitch get to know who I am before me?

Why does she get to know our mother and I don't?

Bile rises in my throat when the realization hits. I have been pining for, dreaming of my *sister* for months now. The instinct to take a disinfecting shower and chop off my right hand is overwhelming. While I'm at it, I may as well gouge my eyeballs out of their sockets.

Standing roughly, I push the table away. Running out of the room, I see Darcy. She tries to talk to me, to grab me, but I shrug her off and head out the door.

It is a dark, cool evening, but I don't feel that now. My breathing is jagged and shallow, clutching at my lungs, begging to survive. Tears wet my cheeks. At times like these, I do wish I had a mother figure. Dad is alright, but he is one of those "tough it out" kind of guys. Not that he would judge me—not that I desire his comfort in this instance.

The cobbled road leads to the woods. I follow it and enter

deeper, perhaps, than I mean. There is an eerie silence that exists in the space just outside the castle. Not here, though. A cacophony of frogs and crickets serenades me while lightning bugs dance along to illuminate a path—I see why Mallory likes it out here so much.

Sadness overtakes me and I crash to my knees. Years have passed since the last time emotion overcame me to this extent.

"Why?" My voice comes out a whine. "It should have been me who grew up with a mother. Mallory wouldn't even be here if she'd stayed with us."

A gust of wind breezes past me, a subtle finger lifting my chin. I shudder at the touch, though it emboldens me to continue.

"And why did my father think it was okay to tell me this in front of her? She doesn't deserve a front row seat to my embarrassment."

"You do not like your sister?" a voice asks.

Without bothering to investigate the speaker, I reply, "She isn't who I thought she was. In more ways than one, it turns out."

A hooded figure appears from the shadows.

"No, she is not—in ways she herself may have yet to understand, but I do."

"Just because she is the heir to the throne prophesied generations ago doesn't give her the right to act this way, to act like she is better than everyone."

A smile appears from under the hood, though it is growing too dark to make out the rest of his features.

"What if I were to tell you that she wasn't the one the prophecy foretold? There is another, meant to usurp her power and lead Nalara to its promised peace."

"I would assume you were lying. Everyone has thought it was her from the moment my mother was pregnant with me. They wouldn't hunt down the wrong woman. It's something set in stone."

There is a beat of silence, followed by a small chuckle.

"There is still much you don't know—much I am willing to teach if you have the desire to learn."

He holds out his hand, beckoning me to grab it with mine. Taking hold, he pulls me to my feet and I follow him into the dark.

CHAPTER FIFTY-ONE
MALLORY

"Well, that went well." My sarcasm is evident. "I don't think it could have gone any better if we'd tried."

Oskar opens his mouth to speak and I roll my eyes, pushing myself from the table with one last gulp of wine. Derrick just stormed out after receiving the biggest news of his life. Someone should follow him if his father won't. Admittedly, I do feel a little guilty about keeping this from him, even though it was Oskar's idea.

At the door, I spot the cook, Daisy or something, and run to her.

"Have you seen Derrick? I know you two are acquainted."

Her icy gaze matches mine. "No."

With that, she walks off.

What does he see in her? She's obscenely standoffish and he's a charismatic goof. Maybe opposites do attract.

If he's not with his girl, he's probably gone out to get fresh air—the dryads will have seen him. Lately, they've gone quiet, but they must make an exception in this instance. They always help in my time of need, though the country itself is in dire need. Reports of magic dwindling in all four corners of Nalara have come in the last week. It's that reminder that almost stops my search, reinvigorating me to focus on what's needed for my coronation.

No.

It's better to hash it out now, get all the family drama over with and then I can focus on important matters.

There are no whispers in the forest—even the animals are silent. With no sound or light, it will be all but impossible to find Derrick out here. Derrick isn't like me; he doesn't thrive in nature. It's likely he saw a creepy forest and turned on his heel immediately. I contemplate doing the same, but by now my eyes have had time to adjust and I see a glow off in the distance.

Could he have had enough time to light a fire?

Probably not, but if he had seen it, he might have investigated. I walk toward the light, about seventy-three yards, give or take, and find myself at the entrance to a cave. Two figures sit around a fire, and at least half a dozen more voices echo from inside the cave. Derrick is one of the figures around the fire, huddled in close beside a hooded figure.

Careful not to make a sound, I take the chance to spy on the pair. What they are saying, I can't make out, although I do spy part of a sigil on the hooded one's back. Inching closer to hear and to try to make the sigil out, the wind whips along my face, pushing me backward, as if guarding the men.

From the gestures Derrick is making, it seems he is in full agreement with what is being said. There is not much for me to do now but to go back.

Do I tell Oskar about this?

As I am leaving, the glimpse of the sigil I'd caught before the wind had kicked up filled my mind. I *had* seen it before. It is the sigil of the Riftclan—enemies to the Twinned Path. Enemies, it seems, of my bloodline. *My* enemies.

CHAPTER FIFTY-TWO
MALLORY

Derrick is gone longer than anticipated, but I remain in the entry hall, waiting to spring my inquisition on him the moment he steps through the door. There is much I want to ask. Most notable being what he was doing with the greatest enemy of my crown.

Ivy waits in the corner, ready to accompany me upstairs. Her training taught her well and, if I were any other royal, I'm sure I would love every whim catered to. Instead, I feel awkward, uneasy with the attention. Everything in me begs to snap at her, ordering her to leave me be. Her eyes betray silent sobs when I turn to look at her.

Why is she crying? I have been with her the whole time.

Whatever her issue, it can wait. Tonight, getting answers from Derrick is the priority. Nothing else matters.

"Ivy," I say with the gentlest voice I can muster, "please go to bed. I do not require your assistance and I am yet unsure how long I will be waiting. It isn't fair to you that I keep you up this late."

She gives me a small nod and descends the stairs. Ivy is with me so often I tend to forget that she resides with the other servants. After my coronation, I will see about moving her to a higher floor.

Two hours after I send Ivy to bed, Derrick comes stumbling through the door. His visage is pale and disoriented, but he does not smell of liquor or otherwise appear intoxicated.

"Where have you been?" I ask, giving him a chance at honesty.

"I was taking a walk."

My eyes narrow, and my voice grows more stern, almost scolding. "Derrick. Where were you? Be honest with me. I know you are hiding something."

Bewilderment crosses Derrick's face and he bursts out in a fit of laughter. It is some time before he calms down.

"What is so funny?"

"You're serious?" He blinks. "You've got to be joking."

A seismic sigh forces its way from my lungs—I am not in the mood to play his games tonight.

"Oh," Derrick almost whispers, "you're not joking."

His eyes search my face, looking for any indication that he is wrong.

"Mallory . . . you don't remember?"

"Remember what?" I ask, more annoyed than curious.

He looks behind him and gestures toward the door. "We *just* spoke outside."

"No we didn't Derrick, you're drunk." I'm tired of this conversation. Bed would have been the smarter option.

"Mal. I don't know how to tell you this without hurting you, but you already confronted me. We were on the lawn screaming at each other moments ago. You seriously don't remember that?"

A puzzled expression must cross my face because he continues. "You told me you saw me in the cave. You saw the sigil on Cadren's back and you figured out what it meant."

Something catches in my throat.

How does he know?

I had been careful—and far enough away that I had been undetectable.

"How—"

"Mallory, you *told* me." His eyes plead for me to remember.

This is just like him—everything is a joke to Derrick Alborian. When he sobers up, I will try this conversation again.

CHAPTER FIFTY-THREE

DERRICK

Tomorrow is my sister's coronation. It has been weeks since we've spoken, and she is convinced I am out to get her since she saw me meeting with Cadren, the leader of the Riftclan. I had tried to tell her that was our first meeting, that he had found me in the woods that night. Of course, I hadn't told her all that we'd talked about— or of Cadren's warning. Or that I have been sneaking out almost every night since to see him.

Darcy and I have split up. I wasn't the same in those days after learning the truth, and she wasn't willing to stick around through my family shit. That leaves me with no one to ask to be my guest at the coronation, though, but with half the nation expected to be in attendance, I'll find someone to keep me company. My father had asked me to be onstage but, given the rift between Mallory and I, I declined. To say he was upset would be an understatement; he was beyond livid and I'm sure I haven't heard the end of it. I'm still ignoring him, there are more important matters to worry about, matters he refuses to acknowledge.

The kingdom is more and more in ruins every day and Mallory remains oblivious. She believes the second the crown touches her head, the world will right itself and magic will flow freely once more. Her goals sound admirable, but her motives raise questions.

What if she doesn't deserve the crown?

Trying to express my concerns to my father is futile; he brushes them aside instantly if they contradict his little plan. A plan I never wanted to be part of—a plan to get my father back in the crown's good graces. But at what cost?

CHAPTER FIFTY-FOUR
MALLORY

"Congratulations, Your Majesty." Ivy's young voice floats over my head as she fastens the last button on the back of my dress.

She steps out from behind me, her reflection in the mirror standing next to mine. Through the stress of coronation planning, the young girl had remained steadfast.

Whatever I'm paying her is not enough.

"Thank you, Ivy." I catch her eyes in the mirror and give her a smile.

My hands run over the lace detailing on the bodice of the butter-yellow dress adorning my body. I'd been afraid that the color would clash with my pale skin and auburn hair, but it worked better than expected. For the first time since entering Nalara, my face is made up, and my hair is pinned in an elegant half-up-half-down hairstyle. Long yellow gloves and simple satin heels finish off the look.

"How are you feeling?" Ivy asks as I stare myself in the eyes and bite my lip.

I release a breath and step off the pedestal, turning to look at my attendant. "This is more exciting than a wedding, and likely just as nerve-wracking."

She laughs politely and squeezes my arm before curtsying. "See you out there, Queen Mallory."

The crown slips easily on my head, like it had been missing all along. Instinctively, my eyes scan the crowd, looking for my brother and his girlfriend. Finding neither of their faces, I focus on the humming in my body. Power emanates from the crown, reverberating down my spine like it's waiting to escape.

For weeks now, I have been preparing for this moment, hoping for the momentous occasion where the crown rests on my skull and the world is fixed. As with everything else, my dreams prove to be in vain.

Foolish girl, nothing comes that easily.

After weeks of preparation, my doubts have subsided but, in this moment, they creep back in.

What if Derrick's right and the prophecy meant someone else entirely?

Will my Ashawill spirit lead my fate to mirror Veyrissa's after all?

The rest of the coronation comes and goes, passing through my mind like water between fingertips. If I'm not intended to miraculously fix the kingdom with my magic, how *am* I meant to fix it?

My thoughts slip away as the music for the celebratory ball starts playing.

CHAPTER FIFTY-FIVE
DERRICK

"May I cut in?" I ask the man dancing with Mallory. It is her fourth potential suitor of the evening. The leeches have been vying for her attention all night, though she hardly pays it any mind, in her usual Mallory way. A stocky bald man at least thirty years her senior hands her over to my outstretched arm.

"Thank you," she whispers stiffly.

"No problem. I thought you could use a quiet moment while maintaining the appearance of doing your duty."

She says nothing and we continue to dance with silence between us as the band begins the next song.

"What is your plan, Mal?" I know I shouldn't ask—not here, not now.

"What do you mean?"

"Well . . . you seemed to think everything would get better the second you were wearing the crown. And, unless you know something I don't, that clearly hasn't happened. What is your plan, moving forward, to fix our nation? What are your campaign promises?" Joking usually works with her to lighten the mood. Not this time; today, Queen Mallory the Shadowbearer is all business.

"Not that it is of any importance to you, but my first plan of action is to bring the leader of the Riftclan in for execution."

My shoulder's tense. *Cadren.* My friend and mentor, set to be executed. Not that Mallory knows how close we've grown in just a few weeks' time—In her mind it was just one drunken meeting in the woods. She has gotten it in her head that I haven't been honest with her, so she can keep thinking that.

"Why?"

"Why not? They are sworn enemies to the Crown. They wish to see nothing less than my downfall. They wish to see the end of Nalara as we know it."

My next words must be chosen carefully. Now is not the time or place to reveal what I know.

"Is that so bad? As far as I can tell, things aren't going great the way they are. Every nation needs a change. Maybe it's our turn and, with your help, we can do that."

"We?"

I have to recover.

"Nalara, the greater *we*—this is beyond the two of us. How are you planning to help your kingdom?"

"It's simple, Derrick, though I wouldn't expect you to understand matters of the state. When we cut down the opposition, we extinguish any spark of rebellion that may exist."

There is a fire in her eyes I don't recognize.

". . . The dryads are dying, Mallory."

The look on her face suggests this is the first time she's hearing such information. My father told her last week. She confirmed she's felt it happening, that they haven't spoken to her directly since Gallivarum.

"You knew that, Mal."

"Perhaps I did, but it must have slipped my mind." She looks bored. She shouldn't look bored, not if she's pretending to care about magic returning to Nalara.

"What is going on with you?" I whisper-yell, hoping to avoid drawing attention from the gathering crowd.

"Whatever do you mean, dear brother?" Her words are laced with venom.

Whatever calm conversation I thought we could have is over now. It's time to say what she needs to hear. "I am sick of giving my cold-hearted bitch of a sister the benefit of the doubt. Your greed is going to be the death of us all."

CHAPTER FIFTY-SIX
MALLORY

"What did you say to me?"

"You heard me, Mal, you are a monster."

The words hit like a punch to my gut. We aren't close anymore, but I never would have suspected Derrick to be capable of such vitriol. He is looking at me like I am the last person on Nalara he'd ever hope to be speaking with.

"How dare you say such things to your queen." My voice carries and I am no longer afraid of drawing attention. The little girl who stumbled down the rabbit hole with two strange men is dead—I am not the damsel in distress or the coward on the run any longer.

"You," Derrick says through gritted teeth, "are not my queen. You are a disgrace to the Crown and to our mother's name."

Something overtakes me and I slap Derrick across his face, the sound echoing through the now quiet hall.

"Don't you ever speak about our mother again. *She* chose me. The *crown* chose me. The kingdom needs me, and you are burning with jealousy over it."

Regaining my composure, I whisper, "And that is not my fault."

A laugh, deeper and more unsettling than anything of which I imagined Derrick capable, escapes his throat. Whether it is a laugh of amusement or malice is unclear.

"You honestly think I am jealous of you?" He spits the words like they leave a bad taste in his mouth. "You are completely unhinged. You don't deserve this. You haven't done *anything* to earn your place on the throne. All you did was be born, a feat as unremarkable as yourself."

"Why wouldn't I have earned this? You were with me at the trials, *brother*."

The laugh returns. "Yes, and I watched you fail them all."

A sharp pain hits my left temple like someone or something is knocking at my memory, fighting to get out. Derrick takes my silence as an invitation to continue.

"You *failed*, Mallory. You wouldn't be here if it wasn't for me and my father. The only reason the Order chose you was because we begged them. Did you wonder why I was in the deliberation room when you entered, despite having not been involved with anything in the castle up until that point? My father and I groveled our humility away, vouching for you—leaving me sick with guilt for what I've done to our people."

"You're lying."

None of this makes any sense. Oskar praised my work in the trials, and the Order told me of their reluctance but only claimed the Sacred Trees themselves as their source of pressure.

"No, Mallory. You know somewhere deep inside that it's true, every word of it. You just don't want to believe it. You don't want to admit that you are a failure once again. It's all you've ever been and all you'll ever be."

A buzzing hits the back of my brain. A white-hot poker stabs at a wall I wasn't aware I'd erected. Waves of nausea pass through me, doubling me over in the middle of the ballroom. The audience fades, pain rising.

"The truth is, Mallory, I know what you are—what you are capable of. I suspected for a long time that something was wrong, but I couldn't figure it out until Cadren showed me the truth."

My eyes narrow at the mention of that rat's name. He has been corrupting my brother with wild tales and unfounded accusations after all.

I knew you were lying.

Derrick smirks, cold and calculated. I fear his question before he even asks it. "Do you know what is almost like a dream, Mallory? The other side of the same coin, if you will. What can be just as easily manipulated?"

I don't answer—I'm not sure where this is going. He laughs again at my silence, a hollow-sounding laugh.

"Memories."

Searing pain shoots through my temple straight into the back of my eyes. The world flashes a bright white, blinding me momentarily. A ringing sounds in my ears, like the aftermath of a bomb exploding.

My senses reorient themselves as Derrick says, "You are a Mnemosyne. It took me too long to see it, but the signs are all there."

"No," I say, finding my voice. "There is none left by blood, and the practice is outlawed."

"Most Mnemosyne go mad and use their power not only on their enemies, but on themselves. And you've been doing it this whole time."

"No—no, that's not true."

"Isn't it, though, Mallory? You erase any trace of the most uncomfortable moments in your life, the moments where you try to run. That's why your life feels so fruitless and mundane. Your life feels meaningless, because pain brings meaning to the good times, and you are too scared to feel the pain.

"The gift of memory magic has been with you since the beginning. When you were young, your mother—our mother—would tell you about Nalara. Your grandmother too. Do you remember that?"

I shake my head.

That can't be true.

"You took our mother's memories of our homeland. You stole her memories of *me*." His voice breaks and sorrow sadness runs through me like a knife.

"How could you *possibly* know that?"

"My father and I were there when it happened. You saw her kissing him and took her memory. Mommy's little girl needed all of Mommy's attention—you were never one to share, I've heard. After that, she looked at my father and I like we were strangers, and it broke him."

"That wasn't my fault. I didn't know what I was doing, if that's true."

"Maybe not. Maybe it is wrong to blame a young girl, but you have been manipulating memories since we arrived in Nalara. You have manipulated my father's. You have manipulated the Order's, and you have manipulated mine.

"The worst part of it all, Mallory, is that you manipulated yourself."

CHAPTER FIFTY-SEVEN

DERRICK

"Tell me about the night we met the Hollowborne."

Mallory looks at me like I am growing two heads, or something closer to ten.

"What do the Hollowborne have to do with this?" she asks.

Not answering, I wait for her response to my question.

"Fine." She throws her hands up. "We heard a noise, went to check it out, and then they called me. They told me they wouldn't speak to me unless you were gone. Then they told me to question everything. Advice I've been heeding our entire journey."

A tired nod is all I can manage to produce—that's exactly how I expected her to remember *her* version of events.

"Mallory . . . they called me. They spoke to me. You ran from their presence when you heard the voices tell you to go—I told you what happened the next day. When you told my father of their warning, I thought you were being malicious, that you were so disturbed by your surroundings you needed to have a handle on the situation."

"That can't be true," she says quietly, her hand resting on her temple.

"Tell me about the ruins—about what happened there."

"I . . . spent a few days alone and learned how to fish from a water nymph so I didn't starve." She sounds unsure, like she is finally questioning her own judgment.

If this wasn't so pathetic, it would almost be comical.

"Mal, you *killed* Maryna in cold blood, the moment she called you Ashawill. I wasn't sure at the time what caused you to do that, but I suspect it was some deeply ingrained defense mechanism. By committing murder against a fellow spirit, you silenced the dryads. The temple that once stood was in worship to the Willow and the water, and you desecrated it."

She looks like she is going to be sick, but her need to argue wins out.

"No, that's not true. I wouldn't—couldn't—murder anyone. Especially not Maryna. She was my friend."

"I *watched* it happen, Mallory." My voice is cold with anger, loud enough to convey the message but quiet enough she feels its weight. "Of course, you made me think it was all a dream—that's the memory you implanted. I was going crazy wondering if I was going crazy."

"My father and I arrived a night earlier than we intended and he thought it best to let you finish your trial alone. Why do you think the trees have grown silent on you? They *all* know what you did on hallowed ground."

I continue, though her body is writhing in pain, an unfortunate symptom of being reminded of the truth. "In Vaelguard—you sent those two men to die without a trial. I know you think you held one. You even tried to get me to believe you held one. And, I did, for a while. But I see the truth now, Mallory. I remember watching you light those matches with a *smile*."

She opens her mouth to protest but no sound comes out.

"Your memory magic no longer works on me—because I have it too. Like you, it went unknown to me for years. The only time I have ever used it unwittingly was to dig up buried memories in others. See, what can be used to hide can also be used to uncover.

"Mallory Nerezza, you fulfilled the prophecy exactly as the fates intended—you are not here to heal the kingdom. You were sent to destroy it."

CHAPTER FIFTY-EIGHT
MALLORY

None of that is true. It can't be. I don't know how to use memory magic, even if I possessed it.

My blood curdles at the thought of intentionally murdering someone. That isn't something I could ever imagine doing.

The pain in my head is searing, and my eyeballs feel like they are about to melt out of their sockets. Even if I didn't believe Derrick at the end of all this, my body does. It holds the memories my brain willed me to forget.

Flashes of the past few months streak through my mind: those eyes, everywhere I was; the portal, how I had purposefully left the two men behind; Thalion, whom I had looked up to; the bridge; the order; the empty room with the windows; all of it. It was all a *lie*, fabricated by my need to feel like I was doing the right thing.

A NOTE ABOUT MALLORY

The Heir to the Hollow Crown is, in most ways, a reflection of the darkest parts of society. It is also a reflection of the darkest parts of me. Mallory, specifically, calls into light my own battle with bipolar disorder and PTSD. Let me be frank, Mallory is not a self-insert. At least, not directly.

Though I intentionally make no mention of her exact diagnosis, Mallory is mentally ill. She is her own person, with her own internal struggles and battles to face. But, more than that—**Mallory is not her mental illness.**

I want to make this abundantly clear:
Mallory is not a villain because she is mentally ill.

She becomes the villain when she refuses to face herself, when she chooses to run from the parts of her that make her uneasy. Her choices reveal her villainy, and Book Two will pull back the curtain on some of the events of *The Heir to the Hollow Crown* the way they really happened.

I very consciously chose not to make Mallory's suffering palatable. The world expects women's stories to be wrapped in pretty pink ribbons. Not this one.

I didn't set out to write a happily-ever-after. I didn't set out to write a version of mental illness that ends with healing and redemption—because not everyone's story ends that way. We will all forever be the villain in someone else's narrative, and I wanted to explore that notion through the lens of something gritty and real.

If you found comfort and camaraderie in Mallory's character, just remember—Mallory became the villain because she wouldn't allow herself to heal. Please give yourself the grace she couldn't.

If Mallory makes you uncomfortable, I understand. She makes me uncomfortable too. And, maybe, that's the whole point.

— G. Marino